Accidental Affair

Leslie McKelvey

ISBN 978-1-936556-44-1

Published 2015
Printed by Black Velvet Seductions Publishing
A division of Savage Publications

Visit us at:
www.blackvelvetseductions.com

To Traci...you've known me 30 years, and for some reason you are STILL my best friend and biggest supporter. I could not have done this without you. You are the sister I got to choose, and I am so blessed to have you in my life.

Love you always!

Chapter One

Laine Wheeler threw an arm across her dog's chest and stood on the brakes as the rockslide tumbled quickly toward her. As the Range Rover shook, she discerned arms and legs flailing, and realized with alarm that it wasn't a bunch of boulders rolling down the steep embankment. It was a person. The front end of the SUV dipped as it shuddered violently to a stop, and the individual landed in a crumpled heap not six feet from her front bumper.

Heart knocking against her breastbone, she exhaled sharply, then looked at Maverick, her half-dog, half-wolf sidekick who seemed as startled as she. Maverick *woofed* softly and put a paw on her arm. Laine took a deep breath, grabbed a handful of thick, gray and white fur, and turned her gaze forward.

The person hadn't moved. She glanced first left, then right, toward the tree line and wondered if there were more people where this one had come from. Both sides of the two lane highway were edged with ten foot wide shoulders hemmed in with 20 foot high embankments topped with thick pine and evergreen. When no other bodies came somersaulting down the embankment, she turned her eyes back to the unknown acrobat.

What the hell was going on? Her pulse ratcheted up a couple of uncomfortable notches. There were no lakes or rivers nearby, and the closest campsite was more than 20 miles away, so what was this person doing out here, literally, in the middle of nowhere? Staring at the rumpled figure, she waited but he, or she, didn't move. Was this a carjacking? An attempted kidnapping?

She gulped and frowned. She glanced at her dog, whose wise, golden eyes were fixed on her. "What do you think, Maverick? Is this a carjacking . . . in the middle of nowhere? And who'd want to kidnap me? My former in-laws?" A short, sharp laugh escaped her. "No, they're happy enough I left Chicago." Her gaze was drawn back to the person in the road. "Maybe they want *you*, Mav." The dog whimpered.

Her brain worked at warp speed, trying to wrap itself around what she'd just witnessed. No matter which idea she entertained, none presented a reasonable explanation for the body lying in the road. She felt the adrenaline hit her bloodstream and took several deep breaths, then opened the door and stepped out.

"Stay there," she said to the dog.

Laine took a step and stopped. What was she doing? The side of a deserted highway was no place to be a hero. She looked at the prone figure for a moment, debating with herself. A low, pained moan escaped the person, and the mournful, gravelly sound spurred her. She squared her shoulders. Right place or not, she wasn't the type to run, and there was no way she was going to just leave an injured person in the middle of the road. She ran around the front of the Rover, looked down at the person for a split second before she knelt at their side. It was a man dressed in camouflage pants and a khaki shirt, and from the stained, disheveled state of his clothes it looked like he'd been rolling in the dirt well before his tumble down the embankment. He lay on his side with his back to her. He wasn't moving, and the silence hung heavy. She waited and as each second ticked off her alarm grew. She hesitated and then pressed two fingers into his neck to check for a pulse. It was weak and thready but it was there, and she sighed in relief. Grasping his shoulder, she rolled him onto his back.

Dark red blood stained the upper left side of his chest and Laine drew back, startled. *That* she had *not* expected. It took her a second to compose herself, and she reached for the collar of his shirt to get a look at the wound. Before she could peel back the material, his fingers snaked around her wrist. She jumped and fell onto her backside, her heart nearly exploding from her chest.

"Please." His grip tightened slightly. "Get the bag and get out of here." He spoke in a hoarse whisper. "They're not far behind me."

Her heart jumped and she glanced toward the tree line, images of high-powered rifles exploding in her head complete with gunshot sound effects. "Who?"

"It doesn't matter. Just get my bag and get it to the FBI." His grip tightened. "What's in that bag is more important than me. Get it and go." He took a ragged breath. "Please."

A finger of fear traversed her spine, but she shook it off. He had obviously hit his head on the way down the hill, and blood loss was no doubt affecting his mental faculties. "Don't be ridiculous," Laine replied, her voice much stronger than she felt. She glanced at the ridge again. "I can't just leave you here."

"They'll kill you," he croaked. "You have to get the bag and go . . . now!"

Laine paused and that finger of fear scratched again, harder. She looked at his dirty, bearded face, searching for signs of the madness his words hinted at, but all she saw there was pain and weariness. She hesitated a moment, and then frowned and squared her shoulders. "I'm *not* leaving you on the side of the highway to bleed to death." She wound his right arm around her shoulders. "Come on, you're going to have to help. I can't lift you on my own."

She knew it was survival instinct more than a conscious decision on his part, but he gathered his feet and, with her help, managed to stand. He swayed, but she held him upright and maneuvered him toward the SUV. She propped him against the side of the Rover, opened the door, and let him fall onto the seat. He moaned in pain, but pulled himself all the way in and curled into a ball. She looked at him for a moment, a shard of doubt worming into her. Her left brain wondered if there was anything to his story, while her right brain scoffed. The delusional always believe *someone* was after them. Then again he was bleeding. Perhaps he wasn't so delusional.

A growl from the front seat drew her attention and Laine looked at Maverick. The dog stood, hackles raised, teeth bared, eyes focused on the injured man. At that moment, he looked more lupine than canine, something she had rarely seen. He was usually such a friendly dog, despite his wolf DNA. She frowned at him.

"Down, boy," she said in a soothing voice. "It's okay."

The dog looked at her for a moment, as if incredulous, but he gradually relaxed. Maverick remained standing, his attention focused on the newcomer, but he wasn't coiled to spring anymore.

"The bag," the man said. "Please." He paused and took a breath, a grimace of pain darkening his features. "They can't get it."

There *they* were again. A shiver of apprehension made her insides clench as Laine wondered who "they" were, and what was in the bag he was so adamant about protecting. A host of questions blossomed on the tip of her tongue, but another look at the front of his bloody shirt reminded her he needed medical attention, and soon. She walked back to the front of the Rover. A few feet onto the shoulder lay a black duffel bag which had seen much better days. She went over to it, and as she bent to take the worn handles, the dull drone of multiple ATV engines reached her ears. For some reason her senses immediately went into overdrive. She paused and listened intently, her anxiety expanding with each passing second. The quads weren't right on top of them yet, but they were headed in her direction and coming fast. She'd grown up in this area and knew four-runners were the preferred vehicles of hunters, fishermen, and campers, but there was something ominous about this sound, though she couldn't explain what. That inner voice she had learned to listen to urged her to move her ass.

She grabbed the bag and tossed it through the open passenger window. Maverick ducked and gave her a reproachful look as the duffel cleared the headrest and landed on the floor behind her seat.

"Sorry," she said to the dog as she climbed in and buckled up. "You can have half my steak, okay?"

The thrashing in the trees grew louder and she heard male voices shouting, though she couldn't understand what they were saying, at least not yet. Instinct told her she didn't want to find out, so she stomped on the accelerator and the Rover leapt forward.

She kept her eyes on the rear view as they sped away, and to her great relief no legion of commandos came bursting out of the pines to take aim at her. Nevertheless, she didn't let up on the gas until she saw the sign for Evergreen Springs, nearly twenty miles down the road.

"How you doing back there?" she asked as they passed the county line marker. She glanced in the rear view mirror and watched as he struggled to a sitting position. Fresh blood continued to wet the front of his shirt and his face was pale and drawn. He vaguely resembled an actor whose name she couldn't recall at the moment, tall and athletically muscular, with brown hair, straight brows, wide-set eyes, and a square jaw.

"I've been better," he ground out. He closed his eyes and leaned his head against the headrest. "Where are you taking me?"

"You need a doctor," she said automatically.

His eyes shot open and his head snapped up. "No hospitals." His head fell back, and when he spoke again, it seemed he was speaking more to himself than her. "They'll be watching the hospitals. Monitoring the police bands, too."

"Who are *they* exactly," Laine asked cautiously, humoring him, "and why did they hurt you?"

He grimaced. "Let's just say we play for different teams."

"And what teams are those?"

"The less you know, the better," he replied. "Just . . . please, no hospitals, no cops, or I'm a dead man."

Laine thought for a moment. "Tell me something," she said. "Are you a good guy or a bad guy?" She watched him and waited for a reply.

"I'm a good guy," he replied.

"Of course you are," she said. "Then again, if you were a bad guy, you wouldn't tell me, would you?" He met her gaze in the rear view mirror and a chill went up her spine. His eyes were clear and gray, the color of charged storm clouds, and something in them told her even if he *was* a good guy he was more than capable of being bad.

"No," he said, "I wouldn't."

He glanced down and she followed the direction of his gaze, gulping when she saw the pistol he held across his abdomen. It was a 9mm with a suppressor on the muzzle. This time, instead of a finger of fear, an entire hand grabbed her heart with icy claws and squeezed. Pictures of all the people she loved flashed through her mind's eye as she cursed herself for a fool, tightened her grip on the wheel, and waited for the shot she wouldn't hear.

"If I was a bad guy," he continued, "I would've simply shot you and taken your car."

"You didn't have a gun when I found you," she pointed out. "If I hadn't gotten your bag, you'd still be unarmed." It was silly to argue with an armed man, but she needed to fight against the adrenaline telling her to stop the car and run. Panic and tears seemed the logical choice, but being raised by a Special Forces father and a grandmother who was an emergency room nurse had drilled the ability to blubber right out of her. Therefore, instead of crying or becoming hysterical, she chose to debate with him. He held the weapon toward her and let go of it, and the 9mm landed on the console between her and Maverick with a soft thump.

"Actually, I did have my gun," he told her. His voice betrayed his weariness, and he closed his eyes. "It was strapped to my leg, not in my bag."

Laine let this revelation sink in. With a deep breath, she picked up the gun, checked to ensure the safety was on and put it in the console. It was silly to be relieved when the lid closed, hiding the weapon from view, but she almost sighed out loud. She could feel her own pulse in her throat as blood sped through her veins, and she reached out to grab a handful of fur. Maverick seemed to sense her distress and moved closer.

"Is this where you tell me where to go, and then kill me when we get there?" she asked. "I'm some sort of . . . doomed taxi driver?"

"I just gave you my gun," he said. "That should tell you I'm *not* going to kill you." He paused and sighed. "You saved my life."

The silence stretched out and her uneasiness grew.

"Ok, talk to me," Laine demanded, unable to stand the quiet. "Is there someplace I can take you, someone who can help? What happens now?"

"Right now," he said, "I think I'm going to pass out."

Laine looked over her shoulder as he lost consciousness and slid down the seat. "Shit." After checking her mirrors, she pulled over to the side of the road and stopped the Rover.

She crawled into the backseat and checked his vitals. When she tried to get a look at the wound, the fabric of his shirt stuck to the bloody flesh and she scowled. "Dammit." She grabbed her water bottle from the drink holder in front. Liquid splashed over his chest, neck and face as she poured it over his shoulder, but he didn't even flinch. *That,* more than anything, scared her. She carefully massaged the wet material and then slowly peeled it back.

Laine sucked in a breath. He'd been shot in the shoulder a few inches left of center just beneath the collarbone, and from the amount blood on his shirt and crusted around the entry wound it had happened a while ago. The seeping bullet hole worried her. No exit wound worried her even more because it meant the slug was still in his shoulder.

"Shit, shit, shit." She looked at Maverick and he whined softly. "Well boy, looks like this one's on us." Maverick's expression was solemn. "Can you handle it?" One wag of his plumed tail was all she got. Laine checked the wound again and sighed. "Right. Home we go."

***

Ripley stood in the middle of the two lane highway. He looked left, then right, and then left again, his temper dangerously close to the flash point. He gripped the AR-15 and wished the weapon would snap in his hands. Perhaps the sound of cracking metal and composite would bring his rage down a notch.

"What do we do, sir?" his second in command asked, from a good eight feet away.

Ripley turned and looked at the man. The four other soldiers made a pretense of combing the surrounding area, but Ripley knew it was only a pretense. It was obvious their quarry was no longer in the vicinity.

"What do we do?" Ripley repeated. "What do we *do*?" He fixed the man with a scalding stare. "We find him, that's what we *do*, Calember. Is that too much for you to handle?"

Calember returned his stare with one of cool composure. "Satellite might have caught an image, sir. We'll have to hump it back to base, see if West got a fix."

Ripley moved till he stood toe to toe with Calember. Then he leaned over until their noses nearly touched. "Call West. Tell him to have an image ready and waiting when we get back. I want to know who picked Vaughn up, where they went, and what they're having for dinner tonight so we can join them for dessert. Is that clear?"

"Crystal," said Calember, as he pulled a satellite phone out of a pocket. He turned and walked away as he dialed.

Ripley stared down the empty highway and cursed. They'd *had* him.

"And we'll have you again," he said under his breath as he focused down the road. "I'll be damned if I'm going to let one man stop me." After a few moments he realized Calember had crossed the invisible eight foot radius line into his personal space and was watching him in silence. Ripley glared at him. "What?"

"West is on it, sir," Calember reported. "I gave him the coordinates and he said, if we have anything, it will be ready by the time we get back."

Ripley put his hands on his hips and stared at the ground. "Good." He slowly lifted his head and met Calember's gaze. "Next time you have Vaughn in your sights, *don't* miss or I'll be putting a bullet in *your* brain."

Calember didn't flinch. "Understood, sir." Ripley gave him a curt nod, and turned to the others. "Form up. Back to base."

***

Jack Vaughn came awake suddenly but remained absolutely motionless, uncertain of where he was and who was there. His head throbbed as he tried to remember what had happened. The last clear picture he had was of marching into the forest with the rest of his squad. The remaining images were disjointed, fragmented. He listened intently and felt mild surprise when he heard a low voice, humming as if from far away. As the mental fog cleared he became aware that he was on his back in a bed, his chest was bare but he was covered with a blanket. The blanket smelled of cedar, a pleasant smell, and his left arm was in a sling. He sensed someone close. He waited, eyes closed, as the presence moved nearer.

The bed dipped and he felt soft skin pressed briefly to his brow and cheeks. Hands. Those hands smelled like Vaseline Intensive Care lotion with an underlying scent of surgical soap. In his line of work surgical soap was something he had become well acquainted with. Was he in a hospital? He listened intently as the hands moved to his shoulder. A hospital would be abuzz with staff bustling and monitors beeping and moans of the ill or injured. There was none of that. Above him was the soft patter of rain, rain on a roof. No, this was no hospital, but where was he? He searched his memory, but all he could recall were Technicolor shards that made no sense. Somewhere in there were a maze of trees, the smell of dirt, dizziness, and the drone of ATVs. His heart rate picked up a few points, but before he allowed himself to become overly concerned, he continued his sightless assessment.

He heard the gentle strains of classical music. Beethoven, or was it Mozart? Beethoven, *Fur Elise* to be exact. Ripley was *not* a fan of classical piano and Jack's pulse dropped a point. One item identified, he started to work on another. He breathed deeply and evenly. The aroma of steak made his mouth water. He also detected apples and cinnamon, and sautéed onions, a strange combination though far from unpleasant. They hadn't had any meals worthy of salivation at the camp that he could recall, and his heart rate eased down again. Slowly, he opened his eyes a fraction of an inch.

The woman didn't notice his scrutiny. She concentrated on dressing his shoulder, the tip of her tongue held tight against the center of her upper lip. Ripley *definitely* hadn't allowed any women at the camp and Jack almost sighed with relief. The pieces of the puzzle were starting to come together.

He guessed she was in her early to mid-thirties, quite attractive with wide hazel eyes, high cheekbones and long chestnut-colored hair pulled into a ponytail. She wore jeans and a T-shirt and around her neck was a delicate silver chain from which hung a silver pendant shaped like a penguin. He looked down at her hands. Her fingers were long and slender with short, neatly trimmed nails, and he could imagine those fingers moving over a keyboard, or skin, with graceful ease.

The sight of the clean, white bandage on his shoulder brought it all back; the race through the woods, the bullet which had, thankfully, missed his head and vital organs, the seemingly endless chase leading to the painful tumble down the embankment to the road. He remembered an SUV stopping just short of running him over. He remembered being helped into a car by someone in a ball cap, and he wondered if the woman was his rescuer. He hadn't gotten a good look at the driver, but he did remember the voice, a *woman's* voice. *Is there someplace I can take you, someone who can help?* His gut told him he was looking at his savior. And his bag . . . that item he had nearly died protecting. His pulse returned to its previous gallop. Where was it?

A dog approached the bed and the memory of being growled at surfaced.

"Hey, Mav," the woman said softly. "He's not nearly so scary now,is he?"

The dog sniffed his hand, turned and walked away, and Jack recalled the voice which had soothed the savage beast before. Those dulcet tones had come from the driver who had saved him.

"*You* stopped for me," he whispered, fully opening his eyes.

She paused in what she was doing and looked at him closely, the way a doctor would look at a patient. When she'd given him the once over, she returned to bandaging his shoulder.

"You left me little choice," she said wryly. "You rolled in front of my car, so it was stop or run you over and I just washed the Rover." She wrinkled her nose. "Then there was all that talk about bad guys coming to get you." She laid a strip of tape over the gauze. "I couldn't very well save you from the villains in the woods just to leave you at some hospital to be murdered by an assassin disguised as an orderly." Her tone was flippant but her expression was serious, and he wondered if she was mocking him. "That would give all good Samaritans a bad name."

"What *is* your name?" he asked.

She hesitated then extended her hand. "Laine, Laine Wheeler. Everyone who knows me calls me Laine, so I guess that includes you now. The dog is Maverick."

He grasped her fingers firmly. "Laine," he repeated holding her hand. "Thank you, though I have a feeling you will regret stopping to pick me up."

A shadow passed across her golden-green eyes which told him she'd already considered that. Instead of commenting on what he'd said, she turned to pick up a small, metallic bowl and gave it to him. He palmed the slug she'd removed from his shoulder and looked at it, a 9mm. He was a lucky man indeed. Had it been a bigger caliber, or had Calember had time to take aim with his rifle, Jack knew he'd more than likely be dead.

"You a doctor?" he asked.

She dropped her gaze and stood. She was tall, at least 5'9", with a shapely figure. "No," she replied in a taut voice, "I'm a vet."

He glanced down at the meticulous bandage, and when he tested his shoulder there was only minimal discomfort. "You do pretty well for a vet."

She walked around the room, straightening as she went. "Well, over the years I've discovered people and animals aren't so very different."

"No," he agreed, "they're not."

He watched as she picked up the torn remnants of his bloody shirt, twisted it in her hands, then crumpled it up and tossed it in the nearby fireplace. The rest of his clothes were already burning on the hearth, and he was surprised he hadn't noticed the fire until this moment.

She seemed nervous now that there was nothing more for her to clean. Jack looked at her as she stood there, arms crossed over her chest, eyes focused anywhere but on him.

"My name is Jack," he told her.

She nodded. "Hungry, Jack?" A small smile tipped the corners of her generous mouth. "I mean, nice to meet you Jack. Are you hungry?"

"Actually," he said, "I'm starving. Something smells fabulous, so please tell me chicken broth and green Jello aren't the specials of the day."

Her smile widened just a bit and she shook her head. "I'll be right back."

She walked through the open bedroom door, and Jack noticed Maverick had taken up a post just outside. The canine stared at him with guarded interest, and his expression seemed to say, "I'm watching you, bud. Make one wrong move and you'll be dealing with *me*."

"Don't worry, boy," Jack told him. "*I* won't bite."

He could hear her moving around and tried to sit up. Heat shot through his shoulder, and he sucked in a breath. He waited for the pain to subside, then carefully eased up and used his good arm to stuff pillows behind his back. He realized with sudden surprise that not only was he bare-chested, he was completely naked. He glanced at the dog, but the animal hadn't moved, nor had his expression changed.

"Chill," Jack said. "I won't hurt your mistress."

Or will I? Jack wondered if Laine Wheeler realized how drastically her life could change now that he had entered it. He was part of a different world, a world glamorized in movies and TV shows, but a real, brutal, uncertain and very dangerous world. Rarely did his path cross with civilians, especially not under these circumstances. Now it had, and he wasn't entirely sure what to do about it.

Nearly eight years of his life had been spent to get him where he was this day. Two years in prison had helped cement his cover first with the motorcycle club, and then with Ripley and his men. His 'conviction' had also cost him his family. He remembered the look of shame on his father's face and swallowed hard. The tears in his mother's eyes had almost been his undoing, but he'd had a job to do.

He had lived and worked alongside some of the most hardened criminals he'd ever encountered, men who had committed every type of crime from embezzlement and fraud to rape and murder. He didn't want to help them, he wanted to put them behind bars, and pretending to be one of them had taken its toll. At this point, having his cover blown was almost a relief. Now, he didn't have to pretend anymore.

His train of thought derailed when Laine entered the room carrying a wicker breakfast tray. She frowned when she saw he'd sat up by himself, but he was too busy with the aroma of beef and onions to care. He hadn't had a decent meal in weeks. Ripley's cook hadn't been much of a cook, and his stomach growled loudly. Laine quirked one arched brow and smiled, then sat the tray across his lap. Before him was a generous serving of what looked like New York steak topped with sautéed onions and mushrooms, roasted red potatoes and green beans with pieces of bacon. A bowl with cinnamon apples was the finishing touch and he licked his lips. She'd even cut the food into bite sized pieces for him.

"Wow," he said as he inhaled the heady fragrance. "Hospital food sure is improving. Are you certain you're not an angel?"

Both brows rose and she blinked. "Um, no, definitely not," she said. She shook her head slightly. "An angel wouldn't make you feed yourself."

"Yes, she would," he replied, indignant. "Angels help you help yourself. They're not supposed to . . . do it for you."

Her eyes narrowed a fraction. "I'm glad you think so. This way you won't be disappointed."

As she turned to leave, several questions popped into his head. What day was it? How far were they from Ripley's base? "Wait," he said. When she looked at him over her shoulder, he met her curious gaze. "Where am I?"

She regarded him silently for a moment and tipped her head to the side, her brows drawing together. "Northern Montana, outside a town called Evergreen Springs, about 20 miles south of the Canadian border." Without another word she left the room. Maverick, on the other hand, didn't move.

Chapter Two

Laine stood in the bedroom doorway and looked at the sleeping face of Jack, last name unknown. She still couldn't remember which actor he resembled, some action hero originally from Australia she thought. There was probably something in his bag to identify him, but it wasn't in her nature to paw through other people's things. Besides, she wasn't sure she wanted to know what was in the bag he had been willing to die for. Then again, maybe she just didn't want to know whether he was really a good guy or a bad guy. Given the fact he hadn't shot her when he very well could have, she wanted to believe the former. Prying into his things could prove otherwise.

She studied him. His hair was dark and thick and brushed his shoulders, and he was athletically built; muscular without being bulky. He had broad shoulders and well defined abs, and the scars on his body told of a life lived hard and fast, though she guessed he was only a few years older than she. She glanced at one of several tattoos. There was a skull with fiery eyes the bullet had marred, and the Harley Davidson logo on his right shoulder blade she'd seen when undressing him. The word "Marauders" ran from his right wrist to his right shoulder and "Motorcycle Club" ran from his left shoulder to his left wrist, both done in elaborate script. The tattoos were real enough, and in her experience the only people who considered bikers "good guys" were other bikers. Also in her experience, the only people who shot bikers were other bikers, or cops.

Laine looked at his face. He was handsome, but not so handsome he wouldn't blend in if he chose to. If he was some sort of undercover law enforcement agent, blending in would be a necessity. If he was just another biker, blending in would still be a handy skill. Motorcycle clubs centered on a "pack" mentality much like wolves. Those who stood out either rose to positions of power or were removed by those who did. After all, each pack could have only one alpha male. Laine chewed her lip and wondered if *that* was why he'd been shot.

She watched him silently, surprised at how strange it felt to see a man in her bed. It had been so long since she'd done more than have dinner with a man, and there was a strange flutter in her stomach which hadn't been there this morning. She wasn't sure if she liked it or not.

Laine knelt down and absently scratched Maverick's ears. The dog had stationed himself outside the room and had refused to move even to eat. She had brought his dinner to him and he'd eaten, though his gaze had found Jack between bites. When done, the dog had pushed aside his bowl and resumed his post.

Now that she was no longer worried about Jack bleeding out, it was harder to ignore the pricks of uncertainty. "What have I gotten us into, eh, Mav?" she asked. She framed the dog's head with her hands, looking deep into his golden eyes. "If the person who shot him is looking to finish the job, I just put us between them and him. Way to go, huh?"

"That'll teach you," Jack said. "I told you to leave me."

His voice was hushed, but it startled her nonetheless and she shot to her feet. She blinked, looked at him and recognized the silent apology in his gaze. "How are you feeling?" she asked as she walked to the bed and sat on the edge. The flurry in her stomach intensified as he fixed those steely eyes on her and her heart did an uncharacteristic flip-flop.

He moved his shoulder. "Not bad, considering," he replied.

Laine reached for a syringe on a tray on the nightstand, but when she took off the cap his fingers grasped her wrist in a viselike grip. He wasn't hurting her, but he was holding her at bay and she couldn't move, not even an inch. Her pulse jumped several points and she gulped, but kept her face neutral. Animals could smell fear, and humans were the most dangerous animals she'd ever encountered. Slowly, with her free hand, she reached for a cotton ball and wet it with alcohol from the pump bottle on the tray.

"Relax," she said softly as she swabbed his right shoulder. "It's justsomething for the pain, and some industrial strength antibiotics."

"I don't need painkillers," he said in a cool voice. "I need a clear head, and painkillers aren't the best thing for that."

Laine met his gaze, but his expression was unreadable, blank. "I gave you some morphine when I removed the bullet," she told him, "to keep you from waking up in the middle of the operation. Now it wasn't much, but when it wears off your shoulder is going to hurt."

"Wouldn't be the first time," he replied.

"No, it wouldn't," she agreed. "I noticed." They battled visually and when he didn't release her, Laine frowned. "Look, if anyone steps foot on this property, Maverick will alert me. That gives us plenty of time to get you into the Rover and out the back way. You don't have to be clearheaded, you have to recover. I can be clearheaded enough for the both of us."

"This isn't your fight," he said.

She gaped at him. "Really? I have a feeling it became my fight the moment I stopped for you, am I right?" When he didn't answer, she scowled. "Will the men who shot you agree it's not my fight, or are you just being optimistic?"

His expression darkened. "You're a civilian."

"Yes, I am," Laine told him, her annoyance growing, "but I'm not stupid. While you were asleep I packed clothes, some food, medical supplies, and cash. It's all in the Rover ready and waiting. Your precious bag is in there too. I'm a woman and I live in the backwoods of Montana . . . alone . . . so I'm armed to the teeth and I know how to use a gun." She paused and met his unflinching stare with her own. "I mean *really* know how. There are weapons within arm's reach of every door and window in this house, and I have the local sheriff on speed dial. Guess it's a good thing he's sweet on me."

Jack still wouldn't release her arm, and she wouldn't look away from his stormy gaze.

"You don't want to do this," he said through clenched teeth.

Laine dropped her gaze, uncertainty like a knot in her belly. This was well outside of her comfort zone, but she had never been the type to back away from something because it was difficult or uncomfortable. Laine closed her eyes for a moment, took a deep breath, and then looked at him. "I already have," she told him, "so deal with it. Besides, it's not like my life here is so great. I'll get you patched up, take you someplace safe, and then we'll take it from there."

"Laine—"

"Look," she interrupted, squeezing her eyes shut, "it's been a long time since I've done anything for anyone but myself, and that used to be a big part of who I was." She met his gaze again, determined. "The people who are after you have no way of knowing you're here, and it will probably take them a couple of days to pick up your trail, am I right?"

He stared at her, and then gave her a curt nod. She gave him a meaningful look, but it was still another minute before he released her. Laine swabbed his shoulder again and injected him. Jack's expression told her he wasn't happy about this, and she gave him a small smile.

"I promise . . . ." She paused and put the syringe aside. "It's not enough to incapacitate you, it's just enough to take the edge off and help you sleep. Right now, sleep is the best thing for you."

"I thought you said you weren't a doctor," he said. "You sound like every doctor I've ever dealt with."

"Judging by the scars you wear, that's a lot of doctors," she replied, as she stood, "or, one *really busy* doctor." She picked up the tray and turned. "If you need anything just call."

Before she moved he grabbed her hand and held it tight. She looked at him in silent question. His face was filled with regret and . . . sadness.

"When we leave," he said in a low, solemn voice, "and we *will* have to leave soon . . . ." He paused and fixed her with an intense gaze. "Think carefully. If you go with me, you may never be able to come back here."

Laine looked out the window into the gathering dusk and thought about that for a moment. She thought of her friends, the people she loved, the simple life she had built for herself. Then she remembered the Laine she had forsaken, the woman she had once been. Taking a deep breath, she met his gaze and squeezed his fingers just slightly.

"Get some rest, Jack," she said with a small smile. "I'll be here if you need anything."

***

Laine pulled the blanket closer around her neck and snuggled into the pillow. Even though it was early September, the nights were already getting cold and she was tempted to fire up the furnace. Instead, she got up and added another log to the hearth, leaning over to warm her hands.

Maverick's soft bark made her head snap up. She straightened and walked down the short hall to where the dog stood by the front door. He looked up at her and woofed again.

The front door was a thick, heavy oak with an inset of stained glass. On either side of the door were floor to ceiling six-inch wide sidelights covered with sheer curtains. Laine pulled back the edge of one curtain and looked out. Two pinpricks of light in the darkness told her there was a car at the end of the driveway, and Laine slowly reached for a pistol hidden in the sideboard to her right. When the vehicle passed beneath a light near the end of the gravel drive she sighed and released the gun. The red and white lights on top of the car told her it was Grant Donovan, the local sheriff who'd been her best friend since kindergarten.

Grant looked like a stereotypical Montana boy; tall and strapping with wide shoulders and large hands, and he looked equally at home in a squad car or a Humvee. He was a crack shot and had the trophies, military and civilian, to prove it. Humble, level-headed, and handsome with thick brown hair and warm brown eyes, he was the one man she'd allowed in her house since moving back to Evergreen Springs.

Laine backed up and turned down the hall leading to her room to check on Jack, last name still unknown. He was sleeping, snoring softly, and she pulled the blanket over his shoulders. When she did his eyes fluttered open.

"Hey," he whispered.

"There's someone here," she said. He started to sit up but she put a hand on his chest. "Don't worry. It's the sheriff."

Jack's brows drew together. "What's he doing here?"

"He comes out to check on me a few times a week," Laine replied. "Don't worry. He's a good guy, too." She straightened the covers. "He'll come in for a cup of coffee then he'll be gone. It's our little routine."

"He the one who's sweet on you?" Jack asked.

Laine thought she saw a spark of amusement in his eyes, but couldn't be sure. She decided to ignore it. "Yes," she replied.

"You sweet on him?" he queried.

She gave him a sharp look. "He's a friend. Now lay here and be quiet, or I may just have to tell him you're here."

"You wouldn't do that," Jack replied.

Her jaw clenched at the note of confidence in his voice, even if he was right. "And why not?"

His eyes narrowed on her face. "If that was your plan you would have gone straight to his office this afternoon." He paused and tipped his head to the side, "Or you'd have taken me to the hospital knowing they'd report me to the police. You did neither, so you won't turn me in now."

His smug tone rankled her and she fought the childish desire to punch him. Instead, she gritted her teeth and shrugged. "Fine. You're right. Now keep quiet, because if he finds you here you're going to have some explaining to do." Before he could reply, she closed the door.

Laine had just put water in the coffee maker when she heard the car stop in front of the house. She hit the button to start the brewing process, walked to the door, and opened it when Grant's shadow darkened the stained glass.

"Well, Sheriff," she began, leaning on the door jamb, "whatever are you doing all the way out here at this time of night?"

Grant's brown eyes twinkled. "Why, ma'am, it is my duty to make sure our residents, even the ones who live in the middle of nowhere, are safe." He removed his hat, leaned over, and kissed her cheek. "So, Lainey, are you safe?"

Laine ruffled his hair and chuckled. "Now that you're here, I am." She stepped back so he could walk past her. Before closing the door, she stuck her head out and looked around, but the night was quiet and undisturbed. When Maverick came to her side and licked her hand, she smiled and shut the door.

The house was a 2-bedroom ranch style cabin. The living room and kitchen were one open space with a granite topped island separating the living space from the cooking area. Grant eased down on one of the bar stools as she walked over to the coffee maker.

"It's almost done," she said as she took Grant's mug from a hook under the cabinet. When she handed the cup to him she noticed his quizzical look. "What?"

"What's wrong, Laine?" he asked. "What's going on?"

Startled by the question, her heart skipped a beat but she kept her face impassive. "What do you mean?" she asked. She took the cream from the refrigerator and put it on the counter in front of Grant. He nodded in the direction of the couch.

"You sick or something?" he asked.

She looked at the couch where her pillows and blankets lay in a rumpled heap. Relief washed over her. She chuckled and shook her head.

"No," she replied. "It's been a long day. I was reading a book and got cold. Something wrong with that?"

He shrugged and faced her. "It's just you're wearing pajamas, it looks like you've been sleeping on the couch, and this is the first time I can remember when you didn't greet me at the door with my coffee in hand."

Laine flattened her palms on the counter. "Sorry to break from tradition, *dear*," she said in a dry voice. "Mrs. Anderson's Labrador had me up at four this morning. Whelped her first litter. Three girl puppies and five boys. You should go pick one up."

He had the decency to look sheepish. "Sorry, Laine. I sounded like a demanding husband just then, didn't I?"

"Just a little," she said, pinching the air with her thumb and forefinger.

"Go ahead," he said as he leaned toward her. "I deserve it."

Laine lightly slapped his cheek. "Yes, you do. Now, the coffee is ready. Full cup?"

"Yep," he said with a sigh. He eased out of his thick jacket, the leather gun belt squeaking with every movement. "Jackson called in sick, *again*, so I'll be pulling a double."

"Aw," she said sympathetically, as she filled his mug. "Should I put the rest of this in a thermos for you?"

"That'd be great." Grant blew on the steaming liquid and smiled. "You are an angel, you know that?"

Laine thought of the conversation she'd had with Jack earlier and shook her head. "Nope. An angel would already have had the thermos ready." She came around the island and took a seat next to him. "So, how are things? Been on any high speed chases lately?"

Grant snorted and took a long swallow of coffee. "Please. I had to pull over old man Ogilvie the other day and tell him to speed up. He was doing 30 on the highway."

"Does he ever go any faster?" Laine asked with a laugh. "I passed him in town one day right there in front of the diner, and it was almost five minutes before he drove by the clinic. It's only a mile from the diner to the clinic, Grant."

"He'd be better off walking," Grant replied with a shake of his head. "One of these days I'm going to have to have him re-exam for his license."

A few moments of silence passed, and Laine looked up as Grant's gaze slid over her, his expression speculative.

"What?" she asked, seeing the direction of his gaze.

"Pajamas," he said. He nodded and wiggled his eyebrows. "It's a good look."

Laine pursed her lips and lifted one brow. "Then you'll *really* like what I *sleep* in, since I don't usually wear these to bed. In fact, I don't usually wear *anything* to bed."

Grant nearly choked on his coffee, and Laine chuckled as she reached for a paper towel. She handed it to him, then stood and walked back around the island to retrieve a thermos. He wiped the dark liquid from his chin and looked at her in reproach.

"You could've waited until *after* I'd swallowed," he told her as he swiveled around toward her. "Sheesh."

Laine laughed and poured the remainder of the coffee into a tall, stainless steel thermos. "Sorry, couldn't resist." She looked at him and chuckled again, shameless in her enjoyment of his discomfiture. "Your face is still red. Did I shock you that much?"

"I suppose I shouldn't be shocked," he replied. "We've known each other since kindergarten and it's not the first time you've tried to embarrass me and succeeded." He drained his mug and put it on the counter. "It's just . . . you haven't said anything like that in a long time." He met her gaze. "You haven't laughed like that in a long time."

That simple statement hit her square between the eyes. As much as she wanted to argue with him, she couldn't. "I haven't, have I?"

"Nope," he told her. "It's a nice sound, Lainey. I've missed it." She stared at him as he stood, walked to the sink, rinsed his mug out and sat it on the dish drainer. "Now come here and give me a hug so I can get back to work."

Laine walked into his embrace and put her head on his chest as his arms wrapped around her. They stood together for nearly a minute. She closed her eyes and silently wished things were different. Grant was one of the finest men she knew, and if they weren't such good friends it would be easy to be more. Finally, Grant kissed the top of her head and she stepped back.

"Keep laughing, Lainey," he told her, as he pressed a hand to her cheek. "I'll see you later."

She smiled. "Yes, you will."

The realization she may have just lied hit her hard, and Jack's words came back to her. *You may never be able to come back here again.* The thought she might never see Grant again made her chest constrict painfully. Laine pushed her burgeoning anguish down and forced a smile to her lips. Grant's eyes were sharper than most, so she kept her feelings well hidden and wound her fingers through his.

"Next time I'll greet you at the door and your coffee will be ready," she said. "Now go catch some bad guys. Lord knows Evergreen Springs is a veritable cesspool of crime."

He kissed her cheek and his gaze lingered on her face for a long moment before he smiled and grabbed his coat. "See ya, Laine," he said.

Laine nodded and walked him to the door. Grant paused and scratched Maverick's ears, and then gave her a small salute as he stepped onto the porch and shrugged into his coat. Laine leaned against the jamb until the car reached the end of the driveway. Her eyes stung and she blinked rapidly, the tightness in her chest expanding until she could hardly breathe. It wasn't until the squad car turned onto the highway and disappeared from view that she shut the door.

Sorrow dropped down on her like a weight and her composure vanished. Tears trickling down her cheeks, she walked to the couch and sat down. She stared into the fire and took a deep, gulping breath as she thought of never seeing Grant again. She had come to depend on him so much since moving back, more than she'd known until this very moment.

"Starting to realize it was more of a life than you thought it was, aren't you?" a quiet voice said from behind her.

Anger sparked in her chest, and that urge to hit him almost overwhelmed her. Laine turned her head and saw Jack standing in the doorway, the sheet wrapped around his waist. At the sight of his pale, drawn face, the anger sputtered and faded. She had made a choice to help him, and blaming him for that would be fruitless. She dashed the tears from her cheeks and jumped to her feet.

"What are you doing out of bed?" she asked. "You shouldn't be up and walking around."

"Sorry," he said, "had to pee."

Laine walked over to him. "No, I'm sorry." She gently took his elbow. "Have you already gone or do you need help?"

He scowled. "I think I know how to pee on my own, thank you."

"Right," she said. "Let's get you back in bed, and I'll see if I can't find you some clothes, unless, of course, you *like* the Roman look."

"No," he replied, "had my fill of togas in college."

To her surprise he allowed her to help him back into bed. She'd thought he would try to be tough and fight her, but he was docile as she fixed the bedding and covered him up. Once he was covered and comfortable, Laine sat on the edge of the bed and pressed a hand to his forehead.

"Well, no fever which is a good sign," she said. "How's the pain?"

"Fine," he said with a frown. "Next time you want to shoot me up, make it straight antibiotics, please."

"Ok, OTC painkillers only," she replied, "unless you request something stronger." She retrieved a bottle of pain medicine from the nightstand, opened it and dispensed two tablets.

"Which I won't," he told her as he allowed her to drop the pills into his mouth.

She smiled and handed him a glass of water. He drank greedily, emptying the cup. Laine let him have another glass then checked the bandage. There was a little seepage from the wound but nothing which concerned her. She'd change the dressing in the morning and give him some more antibiotics at that time. Until then, all he needed was rest.

"You did well, by the way," he told her.

Laine looked at him. "Hmm?"

"With the sheriff," Jack clarified.

"Oh." Laine folded her hands in her lap and looked out the window. "Yeah. I don't think he suspected anything." She started when she felt his hand cover hers.

"I'm sorry, Laine."

Laine closed her eyes as the pain impaled her again. After several long, silent moments she met his solemn gaze and forced a smile to her lips. "If you're going to apologize every ten minutes for something *I* did, I think I'm going to have to inject you with something other than antibiotics and painkillers."

His expression didn't change and his hand kept hold of hers. Laine looked down at his fingers and blinked rapidly as her eyes stung. She swallowed hard, stood, and pulled away. "You should get some rest."

"Laine—"

She didn't think she could stand much more of this. The last thing she wanted was for him to see her cry, but if he looked at her again with that sad, *understanding* expression she knew she'd lose it. He had enough on his mind without adding a weepy female to the mix. "While you're sleeping, I'll see if I can find you some clothes," she said as she made for the door. "I'm sure I've got something around here that will work."

Before he could say anything else, she stepped into the hall and closed the door behind her. Tears fell down her cheeks, and she leaned against the wall taking in huge gulps of air. Maverick nuzzled her hand and whined. She sank to the floor and pulled the dog into her arms, burying her face in his thick coat. She realized with a shock of pain that the dog, too, would have to be left behind. A swirling mix of pressure and sharp twinges beneath her sternum startled her, and she wondered vaguely if that was what getting shot felt like.

It was almost too much, losing her two closest companions in one short hour. She'd known Grant all her life, and she'd had Maverick since he was a pup. She wanted to take the dog along, but they would have to travel light, fast and incognito. An animal like Maverick would draw unwanted attention. The sense of loss pulled her under like a riptide, her lungs labored for each breath.

Anguish grated inside her, all rough edges and sharp corners, as it surged through her chest. It was a feeling she was familiar with, but had hoped to never experience again. Her face crumbled and although she wanted to wail, to vent her despair, she wept softly. Maverick licked her cheeks and rested his chin on her shoulder as if he understood. That simple act only deepened her grief.

"Grant will take good care of you, until I get back," she whispered against the coarse fur. "He loves you and you love him, right?" The knowledge Maverick would be well provided for was one small ray of hope in what seemed a sea of misery. Laine hugged him tighter. "You'll be fine, boy, won't you?"

Maverick woofed softly and leaned against her.

"Well said," she told him. She held him for several minutes, until the sensation of near drowning receded, and then took his furry head in her hands and looked into those intelligent eyes. He licked her nose and she smiled. "Yeah, you'll do just great. Now, come on. Let's get our guest some clothes."

The dog trotted at her side as she walked through the house to the attached two-car garage. Once inside, she turned on the light and put her hands on her hips. The Range Rover took up half the garage. The other half was open and lined with tall, heavy-duty shelves and a workbench. Rows of neatly stacked and labeled boxes sat on those shelves, the contents within untouched and unexamined for nearly five years. The thought of opening those boxes and, thereby, opening her past, made her stomach knot. The memories in those boxes would only be salt in what felt like a gaping wound in her soul, but she had little choice.

Suck it up, Laine, she told herself. She stared at the cardboard boxes for a minute then sighed in resignation. Standing here looking at them would only prolong the inevitable.

She knew exactly what box she needed, and she knew exactly where it was. Her footsteps slowed as she approached the shelves, and when the label "Nick's Locker" came into focus, she stopped. Tears stung her eyes again. Maverick nuzzled her hand and she looked down at him, scratched his ears, and swallowed hard.

"Here goes, boy," she whispered.

Taking hold of the box, she lifted it off the shelf and carried it toward a nearby workbench. With each step her legs grew heavier until it became a physical effort just to move. The panicked, breathless feeling of being pulled under again started to manifest and she fought it, pushing against the tightness in her chest, just to breathe. When she finally dropped the container onto the wooden counter, she realized it wasn't her legs that had been heavy. It had been her heart.

A policeman's uniform was the first thing she saw when she opened the box. She wasn't surprised; she had packed it after all. She stroked the dark blue material for a moment, and then put it aside. Beneath that lay a suit jacket and slacks, a dress shirt, and a blue and red striped tie. She laid the clothing on top of the uniform with great care. Next came miscellaneous items; a pair of sunglasses, a framed photograph of her and some assorted snapshots, a gun belt with no gun, and finally a pair of sweat pants with matching t-shirt, zip-up sweatshirt, a pair of socks and running shoes. The sweats were a nondescript gray, purchased at Walmart, and the faint scent of fabric softener still clung to them. She put the shoes, socks, and sweats aside. After running her fingers over the striped tie, she put the other articles back in the box, but she didn't have the heart to put the box back on the shelf. With a heavy sigh she closed the lid, picked up the clothes and shoes, and walked back into the house. She stood in the doorway for a moment and stared at the box, then turned out the light and shut the door.

Chapter Three

"What have you got, West?" Ripley demanded. Frustration still simmered close to the surface. He picked up a chair and slammed it down next to the work station.

West looked at Ripley and the tech's cheeks brightened as Ripley swept an arm over his desk sending food bags and wrappers flying along with the half-eaten hamburger West had just started eating. Ripley stared hard at him.

"Was able to hack a DOD satellite," West replied, after clearing his throat. His gaze focused on the screen as his fingers flew over the keyboard. "Since Montana is largely unpopulated, there's not a whole lot of surveillance activity, except around the militia groups, and where you were, oddly enough, isn't near any of those locations."

Ripley growled. "The *short* version, West."

"Right, boss." A few more clicks and an image appeared on the screen. "This is all we've got."

Ripley looked at the top of the SUV and scowled. "No plate?"

"Satellite's at the wrong angle," West said. "I can tell you it's a Range Rover because of its distinctive body style, probably 2003-2005, black. If they're local you could get lucky. Doubt there are many of these around that area. If they're passing through, it'll be a lot harder to find out who's driving Vaughn's getaway car."

Ripley studied the picture. "Any image of *who* picked Vaughn up?"

"I might be able to get one, but that will take longer than the allotted window," West replied. "Do you want me to push it?"

"No," Ripley replied. "We'll go low-tech on this one." He turned and scanned the room. His eyes came to rest on Harris, who stood in the back of the room, his shoulder and pectoral muscles bulging out of the wife-beater tank tucked so neatly into the waist of his camouflage pants.

Tall, bald, and vicious, he was not the sort of man anyone would want to meet in a dark alley, or a fully-lit alley for that matter. The animal way in which he devoured his cheeseburger only added to his nefarious air. "Harris. You check out the closest town."

Harris nodded curtly and finished his sandwich.

Ripley swung his head around. "Calember."

Calember came forward. "Yes, sir?"

"Get some teams together and check out every other town between where we lost Vaughn and the Canadian border, then spread out from there. He can't have gone far." Ripley swiveled back to face West. "You, start scanning hospitals in the area and banks looking for larger than normal withdrawals, and see if you can get anything off the police bands. He was wounded and will need medical attention. If you need help take whoever you need from Tech. Let's move!"

***

A flash of light jerked Jack from sleep and he tensed, until a booming thunderclap filled the room with sound. He took a breath and settled back against the pillows as rain continued to fall. At first it was soft, almost velvety, but the intensity gradually increased until it sounded like tiny pebbles against his window. He sat up and looked outside, but all he saw was his reflection. A glance at the clock on the dresser told him dawn was still more than an hour away. He sighed and leaned back against the pillows.

Lightning blazed again and he saw a neatly folded pile of clothes at the foot of the bed. He sat back up and reached for the zippered sweatshirt, wondering if they belonged to Laine's sheriff friend. A matching pair of pants and T-shirt completed the set. She'd even included socks but there was no underwear, a fact for which he was grateful. Wearing another man's clothing was one thing. Wearing another man's underwear was another thing entirely.

Jack moved to the edge of the bed and pulled the sweat pants out of the stack. It took some time and maneuvering to get them on with one hand. By the time he was done, his forehead was damp with perspiration and his shoulder throbbed. He thought about the sweatshirt, but decided not to bother. He'd never be able to get that on by himself. It was then he noticed the shoes on the ground beside the bed. Apparently, his hostess had thought of everything.

The hardwood floor was cool beneath his feet as he walked to the door and opened it. The dog was in the same position Jack had last seen him; parked right outside the door like a silent sentry. Maverick lifted his head and looked at him with those wise, golden eyes. Jack knelt, slowly, and let the dog sniff his fingers. With bated breath he stretched his hand out toward Maverick's head, alert for the growl that would precede a vicious bite to his jugular, but Maverick remained still as Jack scratched his ears. The dog wasn't even tense. His indifference seemed to say he didn't consider Jack a threat.

"Well, you're right there, boy," Jack whispered. "Right now the only one I'm a threat to is me . . . and, unfortunately, your mistress." He scratched the dog's ears for a few more minutes, and Maverick rewarded him with the slightest doggy smile, or so Jack wanted to think. With one last pat to the canine's head, Jack rose and walked down the dimly lit hallway.

Firelight was the only illumination in the main room, and he paused so his eyes could adjust. At the end of the hall on his left was a closed door, to another bedroom he guessed, and another short hall that led to the front door. In front of him and to the left was the kitchen, and to his right, along the back wall, was the sofa where Laine slept, one leg kicked out from beneath the covers and one hand laid flat beneath her cheek. She looked peaceful and young and pretty, and it made him tired to think of what was ahead. A squat, cushioned chair sat directly across from her, and he eased down into it.

Jack knew she didn't realize, at least not fully, what could happen to her life. On one hand, if he could determine his pursuers knew nothing about her, he would be little more than a temporary inconvenience. If the reverse was true, their meeting would become a life-changing event for her, literally. A new name, a new home, a new job. He leaned back and ran a hand over his eyes. He had made a conscious decision to live the life he had, but Laine had been thrown into this because she'd stopped to help a stranger. Hopefully, he would be able to repay her kindness by making sure she could keep her life.

Unfortunately for her, he needed her help. His cover had been blown, and he didn't know who he could trust. Ripley could only have discovered his true identity with the help of a few people, and all of those people were sworn law enforcement officers. Calling in help through the normal channels was not an option. Until he knew who the leak was, he was on his own. He looked at Laine and corrected himself. He wasn't on his own.

He watched her sleep for a few moments and then stood. To keep her safe he had to find his bag. He had to make sure the information he'd nearly died for was still intact, or all of this would be for nothing.

After tossing another log on the fire, Jack glanced around the room. Laine had said his bag was in her SUV. Aside from the front door he had two other doors to pick from, so he made a decision and crossed to the far side of the room. He gripped the knob and twisted slowly, then pulled the door open and stuck his head through. Bingo. The black Rover was there. He stepped into the garage, closed the door quietly behind him, clicked on a light, and walked over to the vehicle. He peered through the window and was rewarded by the site of his bag on the floor behind the driver's seat.

His breath felt trapped in his chest as he opened the door, grabbed the handles, and gently put the duffel on the workbench. With a reverence born of fear and anticipation, he slowly pulled the zipper.

The laptop he took from inside the canvas bag was nondescript, but the information on its hard drive was most definitely not. A glimmer of hope warmed his chest as he turned the computer over in his hands. At least it *looked* intact. However, given the violence of his tumble down the hillside, there was a distinct possibility the machine was worthless. After taking a deep breath, he exhaled slowly and opened the lid. His pulse ratcheted up as he pressed the power button and waited.

Although Ripley's group was only in its infancy, the man had big plans, big money, and big connections. Ripley's organization, his lieutenants, his clients, his terrorist ties, his financial sources, and the training camps he was planning to start around the U.S. and Canada were all detailed on the laptop's hard drive in beautiful, terrifying order, at least, it *had* been. If the information was still intact, Homeland Security would be *very* busy.

As he waited for it to boot up, he glanced around and the glimmer of light on glass caught his eye. On the workbench was an open packing box and beyond that a set of heavy duty shelves lined with more boxes. Sitting on the end of one of those shelves was a white box with green lettering, the type used in offices for storing old papers and file folders. Against the plain brown cardboard of the other boxes it stood out. There was no lid, and the glass covered, framed certificates propped up inside were hard not to notice. He walked over and picked up the one in front. A thick layer of dust could not disguise the ornate lettering on a diploma for Laine Wheeler from Harvard University Medical School. The next honored her for graduating *summa cum laude*. He looked through the rest and found certificates from the American Board of Emergency Medicine, the Fellow of American College of Emergency Physicians, and the American College of Emergency Physicians.

Jack exhaled sharply and a cold shiver of uncertainty wormed up his spine. What reason could she have to lie about being a doctor?

The laptop beeped and the questions about his hostess vanished like shadows beneath full sunlight. Jack placed the diplomas back in the box where they had been and moved to his computer. Holding his breath, he started tapping keys.

It took him only a few minutes to discover the computer had survived his fall down the hill. Relief swept over him when he saw the encrypted files were intact, but his relief was short-lived. Once he knew the computer wasn't damaged, his mind went back to the question of why Laine had lied.

He frowned. "It's none of your business, Jack. Let it go." She'd done nothing to earn his distrust and he knew everyone had a story. Maybe he'd learn hers before it was all said and done. Maybe not. Given his circumstances, he really had no valid reason to pry.

"Oh! There you are," Laine said from behind him. "What are you doing out here? It's freezing."

He realized she was right. "I hadn't noticed," he replied, looking over his shoulder at her, "until now. Woke up and thought I should make sure the thing I was willing to die for was still worth dying for." He nodded toward the computer. "As luck would have it, or not, it still is."

Her expression was inscrutable. "Well, that's . . . reassuring." She wrapped her arms around herself. "Now, why don't you come back inside before you catch your death?"

"You can't treat me for that?" he teased. "I'd think the sniffles would be nothing compared to a bullet hole."

"Yeah, I know what to do for bullet holes," she replied, one brow arched, "the majority of them anyway. The common cold . . . they're still working on that."

He chuckled and faced the computer. "All right, all right. I'll be just a minute."

Laine appeared at his side as if she'd teleported. Jack drew back and looked at her in surprise. He noticed she avoided looking at the monitor as she grabbed his bag and turned.

"Get the laptop, Jack. You can do whatever you need to do inside the house where it's warm. And, I promise I won't watch."

He opened his mouth to protest, but she gave him a pointed look and stood to the side so he could go first. Jack returned her gaze for a moment, then closed the laptop and picked it up.

"Are you sure you're not a doctor?" he asked as he came around the end of the Rover and walked up the two steps into the living room. "You're bossy like every doctor I've ever met."

"I don't usually have to be bossy," she replied as they entered the house and she closed the garage door behind her. She put his bag on the floor beside the desk, moved her laptop, and spun the chair so he could sit down. "Animals are much more compliant, and if they misbehave I just drug them." Before he could say a word, she took the laptop from under his good arm, put it on the desk, and walked away.

Maverick padded over and sat on his haunches, watching as Jack took a seat and opened the computer. He glanced over his shoulder and watched her for a moment as she moved around the kitchen. She started brewing some coffee then walked across the room and down the hall. Jack turned to the computer and studied the screen.

"I'm going for a run," she said from behind him a few moments later. "Want anything before I head out?"

He spun to face her. She was wearing black workout pants and a black windbreaker with white reflective stripes, her hair braided neatly. She plopped down on the couch to put on her shoes and Jack gaped at her. "I'm sorry, you're doing *what*?"

"I'm going for a *run*." She rested her elbows on her knees. "I need to think and . . . running helps me think."

"So, armed men are after me, and now you, and you think it's perfectly fine to go running about the countryside alone and unprotected."

Her expression sobered just a bit. "They have no idea who I am . . . *yet*, right?" She lifted the hem of her jacket, revealing a hip holster with a .38 revolver. "Maverick's going with me, too, but . . . you make the call."

Jack thought about it for a moment and looked out the kitchen window. It was still dark outside. Knowing Ripley, the man would wait until first light before undertaking any large scale search.

He met her gaze. "How far are we from where you picked me up?"

"About 30 miles, why?"

Jack didn't like it, but he could understand her need to run off some nervous energy. If he wasn't wounded he'd probably join her. And, she was right. He doubted Ripley had a clue just yet as to who had saved his skin.

He sighed. "Just . . . stay off the roads and be back here before first light."

Laine stared at him for a moment, then nodded and finished tying her shoes. "Do you need anything before I go?"

"Do you have any writable computer discs?" he asked. "I need to copy some things."

Laine stood and Maverick padded to her side. "Second drawer on the left," she replied as she walked toward the front door. "I won't be gone long."

"I think I'll survive," he said dryly. "Run a mile for me, eh?"

"Will do," she replied. A moment later the door closed behind her.

Jack retrieved the discs from the desk, popped one of them into the drive and a few keystrokes later, the drive started working. While the laptop hummed, he stood and walked into the kitchen with the intent of pouring himself a cup of freshly brewed coffee. He took a mug from a cabinet, and as he shut the door the sparkle of light on glass drew his attention. On the top shelf was a pair of champagne flutes decorated with ornate lettering. His brows drew together, and he reached for the delicate crystal stem. Spinning the glass carefully between his fingers, he read the etching. The flowing script read, "*Nick and Laine, July 7, 2001.*" Below the inscription was a pair of intertwined hearts. It didn't take a rocket scientist to determine what those champagne flutes had been used for. Even *he'd* been to a wedding or two in his time.

So, Laine was not only a doctor, but she was a *married* doctor, or she had been. He remembered her saying she lived here alone. That knowledge did nothing to answer any of the questions in his head, it only added more. He frowned and carefully put the glass back where it had been. He stared at it for a moment, then closed the door, poured himself a cup of coffee, and returned to his laptop.

He'd just sat down when something clicked. Jack looked at the door leading to the garage and put his coffee down. He rose and walked to the door, ignoring the computer as it beeped, demanding a new disc. After opening the door and flicking on the overhead lights, he walked around the Rover and over to the work bench. The box labeled "*Nick's*

Locker" sat there, as if beckoning him. It was a call Jack couldn't resist.

The suit and tie wasn't unusual but the dress-blue policeman's uniform was a surprise, and he was careful not to disturb the meticulously folded material. With that put aside, he came across a framed photograph of Laine and was taken aback by how beautiful she looked in the picture. It was done in black and white and shot from the waist up, a profile view of her in a wedding dress against a dark background. Her hair was swept up into a cascade of shining waves, her expression one of quiet reflection. Below that was a handful of snapshots, and Jack picked them up. The first was of a group of people wearing dirty softball uniforms, Laine in the middle with a huge grin and a trophy. The next was another photo of her, one which had been taken at the beach during what had obviously been happier times. In it she wore a white bikini with a multi-colored sarong tied low around her hips. Her hair was windblown and she was laughing. She looked absolutely radiant.

"What happened to you?" He asked the empty room as he ran a finger over the smiling visage on the photo paper. He stared at the image, as if time would enable it to speak to him. After several silent minutes, he put the photo down and looked through the rest of the box. He quickly found a Polaroid of Laine with a muscular, dark-haired, blue-eyed man, his arm around her shoulders and his cheek pressed to hers. They looked happy and completely in love. Jack had no doubt the handsome guy in the picture was Nick from the champagne flute and the box. The matching wedding bands the couple wore in the snapshot helped solidify his conclusion. Jack shook his head and put the photograph aside.

Past the empty gun belt and other miscellaneous items, in the very bottom of the box lay the final puzzle piece; a badge from the Chicago Police Department that read "Detective", and a flat badge with the photo I.D. of one Nicholas Darrow. Now Jack understood, at least partly.

With a reverence born of respect for fallen law enforcement officers, and his hostess, Jack returned the contents of the box to their resting place and closed it. He thought of putting it back on the shelf, but decided not to. He looked at the box for a moment and turned to leave. Then he realized the photos were still on the workbench. Her image called to him and he picked up the pictures. Part of him said to just put the snapshots back and let it go but, as his hand hovered over the box, he couldn't. He sifted through the photographs until he was staring at the shot of her in the bikini. After a few silent moments of perusal, he slipped the pictures into the pocket of his sweatpants and left the garage.

Jack fed another disc into the laptop, but his mind was not on what he was doing. He stared blankly at the screen as the encrypted files were copied onto the generic CDs, the image of Laine in that white bikini was fixed in his mind. It wasn't the fact she was wearing a bikini and looked great in it. It was her smile and expression that had captured his attention. He took the pictures from his pocket.

The Laine he was acquainted with seemed a ghost of the woman in the photograph. The woman in the picture exuded life, energy and . . . *joy*. It was the only word Jack could come up with. Then again, death had a way of stealing one's joy. He could personally testify to that. Maybe if he could get her safely through this, it would bring back some of what she'd lost. With a heavy sigh, he put the picture back in his pocket and forced himself to concentrate on the task at hand.

He had just extracted the final CD from the laptop's drive when he heard the front door open. A moment later, Laine came into the room, her brow glistening with perspiration, Maverick on her heels. She shrugged out of her windbreaker and tossed it over a barstool as she walked into the kitchen. After retrieving a water bottle and taking a long drink, she looked at him and ran an arm over her forehead.

"I see you survived my absence," she said. "How's the coffee?"

He held up the mug. "Good. Aren't you having any?"

She took another drink and shook her head. "Don't drink the stuff. I only have a coffee maker because Grant bought me one as a housewarming gift when I moved in." Laine finished the bottle, refilled it from a filter pitcher, and put it back in the fridge. "It's more for him and now you, than for me."

Jack smiled. "I can't drink the whole pot by myself."

"Good," she said. "Too much caffeine would be counterproductive anyway. Your heart has enough stress on it without adding caffeine to the mix." She walked over and patted his good shoulder. "Let's work on replacing what blood you lost before you start pushing it through your veins at warp speed, shall we?"

"Aye, cap'n," he replied in his best Scottish accent. Jack drank his coffee and watched as she filled Maverick's food and water bowls. Uncertainty slithered up his back again, which reminded him he'd been snooping, which reminded him of the stolen property in his pants pocket. Guilt quickly slithered in past uncertainty, overwhelming and drowning it. Jack forced a smile and did his best to choke the emotion down. "Dinna think I'll be able t'get much more out o'these engines right now anyway."

Laine chuckled and patted Maverick's neck as he gulped down the water. "Right, Scotty. I'm sure Captain Kirk will understand." She glanced at him. "Are you finished?"

"Aye," he replied. When he saw her raised eyebrow he smiled. "Yes, though I used up all your discs."

"That's fine," she said. "Never used the darn things anyway. Is that all you needed?"

"If you have a large mailing envelope that would be great," he answered. To his surprise, she walked over, opened the bottom drawer and pulled out an Express Mail envelope from the Post Office.

"Anything else?" she asked. "Would you like me to address it for you?"

"Nope," Jack said with a shake of his head. "Right handed."

She handed the envelope over and planted her hands on her hips. "Great. Now, if that's all I'm going to take a shower. Then it will be your turn."

Jack scowled and loudly sniffed his armpits. "What are you trying to say?"

Laine gave him a bored look. "You don't stink, if that's what you're asking. I'm just looking forward to bathing you."

It was too good to pass up, and an unwarranted thrill of anticipation went through him. "Why, doctor," he said with a wicked grin, "I'm looking forward to that, too."

He saw the pink that rose in her cheeks. Less observant eyes would have missed it beneath the flush from her recent run, but it was there and he recognized it. Better yet, she realized he recognized it and her blush deepened. Obviously, she was unaccustomed to having her patients flirt with her. Laine flipped her braid over her shoulder and turned her back to him.

"Nothing I haven't already seen," she said with a sniff of disdain as she walked away. "Or have you forgotten you woke up naked?"

Jack laughed. "No, but I was unconscious then. This will be *so* much more fun."

Laine held her tongue though it really wasn't necessary. She didn't have an acerbic reply or witty comeback handy. Rather than let him see her discomfiture she chose to remain silent and leave with as much dignity as she could. It wasn't until the bedroom door closed behind her that she let her veneer slip.

Her reflection said volumes. Her cheeks were bright with embarrassment and she cursed her fair-skinned ancestors. She didn't want to blush, and she certainly didn't want *him* to see her blush. With an irritated huff she stripped, turned the shower on and waited until the water was steaming, then stepped beneath the flow.

As the water beat into her shoulders, she closed her eyes and let her tension drain away. She'd thought the run would clear her head, and it had until she'd come back. Seeing Jack seated at her desk sharply focused a light on the situation they were in, and it was almost like a slap in the face. While she'd been running, feet padding rhythmically on the ground, nothing but she and Maverick and the passing scenery existed. Now, back in the real world, the danger they both faced was all too clear.

She finished bathing and dried off. After wrapping a towel around her hair and herself, she stepped into the bedroom. The first thing she saw upon entering was Nick's running shoes at the foot of the bed. She paused, transfixed for a moment as memories of the many runs they'd shared flooded her mind. Why hadn't she noticed them before her shower? She *had* put them there, after all. Laine reached for the sweatshirt which lay draped over the end of the bed and held it to her nose. Just below the smell of fabric softener was *his* scent, her husband's scent that only she recognized. How it remained in the fabric years after his death was a mystery, or perhaps she was imagining it. With a heavy sigh, she folded the sweatshirt and put it back on the bed. Soon enough Nick's scent would be replaced by Jack's. Tears stung and she blinked them back. An angry surge of resentment boiled inside her, but she took several deep breaths and let it evaporate. Her pain was her own; Jack had no part in it.

After dressing and drying her hair, Laine glanced at the clock. It was nearly 7 a.m. With one last look at Nick's shoes, she left the room and walked down the hall.

She heard the sound of her printer humming and stood in the doorway as Jack waited for whatever he was printing. When the piece of paper emerged from the printer, he glanced around the desk, took a pen from the holder, and scrawled something on the bottom of the letter. She watched as he tried to fold it, an awkward effort with only one good hand. Laine walked up behind him and plucked the paper from his grasp.

"Allow me," she said. Without looking at it, she folded it and inserted it into the Express Mail envelope, next to the half-dozen or so discs that were already inside. She then ripped off the cover for the adhesive strip and glanced at him. "You *are* done, right?"

He looked mildly annoyed, but nodded. Laine closed the envelope and, to make sure it stayed closed, she took a roll of packing tape from the desk and applied several long strips.

"There. I'll even mail it for you." She turned it over and glanced at the address. "Special Agent Bristol, The Federal Building in Denver." Laine handed the now secure envelope to him. "FBI or ATF?"

He didn't even blink. "Does it matter?"

So he *was* law enforcement, or he worked with them. Laine sat down on a barstool.

"Would you like a bath first, or breakfast?" she asked.

"How about I bathe while you make breakfast?" he suggested with a sardonic twist of his lips. "Unless, of course, you have your heart set on bathing me, as you intimated about twenty minutes ago."

"I *was* looking forward to it," she began in a dry voice, "but the fact you are as well takes all the fun out." They battled visually, and she was rewarded when she saw him fight a smile. Laine relented and smiled too. "I'll run you a bath, help you with your hair and back, and you can handle the rest. Then, I'll redress your shoulder; give you another round of antibiotics, and lastly, food. Sound like a plan?"

"It does," he answered with a nod. "Then, over . . . whatever you make, we can talk."

"About what?" she asked.

He gave her a knowing look. "About the elephant in the room?"

"Oh. *That.*" Laine frowned. "Fine."

"There is one thing I need first."

She looked at him expectantly.

"I could use a haircut," he said. "And a shave."

"You mean you don't always look like a biker dude?" she asked with a small smile.

"I look like what I was supposed to look like," he said, more to himself than her. "That's a plus, I guess."

Their eyes met and the silence stretched out. That single sentence was more information than everything else he'd said put together, and Laine's mind whirled with questions, questions she couldn't ask.

He had the gaze of a raptor, sharp, unflinching, and razor-focused. He also seemed to be reading her mind, or trying to tell her something without words. She didn't know what to make of it. Finally, she forced her eyes elsewhere and got to her feet.

"I think I have some clippers around here somewhere, and a razor. Hope you don't think this is Super Cuts or anything."

"I prefer Great Clips," he replied with a chuckle. "There's one about a mile from my apartment. I'm a frequent flyer there. At least, I used to be . . . a long time ago."

Laine walked into the hallway and over to the one closed door. She opened it, flipped on a light and turned to him. "Well, come on. I am not cutting all that hair in my living room."

She knew exactly where the clippers and razor were, though they weren't usually used on humans. After preparing all the necessary tools she pulled a rolling stool over in front of her and waited. Jack stood in the doorway, looking around the room, and she saw the question in his eyes before he asked it.

"I thought you said you weren't a doctor," he said. "Isn't this an exam room?"

"Where do you think I examine the animals," she asked, "the tailgate of the Rover?" She nodded to the wheeled chair. "Sit, unless you've changed your mind." He looked at her for a moment and then sat with his back to her. "Now, what kind of haircut do you want? I can do a buzz cut or a high and tight, take your pick."

"Just put a number two guard on and buzz me, then trim up around the ears and neck," he replied. "Plain and simple."

"No problem." The trimmers buzzed to life and Laine hesitated. She took a handful of his hair and ran her fingers through it. It was soft and thick, not what she'd expected, and her heart took an unexpected leap. Laine licked her lips and turned the clippers off. "I need to cut some of this first. Hold on."

She grimaced, hoping her voice hadn't sounded as breathless to his ears as it had to hers. Keeping her back to him, she retrieved a pair of surgical shears from a drawer and resumed her position behind him. It took her only a few minutes to trim off most of the long locks then she put the scissors down and grabbed the trimmers. As she did so he advised her to either put the trimmings in the fireplace and burn them, or flush them so no one would know she'd cut his hair. Laine nodded without comment and turned the trimmers back on. Even allowing for the time it took to clean up around his ears and neck, the whole procedure took less than five minutes.

"There," she said, relieved. "Now, for a shave." He remained mute as she lathered up his face and picked up a razor from a shelf inside a nearby cabinet.

"You use that on dogs?" he asked, in a joking voice.

"And cats," she answered as she placed the blade near the base of his neck. He turned to look at her and she nearly cut him. "Hey! Don't do that. I could've severed your jugular."

"Cats?" he repeated, incredulous. "You're kidding, right?"

"Same razor, different blade," she told him. She took his chin in her hand and forced his head back around. "I never use the same blade twice, Jack. Now, hold still."

Laine was very careful as she dragged the sharp razor over his skin. It was a slow, almost sensual process, and she found her thoughts drifting more than once. She remembered doing this same thing for Nick, and many times it had been a prelude to their lovemaking. Laine swallowed hard and tried to focus.

"You okay, Doc?" Jack asked.

She took a deep breath. "Yeah, why?"

"You're trembling," he said in a low voice.

"I'm . . . I'm fine," she replied. She took another breath and continued to scrape at the stubborn whiskers. "It's just . . . it's easy to do this on animals. They're usually sedated and I don't worry so much about hurting them. Now, a person on the other hand . . . ."

"I trust you, Laine," he said softly.

Laine paused and looked down at his freshly shorn head. "You don't even know me."

"I know enough." He looked up at her and gave her a small smile.

Laine gulped and nodded. It took longer to shave his face than it had to cut his hair, but eventually it was done. With a sigh of relief, she dropped the razor in the sink, wetted a hand towel with hot water and handed it to him. He gave her a grateful smile and wiped off the remaining patches of shaving cream. When he was finished, he put the towel in a nearby hamper and smiled at her.

"Damn, that feels so much better." He rubbed his chin with his fingers. "You do good work, Doc, and it didn't hurt a bit."

Laine smiled because it was all she could do. He was even better looking without the whiskers. There was a deep cleft in his chin which had been hidden by his beard, and the lack of facial hair revealed a sharpness in his features even the fullness of his mouth couldn't soften.

"You look good, Jack," she said. She turned her back to him and busied herself cleaning the trimmers and razor. "I'm sure the ladies are all over you, when you're not wounded, that is."

"And even then," he drawled. "I seem to get more action with nurses than anybody."

"I'll bet you do." Laine finished cleaning and returned the cutting tools to their appointed drawers. When she turned he was watching her closely, and she faltered. His gaze was probing, and she couldn't hold it. "Perhaps you should quit getting injured." She dropped her chin to her chest. "Then maybe you'd be able to date someone *outside* the medical profession." She could feel his eyes on her, and the sensation sent a flurry of butterflies bouncing around inside her stomach.

"Oh, I don't know," he replied. "I kind of like people in the medical profession." Then he chuckled. "Given my propensity to get hurt, they're handy to have on speed dial."

Laine forced herself to meet his gaze. "Remind me *not* to give you my number."

"Come on, Doc," he teased. "What if I need a vet?"

She arched one brow. "I hear the Yellow Pages are easy to use."

He gave her a knowing grin and suddenly the room was too small for her. Laine straightened her spine and walked past him.

"I'll get your bath ready," she said over her shoulder. "Or should I make it a cold shower?"

"Only if you're going to bathe me," he answered.

Chapter Four

Jack leaned back in the tub and let the heat of the water soak some of the soreness from his muscles. He was more than just physically bruised; he was mentally and emotionally battered as well. His work had taken a huge toll – the lies, the deception, the constant danger – but those marks weren't as easy to see or deal with. He was thankful he'd run into Laine, and not someone else who might have panicked and cost both of them their lives. Now if he could just keep her from the life he'd led . . . Guilt; cold, dark, and writhing coiled around his heart. It constricted tightly and then expanded to the point he thought he would choke on it. Out of all the bad things that could have happened, this ranked very close to the top of the list. He tasted the regret, like bile. Squeezing his eyes shut, he swallowed hard and scrambled for the only life raft he knew.

"I know I don't talk to you a lot," he whispered, looking at the ceiling with reverence, "and I'm truly sorry for that, but thanks for having my back regardless, Big Guy. A lot of people don't believe in you, but I do. I've been in too many tight spaces and had too many close calls not to know there has to be someone watching out for me, no matter what I've done." Something hard and grating filled his esophagus as the montage of what Ripley's organization had done flashed in his head. He hadn't done anything particularly heinous, but others in the group had and he'd been forced to stand by, watch and feign approval. Shame and remorse washed over him in an icy wave that even the hot water couldn't thaw, but Jack pushed his own guilt aside and focused on Laine. "Now, if you could just look after Laine, too, help me get her out of this . . . ." He paused and took a deep breath. "She's a much better person than I am. She saved my life . . . and she doesn't deserve to be punished for that." He paused and closed his eyes. "Thank you, Lord. Amen."

There was a soft knock on the door.

"Yeah?" he called.

"You okay in there?" Laine asked. "Do you need anything?"

Jack smiled. "No, I'm just soaking. Hot water feels good."

"Ok. Your hair is so short you should be able to get that yourself, but give me a yell when you want me to wash your back."

The thought of her hands moving over his skin sent a sliver of heat through him, followed immediately by a pang of shame. He chided himself and clenched his teeth. "Hey, Doc?"

"What?"

"You don't have to do that," he replied. "I don't want to make you uncomfortable or impose on you anymore than I already have." There was a brief silence, and he could almost hear her inner debate.

"It's no imposition," she said at last, "and I'm a big girl, but thanks for thinking of me. Give me a call when you're ready."

When the water had lost much of its heat, Jack lathered up a bath puff and washed as much of himself as he could. As she had predicted, he was unable to get his back, even with the long-handled brush. It was just too awkward. He rinsed himself then sat back in the water.

He'd felt the tension in her earlier when she'd been shaving him. As an operative he'd been trained to recognize when a woman was attracted to him. Knowing how to use attraction to achieve a certain goal was a vital skill. While he saw some of signs of attraction in Laine, she also sent out contradictory signals. Sarcasm wasn't the best tool to use when trying to gain a person's affection, and she had parried most of his innuendos with alacrity and disdain, a sign she was not drawn to him. Then again, when she'd run her fingers through his hair, when she'd shaved his face, he'd sensed something in her which the male animal in him had responded to; arousal. At first he thought he had imagined it, but his gut knew better. The quickened breathing, the dilated pupils, those were physical signs of sexual tension not easy to falsely manufacture. No, she was attracted to him, at least on some level. Unfortunately, there was something in her that drew him as well. Part of him *wanted* her to touch him, not as a doctor would, but as a woman would. His groin tightened as he imagined her bathing him, her hands moving over his body.

Jack frowned and steeled himself. Regardless of what, if anything, there was between them, they both had more important things to worry about. It would be better to dismiss, or at least ignore, the chemistry they shared. Mildly disappointed, he opened the shower curtain halfway.

"Doc?" he called. "I'm ready."

He heard her footsteps in the hall moments before she slowly opened the door. He glanced at her and smiled when she avoided looking at him.

"Are you decent?" she asked.

He glanced down at the water turned milky-white from the soap. "You can't see anything you've not already seen," he replied, "if that's what you're asking."

"Very funny." She looked at him, and he saw the relief in her eyes when she realized he was indeed decent. She knelt at his side and held out a hand.

Jack gave her the frothy puff and leaned forward. She stroked the mesh ball across his skin, and he closed his eyes as an unwarranted shiver of pleasure ran from the top of his head to his toes. Her movements were languid, sultry, and he wondered if she realized what she was doing to him. He guessed the answer was no, or he doubted she'd still be in the room. Hoping the water was deep enough to keep his growing erection hidden, he started reciting federal firearm regulations in his head.

"How's your shoulder?" she asked.

Jack ignored her, concentrating on . . . some section he couldn't recall. Dammit.

"Jack?"

Her voice was vague in the background of his thoughts, but he answered, "Hmm?"

"I asked how your shoulder felt." Her hand stopped. "Are you okay?"

"Fine," he replied. "It's just . . . I tend to get . . . distracted . . . when a beautiful woman is bathing me. I was trying to concentrate on something less . . . distracting."

There was a brief pause, and then she continued to wash his back. "Oh."

He heard the smile in her voice, but didn't dare look at her. He ground his teeth together and switched to jurisdictional issues and rules for interacting with local law enforcement agencies.

"There. All done."

For some reason her matter-of-fact tone triggered his devilish side. Here he was trying *not* to embarrass himself and her, and she seemed completely oblivious. Seeing her blush would be payback enough for his throbbing groin. "Damn," he said with a slanted look and a small smile in her direction. "Things were just getting good." He was rewarded by the color that crept into her cheeks. To her credit, her expression remained neutral and she met his eyes boldly.

"Let's get you up so you can rinse off."

His grin widened just a bit. "Aren't you worried I won't be decent?"

She pursed her lips. "I'll close my eyes, unless you want to try to stand in a soapy bathtub by yourself and risk even more serious injury."

She was right, of course, and the thought of being even closer to her sent all sorts of wicked thoughts through his mind. He allowed himself a momentary romp through *that* minefield before he clamped down mercilessly on his libido. He nodded, and she opened the drain.

True to her word, she kept her eyes shut as she helped him to his feet, soaking the front of her shirt in the process. Fire shot through his shoulder and down his arm. Jack gritted his teeth and remained mute as she hoisted him up. Throbbing jolts radiated outward from the wound. Without looking at him, she closed the shower curtain.

"There's a towel out here for you," she said as he turned on the water and activated the showerhead. "Call if you need help."

Jack let the hot water sluice over him. When he was certain she was out of hearing range, he let out a ragged breath and closed his eyes. He leaned against the wall and groaned softly, his knees trembling from the pain slicing through his shoulder.

"Damn you, Calember," he muttered. "Although I suppose I should be thankful you're not a better shot."

When the waves of pain subsided, he rinsed himself completely, turned the water off and stepped out. As she'd said, there was a large, plush towel hanging over a nearby towel bar, and he dried himself with it. He tried to hang up the towel when he was done, but it looked more like he'd thrown it over the bar haphazardly. He scowled. Having only one good arm was really starting to annoy him.

By the time he had his sweat pants on and his arm back in the sling, he was shaking, sweat beaded on his brow. Every movement sent heat and stabbing pangs through his upper torso. He sat down on the closed toilet lid and wiped his face with the corner of the towel. He was ready to drop, but the smell of sausage and onions drew him like a siren's song. His stomach growled as he walked down the hall and across the living room to the kitchen. Laine stood at the stove and was sliding an omelet onto a plate as he eased onto a barstool. She glanced at him.

"How are you feeling?" she asked, as she put the plate in front of him.

He said nothing, content to watch as she placed a glass of orange juice and a bowl of diced cantaloupe next to the plate. Jack closed his eyes, inhaled the mouth-watering aromas, and picked up a fork.

"Tired, actually," he finally said as he cut into the fluffy omelet. The first bite made him sigh. "This is delicious. Let me guess. In addition to being a vet, you trained at the Cordon Bleu."

She laughed and poured more egg mixture into the pan. "Hardly. I'm barely a cook." The eggs sizzled and she lifted the edges with a spatula. "Omelet is just a fancy French word for 'toss your leftovers into an egg bath and cook.' My Gram always said you have to work to screw up an omelet."

"Then I must be an overachiever," Jack said with a snort. "I've never made an omelet a *dog* would eat." He took another bite and savored the tang of onions and peppers mixed with the mouth-watering combination of eggs and sausage. "You eat like this all the time?"

Laine shook her head and flipped the omelet. "Only when I have special guests."

"So I'm special?" he asked with a grin.

"Don't read anything into it, Jack," she said flatly. "Jerry's kids are special, too."

There it was again, the contradiction. One minute she was washing his back the way a lover would, the next she was putting him in his place

"Ouch." He took a drink of orange juice. "And here I thought you liked me, a little."

Laine gave him a bored look and scooped her omelet onto a plate. "What I know, I like," she said as she walked around the island and sat beside him. "Problem is I don't know much of anything. Digging a bullet out of your shoulder hardly qualifies as quality time."

"Definitely not a first date activity," he agreed.

"Yeah," she said with a quick grin. "It's usually dinner and a movie, in case you were wondering."

He was starting to see flashes of the woman she must have been, the woman whose picture her husband had obviously plastered his locker with. Sadness blossomed inside him. He wondered what it would take to bring Nick's wife back to life and if he could do something to facilitate that. Then again, it wasn't his place. No matter how much he wanted to know the old Laine, her life was her life. He just had to make sure she was able to keep living it.

Silence prevailed while they ate and as Jack's belly filled up, so did his exhaustion meter. By the time he was finished, he could barely keep his eyes open. His lids drooped and then snapped open when Laine ran her fingers over his brow.

"You look wiped out." She pressed a hand to his cheek. "Let me redress your shoulder, give you some more antibiotics, and then you can get some rest."

Jack took her hand, pressed his lips to her fingers, then gently placed them on the surface of the island and covered her hand with his. "I am tired, but there's still the elephant in the room we need to talk about."

Laine removed her hand from beneath his and took a bite of melon. "Okay. Talk."

Jack watched her carefully, but she was studying her cantaloupe. The sadness in his chest expanded, soft but deeply penetrating. He felt it to his soul. "I don't want to uproot your life unless it's necessary."

"How do we determine if it's necessary?"

"The safest way is to leave," he replied, "today. Gather whatever else we need and go. Once we get where I need to be, we can do a threat assessment to determine what kind of exposure you've had and take it from there."

She nodded slowly and chewed a bite of egg. "Okay. Plan B?"

Jack sighed. "We prepare to leave, get everything we need and be ready, but wait and see if the guys who were after *me* come after *you*."

"Isn't that . . . dangerous," she asked, "letting them get that close before we run?"

"Yes." He massaged his neck absently and sighed. "But if they don't know who you are there's no need for you to run." He could almost hear the wheels spinning in Laine's head as she processed the information.

"Regardless of whether they know who I am or not," she began, "you can't drive yourself wherever it is you need to be, which means I need to take you."

"True, but if *you* don't have to run, *I* don't have to run, at least not right away. That means we can stay here until I'm well enough to drive myself."

Her brows suddenly drew together in a way that told him she was deeply considering their situation. "Not to change the subject, but how would they find out who I am to begin with? We were well out of their field of view by the time they hit that stretch of road."

Frustration swirled in him and he schooled his face into a blank mask. He didn't want to send her into a panic, but he didn't want to lie to her either. "Satellite photos."

Her eyes widened. "They have *satellite* capabilities?"

Jack shook his head. "No, not their own. They do have several very talented hackers who access government satellites. They could possibly retrieve an image. You *do* realize most of this country is under constant surveillance from orbit, right?"

She exhaled slowly. "I don't know which is more frightening: the idea that the bad guys have satellites of their own, or that they can hijack the *government's* satellites."

"They can only access the feed for a few seconds at a time," Jack said. "They could get one, maybe two frames before DOD security protocols kick in and trace the hack. Having the Pentagon breathing down their necks is the last thing they want. They're not going to take any undue risks." He studied her face, noting the tightness about her mouth and the pallor of her cheeks. "Scared yet?"

Laine put her fork down and pushed the half-eaten omelet away. "Yeah, a little." She blinked slowly and flattened her palms on the granite counter top. "Anything else?"

"Yeah." He paused and took a deep breath. "Even if they don't have satellite photos of you picking me up, they know *someone* stopped for me. They're going to do recon of every town within 150 miles of that point—"

"Evergreen Springs *is* the only town within 150 miles of that point." Her eyes widened. "Which means . . . ."

"They will be scouring this town, hell this part of the *state*, looking for me." He frowned. "Eventually they *will* find us. It's only a matter of time."

Laine rested her head in her hands and Jack felt remorse envelop him in a cold, wet cape.

"Who are *they*?" she asked. "If you don't want to tell me, that's fine, but make up a name so we can stop calling them *they*."

Jack looked at her for a moment, debating with himself. He knew he could fabricate a story, a name, an explanation, and she would have no reason to disbelieve him, but the very thought only made the guilt weigh heavier. She had saved his life, risked herself for him, and she deserved to know the truth. Besides, lying would only delay the inevitable. She would find out the truth eventually, and how would she look at him then? The thought of seeing the hurt and betrayal in her eyes was enough to make his decision for him. Jack said a quick, silent prayer, took a breath, and dove in.

"My name is Jack Vaughn and I'm an undercover agent with the ATF." He ran his hands over his hair and felt the dam give way. "The organization I was tasked to infiltrate calls itself CAG, Citizens Against Government. Their leader is a man named Ripley. They're a budding domestic terror group with big backers and even bigger plans. . . ."

His mind flew back to the bombing at the Federal Building in Oklahoma City and the devastation inflicted on so many by so few. Ripley had dozens of trained, dedicated mercenaries at his disposal, and although plans hadn't been solidified as of yet, the mere thought of what the group was capable of sent a blade of pure, icy dread through him. He closed his eyes briefly and took a breath. "I can destroy them if I can get the information I stole into the right hands." He glanced at her. Her eyes were wide and her cheeks pale, and her expression told him she wasn't sure whether she believed him or not. Jack forced himself to continue. "My cover was blown, and not by me." He clenched his teeth. "That means someone who knew about my assignment gave me up. I've got to get that laptop to the main field office in Denver and into the hands of the only person in the world I trust right now."

Laine stared at him for a few moments then took a deep breath. "Well, I'd say that leaves us with *one* choice." She checked his sling. "It'll be at least a week before that arm is of any use to you, and we can't wait that long." She hopped off the barstool. "Let's get you taken care of, and while you're resting I'll get us ready to go."

Jack blinked at her. That was *not* the reaction he had expected. He watched her face carefully, but saw no signs of wavering or uncertainty. Then again, she *was* an emergency physician and probably well accustomed to taking charge during chaotic situations. He shook his head slightly, again amazed at his good fortune. "What are you going to do?"

She seemed to mull that over. "First, I'll take Maverick to Grant's. Grant will keep him for me as long as necessary, even if that means forever."

She glanced at the dog, who was lounging in front of the fireplace. He was alert and watching them, as if he understood everything that had been said. Jack saw the tears that brightened her eyes before she blinked them away, and he felt the sharp steel of regret yet again.

"We can take him," he offered.

"No." Laine shook her head. "A dog like Maverick will draw a lot more attention than just a couple on a road trip. Besides, it'll be safer for him. He goes wolf if someone looks at me funny. I can't imagine what he'd do if someone started *shooting*." She began picking up dishes as she continued. "After I drop Mav off, I'll go to the bank and get some more cash. It's quite a drive from here to Denver, and I imagine credit cards and such are out of the question."

He nodded. "Cell phones, too. They'll be checking the banks and looking for large withdrawals so don't take out more than $500."

A rueful smile curved her mouth. "Guess it's a good thing my dad hated banks and insisted on keeping a couple grand around the house. I couldn't help but pick up the habit." Laine rinsed the dishes and put them in the empty sink. "Okay. No cell and only $500. After that I'll mail your package, get some more supplies, and we'll be out of here before dinner."

Jack cursed himself for putting her in this position, and remorse pulled on him like a riptide. He forced a smile and tried to lighten the mood. "How about after dinner? I doubt any roadside diner is going to be as good as here. I'll even cook, though I may need some help."

The look she gave him said she recognized his attempt to ease the mood, but it wasn't exactly appreciated.

"Oh, the supply thing," Jack said, "don't buy anything you wouldn't normally buy."

"Such as . . . ?"

"Such as men's clothing," he replied. "I can live in these until we get somewhere they don't know you. I mean, how are you going to explain to Marge at the five-and-dime why you're buying men's PJ's or underwear?"

Laine rested her hands on the edge of the sink. "Point taken. In other words, shop for myself."

"Yep," he said with a nod. "Forget all about me."

She gaped at him for a moment then looked away. "If you're finished I'll redress your shoulder."

Twenty minutes later Jack was in bed. He gave Laine a smile as she pulled the covers up around his shoulders.

"Can I have a bedtime story, mom?" he teased.

She eased down on the edge of the mattress and looked at him strangely. "So . . . this is an everyday thing for you?" she asked. "People are trying to kill you and you . . . joke?"

He met her gaze and wished with everything inside him she hadn't stopped to help. The image of her in the white bikini flashed in his mind, pricking his conscience with relentless intensity. Guilt loomed like a shadowy specter, its all-too-familiar presence leaching the strength from his body. Jack pressed his thumb and forefinger into his eyes. "Sometimes that's all I can do, Laine. This job has already taken most of my life. If I let it take my sense of humor, what do I have left?"

"Why do you do it?"

He stared at her, unable to find a ready answer. He felt inept, as if all his hard work and sacrifice had been for nothing, and the tightness in his chest constricted again. In an effort to divert the discomfort he decided to turn the tables. "Why did you become a doctor?"

Her guard went up and her posture stiffened. "I told you, I'm a vet, not a doctor," she said in a tight voice.

He stepped farther out on the limb. "I didn't realize Harvard University gave out degrees in veterinary medicine." He waited for the explosion, but it was much milder than he'd expected.

"You were snooping?"

She sounded hurt, not angry, and Jack felt like an intrusive, meddling son of a bitch. She'd been careful not to pry, she hadn't demanded explanations, and she'd treated him with nothing but respect and care. He, on the other hand, had been selfish and secretive. Shame rasped through him in heated, undulating swells and he ran a hand over his face.

"Not intentionally." He couldn't hold her gaze. "I went to get my laptop and there those fancy diplomas were on the end of the shelf." A rueful chuckle escaped him. "*Summa cum laude.* I'm even more impressed than I was before."

"Well, don't be." Laine stood and took a deep breath. "I knew I should've put a lid on that box." She walked toward the door.

He slipped his hand into his pocket and touched the photographs. *What happened to so completely change you?* He made a decision in that moment as she looked at him with narrow, angry eyes. Working with Ripley had made him an expert in being someone else but it had given him knowledge too. He hoped he could help breathe life back into the woman she'd once been. He prayed she would let him, and that she wouldn't hate him for it. "So, why *did* you become a doctor?"

She paused with her hand on the doorknob. "I became a doctor because I wanted to help people," she said in a low voice. "Consider yourself lucky I forgot why I stopped, or you'd still be lying on the side of the highway."

***

Laine sat in Grant's driveway for a long time, Maverick's head in her lap. The dog's eyes were closed and she stroked his fur, knowing what she had to do but unable to bring herself to do it. She jumped when Grant tapped on her window. She rolled the window down.

"What is it, Lainey?" he asked, concern etched on his handsome features. "And don't say 'nothing' because you've been sitting in my driveway for twenty minutes now. I got tired of waiting and decided to come to you."

Laine swallowed hard, not sure if she could speak. It took her nearly a minute to regain her voice.

"I need you to take Maverick for me," she blurted out, nearly choking on the words.

Grant's brows drew together and he looked at her strangely. "Why?" he asked. "What's going on?"

"Please, Grant," she pleaded, looking him in the eye, "can you watch him for me?"

He appeared taken aback. "Of course, Laine," he said, after a moment of silence. He reached down and scratched Maverick's ears. "Me and Mav get along great, don't we boy?" Maverick licked Grant's hand as if to corroborate the man's statement.

Grant opened the door and stood back as Laine got out. She faced the Rover and slapped her hands against her thighs, and Maverick jumped out, his doggy grin flashing. While he and Grant formally greeted one another, Laine opened the back door and grabbed a tennis ball from the floorboard. She smiled, held it up for the dog to see and threw it as hard as she could into Grant's backyard. He stood next to her and watched as Maverick raced across the lawn and through the open side gate.

"Are you going to tell me where you're going?" he asked. "You have a lot of supplies in back."

Laine glanced at his rugged profile. "On a road trip," she replied.

"Well, that's . . . vague."

"I know."

"When are you coming home?"

She sighed and scuffed the toe of her boot in the dirt. "As soon as I can."

"Again, vague."

"Grant, please."

"I can help if you let me."

"Not with this," she said with a shaky laugh. When she saw he wasn't buying it, she dropped her chin to her chest. "I just need to get away for a while." Tears welled. "What you said last night . . . you were right. I'm not the woman I used to be, Grant. I need to find her again, get her back."

He faced her and studied her closely. The sorrow she saw in those beautiful brown eyes was almost more than she could stand. After a moment or two the sadness left, and he looked at her as if she'd just stabbed him in the chest. Now *that* was more than she could bear.

She gave him a pleading look and said, "Grant . . . ."

He stared at her for a few seconds, then put an arm around her shoulders and pulled her against his chest. Laine buried her face in his neck and wound her arms around him as she tried desperately not to sob. Tears squeezed out from beneath closed lids and she clung to him, inhaling his unique scent and committing it to memory. He smelled warm and clean, like home. The thought that she might never be this close to him again sent despair swirling like a vortex inside her. It pulled her under, threatening to drown her, and her lungs reacted violently to the perceived threat.

Until this moment she hadn't realized how much she cared for this man. It felt like her heart was being ripped from inside her chest by some invisible force. It was a familiar sensation, hot, sharp, and piercing, a sensation she despised but was unable to do anything about.

"Don't go, Laine," he whispered. "Whatever is going on, we can deal with it together."

Laine sniffed and hugged him tighter. "Not this time, sheriff. This is one journey you can't accompany me on." She pulled back and framed his face with her hands. "I love you, Grant Donovan, you know that don't you?" The sheen of tears in his eyes nearly shattered her resolve.

He nodded, and before he could speak she kissed him. As her lips moved over his he pulled her closer, and she cursed herself for not doing this sooner. Grant Donovan, besides being the most honorable man she knew, was a great kisser. His mouth was soft, yet firm and she'd always known he possessed more than his fair share of testosterone just by his height and build. A glacial surge of sorrow, fear, and regret inundated her, and suddenly it was all too much. As if he sensed her withdrawal, Grant ended the kiss and pressed his forehead to hers.

"I've loved you since the third grade, Laine," he said in a hushed voice.

"When you decided girls weren't icky anymore." She smiled. "I remember."

"You're always running away from me," he said. "Why?"

"I don't know, Grant," she replied, "but I promise I'm coming back. I'm coming back and there will be no more running away."

Grant closed his eyes, kissed her brow, and released her. "Then go, do what you have to do. You know where I am if you need me." He turned and walked toward his house without looking back.

Chapter Five

Laine sighed as she put the last bag in the back of the Rover. She'd already been to the bank and the post office to mail Jack's precious package. Then she'd gassed up the SUV and let Eddie the mechanic check all the fluids and give it a once over. She only had one more stop.

While she didn't consider herself a "doctor" anymore, she worked one day a week at the ER and volunteered two days a week at a local clinic to keep her licensing current, just in case. For the trip to Denver she was going to need some more medical supplies, and rather than buy them she decided it would be safer to take them from the clinic. She felt a momentary flash of guilt for stealing, and then dismissed it.

"Hell," she said, "I pay for half the supplies out of my pocket as it is. I'm entitled to take a few items, especially in this situation."

The clinic was a few blocks from the center of town in a residential neighborhood. It was an attractive Victorian building, maintained mostly with donations from several hospital foundations and local charities. The yard was lined with tall trees and thick hedges, like the rest of the homes in the area, giving it a lived in, yet private air. The backyard had been turned into a parking lot, so Laine drove to the rear of the house and pulled into the nearest spot.

The keys to the house were in the center console so she opened it and froze. The silenced pistol lay there and her heart leapt into her throat. The black, brushed metal had a dull gleam that was almost seductive, as if it was whispering, "Pick me up."

Laine did just that. She palmed the weapon, turned it over several times, and then wrapped her fingers around the grip, careful not to touch the trigger. It wasn't that the gun frightened her; she'd been around guns all her life. Oddly enough, it fascinated her. She wondered what stories it could tell, if it could talk.

She slipped the pistol into her purse. After grabbing the keys to the clinic, she retrieved her doctor's bag before entering the building through the back door. Today they didn't open until noon unless there were scheduled appointments, and she'd called Blaire Collins, the clinic receptionist, to verify there was nothing on the books. She had half an hour before Blaire would arrive to open up.

Once inside, she disabled the alarm and started packing. She took bandages, gauze, and all the other accoutrements needed to stitch and dress a wound, marking down what she took on a note pad so she could replace it once she and Jack were safe. When that was done, she went to the locked cabinet where the pharmaceuticals were kept. Morphine, antibiotics, some mild sedatives, several syringes and some prescription strength painkillers were next to find their way into the bag. Laine kept track of those as well. She closed and locked the medicine cabinet, then looked around to see if she'd forgotten anything.

"Nope, I think that covers it," she said to the empty room. She ripped the top few sheets off the notepad, put them in her pocket and closed the bag. A glance at the clock told her she had twenty minutes before Blaire arrived. Laine double-checked each room she'd entered to ensure she'd disturbed nothing and left the secretary a note about the supplies. Then she reset the alarm, stepped outside, and locked the door behind her.

She placed her bag and purse on the passenger seat, then slid behind the wheel and headed for home. Just like a few days ago she had to drive around old man Ogilvie, who was apparently doing his Sunday driving on Thursday. He waved to her as she went by and she returned his wave.

As she passed the city limit sign a strange melancholy overcame her. The quaint billboard which read "Now leaving Evergreen Springs" looked like something you'd see on a picture postcard, and she realized she'd never really *looked* at that sign. It was quintessentially American; white with flowing green lettering and a picture of a white chapel complete with steeple and bell, rolling green hills, bright blue sky, and fluffy white clouds. The sun was rising in the background, and she chuckled as she realized it reminded her of the label on the bottle of Hidden Valley Ranch Salad Dressing in her refrigerator.

"Nice place, Evergreen Springs," said a distinctly male, distinctly *un*familiar voice from the backseat. "At least, it seems so."

Laine jumped and slammed on the brakes as a huge man appeared behind her in the rear view. He scowled as he was jolted against the back of her seat, and her eyes were immediately drawn to the pistol in his hand. It looked familiar, and so did the silencer, but this was a .45 and not a 9mm. *Bigger guy, bigger gun.*

He rested the barrel on her shoulder and rubbed the muzzle against the side of her neck. "Whoa there, pretty lady, calm down. Let's not get carried away."

He looked like a younger, stronger version of Mr. Clean, except for the earring. The stranger didn't have one. He also wasn't wearing Mr. Clean's beguiling smile.

"What do you want?" she asked, though she had a sinking feeling she knew the answer.

"We'll discuss that as we go," he said with a leering smile. "Hell, if I'd known you were some pretty *woman* doctor, I'd have *volunteered* for this job." He licked his lips and rubbed her neck again with the gun. "Now, drive."

"Where to?"

He gave her a look that said she should know where.

"Home," she said.

He grinned, though it did nothing to make him more appealing. It was a serpent's grin, and a shiver went down her spine.

"You reading my mind, pretty lady? Better not do that. You won't like what you find."

A snappy retort entered her mind, but she didn't let it past her lips. Instead, she remained mute and pressed down on the accelerator. Mr. Clean moved to the seat behind her but kept the gun on her shoulder. Every so often he'd press the cool metal against her throat, as if to remind her he was still there.

"So, you fix him up nice?" Mr. Clean asked.

"Who?" she asked, glancing at him in the rear view.

He laughed. "That was good, sweetheart. No inflection, no hesitation. If I wasn't a trained a professional, I would almost believe you don't know who I'm talking about."

"I *don't* know who you're talking about," she replied, focusing on the road. As each mile marker passed her fear grew and her heart pounded harder. She took several deep breaths, but it didn't help.

"C'mon, princess," he drawled, "I have a satellite photo of a black Range Rover picking up a wounded man off this road yesterday. Now, I've done my homework. Shelby, down at the diner, pretty girl that

Shelby, she told me Dr. Wheeler drives a black Range Rover. She also said you were the only one in town who had one, and that you worked at the clinic a couple days a week. Didn't tell me you were a *woman* doctor. Jack always was one lucky son of a bitch." He pressed the muzzle to a spot just below her ear. "Maybe when I'm done with him and *you*, I'll pay Miss Shelby a visit."

Laine knew Shelby Stewart. She'd been elected homecoming queen last year and named Miss Evergreen Springs during the local fair. Shelby worked at the diner where her blonde hair, green eyes and Christie Brinkley smile garnered her quite a good living in tips alone. She was sweet, a little naive, and everyone knew she talked too much. The girl had no idea there were actually monsters in the world outside of her childhood storybooks.

"Leave her alone," Laine said. "She's barely eighteen."

"All the sweeter for the picking." He leered at her. "Although, I personally like a real woman, someone who *knows* what she's doing. I'll bet you could teach *me* a thing or two."

Laine gripped the steering wheel tighter, and thought briefly about running the Rover into a tree. The gunman, however, had buckled his seatbelt, so it would probably do little more than piss him off. Just then she happened to catch a glimpse of her purse on the seat next to her. She'd been so startled by Mr. Clean's appearance that she had forgotten about Jack's gun. Not that it would do her any good. There was no way she'd be able to draw it now before he killed her. But, once they stopped . . . ?

"Now, getting back to the original subject," he said, interrupting her train of thought, "you take Jack on home with you and stitch up that bullet hole in his shoulder?"

"No," she replied. "I did pick a man up, but I dropped him at the ER. I went to park my car and when I got inside he was gone. He must have known it wasn't safe there and left." She met his eyes in the mirror. "I swear to you, I don't know where he is, or I'd tell you."

"Didn't I tell you I do my homework?" he asked, his expression darkening. "I've been to the hospital, and when I was talking to Miss Shelby at the diner some sweet old lady started singing your praises. Told me you delivered her Labrador's puppies, were there for nearly eight hours because it was the bitch's first litter. Said you told her you were going straight home after that, had a steak waiting, if I remember correctly." His face was a thundercloud. "Now, I'd love to keep playing this game with you, and when he's dead I plan to play *several*, but until then, no more lies!"

Laine jumped as he shouted the last and froze when she felt the muzzle of the gun pressed against the base of her skull. "Okay," she said. "Okay, I'll tell you the truth. Just . . . get that thing away from my head."

He returned the gun to its position on her shoulder. "I'm listening."

"He's at my house," she said, her mind working furiously. "He's in the root cellar. It's in the barn out back."

"Root cellar," he repeated, sounding skeptical. "Now, why would you, a good little doctor who volunteers to help sick folk and animals, put an injured man in a root cellar?"

Laine prayed her mouth wouldn't go faster than her brain. "Well, he said he couldn't go to the hospital because someone . . . *you*, I imagine . . . was trying to kill him, and I didn't want him in my house because my boyfriend is the local sheriff. I didn't know how I was going to explain a man with a gunshot wound being in my bed."

She glanced in the mirror and saw him nodding as he stared out the window. Apparently, what she'd said made sense, at least to him.

"Fine," he said after a brief silence. "You just take me to him, and *maybe* I'll kill you quickly." He leaned toward her and she felt his breath on her neck. "I usually toy with my ladies. I like to bring them to the brink, but only to the brink, then I bring them back so I can play some more. You understand, don't you?"

With everything going on, it wasn't hard to summon tears at this point. Laine let them fall and sniffled loudly as she nodded. The man clucked his tongue and made a sympathetic sound.

"I like it when they cry. It excites me." He caressed her hair with his free hand then sat back.

Ten minutes or so later she slowed down to make the turn into her driveway. "This is it," she said. "This is my house."

"Nice place," Mr. Clean commented.

As Laine drove toward the house, she unobtrusively pulled on the blinker lever, enough to activate the Rover's high beams without clicking them all the way on. She flashed them off and on as she drove slowly down the drive, and prayed Jack would see them. If he did, he would know something was wrong. She just hoped he didn't come out the front to see what it was.

Having this man inside her house was the last thing she wanted, so she drove around the side of the house and toward the barn instead of into the garage. She pulled within six feet of the large sliding doors and put the Rover in park, but left the engine running.

"Open the doors, sweet cheeks," Mr. Clean said with a growl, "and no funny stuff or you'll live much longer than you want to."

Laine only nodded, and realized she might actually be able to blubber after all. Her heart was hammering in her chest and her mouth was dry. Her hands trembled as she got out of the car. Once the barn doors were open she turned and looked at her captor. He opened his window.

"Drive her on in, honey," he said with a sweet smile. "Then we can close the doors and have us some privacy."

Laine closed her eyes for a moment, then nodded and got back behind the wheel. The Rover passed through the doors, from light into darkness, from out in the open to hidden, alone, with *him*. The first fingers of panic clutched at her heart. She took several deep breaths, then parked and shut off the engine.

"Close the doors," he said again. "Ain't nobody going to see us way out here, but I prefer to err on the side of caution."

When Laine exited the vehicle, so did Mr. Clean. He moved to the side as she walked past him. The next scene in this little drama played out in her head as she pulled the barn doors shut. She wondered if she could possibly pull off what she was thinking. Did she have even the slimmest chance of getting the drop on a trained mercenary? Then again, she didn't have much choice but to try.

Laine had deliberately left her car door open, and Mr. Clean stood to the left of it, one hand resting on the top of the door frame. She swallowed hard and tried to be as non-threatening as possible as she approached him. He watched her out of the corner of his eye, and scowled when she leaned across the driver's seat to reach for her purse. Immediately the gun whipped around and found a tender spot between her shoulder blades.

"What do you think you're doing?" he asked in a deadly voice. "I said no funny stuff."

"The keys to the cellar are in my purse," she replied, holding her hands up. "Unless you want to break down the door, we need them."

It was nearly ten seconds before he spoke. "Fine, but watch yourself. One wrong move and it will be *days* before I kill you."

Laine nodded mutely and reached for the purse. She took the strap with her left hand, and put her right hand inside the bag. The gun was easy to find since it was a lot bigger than a lipstick, and she wrapped her fingers around the grip, flicking the safety off with her thumb. With exaggerated slowness she backed out of the Rover and turned toward him. He growled, grabbed the strap, and jerked the bag from her. Laine held her breath.

"Give me those keys," he said as he searched the inside of her purse, the muzzle of his pistol angling toward the floor as he did so. He never noticed the gun in her right hand. He didn't even notice it when she leveled it at his chest. Several seconds passed before he froze, his eyeballs swiveling to look at the pistol.

Laine grit her teeth. "I know you wanted to . . . *explore* this relationship," she said, her voice barely above a whisper, "but I think *I'm* going to have to kill *you. Now.*"

She squeezed the trigger just as she'd been taught all her life, and there was a soft "pfft" as the pistol fired. Mr. Clean looked at her in shock. Laine fired again. He seemed frozen, but then the spell broke and he fell backwards.

Strong fingers wrapped around her wrist, and she nearly jumped out of her skin, the gun discharging again as she reflexively squeezed the trigger. Jack stood to her right, on the other side of the open driver's door, reaching around the frame, his eyes filled with concern and fear.

"Give me the gun, Laine," he said in a whisper. "It's over."

Laine didn't realize she'd been holding her breath until she took one, and her knees nearly buckled. Jack took the gun, dropped it on the ground, then closed the Rover's door and pulled her to his chest.

"Breathe, sweetheart," he said, "breathe."

Laine gasped, and the sobs she'd held back earlier with Grant burst from her as if they'd been forcefully expelled from the deepest part of her soul. She fell to her knees and Jack went with her, but he didn't let go, his right arm held her tightly. Laine pressed her face against his chest as her body shook with the force of her emotions.

"That's it," he said in a low voice, "let it out. Let it all out." He stroked her hair and laid his cheek on top of her head. "It's over. You're safe now, and I won't let anything else happen to you. I swear on my life I won't."

They stayed on the floor until she had nothing left in her, his voice whispering soothing, nonsensical words in her ear. Laine closed her eyes and listened to his heartbeat, slow and steady. It calmed her. Jack moved to a sitting position with his back against the Rover and pulled her onto his lap. Laine curled up against him as he draped his arm across her body.

"Hey, Doc," he said softly, "You're not going into shock, are you?" He pressed his hand to her forehead.

"No," she replied. Out of the corner of her eye she looked at Mr. Clean. "Is he . . . ."

"Yeah, I'm pretty sure he is."

"He was in the back of the Rover," she said, and the memory of her fear made her stomach knot. "I left the clinic and drove halfway home before he said anything." She looked at Jack in disbelief. "I didn't even know he was there, Jack. I didn't have a clue."

"Did he say how he found you?"

"He said he talked to Shelby Stewart," Laine replied, "at the diner, and she told him where I worked." She shook her head. "Shelby would have tea with the devil himself if he smiled and asked politely. She's a sweet girl and everyone loves her, she just . . . talks too much."

"Does Shelby know where you live?" Jack asked.

"No," Laine answered.

"Which means he didn't know," Jack said, more to himself than her.

Laine was remembering the feel of the gun to her head, and squeezed her eyes shut. A tremor ran through her. "How could I not have known he was there, Jack? He was *six inches* from me, and I never suspected."

"Your mind was elsewhere, Laine," Jack said. "Don't beat yourself up."

She looked at Mr. Clean. "Do you know him?"

Jack sighed and put a hand on her cheek, turning her gaze away from the corpse. "Yes, and be glad you don't." He tipped her chin up and looked in her eyes. "Right now I don't care about him, Laine, I care about you." He studied her face. "Are you okay?"

Her eyes welled with tears. "I just killed a man, Jack. No, I'm not okay." She wanted to look away from that raptor's gaze, to bury her face against his chest, but he wouldn't let her.

"It was self-defense, Laine," he said, from between clenched teeth. "Do *not* feel guilty about this. You look up the word monster in a dictionary, and you'll find that man's picture." His expression softened and his fingers stroked her skin. "If you hadn't shot him, he would have killed us both. While *my* death may have been quick and relatively painless, *yours* would not have been so easy."

I like it when they cry . . . . Her face crumpled and the tears slid down her cheeks.

"I know," she said, pressing her face into his neck. "He told me as much."

He cupped her head with his hand. "Then let it go," he said. "You did what you had to do, and you saved us both."

Laine didn't think she had any tears left, but she was wrong. It seemed like forever before the waterworks dried up. Jack said nothing. He simply held her and let her cry.

When she was completely wrung out, she disentangled herself from Jack's embrace and sat next to him on the ground. She glanced at the dead man and then laid her head on Jack's shoulder. "You know what this means, don't you?" she asked in a hushed voice.

"What?"

"They know where I am."

Jack looked at her for a moment then looked at Mr. Clean. "Maybe, maybe not."

He got to his feet and walked over to the dead man. First, he checked for a pulse and then briefly examined the wound. "Nice shot, Doc. Got the pumping station with round one. He hardly bled."

"Thanks," she said, her voice laced with sarcasm. "That's what I was going for." She got up and moved to his side, taking a deep breath as she looked into those lifeless eyes. He didn't look so menacing now, but still a shudder ran up her spine. As if sensing her distress, Jack closed Mr. Clean's eyelids.

He started checking the many pockets on Mr. Clean's black BDU's. After about a minute he found a cell phone, but it was like no cell phone Laine had ever seen. Jack pumped his fist once and showed it to her.

"Satellite phone," he said. "Now we'll be able to find out if they know where you are, or if only *he* did."

He started punching buttons until he pulled up the call list. Jack scrolled through them.

"When did he find you?" he asked.

"Around 11:40," Laine replied. "He must've sneaked into the Rover while I was inside the clinic getting supplies."

"Last call he made was before 11:00." Jack pushed several more buttons. "That means they may know you're in Evergreen Springs, they may even have your name, but they won't know where your house is because he didn't. Had he called CAG once he got his information, it would've taken West, their head computer tech, mere seconds to find you, which tells me he didn't call. Had this guy known your address he never would have approached you in broad daylight in the middle of town. He'd have come here and killed me, then waited for you." He gave her a meaningful look. "That gives us some time. Let's get out of here."

"What about him?" Laine asked. "We can't just . . . leave him here."

"Yes, we can," he replied. "When Ripley's team gets here, they'll take care of their departed colleague. They don't want the cops getting involved in this because they don't want that kind of attention. They certainly won't want the police to have *this*." He waved the sat phone in the air then tucked it back into Mr. Clean's pocket. He walked up to her and cupped her elbow. "We need to get out of here and, preferably, in something other than the Rover. Do you have another car?"

Laine nodded and walked to the back of the barn, Jack beside her. There, hidden in the shadows stood a blue Suburban with tinted windows, and aside from the dust it looked to be in pristine shape. She glanced at him. "Will this work?"

For an answer, he turned to her and kissed her squarely on the mouth. Laine was too startled to react, and just when her body caught up, he drew back and chucked her under the chin.

"And here I was worried we'd be stuck in some cramped sub-compact," he said with a grin. "You, Laine Wheeler, are a girl after my own heart. Now, come on. Let's get the heck out of Dodge."

Startled, Laine stared at him as he turned and walked away, her lips still tingling.

***

It was just after two p.m. when they were ready to leave. The Suburban was packed and Jack was already inside it, waiting for her. They'd put the Rover in the garage, as she usually did, and other than some clothes, toiletries, a picture of Maverick, and the box from Nick's locker, she was leaving everything behind. She knew she should go through Nick's box and take the few items that meant something to her, but she just didn't have the energy. Later, when this was all over she'd put those ghosts to rest. Maybe.

She double-checked the locks, turned off the furnace and the water heater, set the timer for the lights, and then stood in the middle of the living room. That same melancholy from earlier came over her as she looked at the cozy home and wondered why she'd never appreciated its simple beauty until now. She was only leasing it from Grant, but it was a good home and she was sorry to leave.

Her steps were slow and measured as she exited through the front door, then closed and locked it behind her. It was silly to think a deadbolt would keep Ripley and his men out, but she couldn't leave without securing it. With a final glance around the yard, she climbed into the driver's seat and they were off.

"You okay back there?" Laine asked.

Jack was sitting in the back on the passenger side, concealed from view by the tinted windows. She felt him watching her and kept her eyes focused on the road.

"I'm fine," he said. "How are you? It's been a rather . . . eventful day for you."

"You have a gift for understatement," she replied. "I'm fine." She was lying, and she knew he knew she was lying, but what else could she say? What could he say?

She paused at the end of the driveway, looked both ways, and then looked at her house in the rear view. For a moment she was caught off guard and her eyes stung as she stared at the homey cabin. Mr. Clean had been right; it really was a nice house. She wondered if she'd ever see it again.

Chapter Six

The distance from Evergreen Springs to Denver was nearly a thousand miles, so Laine guessed it would take two days to reach their destination, barring any unforeseen problems. This meant they would arrive in Denver sometime on Saturday. At least the drive was scenic, a plus for any journey. She glanced in the rear view and saw Jack was dozing. After popping a CD into the player, she set the cruise control to match the speed limit and settled in for the long haul.

In the mountains, darkness fell quickly and today was no exception. The digital clock read 6:03 p.m. and already the sun had dropped behind the rugged peaks to the west. The sky was light above them, but in the curves and crags of the Rockies, light was kept out despite its valiant effort to reach the ground. It looked odd. Straight up — it was bright blue. Straight ahead — it was almost night time.

They'd been on the road for close to four hours and, even though she hadn't eaten since breakfast, Laine wasn't even close to hungry. In fact, the farther they got from home, the more tense she became. Several times she had to take her hands off the wheel, one at a time, and shake them to get the feeling back in her fingers. She tried to relax, but as soon as she stopped focusing on her grip the white knuckles returned, as did the memories of what had happened earlier. She supposed she should be happy she was coherent enough to drive. Tonight she'd sleep and in the morning things would look better. They might not *be* better, but they had to at least look that way.

Behind her Jack yawned. "Hey." He stretched his good arm and sat up. He tried to look out the window, cupping his hand around his eyes. "Where are we?"

"Not in Denver," she replied. "How are you feeling?"

"Shoulder hurts," he said, "but not bad. How are you? Ready to let me drive?"

Laine chuckled. "Right. I'll pull over and you can take the wheel. Oh, wait, I forgot. I took a bullet out of your shoulder about 24 hours ago, so . . . no. I think I'll keep control of my vehicle, thank you very much."

"Fine," he said with a wry twist of his lips, "be that way. Hey, where are the water bottles?"

"They should be right behind you," she replied. "Grab me one, would you, please?"

"You got it, boss."

He reached behind the seat into the cargo area and came up with two water bottles. Laine watched as he tried to open one and was unsuccessful. He made several attempts; bracing the bottle against his ribcage with his sling, trying to hold it with his useless left hand while opening it with his right, but no luck. Laine chuckled at his frustration.

"Give them to me," she said. "I'll open them."

"I have an injured shoulder." He scowled at her. "That doesn't mean I'm completely useless." He held the bottle between his knees and the cap came off with one twist. "See? I told you." He handed her a bottle, then opened his and took a long swig.

"We should probably stop soon," Laine said.

"How far have we come?"

She checked the trip meter. "About 250 miles," she replied.

A slight frown creased his brow. "I think we should put more distance between us and them."

"Well, I can drive all night, but stops are few and far between out here," she said. "There might be a service station at the next exit, and then we won't see another for two hundred miles." She looked down at the gas gauge. "We're going to have to stop for gas anyway. The Rover was full, but this thing had just over half a tank. We've got about an eighth of a tank left."

Jack drained the water bottle, capped it and put it back in the cargo area. "Tell you what," he said, "when we stop for gas we ask the attendant how much farther it is to the next motel. If it's less than two hundred miles we go, if it's farther, we stop right there."

Laine was so tired she would've been happy to stop on the side of the road and sleep, but it made sense to put more distance between them and Mr. Clean's friends. "Whatever you say." She reached for her

purse, retrieved a bottle of ibuprofen out of it and held it out to him.
"Here. Take a couple of these. If you need something stronger when
we stop, I can help."

His brows drew together. "Hey, what'd I say about that?"

"Keep your pants on, Jack," Laine said with a wry smile. "The
morphine is for me. I might let you have a couple Vicodin if you're nice."

"No thanks." He shook his head. "I'm good."

He took his medicine and they drove in comfortable silence for a
while. The CD that was playing ended and Laine looked at him in the
mirror.

"You know," she said, "you never did answer my question."

Jack rubbed his chin. "Hmm. Well, you haven't asked me very many
questions, but I'm afraid I need a refresher."

"Why do you do it?"

His expression became guarded and he glanced out the window.
"That's a simple question with a very complicated answer." He looked
at her out of the corner of his eye. "Got anything easier?"

"Never mind," she said. "I didn't mean to pry."

He sighed and ran his hand over his face. "I'm not being evasive,
Laine," he said. He was quiet for a moment. "It's just . . . I'm not really
sure I *know* why I do it anymore. It seems like no matter what lengths
we go to, the bad guys are always one step ahead and innocent people
suffer for it."

"Do you ever think about walking away?" she asked.

He met her eyes in the mirror. "Every day." His eyes narrowed. "What
about you? You *did* walk away. Why?"

Laine focused on the road, unable to maintain his gaze. "That's a
simple question with a complicated answer. Got anything easier?" There
was a pregnant pause, and Laine glanced at him. He was watching her
carefully, as if debating whether or not to ask something.

"Go on, spit it out," she said.

He hesitated. "Tell me about Nick," he said after a brief pause.

Laine's head snapped around and anger bloomed in her chest. "You
were snooping." She turned back and gripped the wheel so tightly her
hands went numb up to her elbows.

"Not really," he said with a sigh. She skewered him with a gaze via
the rear view, and he dropped his chin to his chest. "Well, yeah, but . . .
not like you think."

"Then educate me." She didn't hide the tremor in her voice. Tears stung her eyes and she thought about pulling over so she could hit him. She flexed her fingers and clenched her jaw.

"When you went running this morning," he began, "I went to get a coffee mug out of the cabinet and saw the champagne flutes on the top shelf."

Laine blinked rapidly and a tear slid down her cheek. The etched glasses. She'd forgotten they were there.

"I read the engraving on the crystal and remembered seeing a box in the garage." He jerked a thumb toward the box in back. "That box. These are his clothes I'm wearing, aren't they?"

Her chin began to tremble and tears obscured her vision. A pain she'd thought she'd gotten past tore through her heart and blazed a trail of agony through the rest of her until she thought she'd be sick. Suddenly she needed some air. They were just passing an off ramp, but Laine slammed on the brakes and jerked the wheel. She skidded across the gore point and up the ramp, the Suburban shuddering to a halt at the stop sign. She saw a gravel turnout and pulled into it. After putting the vehicle in park, she jumped out.

The cold night air was a stark contrast to the warmth of the car, but Laine hardly noticed. All she knew was she needed some distance. She walked to the edge of the turn out and looked down the ramp she'd just rocketed up. The highway was empty and a veil of loneliness settled over her. Her breath turned into frothy puffs, and she wrapped her arms around herself.

"Laine."

She felt him standing behind her, and it took all her self-control not to turn and deck him. "Don't, Jack," she said from between clenched teeth. "Just get back in the car."

"I'm sorry," he said. "I was out of line."

"Yes, you were," she replied. "Now get back in the car."

He stood there for a few moments, and then she heard him turn and walk back to the Suburban, gravel crunching under Nick's running shoes as he went. Laine dashed a hand over her eyes and looked into the heavens. Night was starting to assert itself and the color finally seemed to deepen, going from sunny sky blue to deeper blue and then to indigo. The brightest stars began to show themselves, but for now they were only faint twinkles. Laine turned and looked into the southwest at Venus, the only heavenly body that was truly shining in the dusk. When the sun finally decided to move out over the Pacific and leave them in darkness, that planet would be the brightest object in the sky. She would often look into the heavens at night and imagine Nick was up there looking down on her. Usually, the thought was comforting. Right now, it didn't help at all.

The cold started to burrow through her sweater and she took a deep breath. Laine ignored the chill and watched Venus for another moment, picturing Nick in her mind. Closing her eyes, she let Nick's presence, whether real or imagined, calm her. She could almost feel him stroking her cheek and hear him whisper, *"It's okay, baby. I'm here and you're going to be fine."* She started to shiver, but glanced at Venus one last time. It twinkled. With that final reassurance, she got back into the SUV, started the engine, and started driving.

She sensed Jack's gaze on her as she took the ramp and got back on the highway, though he said nothing. They drove in silence and Laine never even looked in the mirror. Roughly thirty miles down the road they came upon a truck stop and she pulled off the highway. Big rigs lined the large parking lot, motors idling, refrigerator units humming. Laine drove past them to the self-service gas pumps. After shutting off the engine she grabbed her purse and moved around to the pump. She took her credit card from her wallet and was about to swipe it when she realized what she had almost unwittingly done. Pausing, she looked at the plastic square for a moment before returning it to its slot in her wallet. A cold numbness took hold of her as she took a handful of cash and walked inside the 24-hour convenience store to pay.

It took nearly five minutes to fill the Suburban's tank. The air seemed to get colder with each tick of the gas pump. Laine watched the numbers whirl, but her mind was a million miles away. When the pump shut off, she jumped. It took her a second to realize the tank was full. She put the nozzle away and replaced the gas cap.

Laine looked at the rear window as the pump spit out a receipt. She hesitated a moment and then opened her door and stuck her head inside. For a second her mind blanked as her anger tried to reassert herself, but she took a deep breath and swallowed it. Now was not the time.

"Do you want anything?" she finally asked in a clipped tone. "Sandwich, soda, chips, candy maybe? They have a Subway in there if you're hungry."

Jack didn't look at her. "A ham and cheese sounds good. And water is fine, thanks."

His voice was low, and even though he said nothing more Laine heard the unspoken apology in the subdued tones. He glanced at her then turned his gaze to his lap, but the flash of regret in his steely eyes was unmistakable. Something else glimmered briefly in those silver depths, something she couldn't quite pinpoint, and then it was gone. She blinked, nodded, and walked into the mini-mart. After receiving her change from the clerk, she approached the Subway counter. She ordered a double ham and cheese for Jack on whole wheat, and a meatball sub for herself, and while they were being made she grabbed a few bottles of Coca-Cola, a few bottles of Sprite, two bottles of A&W Root Beer, and a small bag of ice. After paying for her purchases, she walked back out to the Suburban.

She drove away from the gas pumps and parked in a dimly lit corner of the parking lot that had a view of both incoming and outgoing ramps. She shut off the engine and handed Jack his sandwich.

"Double ham and cheese with the works," she said. "I figured if you didn't like any of the toppings you could just take them off."

"No need." He unwrapped his food. "That's just the way I like it. Thank you."

Laine looked at him for a moment, but he didn't return her gaze. A splash of guilt dampened her anger further. His expression reminded her, oddly enough, of a puppy sorely chastised when caught chewing on the owner's favorite shoe. His actions hadn't been deliberately hurtful, and the owner *had* left the shoes in plain sight. She sighed softly, got out of the Suburban and walked around to the back.

In the cargo area was a medium-sized ice chest, and she took it out and put it on the ground. She then retrieved the bag of sodas and ice, put the sodas and some water bottles inside the chest and dumped the bag of ice over them.

"Want something other than water?" she asked him. "I have Coke, Sprite and A&W Root Beer."

He finally looked at her, but only briefly, his mouth full of sandwich. She waited until he finished chewing.

"Root beer, please," he said.

Laine tossed him the icy bottle and he caught it with one hand. She then grabbed a Coke and put the lid on the chest. Once the cooler was safely stowed she closed the rear hatch and got back behind the wheel.

By the time she started her sandwich he was almost done with his. She glanced in the mirror and watched as he popped the last bite into his mouth and washed it down with a long swig of root beer. It was odd, but her anger had pretty much evaporated. She couldn't blame him for being curious; she was curious about him after all. He simply had the courage to ask. She, on the other hand, did not.

"There's a motel over there," Jack said with a nod to his right. "We can stop here, if you like. It's been a long day and you must be exhausted." He chuckled and met her eyes in the mirror. "I have to keep reminding myself you're not a pro at this. It's easy to forget."

"What do you mean?" she asked.

"You're always so . . . calm," he replied. "I mean . . . when I told you your life could change completely, you acted as if I'd simply said the roast needs to bake at 450 for an hour." He paused, and his gaze became solemn. "I imagine that's what makes you a good doctor."

"It helps," she admitted. "But I learned something about myself today."

"What?"

A snow flurry danced outside and Laine watched it for a moment. She wasn't surprised by the sudden appearance of the frozen precipitation. In the mountains the weather was unpredictable, and even in late summer snow sometimes fell. The flakes quivered in front of the window, and then disappeared.

"Before this afternoon," she said at last, "I didn't think I had the ability to panic, and crying is certainly not high on my list of activities. Now, I know I can do both." She sighed and absently rubbed her neck. "With exceptional skill, and troubling ease, I might add."

He leaned forward and put a hand on her shoulder. "No," he said in a low voice. "If you had panicked, we'd both be dead." He squeezed her shoulder and sat back. "That trick with the lights, by the way, brilliant."

She turned in her seat and looked at him. "You saw them?" When he nodded she shook her head. "I had hoped you would. I was just praying you wouldn't come out the front to see what was wrong."

"I almost did," he said, "until I looked out the kitchen window and realized you weren't alone. That scared the shit out of me, especially when I saw who was with you."

"You recognized him even before you came into the barn?"

Jack nodded and his expression darkened. "There's only one guy in the unit who looks like that."

"In my head I called him Mr. Clean," Laine said. "Who was he?"

"Reed Harris," Jack replied with a small sigh. "He's a convicted felon with a rap sheet as long as both our arms." He grimaced. "The majority of his offenses were crimes against women, and what he did to them usually left them too frightened to testify . . . or dead."

Laine closed her eyes and exhaled slowly. "I can only imagine. He said some awful things in the car."

"I bet. I spent some time around him, unfortunately, and he was the type who liked to brag about what he'd done." He shook his head and turned his gaze out the window. "If you'd known what he was capable of, you'd have shot him again just to make sure the first ones took."

They drifted into contemplative silence and Laine finished her sandwich. After she finished her soda, she gathered the trash and tossed it in a nearby receptacle.

"So," Jack said as she slid back into the driver's seat, "we going to call it a night?"

"No," Laine replied, starting the engine. "The clerk inside said there's another truck stop with a motel about 150 miles down the road. I think I can hang on for another few hours. You?"

"Press on, oh fearless leader," he said with a smile. "You're the boss."

Laine arched one brow and glanced at him. "And don't you forget it."

***

Calember stared down at the body through his night vision goggles with disinterest as the rest of his team searched the barn. They'd followed the GPS chip in Reed's satellite phone to this position when he had failed to check in. Although Calember was surprised to find the man dead, he wasn't at all sorry. Reed had been good for what Ripley had hired him to do, but that didn't make him likeable.

"You think Jack got him, sir?" Harmon asked. The man pulled a sandwich out of his pack and downed half of it with one bite.

Calember watched him chew for a bit then rolled his eyes and shook his head. Standing over a dead teammate, and Harmon was more interested in filling his belly than his fallen comrade. Ripley really knew how to pick them. "Probably," he replied. "It would be poetic justice if the doctor killed him though, wouldn't it?" The thought was oddly satisfying and more than a little amusing. He chuckled. "Reed Harris, rapist and sadist extraordinaire, killed by a practitioner of the healing arts, and a woman. You just can't make this shit up."

Harmon finished his egg salad. "So, what now, sir?"

From the tone of Harmon's voice, Calember could tell the man was no sorrier to see Reed go than he was. He stared at the corpse and briefly considered giving him a pseudo-Viking funeral. But, the smoke and flames would only draw attention, and frankly, Harris wasn't worth that much bother.

"Have Marx and Brannagan sanitize in here, take the body back over the ridge to the Jeep," Calember said at last. "We'll check the house and see what we can find out about our elusive doctor."

"Sir, hasn't West been doing a complete background since we got her name from Mr. Clean here?" Harmon asked with a smirk. "That should give us all the info we need, right?"

"Perhaps, but the devil is in the details," Calember replied flatly. "You're not going to get details from a background check, Harmon." He flicked a finger against the front of Harmon's goggles. "Remember that."
***

Jack had to admit by the time Laine pulled into the motel parking lot, even he was exhausted. It wasn't 11:00 p.m. yet, but it felt like it had been years since he'd been in a bed. He knew his lack of strength was due to the gunshot wound and blood loss, but that didn't make him hate it any less.

He stayed in the car while Laine got them a room. From where he sat the clerk looked rumpled and tired, and it seemed to take longer than necessary. The man and Laine exchanged a few words and the clerk frowned. A sliver of apprehension wormed through him as the conversation continued for about another half minute. When Laine came back out to the Suburban she appeared frustrated.

"What's wrong?" he asked.

"Asshole wanted a credit card and I.D.," she replied with a scowl. "I *am* not giving him a credit card, so he wants a $200 deposit in cash, as if the *entire room* is worth that much. I told him I lost my I.D., so he wants my *husband's* identification."

His brows rose. "Husband?" Jack repeated, surprised.

She kept her gaze averted and nodded. "I thought a woman traveling alone might draw more attention." She shrugged. "A husband and wife, however, not so much."

Something inside him warmed and he fought a smile. "That's good, but I don't have any ID."

"I know."

She opened the glove box and grabbed a manila envelope. He watched as she took out a few bills and stuffed them in her pocket. Then she started digging in her purse.

"What are you looking for?" he asked.

After a few moments she pulled out what looked like a man's wallet. He saw the flash of pain in her eyes before she opened it and took something from inside.

"It's Nick's wallet," she said with an almost sheepish expression. "Ever since . . . ." She paused and took a breath. "I keep it in my purse. I don't know why."

She looked at the hard plastic card and Jack saw the sheen of tears. He wanted to kick himself. He knew he wasn't responsible for her husband's death and the grief that went along with it, but he *was* responsible for putting her in the position to face those feelings again. No matter how much he wished otherwise, there was nothing he could say or do to make it any easier.

"You don't have to explain anything to me," he said softly.

"I know." She sandwiched her husband's driver's license between her palms. "Be right back." She closed the door and walked away.

He watched as she paused before re-entering the motel office. She took a deep breath, pasted a calm, slightly annoyed look on her face, and pushed through the swinging glass door. This time she returned with a key.

"Got a room on the backside of the motel, first floor," she said as she got into the Suburban. "He said it was the 'honeymoon' suite." She snickered. "Probably means the bed has 'magic fingers' and a mirror over it."

Jack couldn't resist. "Sounds promising." He smiled. "Got any quarters?"

She glanced over her shoulder at him, and he was glad to see that the haunted expression was gone.

"Don't even go there," she said flatly.

In less than a minute, Laine pulled around behind the building and backed into a parking space against the fence at the rear of the motel. Jack groaned as he got out and stretched his legs. Laine was immediately at his side.

"You okay?" she asked.

"Fine," he said, arching his back. There were several loud pops and he groaned again. "I think I'm going to need those magic fingers."

She started taking bags out of the Suburban. "What do you want me to bring?"

"I don't have anything besides my duffel bag. Other than that and your sweet self, I need nothing else."

"All right," she said as she handed him the key. "We're in room 126. Why don't you go ahead and I'll bring the bags."

A flash of annoyance sent a snappy retort to the tip of his tongue and he bit it back just in time. "I *can* carry something."

Laine straightened and looked him in the eye, a small smile dancing about her mouth. "Fine." She handed him his bag. "Now go. I can get the rest."

He bit his tongue again as his irritation grew, but he did as he was told. She had parked well away from the room, and again he had to remind himself she was not a professional. "Must watch a lot of spy movies," he muttered to himself.

As expected, the room was a virtual carbon copy of every cheap motel he'd ever stayed in, only gaudier. The difference between this room and the many others he remembered was the brothel inspired décor. He didn't know Laine well, but somehow he doubted she'd ever stayed in a motel room that looked like this. Imagining her reaction made him smile. Then there was the bed, the *only* bed, the bed they would no doubt share. It was large, circular, covered with a red velvet comforter, and it did indeed have "Magic Fingers." The headboard resembled a bad Valentine's Day card with elaborate gold-filigreed Cupids and hearts. The wallpaper looked like it had come straight from a whorehouse. Other than the bed there was a small, circular table in front of the window with two matching chairs covered in worn vinyl. A narrow dresser sat against the wall with a TV on top. Next to the dresser was a door Jack knew led to another door that opened into the next room. At least it smelled clean, which was a plus. He dropped his bag on the table and closed the curtains. A few seconds later Laine entered and closed the door behind her.

"I'm bummed," Jack said. "Magic Fingers, but no mirror."

She chuckled and put her bags down on the dresser. "Sorry to disappoint." She looked around the room, then at the bed, and the horrified expression on her face made him laugh.

"Bet you're wishing you'd gotten a room with two doubles now, aren't you?"

She ignored the remark. "Don't even touch that comforter," she said. With her thumb and forefinger she grabbed the corner of the spread and pulled it off with one swift jerk. She then kicked it repeatedly until it was in a rumpled pile in a corner. "Yuck. I'm going to get the sleeping bags out of the car, and the antibacterial wipes. Be right back."

While she was gone Jack used the restroom. He was washing his hands when she walked in with two sleeping bags. She put them on the table next to his bag.

"Let me use the bathroom, then I'll check your shoulder," she said. "Why don't you take a seat?"

"You got it, Doc."

Jack sat down in one of the chairs by the round table, unfastened the sling and took it off. He flexed his arm before he unzipped the sweatshirt and removed it as carefully as he could. He examined the neat gauze and looked up when he heard the bathroom door open. Laine washed her hands before taking her doctor's bag from the dresser. She sat on the edge of the mattress across from him, opened the case and snapped on a pair of latex gloves.

"All right," she said as she slowly peeled the tape, "let's see what's going on here." She looked at the gauze. "Leakage has almost completely stopped, and there are no signs of infection which is good." She gently pressed on the wound and looked up at him. "How does that feel?"

"More like a bruise than a gunshot wound," he replied.

"Move it around a bit."

He moved his arm slowly backward and forward, and then side to side. Laine stood, took his hand and lifted it so his arm was straight out to the side. "That hurts a little, but not much," he said. "Want to try something else?"

"Hold your arm out just like that."

He did, but he only had the strength to do so for a few seconds. His muscle gave out and his arm dropped to his side. "Dammit."

"Relax, Jack," she said. "Your injury was mostly soft tissue damage. You should expect some weakness for a while, until things are healed up." Laine pursed her lips. "Can you lift your arm over your head?"

Jack grimaced and raised his arm until it looked like he was saluting Hitler. He held it there for a few seconds before he put it down.

"Did that hurt?" she asked as she sat down and started pulling things out of her case.

"Yeah, but not nearly as much as it did yesterday." He watched as she picked up a syringe and a small glass bottle. "Antibiotics?"

"Yes, sir," she replied. She filled the syringe, tapped it a few times and depressed the plunger to ensure there were no air bubbles, then wiped his shoulder with an alcohol soaked pad. "Little pinch."

He studied her face as she injected him; the smooth texture of her skin, the spatter of freckles across her nose, the flecks of green and gold in her eyes. He remembered the flash of pain in those eyes, the pain *he* had caused. Not only had he upended her life, he had also hurt her by prying into what was obviously a painful past she wasn't ready to face. He wanted to kick himself . . . again.

"There," she said. She placed the used syringe inside a portable bio-hazard receptacle. "Let me clean this, put on a fresh bandage and you're done."

"Good. I'm exhausted." Jack gave her a rueful smile. "You're probably more tired than I am." He watched her as she soaked some gauze pads with alcohol. Her expression was professional, like that of any doctor treating a patient, but he had a feeling much more was going on beneath the surface. She met his eyes briefly and he saw the shift before it was carefully masked. He grabbed her wrist gently when she reached toward him. "Laine, I'm sorry," he said suddenly. "I didn't mean to hurt you."

She didn't even hesitate. "I know, Jack. You're forgiven."

He was surprised it had been that easy. He had expected anger or grief or, at the very least, indignation. His hand dropped into his lap. Her calm acceptance made him feel worse, especially when he thought of the pictures he'd taken. He didn't deserve her forgiveness.

His throat tightened and words failed him, so he kept his mouth shut and stared at her as she bandaged his shoulder. Even when she had finished he couldn't take his eyes from her face. Laine frowned as she put her supplies back in the case and removed her gloves.

"What?" she asked. She stood and placed the case next to the TV. She sat down on the edge of the inexpensive dresser and crossed her arms over her chest.

Jack hung his head, unable to hold her gaze. He knew this wasn't the right time to come clean – she was tired, emotionally drained, frightened – but he didn't foresee the right time presenting itself anytime in the near future. At least here she could take his head off in relative privacy if she chose. He took a deep breath.

"Before you say you forgive me, I have to show you something." She said nothing as he reached into his bag and pulled out the pictures he'd found in the box marked "Nick's Locker." He looked at them again before he handed them to her.

Her expression was inscrutable as she took the photos, but her eyelids fluttered slightly.

He wasn't the type to blush, but heat crawled up his neck as shame grated hotly against the inside of his chest cavity. It left raw, bloody claw marks as it climbed into his throat. He swallowed hard. "I found those—"

"I know where you found them," she said in a hushed voice. "Why do you have them?"

Jack was at a loss. He wasn't sure he could explain to *himself* why he'd taken the photos. He certainly couldn't explain it to *her*. Head bowed, he sat and rested his elbows on his knees. "I don't know," he admitted. "I just . . . ." He looked at her and realized he owed her *some* sort of explanation. Hell, he owed her his life, and he wouldn't blame her a bit if she decided to walk. "I guess . . . I want to know who *she* is. I want to know who *you* are, and after seeing the diplomas from Harvard, I knew you weren't going to tell me."

Her chin trembled and a single tear slid down her cheek. "Just because I'm helping you, that doesn't give you rights to my life." She put the photos on the dresser. "Besides, you know who I am." She paused and met his gaze. "*That* woman is dead."

That flat statement sparked something in his chest, and angry heat burned through the disgrace he'd been choking on. "Your husband *loved* that woman," Jack said, frowning. "Anyone could look at that picture of the two of you and know you were his whole world." He took a step toward her. "She didn't die with him."

"Maybe she did."

Fury and sorrow battled inside him, one hot, one cool, and the conflict only added to each. "Only if you let her. Do you think that's what Nick would've wanted?"

"Don't." She shook her head and narrowed her eyes. "Don't you dare."

Jack couldn't let it go. "Answer the question, Doc."

"Why do you care?" she asked, eyes brimming, "and what business is it of yours?"

He scowled. "Until we reach Denver and I get you someplace safe, you *are* my business." Taking a deep breath, he dropped his gaze. "And, I *do* care." He met her disbelieving eyes. "I know what it's like to not be who you are. It's not living, Doc, it's *existing*. Just looking at those pictures, I know your husband would have wanted more for you."

She stood. "My past has *nothing* to do with this," she said flatly.

"I want more for you, too."

Tears spilled unheeded and she stared at him with wide, anguished eyes. "You have no right," she whispered.

Jack could relate to her pain and her reluctance to face it. "I know what it's like to lose the people you love, but letting their loss change who you are dishonors their memory." He sensed a chink in her armor and tried a different tactic. "You saved my life, Laine," he said softly. "Let me help get yours back."

Laine stepped back from him and shook her head. "Why don't you stick to ATF operations, and leave the pop psychology to those who are trained for it." With that, she turned on her heel and went into the bathroom. He heard the soft thunk of the lock as she locked the door behind her.

Chapter Seven

The room was dark and quiet when Laine opened the bathroom door. She half expected Jack to be asleep, she was hoping for that, but he wasn't. He was sitting on the edge of the bed with his back to her, and, to her surprise, with a bottle of beer in his hand. She watched as he took a long drink, finished it, and grabbed another from several sitting on the table. Apparently, he'd visited the restaurant/bar next door while she'd been in lockdown. Anger flared briefly. He shouldn't have exposed himself and put himself in more danger by leaving the room, but she didn't have the energy to maintain the heat of her anger and it quickly sputtered out. With a sigh she let it go and, oddly, felt lighter when she did.

She couldn't remember a day when she'd cried so much or so hard, not even when her husband had died. She was drained, but in a way she felt better. Part of her was mad as hell at Jack, but there was that still, small voice, the one she had learned to listen to, that said Jack was absolutely right.

She wasn't blind to the fact that she was a shell of the woman Nick had loved, and she could imagine the scowl on Nick's face if he could see her. Grant had commented that he hadn't heard her laugh in a long time. She'd allowed her grief to overtake her, to infiltrate her life and change her into someone she didn't know. What she *did* know was it was time to re-join the land of the *living*, and not just the *alive*. With slow, deliberate steps she walked to the end of the bed.

"I always seem to be apologizing to you," he said in a low voice. "You're right. I have no right to pry into your life, Laine. I'm sorry, and I promise I won't ask you any more questions. I know you won't believe this, but the last thing I want to do is hurt you."

Laine looked at his strong, bare back for a moment then sat on the end of the mattress and faced him, though she didn't look at him. "I understand your curiosity," she said after a moment. "I'm curious about you, too." She grabbed a beer, twisted off the cap, and took a drink. "That part of my life . . . it's . . . it's not something I talk about." She rested her elbows on her knees. "I've *never* talked about it, not even to Grant. It's, um . . . it's painful."

"I get it, Laine," he said, "And I think I know the basics, just not the details."

She chuckled ruefully. "Yeah. The devil is in the details." She took another drink and closed her eyes as the bubbly liquid cooled her throat. "Y'know, maybe when this is all over, we'll have a sit down, a couple of drinks, and I'll give you my life story. Until then, let's concentrate on getting to Denver in one piece." She glanced up at him. "Deal?"

He smiled and held out his right hand. They shook hands then he lifted his bottle. "To you," he said with an amused glint in his eyes. "The only woman I know with just as many secrets as me."

A smile curved her mouth and she tapped her bottle to his. "To secrets."

They drank in comfortable silence. When Jack finished his beer he put the empty bottle in the trash and stretched. He looked at the bed, scratched his head and gave her a crooked grin.

"Okay ," he said, "how are we going to work this?"

"Like adults," she said in a wry voice. "Why? Worried you won't be able to control yourself?"

Jack pursed his lips. "I was more worried about *you*, actually," he teased. "After all, I am wounded and helpless."

Laine laughed. "Helpless? You mean helpless like a pit bull, right?"

"More or less," he replied with a chuckle. "So, adults?"

"Last time I checked." She arched one brow. "At least, I know *I* am."

"I am, sometimes," he admitted, "and tonight will be one of those times."

"Good," Laine said. "There's an extra toothbrush in my bag if you want it. I'm going to run down to the truck stop and get you some clothes." She studied his physique for a moment. "Let me guess, 34 waist and 36 length."

His brows drew together. "How did you know that?"

"That's what my husband was," she replied. "It wasn't much of a leap." She glanced at his feet. "Do the shoes fit?"

"Well, your husband had a half size bigger foot than me," Jack replied, "but they work. There's no need for new sneakers."

"Maybe not," Laine said as she got to her feet and swung her purse over her shoulder, "but if we meet up with any nefarious individuals and need to run, wouldn't it be better to have the right size shoes?"

He narrowed his eyes on her face. "You think of everything, don't you, Doc?"

"I try," she said with a smile. She reached into her overnight bag and pulled out a fresh toothbrush and a tube of toothpaste. "Here. I trust you can make do with the little bitty soaps?"

"I'll make do," he said dryly. "I know those miniature beauty bars are going to wreak havoc on my dewy complexion, but one makes sacrifices where one must."

Laine chuckled and rolled her eyes. "Glad to see you can adapt. I'll be back in a few."

The truck stop was only a mile or so down the road, and it was one of the larger establishments with a 24-hour restaurant, a large convenience store, showers, and overnight accommodations for the truckers. Before going inside, Laine gathered her hair into a ponytail and tucked it all inside a San Francisco 49ers ball cap. Then she zipped her jacket all the way up, left the Suburban, and locked the doors.

The convenience store was like a mini Walmart, with everything from snacks to shoes, clothes to motor oil, and cosmetics to radiator fluid. Laine picked up a basket near the register and nodded to the clerk. The man gave her a disinterested look and returned to his magazine.

Laine looked through a rack of khaki pants and found a pair to fit Jack, then grabbed a short-sleeved button up shirt, another t-shirt, and a jean jacket. There wasn't much of a shoe selection, but she found a pair of work boots in his size and took them, tossing a couple pairs of socks and a 6-pack of men's underwear into the basket as she went. She was walking toward the register to pay for her items when the front doors opened and three men strode in.

Normally, she wouldn't have given them a second look, but the military haircuts and sharp, searching gazes made them stand out amidst the tired truckers and bleary-eyed travelers. She noticed one of the men was wearing an earpiece. It wasn't a Bluetooth that much she was sure of. The pigtail wire that ran from the end of the earpiece and disappeared beneath his shirt collar was a dead giveaway. She'd watched enough episodes of 24 and Alias to know what it was. The fact they were wearing all black and resembled a SWAT team that had just gotten back from a raid didn't hurt either. Laine grabbed a book from a rack and started perusing the back cover, trying to blend in. From beneath the brim of the ball cap, she watched their every move.

The tallest man walked into the restaurant and one of his buddies approached the cashier. Her heart rate jumped when the guy by the register took what looked like a photograph from his pocket and showed it to the clerk. A tremor ran through her as adrenaline hit her bloodstream. The bored employee looked at the picture, shook his head and turned his gaze back to *Guns and Ammo*. Laine bent over and pretended to tie her shoe as the man in black turned and scanned the store. If he noticed her he gave no sign, and after a few moments perusal, he left the shop to join his cohorts.

"You find what you're lookin' for?" a male voice asked from behind her.

Laine's head snapped up and she looked into the face of the clerk.

"Almost," she said as she rose, using her best Southern drawl. "Now if you'll just point me toward the anti-diarrhea medicine I think that'll just about do it." She looked around quickly, leaned toward the clerk and whispered, "Hubby had some bad chili in Cheyenne. Let's just say, if it weren't for that chili, we wouldn't be havin' to buy him a new set of clothes and I wouldn't be needin' to steam clean our rig's interior once we get home to Missoula, if'n you know what I mean."

A look of disgust crossed the clerk's face and he pointed to his right. "Medicine and stuff's over there." He shuffled away and returned to his chair behind the counter.

Laine was secretly surprised. If that man had shown the clerk a picture of her, then she'd just experienced what could only be divine intervention. Apparently, the attendant either hadn't looked at the photograph, or he had and still didn't recognize her. Then again, perhaps they'd shown the guy a picture of Jack. Either way, she heaved a sigh of relief and made her way to the toiletry department. After picking up some anti-diarrhea medicine, she paused in front of a rack of women's hair color. On impulse, she grabbed a box, *Ravishing Ruby*, and added it to the basket.

The cashier barely glanced at her as he rang up her items. Even when he scanned the hair color he didn't blink. Once she paid and he'd bagged the items, she gave him a smile and walked out.

Her heart was still racing and her gaze scanned the parking lot as she walked toward the Suburban. She noticed a large, black SUV out of the corner of her eye with its running lights on, steam puffing out of the tailpipe, parked facing the truck stop entrance. Instinct told her the men from the store were in that vehicle. She tried to appear as normal as possible as she got into her car, started the engine, and pulled onto the frontage road.

She kept her eyes on the rear view as she drove away. The SUV did not follow her. Regardless, she watched the mirror until she was parked at the motel. When she entered the room Jack sat up in bed and clicked the TV off. Damn. She'd been hoping he'd be asleep.

"Everything okay?" he asked.

She saw the concern in his grey eyes, and the dark circles beneath them. Laine knew if she told him about the guys at the truck stop they'd be back on the road, and she wasn't sure he, or she, could handle that. Fumes and adrenaline were all that fueled her, and even though she doubted she could sleep she needed a break, even if it was only a couple of hours. "Fine," she lied. She removed the clothes from the bags, pulled the tags off, and stacked them neatly on the armoire. "Now you can wear something other than sweat pants."

"Thanks."

"You're welcome." She looked at him for a moment then pressed a hand to his brow. "I'm going to take a shower. You should rest."

He covered her fingers with his. "Now that you're back I might be able to close my eyes for a few." He pressed his lips to her palm and released her. "But you need some rest, too, Doc. After you shower, wake me up so you can get a few zees."

Laine nodded and took the bag containing the hair color. "I'll do that. Now lie down and try to sleep. If you want that shoulder to get better you need it."

***

Laine pulled the neck of the robe tighter and took the towel from her hair. She absently rubbed the damp, freshly colored strands as she walked to the edge of the window and peeked through the inch between the curtain and the wall. She froze.

Cruising slowly through the parking was the black SUV she'd seen at the truck stop. They were going so slowly they made old man Ogilvie look like a NASCAR driver. The windows were all heavily tinted, even the front ones, so she couldn't tell how many people were inside.

"Jack." She spoke in a whisper and didn't move for fear they might notice. "Jack, you need to get up." To her surprise he was at her side almost instantly.

"What is it, Laine?" He peered through the narrow opening.

"That SUV cruising by," she began, "it was at the truck stop when I was there."

"So?"

"Well, I think they're friends of yours." She felt him tense.

"Why?" he asked in a low, accusing voice.

She glanced over her shoulder, but he wasn't looking at her. His hawk-like gaze was fastened on the SUV.

"When I was in the store buying your clothes three guys dressed like SWAT commandos came in. I wouldn't have paid them much attention, until I saw the earwigs."

He met her eyes. "Are you sure?"

She looked back to the car. "Yeah. Sound familiar?"

"Why didn't you tell me?"

Heat inched up her neck and she ran a hand over her eyes. "Because they didn't see me and they didn't follow me back. I figured we were safe . . . for a couple hours at least."

His gaze impaled her, but he pressed his lips into a thin line and remained mute. He grabbed his laptop, put it on the bed, and turned it on. His brows were drawn together in a scowl and she waited.

"Come here," he said, his eyes focused on the computer.

She went to his side and looked at the screen. On the monitor was a photograph of a group of men, similar to pictures she'd seen of Grant's squad he'd taken while deployed in Iraq, only these guys weren't wearing U.S. military uniforms. She leaned over and scanned the faces.

A cold, hard stone of dread settled in her stomach and the realization of what she'd done sent nausea swirling in her belly. Her hand trembled as she reached toward the screen. "This one, and . . . this one were the only two I got a clear look at." She straightened and took a deep breath. "We're in trouble, aren't we? Maybe we should call the police."

"And say what?" he asked. "If the cops show up here, it'll only spook them and give them a reason to come back."

Her throat tightened. "Jack, I'm sorry . . . ."

"It's not your fault, Laine." He rose in one fluid motion and went back to the window. He was careful not to move the curtain. "Shit."

He whirled from the window and sat down on the edge of the bed. Laine could tell he was trying desperately to figure a way out of this, his eyes darting back and forth as he pressed his thumbs into his temples and vigorously rubbed his forehead. Finally, he stood up and went back to watching the SUV.

"Get your stuff together," he said. "As soon as they go around the corner of the building, we run for the Suburban and get out of here."

"You really think we can outrun them?" she asked, incredulous.

"I don't know," he replied. "It's better than sitting here and waiting for them to come to us."

Laine stared at him. "How would they find out we're here?"

"They're checking license plates," he said. "Ripley probably has teams on every major road in and out of Evergreen, and it makes sense they'd be checking all the truck stops and motels. They haven't gotten to the Suburban yet, but when they do they'll run the plates, and when they find out who it's registered to . . . ." He paused and looked at her. "It won't take much for that night clerk to tell them which room you're in."

Laine felt a surge of relief. It must have shown because his eyes narrowed on her face, and he watched her as she walked to his side and looked over his shoulder. The men in the SUV had passed out of their field of view, but for some reason she knew they weren't far away. She could *feel* them.

"It's not registered to me," she said.

He turned to her. "What do you mean?"

She met those silver eyes and realized suddenly how close they were, and that he was shirtless. He really was a fine male specimen. Mortified at the completely inappropriate thought, Laine closed her eyes, forced herself to focus on the problem at hand, and took a small breath.

"It's not registered to me." She steeled herself and met his gaze. "It's Nick's car, and Mr. and Mrs. Nick Darrow are registered at the motel."

He seemed to stare right through to her soul, and she swallowed hard. Then he grinned.

"Laine Wheeler, I think I love you." He cupped her head with his hand and kissed her again as he had earlier that day. This time her body reacted more quickly. Shivering pulses traveled along every nerve ending. After giving her lips a loud smack, he walked past her and started to put his computer away. "That'll buy us some time, but not much. We still need to get out of here. Once Ripley got your name he assigned West to get every scrap of information he could find on you. Eventually he'll connect you to Nick. He might already have . . . ." He froze then turned back to her. "What did you do to your hair?"

"What?" Laine asked innocently. "You don't like redheads?"

He stared at her for an uncomfortable moment, and then a wicked gleam entered his eyes. "Actually, I *love* redheads, and you've got the coloring to pull it off." He walked over to her and lifted a damp lock of hair from her shoulder. "For me, Doc? You shouldn't have."

Laine scowled at him and batted his hand away. "Don't flatter yourself, Agent Vaughn." She stepped around him and walked toward the bathroom. That brief contact with his mouth had set her nerves tingling, but there was no way she was going to let him see that. Before closing the bathroom door, she gave him another scowl. His low chuckle caused her to put a little more force behind closing the door than was necessary.

After she changed into a pair of sweats and a tank top she braided her hair. She left the sanctity of the bathroom braced for more of Jack's semi-flirtatious behavior. She glanced at him, but he wasn't looking at her. He was standing at the side of the window, his eyes focused on the parking lot.

"Do you see them?" she asked, almost afraid of the answer.

"They just finished making their round," he replied. "They've stopped by the motel entrance. Keep your fingers crossed. If they drive off it means they haven't put you and Nick together yet."

"Or they're driving off so they can come back on foot and kill us," she said as she stuffed her robe and other clothes into a bag.

"Perhaps," he said absently.

She frowned. "What are you planning, Jack?" she asked. "You don't seem worried about the possibility of them doubling back."

"They won't try anything here." He shook his head. "Too many possible witnesses. If they are onto us, Ripley will tell them to wait until we're somewhere they can take us out with relative assurance of it being anonymous."

"Why would he do that?"

Jack looked at her, and the coldness in his eyes made her blink. "Because that's what I'd do." He gave her a grim smile. "There are a lot of mountainous, two-lane, semi-deserted stretches of road between here and Denver. Why risk a frontal assault on a half-full motel when you can just run someone off a cliff and keep driving?" He returned to his watch post.

Laine gulped. He was right. The road to Denver could be a dangerous one, with windy mountain roads and empty, forlorn lengths of highway. They would be a much easier target out there than in here. Oddly, the thought wasn't at all reassuring.

"So, what now?"

"You packed up and ready to go?" he asked.

"I've only got the one bag," she replied.

"Then get some sleep."

One brow rose. "What? You're kidding, right?"

He shook his head but didn't look at her. "Nope. Get some rest, Doc. You didn't get much sleep last night and tomorrow may be a longer day than today, so at least try." He glanced at her and cocked one brow. "I can sleep while you drive. You can't drive while you sleep."

"The men who want to kill you, *and* me, are in the parking lot and you want me to sleep." She shook her head, but lay down on the bed. It was a little bumpy but otherwise comfortable, and she pulled the sleeping bag up around her shoulders, turning her back to Jack.

She heard the sound of coins and a moment later the bed started to vibrate. Laine rolled over and looked at him, incredulous. He met her disbelieving gaze with a boyish smile and a shrug.

"Couldn't hurt, right?" he asked. "By the way, they drove on."

Laine said nothing as he returned to his post by the window. He leaned one shoulder against the wall and peered through that narrow gap. She watched him for a moment, then rolled onto her side and curled into a ball. It wasn't long before the Magic Fingers did their work, and, despite her belief that she'd be unable to sleep, she was sound asleep.

***

It wasn't hard to get the outlet to short out, and Jack waited as sparks and smoke started to curl from the plug. There were more sparks and a soft *whoosh* as a small finger of flame lazily explored the wall. The finger grew and multiplied and Jack didn't wait any longer. He returned the dresser to its original position, quickly crossed the vacant room and went back through the connecting doors, locking each as he went. After snapping off the latex gloves he'd taken from Laine's bag, he flushed them then moved to the side of the bed.

She had actually fallen asleep, and he smiled as he eased down on the edge of the mattress. He wished she could always look so peaceful, her face soft and untroubled with just a hint of a smile. Jack wondered what she was dreaming about, and if he might be part it. He shook her gently and she bolted upright.

"What? Are they back?" she asked, her eyes hazy with sleep.

He gripped her shoulder and forced her to look at him, then pressed a hand to her cheek. "It's okay, Laine. We just need to get ready to get out of here."

She squinted at him and rubbed her eyes. "What's going on?"

He gave her a grim look. "I don't think you're going to be getting your deposit back."

"Why—"

The shriek of a smoke detector tore through the quiet night and she jumped. Her eyes flew to the adjoining door, then to his face.

"Tell me you have something to do with that."

He gave her a nonchalant shrug and a smile as he picked up the phone and dialed the office. "Yeah, hey this is room 126. The fire alarm is going off next door." He paused as the clerk responded. "Ok, thanks." He looked at her. "Get up, Laine. It's almost time for us to go." Jack got out of her way and she stood. When she moved to put her shoes on he stayed her hand. "Don't. Everything else is put away except your sleeping bag. When we leave, it has to look like we just grabbed our stuff and ran. Oh, and I'll be driving, at least until we get out of sight."

"What did you do?" she asked.

"Created a diversion," he replied. "It'll be easier to slip away from our pursuers if there are fifteen other cars trying to get out of here instead of just one." He could tell by the look in her eyes she was nervous, but she kept her cool and sat down.

"So, what are we waiting for?"

"Well," he said, "the clerk said he'd check it out, that it's probably a malfunction. When he comes to investigate and discovers there actually is a fire, he'll start banging on doors." He grabbed the plastic bag from the truck stop and gathered all their trash, what little there was. He used the handles of the bag to tie it closed, then stuffed it, and the stack of clothes she'd left for him, all but the button-up shirt, into his duffel. "Once he lets us know there *is* a fire, we grab everything and head for the car." He saw a shadow of fear pass over her face.

"And if they're watching?"

"Well, hopefully they won't recognize the short-haired, clean-shaven guy and his redhead wife as they scramble to get out of a burning motel." He carefully put on the shirt, leaving it unbuttoned, and paused when he saw she was frowning. "What?"

"Where's your sling?" she asked. "You need to keep your arm as immobile as possible or you risk tearing open the wound."

"They know they shot me, Laine," he said. "Once we're away from here, I'll put it back on, but until then we can't afford to stick out."

The door to the adjacent room banged open and Laine jumped. Jack moved to the bed and lay down, motioning for her to do the same. To her credit, she didn't hesitate, even when he indicated she should cuddle up next to him. She snuggled down without saying a word, and her head on his shoulder was a welcome pressure. He closed his eyes for a moment to enjoy the contact.

She started violently when someone banged on the door. Jack put a finger to her lips and quickly rose. He moved to the door and opened it a crack.

"Yeah?" he asked.

"You need to get out now!" the frantic clerk said in a rush. "There's a fire in the room next door!"

Jack widened his eyes. "So, it's not a malfunction? Shit!" He looked over his shoulder. "Get up, honey, there's a fire."

The clerk had already rushed off and Jack could hear the man pounding on other doors and yelling fire. The sound of distant sirens made Jack smile, and he closed the door.

"Ok, Mrs. Darrow," he said. "Grab your shoes and your bag and let's get out of here."

He threw the sleeping bag over his injured shoulder and grabbed his duffel as Laine picked up both her bags, her tennis shoes sticking out of the top of one. With bare feet, looking like they'd just been roused from a sound sleep, Jack followed Laine as they left the "honeymoon suite" and jogged to the car.

"Keys," Jack called to her when he reached the driver's side door. His shoulder throbbed, but he ignored it as Laine threw the keys to him over the hood. He quickly unlocked the door, punched the button to unlock the rest of the Suburban, then jerked open the back door and heaved the sleeping bag and duffel inside. Laine followed his lead, but he saw the fear in her eyes as she did so. She gasped and jerked upright when a window in the burning room shattered and yellow flame leapt out, casting a golden glow over them.

"Laine," he said. She didn't respond, her gaze locked on the burgeoning blaze. He raised his voice a little, but not enough to carry past her. "Laine."

She looked at him, and their eye contact seemed to break her trance. She gave him a short nod, heaved her bags inside, and closed the door. She got into the front passenger seat and Jack slid behind the wheel, sucking in a breath as he jarred his shoulder. The pain paralyzed him for a second before he jerked the door shut, jammed the keys into the ignition, and started the engine.

"Do you need any help?" she asked, buckling her seat belt.

"No," Jack said through clenched teeth as he buckled up. He put the Suburban in drive and pressed down on the accelerator.

Around them the motel became a scene of utter chaos. The clerk ran around, screaming into a cell phone as other guests rushed to evacuate the burning building. In the short time since they'd left their room, the fire had spread and now the orange glow was coming from the room above and from inside their window as well. He looked at Laine out of the corner of his eye. She seemed transfixed, her wide-eyed gaze taking in the scene as if she didn't believe what she was seeing. The light from the flames made her hair look like liquid copper and gave her eyes a golden cast. He shook himself and concentrated on getting out of the parking lot without crashing the Suburban.

When they turned out of the lot, they met the fire engine as it roared onto the scene. Jack grimaced and spun the wheel to keep from colliding with the huge vehicle. Laine braced a hand against the dashboard as the Suburban yawed wildly, then righted itself. A grunt of pain escaped him and she was immediately alert.

"You okay?" she asked.

"I'll be fine, Doc," he ground out, "but as soon as we can arrange it, you're driving."

He concentrated on making it to the highway and keeping an eye out for their friends as Laine dug in the glove compartment. She came up with a map, opened it, and flipped on the front passenger light. The tip of her tongue held to the center of her upper lip, she perused the map, her finger running down one line, then the next. He remembered that was how she had looked when he'd first seen her, and couldn't stop a smile.

"We should get off the main highway," she said, her brow furrowed in concentration. "If I remember correctly . . . yep, there it is." She looked away from the map, peering intently out the front window until they passed the next exit. That gave her her bearings, and she returned her gaze to the map.

"Ok, good. We haven't passed the exit." She glanced at him. "You averse to adding a few miles to our trip?"

"I'm not averse to anything that will help us get to Denver in one piece," he replied, his gaze on the rear view.

"Any sign of them?" she asked.

He heard the trepidation in her voice and shook his head. "No, not yet," he replied. "How soon can we get off this road?"

He could almost hear the wheels in her head as she did the mental calculations. "About five miles up the road is a turn off for Route 23. It's a two lane road that backtracks west before turning south." She pursed her lips. "It'll add another hundred or so miles to the trip, and at least another two hours."

"Whatever," he said, pain flaring as he pulled his left arm close in to his side. He let out a slow breath and kept driving. "Just let me know when to exit. You're the navigator until then."

Chapter Eight

The Suburban rolled to a stop behind the stand of trees about a mile off the highway. It was nearly four in the morning. They'd only been on the road about 15 minutes, but for some reason it seemed much longer. Laine watched Jack's face as he put the vehicle in park and turned off the engine. Harsh lines bracketed his mouth and the faint sheen of perspiration dampened his brow.

"Stay put," she said.

Laine got out and climbed into the backseat. It was dark outside, as dark as pitch, so she moved more by feel than sight at first. After putting their bags into the cargo area, she spread the sleeping bag out on the seat and grabbed her doctor's kit. She put it on the seat and climbed across and out the other side so she could open the driver's door.

"Come on, Jack," she said gently.

He said nothing as he eased out from behind the wheel and stood, his left arm held tight against his side, his forearm lying over his stomach.

"Let's get this off so I can take a look." He hissed in pain as she helped him out of the shirt. "Now, get in back." She tossed the bloodstained garment on the front seat while Jack gingerly eased onto the edge of the back seat. A low moan escaped him and she frowned.

She reached down and turned on the interior lights.

"Don't, Doc," he said in a tight voice. "We may be away from the road, but at this time of morning, even the dome lights will stand out like a beacon. You have a flashlight?"

"Yeah," she replied as she turned off the lights. "Now, sit."

When he sat down, Laine reached around him into her doctor's kit. She retrieved a small flashlight and put it between her teeth as she checked the wound. Fresh blood was clotted around the opening. She needed to re-stitch the bullet hole, but his breadth filled the doorway and gave her no room to work. She took the flashlight out of her mouth and scowled, hands on hips.

"Tailgate."

Again, he said nothing, he merely obeyed. That, more than anything else, told Laine he was hurting. She opened the back of the Suburban and got her kit. He sat and closed his eyes, leaning his head against the frame as she examined his shoulder more closely.

"Well," she said as she put the flashlight down, "you've pulled four stitches."

He scowled at her. "I didn't *do* anything. How could I pull four stitches?"

"I told you your arm needed to be in a sling," she replied. "Running across the parking lot and throwing bags around certainly didn't help." She picked up the penlight again. "Look at me."

"No problem," he said with a hint of a smile. "I like doing that."

One brow rose as she checked his pupils and his pulse. "On a scale of 1-10, what's your pain level?" she asked.

"Four."

Laine pursed her lips. "You're sweating, your teeth are clenched, and your heart rate is up." When he rolled his eyes and looked away, she gripped his chin in her hand and forced his head up. "What's your pain level? And I want the truth."

They battled visually for a few moments then he frowned. "Eight."

"I thought so," she said. "Well, the good news is you'll live."

A mischievous twinkle glimmered in his eyes. "And the bad news?"

Laine smirked. "You'll live . . . and I'm going to have to fix your stitches." She glanced at the wound again. "I'll give you a local, but you're going to need something stronger than ibuprofen afterwards."

His frown was back. "I thought we talked about this."

Laine gave him a frown of her own. "No, *you* talked. Now you're going to listen." She paused, and he pressed his lips into a thin line when she continued. "You were shot less than 48 hours ago, Jack. You should be in a hospital bed with your arm in a sling, a morphine dispenser and pretty nurses to rub your feet and give you sponge baths."

"But I'd rather be with you."

His quiet words caught her off guard, and she completely forgot what she was going to say next. Her mouth worked soundlessly a few times then she snapped her jaws shut. Unable to hold that stormy gaze, she started pawing through her bag.

"That's sweet," she said when she regained her voice. "Now, I'm going to give you a local anesthetic, but afterwards, you're getting Vicodin or morphine, take your pick."

"Doc—"

She pressed her fingers to his mouth to silence him, and was unprepared for the electric tingle that shot up her arm. For a moment she lost her voice. "Stop arguing with me," she said. "We'll be on the road for a while, so you can sleep. Now, which is it?"

He kissed her fingers and Laine inhaled sharply. She felt frozen, rooted to the spot as he covered her hand with his and pressed his lips to her palm. Then he flattened her hand against the warm, smooth skin of his bare chest and covered it with his.

"The lesser of the two," he replied in a low voice.

All Laine could do was nod. She pulled her hand gently from beneath his and snapped on a pair of latex gloves. Per her instructions, he held the penlight for her as she loaded two syringes; one with anesthetic and another with antibiotics. She then swabbed the area with a pre-wrapped alcohol pad, gave him both shots, and disposed of the needles in the portable sharps container.

"Thanks," she said as she took the light from him, unable to meet his eyes. She fished in her bag for the right bottle, and handed him two pills.

"Let me get you some water." After grabbing an ice-cold bottle, she twisted off the cap and handed it to Jack. "Take the pills and drink all of this."

"Yes, ma'am," he said with mock gravity.

Laine glanced at him and fought a smile when she saw the boyish grin. He saluted her with the bottle before downing it.

As he drank, Laine lay out a sterile pad and arranged what she was going to need on it. She poured about an inch of alcohol into a small basin, then threaded a needle with sturdy surgical thread and dropped them both into the liquid. A small pair of scissors and some tweezers joined the needle in the alcohol bath. When she finished arranging her tools, she waited until he emptied the water bottle.

"Here we go," she said. He tensed just slightly and nodded. Laine probed his shoulder. "That hurt?" When he shook his head, she pressed harder against the stitched area. He didn't even flinch. Laine looked at him for a moment longer. "Okay. Let's begin."

Holding the flashlight between her teeth, she first removed the old stitches, carefully snipping with the scissors. When the last stitch gave way, she used the tweezers to remove the old thread, depositing the stained strands on a corner of the sterile pad opposite her instruments. When the stitches were gone, she took the flashlight from her mouth, did a more thorough inspection of the wound and cleaned it again.

"Looks good," she said.

"Do you know your eyes change color?" he asked.

Laine's hand froze and her gaze met his. Scant inches separated their faces, and she could feel his breath on her cheek. "No, I didn't know that," she said at last as she returned to her work.

"They do," he informed her. "This afternoon in the barn they were a deep green color. Now they're more . . . green-brown. When you're mad, they turn golden."

Odd, she thought. She'd been married to Nick for eight years, and he'd never once mentioned that.

"How can you see my eyes in this light," she asked, "or should I say lack thereof?"

"I can see."

Laine shook her head. "I think the Vicodin is getting to you."

She picked up the needle. It took her about five minutes to re-stitch the wound, and Jack sat silent and unmoving for the entire ordeal. Thanks to the anesthetic it bled very little which made the going easier. Once she finished, she disinfected the wound again, put on a fresh bandage and started to clean up. He watched her closely, his expression unreadable.

"I guess they're right," he said, more to himself than her.

Laine removed her gloves and rolled them into the sterile pad along with the old stitches and other trash. "What are you talking about?" she asked as she put the garbage in a large zip-top bag and sealed it.

He caught and held her gaze. "All my life people have told me I'm a lucky SOB," he said. "I guess they're right."

"About the lucky or the SOB?" she asked. A small smile lifted the corners of his generous mouth, and Laine found her gaze drawn there, almost against her will.

"Both," he replied with a ghost of a chuckle.

She blinked when his finger traced from her cheekbone to her jaw.

"Every time I get in a situation where I should be a goner," he began, "I somehow manage to get out of it. It may be by the skin of my teeth, but somehow I manage."

Laine gulped. His touch was feather light, like an errant spider web brushing her face. "That's a good quality to have in your line of work, I'd imagine," she said, her voice hardly more than a breathy whisper. She cleared her throat. "You'll live longer with a skill set like that."

"This is one scrape I wouldn't have gotten out of without you." He pushed her braid back over her shoulder.

When he rose, Laine felt very small standing next to him. It wasn't that he was so much taller than she was, it was just *him*. She had no doubt when he entered a room people turned to look. His presence, his aura, was tangible, as tangible as his physicality. She stared at the cleft in his chin, unable to move her eyes any higher.

Jack put a finger under her chin and tipped her face up. He looked down at her, and there was such warmth in his silver gaze she couldn't help but smile.

"Your husband was a very lucky man," he whispered as he lowered his head. "And so am I."

Laine closed her eyes and part of her hoped he would kiss her. When he pressed his lips to the corner of her mouth and moved away she almost reached out to pull him back.

"Thank you, Laine," he said.

"You're welcome," she replied. She hid her disappointment behind a smile and prayed he couldn't hear the pounding of her heart.

Jack sat back down and closed his eyes with a sigh. He didn't look at her when she helped him get his arm back into the sling. She adjusted the straps, securing his arm to his torso so it wouldn't move. He sat there, silent and compliant.

"Why don't you lay down on the backseat," she suggested.

He nodded without looking at her. She continued to put her things away, and was almost done before he finally stood and shuffled to the rear door. Laine closed her doctor's bag, stowed it in the cargo area and shut the tailgate.

She walked around to the driver's side, and stood in the open rear door for a moment. Jack was curled up in his familiar ball and she smiled. She grabbed the corner of the sleeping bag and, with a flick of her wrist, settled it over him.

"Thank you," he said.

"You're welcome."

***

It was close to noon when Laine pulled into a small town somewhere north of Casper, Wyoming. She was so tired her eyelids felt like they were made of sandpaper. Since they'd left the motel she'd driven without stopping except for gas and bathroom breaks. Jack was dozing in the back seat, but when she pulled into a fast food restaurant parking lot he came fully awake and sat up. She rested her brow against the steering wheel and didn't bother to turn off the engine.

"Where are we?" he asked, looking around.

It was a bright day, the sun high in the cloudless azure sky. From what she could see, this little hamlet was pretty much like every small town in this part of the country: hardly more than a village snuggled in the crags of the mountains. She'd missed the sign noting the name and population, but she doubted there were more than five hundred people. The McDonald's sat on the north edge of town and she could see the south edge of town from where she was. The road was a two lane stretch of patched asphalt with one stoplight at a four-way intersection, the single red bulb blinking on and off. The place looked virtually deserted.

"I don't know," Laine admitted, peering through the window. "Somewhere north of Casper."

"You okay, Doc?" he asked.

Laine closed her eyes and leaned her head against the headrest. "I'm just tired, Jack." She chuckled. "I really must be getting old."

"Why do you say that?"

"In med school I could go for days without sleep," she replied with a sigh. "Especially during internship and the endless rotations. Now if I don't get at least six hours of sleep a night I'm useless." She looked at her reflection in the rear view and smoothed back the stray hairs that had escaped her braid. "I don't know how I did it."

He snorted in derision. "You must've done pretty well, Miss Summa Cum Laude."

Her eyes were dry and scratchy and it hurt to blink. She yawned loudly and rubbed a hand over her face. "You hungry?"

"Double quarter-pounder with cheese, please," he replied.

She glanced at him over her shoulder and scowled at his sunny smile. "Well, at least you have an appetite, which is a good sign."

"I admit I am not one to turn down a meal," he said.

"You want fries with that?" she asked, her voice laced with sarcasm.

For some reason, the fact he seemed wide-awake and in a good mood rankled her. They were running for their very lives, being hunted by domestic terrorists, and he looked as bright and alert as a four-year-old on Christmas morning.

"You're not a morning person, are you?" he teased.

Laine threw him a withering glare. "Is it morning? I've kind of lost track."

He laughed. Laine looked in the rear view and watched as he shrugged into the button-up shirt. She wondered if he'd ask for help, but he didn't. His fingers moved with surprising dexterity and it wasn't long before he had the shirt on and halfway buttoned.

"Allow me," he offered with a grin. "What would you like to eat?"

"Don't even think it." She rubbed her eyes again. "That's why God invented the drive-thru."

His brows drew together and that hawk-like gaze focused on her. "You sure?" he asked. "I'd be more than happy to go get you a Happy Meal."

She scowled. "Why? You think because it has the word 'happy' in it that it will somehow improve my mood?"

"No," he said with a chuckle. "I imagine only sleep and not having crazed killers chasing you will do that."

Laine rolled her eyes. "Seat belt, Agent Vaughn." She watched him in the rear view as he buckled his seat belt and fought a smile. Their eyes met in the mirror. He gave her a wink and she shook her head.

Fifteen minutes later Jack held the two red and white take-out bags as Laine opened up a sleeping bag and spread it on the ground beneath a towering Rocky Mountain Maple. They had stopped near the banks of a river just south of town, but this late in the season the waterway was hardly more than a big stream. She knew come February or March, however, the spot where they were standing would be close to the water's edge, if not under it. She watched as Jack dropped the bags, sat down and started distributing the food.

Laine arched her back and stretched, weary to the bone. The maple had yet to surrender its leaves to fall, the foliage providing a thick canopy overhead. It was cool beneath the tree. Looking at the idyllic scene, Laine found it hard to believe what was happening to her life. This shady spot was so peaceful and serene it diametrically opposed the chaos following her. The gentle gurgle of water over rocks was usually soothing, but for some reason, today it bothered her. Her body was still in fight or flight mode, and this calm sanctuary seemed false, as if someone had created it as a distraction to lull her into a sense of security she knew she shouldn't have.

"I'll get the drinks," she said absently. He bounded to his feet so quickly she jumped.

"Sit down," he commanded, fixing her with a scowl. "*I'll* get the drinks."

She pinched the bridge of her nose. "Jack—"

"*Sit.*"

Before she could protest, he walked the ten or so feet back to the Suburban, and returned with two large drinks. She sat and reached for the cups he extended to her, holding his while he sat down.

"Now," he began, flipping out a napkin, "we feast."

Despite her fatigue she found his childlike enthusiasm infectious. She took a long drink before she popped a couple fries into her mouth. More than anything else, even food, she wanted to sleep. As she chewed, she wondered when she would get that chance.

As they ate, she felt some of her tension drain away. With each bite of her burger her eyelids grew heavier. She finished her cheeseburger, gathered her trash, and stretched out on the sleeping bag beneath the arms of the giant maple.

"Don't let me sleep long," she murmured. "We have to get back on the road."

Her eyes closed and Jack smiled to himself. He watched as her breathing evened out and deepened. The change in her appearance was visible as the last traces of tension left her face and body. When a faint smile curved her mouth he knew she was asleep. She needed it. He would have suggested a nap break while they were eating, but somehow he knew she'd refuse. Letting nature take its course had been much easier.

When he finished eating he gathered the trash as quietly as possible and put it in the Suburban. While there he retrieved his pistol from his bag and slipped it into the waistband of his sweats. When the gun was secure, he returned to her side and lay down.

Jack put his right hand behind his head and stared up at the maple leaves overhead. Some of them were starting to turn from green to gold, but just around the edges. He took a deep breath and listened to the river. The last camp he'd been to with Ripley had been near a river, and some of the guys had complained that the sound of running water made them want to pee, but it didn't bother him. He found it relaxing.

As his mind drifted back to that last camp, he tried to pinpoint the moment his cover had started to unravel. His background had been meticulously detailed, the motorcycle club had enthusiastically vouched for him, and he'd been *very* careful to play the part of an outlaw biker. As he replayed the past years he knew he'd done everything right.

He remembered the moment it had started to go downhill.

"What are you doing out here, Jack?" Ripley had asked from behind him. "The rest of your squad went into town for some R&R."

Jack looked at the river and continued to oil his gun. "Good for them," he replied. "When they come back, drunk and puking, my gear will be ready, my uniform pressed, and I'll be asleep." He glanced over his shoulder at Ripley. "Unless, of course, you want me to join them so I can be as useless tomorrow as they will be."

Ripley laughed. It was a sharp sound, but not without humor.

"You're a strange one, Jack," the man said, "but I have to admit I like your style. Your dedication is . . . refreshing."

Jack gave his commander a curt nod. "Thank you, sir."

Laine murmured in her sleep and rolled toward him, breaking his reverie. He tensed when she snuggled against his side, her hand flattening on his belly. Jack held his breath and waited a moment, but she didn't move again.

He had read the disappointment in her gaze when he hadn't kissed her after she'd sewn him up again, though he knew she'd never admit it. Truth be told, he had wanted to kiss her, but given what was going on, he wasn't about to push *that* boundary. He was the professional and he had to remain professional, or they could both wind up dead.

She moved closer and her head came up onto his good shoulder. Jack looked down at the top of her head, then draped his arm around her and pressed a kiss to her brow. Her lashes were dark against her cheek, and he realized with surprise she'd even dyed her eyebrows. The color looked good on her; different, but good. He picked up the braid and ran his fingers down it, enjoying its softness. When she undid the braid her hair would be a cascade of waves. He pictured in his mind what she would look like with those red tresses loose around her shoulders and her hazel eyes smiling. The image sharpened his attraction and his gut clenched. Jack took a deep steadying breath and closed his eyes.

They lay together for several hours, and during that time Laine hardly moved. Jack enjoyed the familiarity, and the closeness of another human being. He had given up so much to pursue Ripley's organization, his family, most of his friends, and the ability to be honest with *anyone*. The fact he didn't have to hide with her opened up a part of him he'd kept tightly locked up for years. The sensation was liberating, and frightening, but he craved more.

Jack liked the way she fit against him and the fact she trusted him enough to sleep so close to him. She had no reason to trust him, not really, but he felt her trust as surely as he felt her head on his shoulder. Even odder was the fact he trusted her completely. His body was relaxed despite their close contact. He knew that when a person was used to sleeping alone, it took some time to become accustomed to sleeping with another person.

This was different. In the short time he'd known her, they'd built a level of trust that only came from going through dangerous and harrowing experiences, much the way soldiers who barely know each other become best friends after one combat mission together. The difference here was Laine was not a soldier, *he* was. An arrow of sadness pierced him. He had voluntarily given up everything to do his job, but she'd been thrown into this through a twist of circumstance. Unfortunately, that twist of fate might require that she give up just as much as he had. Jack closed his eyes briefly and vowed to make sure she lived to become a civilian again.

Although he would have been content to stay there with her all day and night, he could tell from the angle of the sun that it was around three in the afternoon. If they wanted to reach Denver at a decent hour they needed to get moving. He pressed another kiss to her brow then gently shook her.

"Laine," he said in a low voice, "get up. C'mon, Doc, we've got to go."

Her eyes fluttered open. She yawned, and then looked up at him with a wide, sleepy smile. When the haze cleared, her brows drew together. She sat up and looked around.

"What time . . . ." She glanced at her watch and her head snapped around. "Three hours? You let me sleep for *three hours*?"

He leaned up on his elbow. "You needed the rest. Besides, we're almost to home plate so I figured it would be all right."

"Almost to home plate?" she repeated. "How do you figure?"

"Well, we're only about 20 miles north of Casper, and it's less than 300 miles from Casper to Denver," he answered matter-of-factly. "It's what – three o'clock?" He waited for her terse nod. "We leave now, factor in time for gas and bathroom breaks, and we should be in Denver by about 10 o'clock tonight. Eleven o'clock tops."

She stared at him for a moment, looked at the river, and returned her gaze to him. "Wow. I didn't realize we were so close. That went a lot faster than I anticipated."

He stood and extended his hand to her. "Time flies when you're having fun, Doc."

When she placed her fingers in his, he pulled a little harder than he realized, putting her off balance. She fell against him, her hands on his chest. Jack's arm automatically slipped around her waist and their eyes met. Electricity crackled between them and he allowed himself a moment to enjoy the feel of her against him while he ignored the warning bells that went off in his head. His inner voice screamed at him to remain professional, but as he looked into those hazel eyes with their flecks of green and gold he didn't want to be professional. He wanted her.

"Sorry, Doc," he said in a low voice. "Guess I don't know my own strength."

Laine didn't move and he splayed his fingers over her lower back. It was one of those defining moments, the moment in the story where the hero kisses the girl. He felt drawn to her, his gaze pulled inexorably to her mouth with its ripe, generous curves. He desperately wanted to kiss her, to feel her mouth beneath his, but he shouldn't. It wasn't right, or fair. He had pulled her into a completely foreign environment, one in which she was running for her life and emotionally vulnerable. He wanted to move away from her, to rein in the desire that was building inside him, but he couldn't.

Laine blinked slowly, her breaths short and shallow, her eyes locked with his. His pulse jumped when she tipped her face up and moved closer to him, her lashes fluttering down. A battle raged inside him. Jack, the man, wanted to kiss her with everything he had and then some. On the other hand, Agent Vaughn knew he shouldn't. This wasn't the time or place. She wasn't some biker chick to whom commitment meant nothing more than being given a carton of cigarettes for her services. This was a woman he cared for. He hadn't known her two full days, but he cared for her, more than he wanted to admit.

Her hands ran slowly up his chest and over his shoulders, her body pressing against his. Her fingers stroked his neck as she lifted onto her tiptoes, bringing them face to face. As she moved to kiss him, Agent Vaughn finally won out.

"Laine," he said just before her lips touched his.

Her eyes opened and the passion he saw reflected in those golden-green pools almost undid him. Clenching his jaw, he released her and stepped back. He saw the flash of surprise and hurt before those emotions were carefully masked. He wanted to kick his own teeth in when color rose in her cheeks and she backed up a step.

"Laine—"

She shook her head and looked away. "I'm sorry, Jack," she interrupted. "I shouldn't have . . . ." She closed her mouth and glanced at the river. "I'm sorry. I apologize if I offended you."

"You didn't—"

"We better get going," she said. "Wouldn't want to miss our date with destiny, now would we?" She bent over to grab the corner of the sleeping bag and her gaze fell on the gun. Her fingers gripped the barrel of the weapon and she extended it to him, butt first. "Can't forget this."

He took the pistol, shame and regret gnawing at him once again. "Doc—"

"Why don't you get back to the Suburban?" Her voice was flat, devoid of emotion. Her request had been more a command than a question. "I'll roll up the sleeping bag and be right behind you."

She turned away from him and it took all of his strength not to grab her and turn her back. Jack, the man, wanted to kill Jack, the agent. He stared at her for a while longer, but she didn't look at him. He turned and strode back to the SUV, hating himself more with each step. Guilt churned in his gut, the tightness radiating into his chest. He hadn't meant to start this, but he definitely could have handled it better. All she had done was respond to what she thought was an invitation. If he was completely honest, it *had* been an invitation. Jack cursed himself, opened the rear passenger door, and glanced over his shoulder. He watched, dejected, as she shook out and rolled the sleeping bag with the efficiency of someone who did it often.

He knew she viewed his sudden retreat as rejection, as a sign he wasn't attracted to her. She couldn't be more wrong.

Chapter Nine

Calember leaned against the wall and watched his commander with a knowing eye.

"You *had* them," Ripley said in a low, cool voice, his back to the three man team which had just reported in. "There they were sitting in a cheap, roadside motel, blissfully unaware that death was in the parking lot." He spun around. "Oh, wait! Death wasn't in the parking lot, it was *you* three!"

Calember had seen this before and felt a spurt of pity for the three men facing Ripley's wrath. He knew enough to stay on the opposite side of the room. Ripley appeared normal, he sounded a little angry but not too much, and his expression didn't reveal anything more frightening than mild annoyance. It was like an earthquake which hadn't reached the surface yet. Tectonic plates were heaving and shaking below, but the people above had no idea what was coming. He tensed as Ripley's gaze scoured the three men, and he knew his commander was making what would be, for one of them, a life-ending decision. Wait for it, Calember thought. Wait for it . . . .

The gunshot split the air, and he jumped even though he'd been expecting the shot. The squad leader went down like a tree that had just been felled, a small hole over the left eye. The other two men remained at attention, but Calember could see them shaking from his place on the back wall.

"West forwarded all the information to *all* the teams once he got it," Ripley continued. "The doctor helping our wayward compatriot, Dr. Laine Wheeler, was married to one Nicholas Darrow, former detective with the Chicago Police Department. Did the name Nick Darrow not jump out at you while you ran the plates in that lot, Davidson?"

"Sir," Davidson said in a hushed voice, "we were already through the motel lot when West sent us the update. We went back as soon as we got it, but . . . ."

"But what?" Ripley asked.

The smile Ripley wore would entice even the most cautious little girl into his car, no candy needed, but Calember knew what lay behind it. It was probably the same smile a black widow spider used just before mating with and then killing her mate.

"They'd already left, sir," the man squeaked.

"They'd already left," Ripley repeated. He rubbed his chin and paced back and forth a few times. "The initial report says you went through the motel parking lot at roughly one a.m, is that right, soldier?" The man nodded and Ripley continued. "The fire at the motel was called in just after three a.m." He got nose to nose with Davidson. "Where the hell did you go that it took you so long to return?"

Sweat trickled down the side of both men's faces and Davidson paled visibly.

"We . . . um, we went . . . farther down the road . . . headed south . . . ."

"And did what, soldier?" Ripley asked, his polite tone belying the blazing rage in his eyes. "What did you do farther down the road, headed south?"

"We stopped to eat, sir," Davidson replied in a voice so low Calember almost couldn't hear him.

"And when you saw the report from West, did you stop eating immediately and rush back to the motel?"

Davidson shook his head, his face a mask of misery. His eyes were glued to his dead comrade, and Calember knew the man saw his own life flashing before his eyes at that moment.

"So you saw you had a match on the names," Ripley began, "and didn't think it important enough to put down your tuna melt and race back to the motel where Jack Vaughn, traitor to the cause and undercover federal agent, was *sleeping*?" Ripley began to pace again, signaling the next evolution in his rage.

Calember didn't bother to point out that Jack hadn't been sleeping, or he and Dr. Wheeler would still have been at the motel. From what Garner, the now-dead squad leader had told him, his team had arrived just after the lead fire engine. It was apparent to him that Jack had started the fire as a diversion to aid in his escape, which meant he had to have seen the surveillance team. Calember despised Jack for his betrayal of the cause, but he had to admire the man's resourcefulness and his luck.

Regardless of what had or hadn't taken place at the motel, the squad leader had to suffer the consequences for the team's mistake, if not for letting Jack get away, then for being seen by Jack in the first place. It would do no good to argue. Ripley was not known for his reasonable nature.

When the second shot rang out, Calember was shocked. Ripley was more pissed off than even *he* had assumed. Usually, only the squad leader paid the ultimate price. The other two would be punished either by confinement, hard labor, or whatever else struck Ripley's fancy at the time. Now, Davidson stood alone. Calember felt a fleeting ghost of uneasiness, and then a strange thrill of what he could only describe as anticipation. This was a level of angry he had never seen before. Then again, they'd never been infiltrated and betrayed by a federal agent before. This was uncharted territory.

Ripley pointed the 9mm at Davidson. As much as the man's knees were knocking Calember was surprised he could remain upright, but, to his credit, he did. Without another word, Ripley pistol whipped Davidson twice, then changed his grip and brought the butt of the gun down on Davidson's head. The man crumpled, but Calember saw he was still breathing. Ripley met his gaze, holstered his weapon, and spun around to face the giant U.S. map that covered nearly the entire wall. Ripley put up a hand and twitched his first two fingers. Calember recognized his cue and walked forward over the fallen men to stand at his commander's side.

"Here's the motel," Calember said, pointing to the spot on the map. "I've dispatched teams to go down all major roads headed south towards Boulder and into Utah."

"They're going to Denver," Ripley said, appearing as calm as if nothing had happened.

"Denver?" Realization dawned and Calember almost slapped himself in the forehead. Of course.

Ripley looked at him as if he were daft. "The pigeon is flying home, Calember. The FBI and ATF both have main field offices in the Federal Building in Denver."

"I'll deploy two squads to Denver right away," Calember said, his stomach twisting uncomfortably. He'd known the FBI and ATF had offices there, and he should've realized Jack would want to get there. Thankfully, Ripley seemed too preoccupied to notice his lapse.

"First, notify our asset in Denver. Then fly four squads down. Make sure they leave the uniforms at home." Ripley gave him a pointed look. "Have them start at the Federal Building and fan out from there." His eyes narrowed on the map. "Spin the web, Calember, and let the flies come to you."

***

Laine focused on the highway without really seeing it, her mind replaying her gross misstep. Since leaving their picnic area, they'd barely spoken two words. Unfortunately, this just gave her more time to ruminate on what an idiot she'd been.

"When we get to Fort Collins, we need to stop and pick up a few things," Jack said as they passed the mileage sign that said the city was 15 miles out.

"Okay," Laine said. "Where?" She glanced in the rear view, but he was looking out the window.

"Walmart, Target, wherever," he replied.

Laine fumbled through her purse with one hand until she found a small spiral notebook with a pen stuck through the wire binding. She held it out to him.

"Here," she said. "Write down what you need." It was several seconds before he took the notebook from her outstretched hand. "We'll stop for gas, and I'll ask the attendant where the nearest Walmart is."

He didn't reply, but she heard the scratching of the pen. She glanced surreptitiously at him every few seconds and if he wasn't writing she could tell he was thinking, ticking off a mental list, his grey gaze focused somewhere on the horizon. Obviously, he'd already forgotten her blunder. The feeling of being summarily dismissed hurt, regardless that the logical part of her brain knew she was being ridiculous. Jack had more important things to concentrate on than her bungled attempt at kissing him.

Laine groaned inwardly and cursed herself for a fool. She used to be so good at reading people; she'd known Nick was going to ask her out before he did. But she'd been wrong with Jack, and she still felt the sting of his rebuff. It had seemed like the perfect moment when she'd fallen against him, but apparently she'd read that wrong. She scowled and blamed Lifetime Television. How many times had she watched that sort of scene play out in some made-for-TV movie, and told herself with a roll of her eyes that those things didn't happen in real life? She huffed and tightened her grip on the wheel.

"Did you say something, Doc?" Jack asked.

"No, Jack," she replied in a tight voice. "Not a word."

She glanced in the rear view and caught the flash of regret in his eyes before he turned to stare once again out the window. Well, at least that was something.

She pulled off the freeway long enough to get directions to the closest Walmart, use the restroom, and fill the Suburban's tank before returning to the road. Half an hour later she exited the highway and drove west, the direction the clerk at the gas station had said she needed to go. Sure enough, even from the off-ramp she could see the huge building with its sprawling parking lot. She parked in the middle where there would be plenty of people coming and going and Jack would be relatively safe. After shutting off the engine, she took the money from the glove box, put it in her wallet and grabbed her purse.

"I'll be right back."

He didn't look at her. "I'll be right here."

Once inside, she went straight to the electronics department. In her cart she deposited a couple of disposable cell phones, a handheld GPS unit, a small digital camcorder, and a pair of inexpensive binoculars. She then made her way to the clothing department where she picked up a pair of men's dress slacks, a jacket, a button up shirt and tie, a belt, a skirt/jacket combo, and a short-sleeved, low-cut blouse. Once she had all the clothing Jack had asked for, she meandered around, gathering the remaining items on her list. She picked up a pair of heels for her and some dress shoes for Jack, pantyhose and a pair of men's dress socks, a large black suitcase with rollers, and a laptop bag. Some miscellaneous toiletries and cosmetics, and other small items, completed her shopping. After marking everything off the list and double-checking it, she went to the front of the store where the check stands were and picked what looked to be the shortest line. All in all, it took her only thirty minutes to get in and out.

Jack watched from the backseat as she unloaded everything, his face a blank slate. She wished her insides felt as placid as his features looked.

"Did you have any trouble?" he asked in a neutral voice.

"No," she replied. "In and out, list complete."

"Good," he said. "Hand me the electronic gear so I can get them up and running while you get us back on the freeway."

Laine found the bag with all the gadgets and handed it to him. He immediately busied himself opening boxes and pulling out manuals. Laine watched him for another moment before she shut the back of the Suburban and slid in behind the wheel. She didn't speak until they were back on the interstate.

"So, I imagine you have some sort of plan," she said. "Mind giving me some of the details, or are you going to hide me away in some safe house while you take care of everything?"

"Unfortunately for you," he began, "my lack of one usable appendage makes your participation integral." He glanced up and briefly met her gaze in the rear view. "How much cash do you have left?"

"I didn't count it," she replied, "but I spent nearly $900 in Walmart. We started with $2500, and between gas, food, lodging and our recent shopping spree I'd estimate we've got about $800, maybe a little less. I'll check when we make our next stop."

"Okay," he agreed, "that should be enough." He was silent for a moment. "About the money. You'll get every penny back."

"I wasn't worried about it, Jack," she said, insulted he'd even mentioned it. "Even if I didn't get it back, $2500 is a small price to pay for your life."

He seemed to understand he'd said the wrong thing. "I'm sorry, Laine, that came out wrong."

"It's okay. Everyone makes mistakes."

"Some more than others," he muttered.

The flash of self-reproach she saw on his face should have brought her some measure of satisfaction, but it didn't. The tension between them was so thick it was like a giant inside the car. She felt the squeeze of it on her heart. She knew to survive they had to work together, but how could they do that without looking at or speaking to one another?

She looked in the rear view mirror but he was staring out the window. "So," she said "what's the plan?"

He turned his gaze to the GPS navigation unit she'd purchased. "Well, first we need to change clothes." He started pushing buttons on the GPS unit. "Drive to Denver International Airport and park in the long-term lot."

"Planning a trip, are we?" she asked, suspicious.

"Sort of," he replied. The monitor beeped a few times and he nodded, as if satisfied with his work. He then turned to the cell phones. "We're going to the airport and buying two one-way tickets to Los Angeles."

"Friends there?"

"Co-workers," he answered. "I was working out of L.A. when the chance to infiltrate Ripley's group came about."

Laine was confused. "So, why are we going to Denver?"

"Denver handles all operations in the central region, including Montana," he said. "I was introduced to Ripley's second, a guy named Calember, while I was undercover with a biker gang in L.A. Denver is where the op was put together, and someone there blew my cover."

"So," Laine said with a sigh, "are we staying in Denver or going to L.A.?"

"We're buying tickets to L.A., and then we'll take a cab from the airport to a hotel in downtown Denver." He glanced at her. "Something close to the Federal Building."

The light bulb went on. "Throwing them off the scent?" Laine asked.

Jack snorted as he started pushing buttons on the phones. "Doubt it," he said. "Diverting their attention temporarily, perhaps. Ripley will send some men to L.A. just to be sure, but he knows we're heading to Denver, and he knows why."

"Then what chance do we have?"

"If their resources are divided, that's fewer men for us to deal with," he replied as he dialed the phones. A small smile curved his mouth. "There. At least now we can communicate without West tracing us." He handed one of the phones to her. "I'm speed dial number 1."

Laine dropped the phone into her purse. The three hours of sleep she'd gotten was evaporating, and her brain was spinning with 'what-ifs.' "I'm assuming you have some sort of plan for *after* we get to the hotel."

"Working on it," he said. "I've never actually been in this sort of situation before."

She looked at him in the mirror as her heart somersaulted. "What about all the getting out of situations you shouldn't have?"

"In *those* situations I always had someone I could call for help," he said, a fierce gleam in his raptor-like gaze. "Having a traitor give me up . . . that's new."

Laine took a deep breath and processed that piece of information, filing it away. "What do you need from me?"

Jack was silent for a moment. When she looked at him in the rear view, she saw something in his expression that made her blink; desire. It was gone so fast she was certain she had imagined it, and when he spoke he sounded cool and professional.

"I need you to keep doing what you've been doing," he replied, "going with the flow, following my lead, leading when you have to." He gave her a ghost of a smile. "Be yourself, Doc. It's gotten us this far, hasn't it?"

"Right." She exhaled slowly. "So, to the airport. Why don't you fire that thing up and give me some directions?"

He brightened. "That's right. I'm the navigator now, aren't I?"

***

Laine cursed as she ripped her pantyhose. With a snarl she yanked them off and tossed them on the floorboard. "I hate pantyhose. Guess it's a good thing I shaved my legs last night."

"When did you do that?" Jack asked from the backseat.

She looked over her shoulder and was surprised to see he was nearly dressed. Instead of sweats, he had on the dress slacks she'd bought, and he had his white dress shirt almost buttoned. They were parked in the long term lot at Denver International Airport, hidden from prying eyes by the shroud of darkness. It was almost 9 p.m. They'd made better time than either one of them had anticipated.

"Um, last night while I colored my hair," she said absently as she slipped into the black pencil skirt and zipped it up. She reached for the hem of her tank top then glanced at Jack in the rear view. "Eyes closed, please."

Jack gave her a wicked grin and then obediently closed his eyes. He continued to button his shirt with surprising dexterity, and Laine was momentarily transfixed by the movements of his fingers. She shook herself, then yanked the tank top off and slipped her arms into the sleeves of the red blouse.

"Ok, you can look."

"Why?" he asked in a teasing voice. "You're covered up *now*."

Laine looked down at the plunging neckline with dismay. "That's what you think," she said flatly. "I knew I should've gotten the other blouse . . . ."

"Relax, Doc," Jack said. "A little cleavage will not hurt our cause. It may even help."

"Right," she agreed with a roll of her eyes. She spun to face him and gestured to her chest. "Emphasis on the 'little cleavage'."

She hadn't donned anything this low-cut since college, and she was surprised that Walmart, a store known for its wholesomeness, carried such a garment. When Jack whistled softly, she turned a glare on him.

"Sorry, Doc," he said with a shrug and a boyish smile. "I like it, and so will every other red-blooded male who catches a glimpse."

"That isn't the kind of attention I want," she snapped.

He chuckled. "Laine, if they're looking at your décolleté, they won't be looking at your *face*, which is a good thing. Now, you're going to have to help me with the shoes and the tie."

Laine rolled her eyes and slid her red high-heeled pumps on. She checked her make up in the rear view, put on the modest jewelry she'd purchased, including a wedding band, then got out of the Suburban and opened the back door. His eyes did a vertical scan and he nodded in approval.

"Looking good, Mrs. Vaughn," he said. "You clean up real nice." Jack handed her the socks, she put them on his feet, and then put his shoes on him.

Laine pursed her lips, "You're not so bad yourself, Agent Vaughn." He handed her the tie and scooted out of the SUV to stand in front of her. She watched as he slid the matching wedding band on his ring finger with a small smile. The moment was surreal.

Laine pursed her lips, flipped up his collar, and started on the double Windsor.

He looked delicious. If she were to put the Jack she'd first met next to the Jack she saw now, they would look like two completely different people. The first Jack had looked every inch the biker, while this Jack looked like a Wall Street executive, if you discounted the five o'clock shadow. She finished the knot and flattened the tie against his chest.

"There," she said, "all done."

"Not quite," he said in a low voice.

She froze when he reached around her and grabbed her braid. With those extremely dexterous fingers he slipped the band off the end of the braid and began to sift through her hair. He did it slowly, working the strands loose with careful, measured strokes. Laine met his gaze and her pulse jumped. That flash of desire she thought she'd seen earlier was back, and she gulped. She chided herself for responding to him at all. A smile curved his mouth and she wondered if he could hear her heart pounding. She wanted to close her eyes as he massaged her scalp, but she forced herself to return his stare with one of cool indifference.

When he was done he arranged her hair around her shoulders, his eyes never leaving hers. "Beautiful," he whispered. "You're a knockout, Doc."

The compliment caught her off-guard. He stepped away from her, and Laine wanted to pull him back. Instead, she dropped her gaze and gave him a nod, fighting to stay upright as her body wanted to sway toward him. "Thank you."

"You're welcome. Now, let's get this show on the road."

Laine turned on her heel and walked to the back of the Suburban. She pulled out the suitcase they'd packed with their combined belongings, pulled up the handle and hung the laptop bag over it. Jack would take those, leaving her with her purse and doctor's kit. She'd wanted him to wear the sling, but he had convinced her otherwise, citing their need to remain as inconspicuous as possible. He could easily maneuver the wheeled suitcase with his good hand, and to anyone who noticed they would look like any other couple. She looked at the box of Nick's belongings for a moment, and decided now was as good a time as any to move forward. She threw a sleeping bag over the cargo area and closed the tailgate. After retrieving her purse and doctor's bag, she locked the Suburban and turned to him.

"Let's go."

They spoke little on the shuttle ride to the main terminal. His eyes scanned the terminal, his gaze sharp and probing, as Laine purchased their airline tickets. She used her credit card to pay, glancing at Jack as the attendant checked her ID and then printed their boarding passes. Once the tickets were in hand, she grabbed a couple of luggage tags and they walked toward the escalator leading to the security checkpoint.

"Everything okay?" she asked as he fell into step beside her.

"As far as I can tell," he replied. "Haven't seen any familiar faces."

"Good." They paused at the base of the escalator, and Laine attached the tags to the handle of the suitcase and laptop bag. "Let's get out of here."

Instead of going up, they bypassed the escalator and headed outside. Once there they flagged down a cab. The yellow car pulled over and a man of African-American descent stepped out. The gray at his temples said he was at least middle-aged, probably older, but it was hard to tell. He was tall and heavy set and wore rainbow colored suspenders with his blue jeans, but regardless of his dress he had a gentlemanly air about him. He flashed them a big smile and opened the trunk.

"Hello, folks," he said in a deep, resonant voice that Laine imagined would carry a tune exceptionally well. "I'm Lionel. Welcome to Denver. First time here?"

"No, Lionel," Laine said before Jack could utter a word. "This is my third trip, and I have to tell you, I love it here."

"Well," Jack began, "it's my first time, but my wife just raves about it. We're thinking of moving."

Lionel grinned and put the laptop case in the trunk. "You'll be glad you did." He hefted the large suitcase and maneuvered it in next to the laptop. "Moved here twenty-three years ago and never regretted it." When he reached for her doctor's bag Laine smiled and shook her head. He rubbed his chin. "Something important in that bag?"

"It's just my medical kit, why?" Laine asked, trying not to appear overly suspicious.

"You a doctor?" When she nodded he gave her a knowing smile. "Been driving doctors all day, but I haven't seen many bags like that one there." He closed the trunk and opened the door, wiggling his eyebrows at her. "Wish *my* doctor was as pretty as you."

Laine blushed and slid into the cab, and Jack carefully eased in next to her, air hissing from between his teeth. Lionel waited until he was fully inside, then closed the door gently but firmly.

"You okay?" Laine whispered. Jack gave her a small smile and nodded.

"Well, then," Lionel began as he got behind the wheel, "guess you're here for that conference." When Laine didn't reply, he started the engine and checked his mirrors. "The big medical conference they're having at the Ritz?"

"Yes," Laine replied. "As a matter of fact, I am."

Lionel looked at Jack in the mirror. "You a doctor, too?"

"Nope," Jack said. "I let the little woman do the heavy lifting. Me, I'm an architect."

Lionel laughed. "So you're just along for the *ride*," he said in a voice laced with hidden meaning. "I envy you, son."

"Don't," Jack said, fixing her with a petulant look. "She actually *attends* all the meetings, leaving me alone in the room with nothing to do but commiserate with the mini-bar."

"Oh, sweetheart," Laine said in a sultry voice, "I promised to wear you out tonight, so you'd sleep through the meetings tomorrow." She leaned toward him and nibbled his earlobe. "You go ahead and envy him, Lionel. He'll have nothing to complain about." She glanced at the cabbie. "You don't mind if I start now, do you Lionel?"

Lionel guffawed and pounded one hand against the steering wheel as he pulled into traffic. "No, honey, you go right ahead. You got plenty of time, and I don't see anything."

Since Jack had baited this trap and then walked into it, Laine decided to play along. Part of her wanted payback for his toying with her, and part of her was just thrilled at the opportunity to kiss him and have a plausible excuse for doing so. She eased onto his lap, careful not to move his shoulder.

"Laine, what are you doing?" Jack asked in a whisper.

"Going with the flow," she replied softly, her mouth near his ear. She carefully lifted his left arm and laid it in her lap as she wound her left arm around his neck. "Following your lead." She kissed his jaw and was rewarded by his sharp intake of breath. A low ache sharpened in her belly and a sense of euphoria washed over her as she pressed a hand to his cheek and turned his face to hers. "Leading when I have to . . . ."

This time when she kissed him, he kissed her back. Heat sizzled through her with such force she could almost hear the crackling. She didn't care if he was only playing along or really wanted to kiss her, it felt real regardless. His right hand splayed across her back, pressing her closer. His lips were soft and warm, and she felt the sensation of air rushing by, as if she was falling from a great height. Suddenly she wasn't kissing him anymore, he was kissing her. Her limbs went rubbery, her skin flushed, and she was helpless to fight it. When he pulled away, it was all she could do not to pull him back.

"Hey, Lionel," he said, his gaze fastened on her mouth, "how much time *do* we have?"

"About twenty, twenty-five minutes," Lionel replied with a hearty laugh, "Unless you want me to take the *long* way."

Jack looked at her, but his expression was inscrutable. "That's okay," he told the cabbie. "I think we should go straight to the hotel. Half an hour's a good start, but for what I've got planned . . . I need a *bed.*"

"Amen to that, brother," Lionel agreed. He laughed heartily and pounded the steering wheel again. "Amen to that."

"And, Lionel, you may want to turn the music up. We don't want any accidents on the expressway."

"No, sir," Lionel said with a deep chortle. "We certainly don't want that." The cabbie shook his head and turned the volume of the radio up.

"Now," Jack said, his gaze swiveling back to her, "where were we?"

Laine couldn't tell if Jack was serious or not, but when his mouth descended on hers again, it didn't matter. All she could think of and all she could feel was Jack, the steel-muscled legs beneath her, his left hand curled lightly around her right hip, his lips on hers. Her breasts tightened when his tongue traced the outline of her mouth, and a small gasp escaped her. That gave him the entrance he needed.

He explored her mouth as if they had all the time in the world, and not a thing to worry about but each other. There were no terrorists, no assassins, and no cab drivers chuckling in the front seat. Heat fanned over her skin as if a desert wind had found her in the middle of Colorado.

His hand crept up her back and fisted in her hair, gently pulling her head back. Laine stifled a moan when his mouth trailed down her throat, leaving hot, wet kisses on the pulse racing there.

"Be careful what you wish for, Laine," he whispered. "You may get it."

Her limbs felt heavy and it took more effort than normal to pull her head upright and look him in the eye. "Be careful what wishes you grant, Agent Vaughn. You may get more than you bargained for in return."

A grin lit his face. "Is that a challenge?"

She lifted one brow. "It's an invitation. After all, you've been flirting with me since we met. Turnabout is fair play."

He gave her a slanted look. "I think taking advantage of a wounded man in the back of a cab with a complicit driver is more than flirting. It's coercion at the very least."

Laine narrowed her eyes on him and pulled back a bit. "All you have to say is no, Jack, and I'll return to my seat and leave you in peace." She studied his face. "Is that what you want?"

"You're sitting in my lap, Laine," he said with a wry twist of his lips. "If you can't tell what I want, then you haven't done very much of this. What I *don't* want is to be distracted if Ripley's men catch up with us, and *you* are distracting. I would think you would understand my need to remain professional in this situation."

He might as well have slapped her and dumped a bucket of cold water over her head. She stared at him. The implacable mask was back in place and his expression was cool. Rejection impaled her for the second time that day, pain blossoming in her chest.

"Well," she began in a hushed voice, "that says volumes, doesn't it?"

She searched his face for any softening and found none. "Why don't you just tell me what you really think of me?"

Anger flared hotly in her chest, but what was worse was the fact she still wanted him. Desire still hummed through her, driven even further by the jolt of growing, red fury. Suddenly she needed to feel something else, *anything* else. She hesitated a moment, then hauled off and slapped him. Her fingers stung and shocks of pain traveled through her hand to her wrist. He looked at her in astonishment, but she ignored his reaction.

"How dare you!" she demanded, loud enough for Lionel to hear. The music inexplicably went down. Laine pushed his good arm away and returned to her seat, crossing her arms over her chest and turning her back to Jack with a loud huff. "I told you, he's only a colleague! I am *not* sleeping with him!" She blinked back tears, and while they were for effect, they were real enough.

"Laine . . . !"

"Just stop, Jack," she said in clear, cold tones. "This was supposed to be a romantic getaway, but you just had to get your dig in. I have *never* cheated on you, but you just won't believe me." She swiped at her eyes and sniffed loudly. "Lionel, how much longer?"

"Another twenty minutes or so, miss," he said. There was a note of sadness in his voice. "You need a Kleenex, or something?" He held up a small box of tissues.

Laine took several and dabbed at her eyes. "Thank you, and could you hurry please?"

"Sure thing, miss," he replied as he cast a withering glance at Jack in the mirror. "Sure thing."

Chapter Ten

The Ritz Carlton was abuzz with activity, even though it was after 10 p.m. when Lionel pulled up in front. Light spilled through the enormous plate glass windows at the front of the hotel. Jack stacked the bags as Lionel pulled them out of the trunk, then he handed the man a hundred dollar bill, one of several Laine had slipped into his pocket. Jack told him to keep the change and the cabbie nodded his thanks, but when Jack turned, the man grabbed his arm lightly.

"Excuse me for saying so," Lionel said, "but you have a beautiful woman there. Now, I know what it's like to love a beautiful woman, it's hard sometimes, but it's worth it. You go and apologize and do whatever you have to do to make things right. She loves you, I can tell. Ain't no bigger fool than the man who pushes the woman who loves him away for no better reason than petty jealousy. No bigger fool on earth."

Jack studied the man's face, and then extended his hand. "You're right, Lionel, and thank you. You are a gentleman and a scholar."

The big man shrugged and smiled. "Well, I don't know about that, but I almost lost my Maisie for the same reason. I got on my knees and asked her to forgive me, and we've been married 37 years now. Best decision I ever made."

"Jack," Laine called from the front door of the hotel.

"Thanks again, Lionel," Jack said with a smile. "Maybe I'll get lucky yet."

Lionel chuckled and shuffled back to his car. Jack watched him another moment, then turned and looked at Laine. She stood outside the main doors, watching him, her expression neutral. Lionel was right, she was beautiful. He thought of the way she'd kissed him and wished desperately he had met her in a different time and place. For the hundredth time since meeting her, Jack, the man, wanted to kill Jack, the agent. That droning voice had begun to lecture him as soon as he'd kissed her, and somehow Agent Vaughn's voice had escaped his head through his mouth. The wounded look she'd given him had hurt more than her slap, but he knew he'd deserved it. He rubbed his still stinging cheek absently, and took hold of the suitcase's handle and made his way toward her.

"Well, here goes nothing," he said. He gave her a small smile. "Time to see if my plan is going to work."

"What *is* the plan?" Laine asked.

"Well, we're not staying here," he replied. "We're getting a room, but we're not staying here."

She studied his face a moment. "So, where *are* we staying?"

He nodded to the high-rise hotel across the street. The sign read "The Montbleu," and it looked just as swanky as the Ritz. "That's where we'll be sleeping, but we'll take care of that in a little while. Right now, take the bags and wait in the lobby. After I get the key, follow me to the elevator."

"What are you going to do?"

"Bait a trap and see if I get a nibble," he replied.

She nodded and walked away, her heels clicking on the polished marble. Jack watched her go, admiring the graceful sweep of her legs and the firm, rounded bottom showcased by that tight, black skirt. He remembered the feel of her on his lap, the pressure of her breasts against his chest, and mentally kicked himself. They were running for their lives, and he was salivating over the woman who had saved him. He had to protect her, and all he could do was wonder if the rest of her was as soft as the skin of her neck had been. He really, *really* wanted to find that out.

"You're losing it, Jack," he muttered. "Get your head on straight, or you're not going to make it through this."

He watched her until she'd taken a seat in the lobby before he walked into the hotel. It was obvious there was a convention in town. A large sign pointed the way to the conference registration area. Almost everyone he saw had one of those paper name tags that read "My Name Is . . . ." The enormous lobby was filled with people, chit-chatting, drinks in hand, as if a party from elsewhere in the hotel had overgrown its bounds and spilled into this room. He quickly scanned the area and then approached the desk.

"Can I help you, sir?" the clerk asked.

"I don't have a reservation," Jack began as he put the laptop on the ground and fished his wallet out of his pants pocket. "I'd like a suite, one facing the street, if you have one available."

The young woman tapped on the keyboard in front of her, her eyes glued to the screen. "I do have a few suites available, but they're our Ritz-Carlton suites."

"Top of the line," Jack said as he pulled his credit card out and handed it to the clerk. "All the better."

"And how long will you be staying with us, sir?"

"Just the night," Jack replied, "but I need a late check-out, around 2 p.m. Whatever it costs." He leaned an elbow on the counter so he could peruse the room while the clerk ran his card. He noted every face, every casual movement, and every snippet of conversation he overheard. He glanced at Laine. She was talking with a distinguished middle-aged man seated across from her. To her credit, she looked completely at ease, even friendly, and Jack was surprised at the spark of jealousy that flared briefly in his chest.

"There you are, sir," the clerk said as she slid a key card across the counter. "Top floor, Suite 3687. Would you like your bags taken up?"

"That won't be necessary," Jack replied as he palmed the card. "All I have is my laptop." He glanced at Laine again and gave her a nearly imperceptible nod. She lifted her eyebrows in return.

"Thank you," Jack said. The clerk nodded and turned to another customer.

As he picked up his bag he saw Laine had preceded him to the elevators. He was again amazed by how easily she dealt with the situation at hand. He could easily mistake her for a fellow agent, but he wondered if she realized what a dangerous role she was playing.

They were alone in the elevator, and once the doors slid closed Laine sighed and looked at him.

"Now what?"

"First, I bait the trap, then we need to get a room at the hotel across the street," he replied. "It should be on the same level as this one and facing this hotel, which probably means a suite. That won't be easy. They're going to want a credit card and identification, no matter how much cash you flash at them, but using a card will tell Ripley we're there." Her brows drew together, and Jack could almost hear the gears in her head start to spin at warp speed. "What?"

She looked at him out of the corner of her eye. "I may be able to take care of that."

"How?"

Laine chewed her lip for a moment. "My brother-in-law."

Jack leaned against the rear of the elevator and shook his head. "No. They'll be able to trace that."

"Maybe, given some time," she said, "but not right away. Brian and Nick are half-brothers; same mother, different fathers. He's four years younger than Nick and has a different last name."

"How could he help?"

"He runs a pharmaceutical company," Laine said.

She looked at him as if he should know what she was inferring but he didn't. When he shook his head and shrugged, she continued.

"This convention is being put on by pharmaceutical companies who pay for the doctors to come here for a weekend so they can pitch their latest drugs. The hotel wouldn't think twice about a pharm company booking a last minute suite for a VIP, and neither would your friends. With the room guaranteed to the company, the hotel won't be interested in my name and ID. We'll be completely anonymous."

Jack thought about it for a moment, almost afraid to give birth to the hope that so desperately wanted to burst forth. "Would he do it, without asking any questions?"

Laine faced him. "If I ask him, he will."

The elevator doors opened. "Then make the call."

He stalked to the room and held the door for her. She immediately tossed the bags down and pulled the cell phone out of her purse. Jack took the laptop to the desk, plugged in the internet cable and turned it on. As he waited for it to boot up he listened to Laine's one sided conversation.

"Yeah, Brian, it's great to talk to you, too. I'm sorry it's been so long."

She paused as her brother-in-law said something.

"I'd love to chat, sweetheart, but right now I'm in kind of a bind and I need your help."

Laine glanced at him as she paused again, listening intently.

"Yes, I need you to call the Montbleu Hotel in Denver and book a room on the thirty-sixth floor, or as close as possible, and it needs to face the street. I need you to use the company credit card, and I need you to do it ASAP. Also, it would be best if you called from work."

A frown flitted across her brow and she glanced at her watch.

"It's almost Saturday. What are you still doing at the office?"

She sat down on the plush couch and flipped off her shoes, rubbing her feet as she listened.

"I can't tell you why. I'm in trouble and I really need you to do this for me, please. I can't have the front desk asking me for ID."

Jack watched as she straightened, her brows drawing together as she looked down at herself.

"A black skirt, red satin blouse, and red heels, why?"

After a few moments she smiled, and gave Jack a nod.

"Well, then you may want to know I have red hair now." She laughed and leaned back against the cushions. "As soon as everything's straightened out, we'll take a trip to the lake house, and I'll tell you the whole story. It's quite a nail-biter, actually. I may even write a book someday."

She paused again and Jack saw the sheen of tears in her eyes.

"I love you, too, little brother. Give my love to Marina and the girls. Okay, bye." She hung up the phone, closed her eyes, and exhaled. "One room, coming up."

"Why did he want to know what you were wearing?" Jack asked.

"So he could tell the clerk to keep an eye out for me when I show up to collect my key," she replied. "He said if the desk gives me any trouble to call him back and he'll take care of it. As of now, I am an official representative of Tauscher Pharmaceuticals."

Jack studied her and saw the weariness in her face. "You sure you're a doctor?" he teased. "I could swear you've done this sort of thing before."

"Nope," she answered. "I'm just a devout fan of *24* and *Alias* and shows like them." She opened one eye and scowled. "I can't believe I used to think this kind of stuff was exciting."

Jack chuckled. "Yeah, it's amazing how your perceptions change when you have to live it, isn't it?"

"You can say that again." She rubbed her feet a little more, then slipped her heels back on and picked up her handbag. "Well, I'm off to get the key."

"Good," Jack said as he turned to the laptop and started typing. "I think by the time you do . . . the limit on this suite will be very close to maxed out."

She walked over to him and rested a hand on the back of the chair he was sitting in. "What are you doing?"

"The information I have on Ripley is what he's really after," Jack said as he opened an internet browser and started clicking away. "Me, I'm just the cherry on top of his sundae. Killing me is secondary to getting his hands on what I have in this computer."

"So, you're going to what? Upload all your files to the worldwide web?"

"Not quite." His gaze was fastened on the screen. "West, Ripley's head computer geek, taught me a few tricks during my 'review' period with CAG. Ripley thought it would be safer for me to work in tech while they decided if I was trustworthy and ready for field work."

Laine whistled softly. "I have a feeling he's going to regret that decision."

"I plan to make sure of it," Jack said. "As we speak, the encrypted files I have are being e-mailed to every top level agent at ATF offices in Denver, Missoula, Los Angeles, and Seattle, in case the ones I mailed don't make it. I'm also sending them to the FBI, and the general inbox at Langley will be getting their copy shortly."

"Do you think that will stop him from coming after you?"

"No," Jack replied. He turned and looked up at her. "It might take his eyes off *you*, though."

She straightened, and he could tell she didn't know what to say to that. She started to pace, her skirt swishing softly with every step. Glancing at him, she nibbled on her thumbnail. He knew she was confused by the mixed signals he was sending, but he didn't have time for the kind of full disclosure that would ease her mind.

"Oh," was all she said.

He turned back to the laptop. "Go get our key, *Mrs. Vaughn*, and take the suitcase, please. Once I'm done with this we need to be the hell out of here."

She nodded and walked to the door. "Jack," she said over her shoulder as she stepped into the hall.

"Yeah?"

She opened her mouth to speak but nothing came out. After a moment she licked her lips and looked at the floor. "I'm . . . I'm going to want a look at that shoulder when we're settled. Keep that arm immobile."

Disappointment swirled inside him at her business-like tone, but that was something he'd just have to deal with. He had asked for it, after all.

Choking down his own frustration, he forced a smile and nodded. "You got it, Doc."

Laine walked to the elevator, her mind in a whirl and her insides twisting like a ship's sail in a hurricane. She wasn't accustomed to being confused . . . about *anything*. It made her nervous, jumpy, and unsure of herself, and she didn't like it at all. One way or another, she was going to have a conversation with Jack about what was going on between them. She realized, though, they both had more pressing matters to deal with, so she was willing to put it aside, for now. As she waited for the elevator, she scanned the hallway, noting the security cameras. There were three; one by the elevators, one in the center of the hall and one near the door leading to the stairs. A bell rang and the doors slid open.

In less than three minutes she was walking through the front doors of the Montbleu, and it was indeed just as swanky as the Ritz. The floors were highly polished and made of black marble veined with pale pink. Thick rugs dotted the floors, and groupings of cushy black and white couches throughout the lobby formed intimate seating areas situated around square black tables decorated with elaborate candle arrangements. Large crystal vases overflowing with brightly colored blooms lent their subtle perfume to the room, and added spots of color to what would otherwise be a stark color scheme. The high ceiling was mirrored, and light from fine, crystal chandeliers was reflected around the room, making it bright but not garishly so. The soft notes from a piano floated through an open set of double doors to her right at the far end of the lobby. This hotel was also busy. People sat on the black and white couches conversing in muted tones, others wandered in and out of the bar, but the air was more subdued than at the Ritz. Laine gazed about the lobby, and walked to the registration area.

The man behind the front desk had just hung up the phone, and when she approached he brightened and smiled. He was probably thirty, blonde, blue-eyed, and well-built.

"Ms. Garrett from Tauscher Pharmaceuticals, I presume," the man said. His voice was deep and pleasant and he spoke with an Australian accent.

Laine made a mental note of the name Brian had used for her and read the clerk's name tag. *Steven Curry, Front Desk Manager*. She smiled and leaned her elbows on the marble counter, giving him a good view of her cleavage. "You presume correctly, Mr. Curry," she said in a low, seductive voice. "I am hoping you just finished speaking with my employer, and have a room waiting for me. It's been a very long, very trying day, and I am so looking forward to a drink and a long, hot bath."

Curry nodded and placed a registration card on the counter. "Mr. Forrester said to give you a suite on the top floor, facing the street, and he said to give you anything and everything you need." He plucked a pen from behind the desk. "All I require is a signature right here," he paused and pointed, "and you are all set."

Laine took the pen and signed *L. Garrett* on the line with the "x", then returned the pen to the man. "There you are, Mr. Curry."

"Please, ma'am," he said with a glance at her breasts as he handed her a key card, "call me Steven. If you need anything, anything at all, you let me know."

She licked her lips slowly, and noted the spark in the manager's eye when she did so. "I will do that, *Steven.*"

He seemed a little flustered, and quickly picked up a paper showing the hotel floor plan. He flattened the map on the counter and pointed. "You're on the 37th floor, right here. Mr. Forrester requested the 36th floor, but all the suites on that level are occupied. Your suite is nicer anyway. I gave you an upgrade, no charge."

Laine glanced at the floor plan, then looked at him with a smile and purred, "Perfect."

"Would you like me to take your bags for you?" he asked. "I'd be happy to escort you to your room."

Laine thought about it for a moment. "I'm not going up just yet, but I'd appreciate it if you could have my bags taken to my room." She gestured toward the open doors on the far side of the lobby. "That is the bar, yes?"

"Yes, ma'am," Curry replied.

"Wonderful," Laine said with a sigh. She gave the man a sidelong glance. "You wouldn't be able to . . . join me, would you?"

To her surprise, color rose in his cheeks. He grinned and shook his head, and Laine half expected him to say, "Aw, shucks."

"I'm afraid I can't, Ms. Garrett," Curry replied. "I appreciate the invitation."

"Shame," Laine said with a small sigh. She tipped her head and considered him for another moment. "Thank you for your help, Steven."

He gave her a nod and took another glance at her bosom. "You are most welcome."

Laine gave a sultry smile. "I'll be certain to tell your General Manager you are a model employee, capable of handling greater responsibility than that of a front desk manager." She leaned toward him and his eyes widened slightly when her breasts nearly popped out of her blouse. "I'll also be sure to let my employer know of your unwavering commitment to excellence. With a phone call from *him*, a promotion for you can't be far behind."

Steven Curry gulped and nodded. "Thank you, ma'am. I'll have your bags taken to your room now." He motioned to a bellhop, and the young man scurried forward.

Laine handed Steven Curry a $50 bill, then handed the bellhop a twenty. With a small wave, she sauntered across the lobby to the bar.

The interior of the bar was dark, the room filled with two-person tables topped with red glass candle globes. The bar itself lined the wall to her left, going back some forty feet to a window overlooking the street. To her right was a small stage with a shiny black *Steinway*. There were few empty chairs, but there were several spots open at the bar. She glanced at the handsome young man whose hands moved with ease over the piano keyboard. She then pulled out the cell phone and dialed. Jack picked up after the second ring.

"Mission accomplished," she said.

"Good." He paused and she could hear him tapping on the keyboard. "I'm almost finished here. What room are you in?"

Laine glanced around the dimly lit room. "I was thinking you should meet me in the bar. We'll hang out for a few minutes then go to the room. That way, it will look like I picked up a stranger."

There was a brief silence. "Y'know, Laine," he began, "if you ever decide to give up medicine, I'm sure there's a slot at some intelligence agency you'd be more than capable of filling."

"You say such sweet things to me," she said. "I'll be sitting at the bar."

"See you soon."

Laine hung up the phone and slipped it back into her purse. She took another long look around the room then walked over to one of the vacant bar stools. She tapped the shoulder of the man nearest her.

"Excuse me, is this seat taken?" she asked.

He was probably in his mid to late forties, handsome in a hawkish way with dark hair and eyes, dressed in a designer suit. He perused her openly from the top of her head to the toes of her red pumps. His gaze was sharp and probing, and lingered on her bosom for several moments longer than was polite or necessary. His features were hard and he had a cynical air, and when he smiled he reminded her of a viper.

"Even if it was taken I'd let you have it," the man said. "Help yourself. I'm Dr. Livingston, but you can call me Brad." He extended his hand and she shook it.

"Thank you, Brad," she replied. "I'm Violet."

He nodded, his gaze once again sweeping over her. "I've always loved those flowers, and the color."

Laine forced herself not to roll her eyes. "Why, thank you." She sat and turned away, making a pretense of looking for the bartender.

"Are you here for the convention?" he asked.

"Not exactly," Laine replied absently without looking at him. "You?"

"Yes," he said. "I'm a neurologist. Work for Cedars Sinai in Los Angeles." He paused, and when she didn't reply he continued. "You know, where all the movie stars go?"

"Do you work with any celebrities?" she asked. Laine couldn't have cared less, but she knew once he got talking about himself he would be unlikely to stop. She was right. She looked at him and nodded when appropriate, inserting "Really?" and other key words to keep him going without really listening. Every few moments she'd glance over her left shoulder out the doors, and when she saw Jack walking toward her she could barely contain her sigh of relief.

"Enough about me," he said, as if he sensed her boredom. "Can I buy you a drink?"

"Hmm." Laine turned her gaze to the rows and rows of bottles. She saw one she recognized. "I don't know. You may not want to do that."

He swiveled his chair toward her. "And why wouldn't I want to buy a pretty lady a drink?"

"Well," she began, "because I'm partial to that 30 year old Laphroaig Scotch whisky. Since it's almost $700 a bottle, I can't even imagine what they'd charge for a glass." Her father-in-law had drunk that same whisky and had made certain she knew how much it cost.

"I'll buy you one," a familiar voice said from her left elbow. "Hell, if you're half as good a conversationalist as you are a judge of whisky, I'll buy you *two*, but only if you join me."

Before Brad could say a word, Laine turned her back to him and faced Jack. The neurologist was silent for a moment, then huffed and returned to his previous conversation. Laine mouthed a silent 'thank you.' Jack winked at her and offered her his arm. She put her hand in the crook of his elbow and walked with him to a table near the window overlooking the street.

He motioned for a waitress, and Laine's eyes widened slightly when he did indeed order the Laphroaig. After the server put two glasses of the dark liquid in front of them, he handed the woman three C-notes and lifted his tumbler.

"To you," he said. "And whenever you drink this in the future, I pray you remember me, your humble admirer, with fondness."

Laine took a small sip and let the sweet, smoky liquor warm her throat. She took another drink and contemplated the glass as a vision from her past filled her mind.

"And what memory does this trigger?" Jack asked in a low voice as he leaned toward her.

"Nick's stepfather drinks this," she replied. "The first time I met him he offered me a glass, and when I declined he said, 'That's probably best, dear. No doubt your palate would not be accustomed to scotch that costs more than $600 a bottle. Perhaps something else, something more in your . . . range?'" She chuckled. "Nick was furious."

"I would be, too," Jack said with a scowl. "Why would his father say such a thing?"

Laine chuckled and took another sip. "Because I'm from the wrong side of the tracks, Jack."

Jack scoffed. "That's ridiculous. You're sure this man actually met you, right?"

"Oh, he met me," she assured him, "and from day one he disliked me, he and his wife both." She put the glass down and trailed one finger around the rim. "It didn't matter to him I graduated from Harvard with honors and was a doctor in one of the best hospitals in Chicago. I had the prestigious diploma and a fine résumé, but I didn't have the *pedigree.*"

"Pedigrees are for dogs," Jack said flatly.

"Or for rich people who send their children to the finest private schools and universities," Laine said with a smile. She looked at him. "Nick went to Yale and graduated with honors. His stepfather expected him to become a corporate lawyer and work for the family import-export business."

"So, how did he end up a cop?" Jack asked.

Laine shrugged. "It's what he wanted to do. He told me he realized he didn't want to help rich companies become richer, he wanted to make a difference." She chuckled and took another sip. "His stepfather was furious, so Nick said. He still hadn't fully accepted Nick's career choice, and when I came into the equation, *well* . . . ." She paused and shook her head. "You can only imagine. After all, my father was just a lowly soldier. Nick's stepfather, Adam Forrester, was a captain of industry. Brian and his family are the only ones I still have any contact with. After Nick died, I no longer existed for anyone else."

"I'm sorry, Laine," Jack said in a low voice, his eyes on his drink. "You deserve better than that."

Laine looked at him, and it was on the tip of her tongue to tell him to heed his own words. This, however, was neither the time nor the place, nor would it be entirely fair. She kept quiet and took another drink.

They finished their scotch in silence. When Jack put the empty tumbler on the napkin, he stood and held out his hand. "Dance with me, Doc?" he asked.

The pianist was singing a tune she'd heard on the radio, a moving ballad about a man finding the love of his life. His rich baritone gave the words depth, and despite the fact it was originally a country and western song, it seemed appropriate even in this modern, city setting. Laine looked at Jack's hand and then looked at him. Finally, she nodded and slipped her fingers into his.

The dance floor was about fifteen feet square, and they were the only ones on it. Jack carefully placed his left hand in the small of her back, and took her other hand in his. As they moved over the parquet wood squares, he gazed down at her, the corners of his mouth tipped up in a slight smile. There was warmth in his eyes and Laine was captivated by it. Heat swirled inside her when she felt his gaze linger on her mouth. As her body swayed toward him, her heart thumped uncomfortably. Somehow she recognized the warning and caught herself just before she laid her head on his shoulder. She wasn't sure she could handle another rejection. Taking a deep, steadying breath, she gathered her resolve. He was not going to do this to her, not again. She forced herself to remain upright and aloof, though that was the last thing she wanted to be with him. Despite his earlier rebuffs, she wanted to believe he felt the sparks flashing between them as she did.

The song ended and he held onto her for a few moments, his eyes searching hers. Laine hoped he couldn't see what she was feeling. Knowledge was power, and if he knew how much she wanted him right now. . . . She wasn't ready to give him that kind of power over her.

"We should probably head upstairs now," she said in a low voice.

He stared at her for a moment longer. "After you," he said at last.

As they made their way out of the bar, they passed Brad, the neurologist from L.A. Jack stopped behind him, tapped his shoulder, and grinned when the man turned and scowled.

"Next time," Jack said as he slid an arm around her waist and pulled her tight against his side, "spring for the good stuff. The reward is well worth the expense."

Laine didn't stay to see Brad from L.A.'s reaction. She walked toward the doors, Jack's hand on her hip. When they were away from the bar, she chuckled. "That was mean," she said under her breath, even as she smiled. She looked at him out of the corner of her eye. "Nice."

"Sorry," he said. "Couldn't resist."

After they stepped into the elevator, she pushed the button for the thirty-seventh floor. Unable to meet his gaze, Laine kept her eyes trained on the numbers as they blinked on and off in sequence as they ascended. She felt him watching her, but was afraid she'd give herself away if she made make eye contact. As much as she wanted to be mad at him, as much as she wanted to be cool and unapproachable, there was something about him which scattered her defenses. Despite what had happened earlier, she wanted him to kiss her again. Truth be told, she wanted him to do much more than kiss her.

"What's wrong, Laine?" he asked in a low, velvety voice.

She glanced at him then turned her eyes back to the numbers. "Nothing, why?"

"You're scowling, and your eyes are gold."

Laine straightened her spine. "I'm tired, Jack. It's been a rather eventful couple of days."

"Yes, it has," he said, in the same soft, buttery tone, "but, that's not it." He paused and she felt his scrutiny as if his hands were moving over her, not his gaze. "You're angry with me."

"I have no reason to be angry with you, do I?" she asked.

"Oh, I don't know," he replied. "I've turned your life upside down, nearly gotten you killed, forced you into a position where you had to kill to defend yourself, and now you have to choose between the life you know and simply living." He paused. "I think that would be enough to piss just about anybody off."

You forgot to mention the mixed signals or the kissing or the proverbial slap in the face or the fact that I want you so much I can't stand it. "Yeah," she agreed, pushing the unwelcome thoughts aside. "I already warned you what would happen if you apologized again." He was still watching her, so she changed the subject. "How's your shoulder?"

He chuckled. "Ah. Very diplomatic, Doc."

The elevator stopped so smoothly that if the bell hadn't rung and announced their arrival on the 37th floor, Laine wouldn't have realized the ride was over.

"I'm not a diplomat," she replied as she left the elevator bay and walked down the hallway toward the suite. "I'm a doctor."

"The two aren't so different," Jack said from a step behind her.

Laine ignored him. She wasn't in the mood to verbally fence with him; her brain was exhausted, her emotions were raw, and she was so confused she could hardly remember her own name. She was painfully aware of his presence behind her. She wondered what would happen once they were safely ensconced in their room. Would he let down his guard or keep his shields firmly in place? Would she be strong, or give in to the seemingly irresistible temptation he presented and set herself up for a fall once again? The thought of more rejection, of more tension between them made her ache inside.

Finally, after what seemed like a mile-long hike, they reached the door to their suite and Laine took the key card from her handbag. Before she could insert it into the lock, Jack put a hand on her arm.

"Let me go first," he said. "That way, if there are any surprises, you'll still be alive to fix me up again."

Laine tossed him a glare. "That's not funny."

He caught and held her gaze, those grey eyes piercing to her very soul. He stared at her for what seemed forever before he lightly plucked the key card from her fingers. "It wasn't meant to be funny." He took her arm and steered her away from the door, clearly positioning her out of the line of fire should someone be inside the room. He gave her a look that said to stay put and slid the key into the slot.

Chapter Eleven

Jack had no doubt Laine would stay where he'd put her, so she wasn't a concern as he slowly opened the door and entered the suite. Inside the lavish room, the curtains had been pulled, a fire crackled merrily in the fireplace, and the lights had been dimmed, giving the luxurious surroundings an even richer and more romantic feel. Thick, cream-colored carpet deadened the sound of his footfalls, and his eyes quickly took in the details of the suite. Directly in front of him was the sitting area, with a large couch and two wing-backed chairs flanking the hearth. A desk with rolling chair sat near the window. Everything seemed to be in perfect order. To his right was the kitchen, and an open set of double doors past the kitchen revealed a full-sized dining table and eight chairs. Seeing and hearing nothing out of the ordinary, he moved away from the door and let it close silently behind him.

He looked into the dining room and found it empty. After checking behind the curtains in both rooms, he crossed the sitting area to the closed double doors that led into the bedroom. He listened at the door for a moment, then wrapped his fingers around the knob and turned it as slowly and as quietly as possible. He tensed as he pushed the panel inward. When no one shot at him or sprang out from hiding, he stuck his head in and looked around. The room appeared empty.

A king-sized, four-poster, canopied bed dominated the space. Lengths of sheer white fabric hung from the dark wood beams to the floor, and on either side of the frame was a set of shallow steps. He moved to the end of the bed and looked beneath the enormous piece of furniture. Behind him sat an armoire and a matching dresser, both empty. To his left was another door which he figured led back out to the hallway, and to his right was the bathroom. Jack walked over, listened at the door, and stuck his head in.

As if the rest of the suite hadn't been opulent enough, the bathroom was the *pièce de résistance*. The floors and tiles were a muted gold, and he could see his reflection in almost every surface. The bathtub was the crown jewel, more like a pool than a tub, centered in front of a spotless window which took up most of the wall overlooking the street. Candles lined the marble surround, their flickering light glittering off the pristine glass. He could easily imagine Laine in a place like this, drinking $100 tumblers of 30 year-old scotch, and soaking in the Jacuzzi tub up to her neck in bubbles. It was a nice picture.

The thought of her gave him a pang of guilt and he scowled. He knew why she was angry with him, and she had every right to be. Hell, he was angry with himself. He seemed to lose his mind whenever she was near.

The conflicting emotions of fear, desire, anger, and sorrow, spun inside his chest in an ever-expanding ball of fire and ice and contrasting colors: black, white, red, and blue. The sensations overwhelmed him at times, until he could hardly breathe. As he walked back to the bedroom, he glanced at the bed, and a picture of the two of them, naked and entwined, flashed in his mind. Something shuddered violently as not only his body but also his soul responded to the erotic image. That coiling ball of emotion swelled until he felt his heart pressing against his spine. He ground his teeth together and willed the image, and the feelings, away. Once he regained some control, he turned off all the lights and walked to the main door. After taking several deep breaths, he turned the knob and let Laine in.

"What's going on, Jack?" she asked as she stepped into the room. "Why is it so dark in here? Turn on some lights."

"Not yet," he replied. With four long strides he crossed the room and stood before the curtains. He took two fingers and moved the heavy drape aside about an inch. When she moved to stand behind him he felt her presence, but kept his eyes forward.

"What is it?" she asked in a low voice.

Jack looked across at the Ritz. "Just checking to see if my trap worked," he replied.

He watched the darkened windows of the suite he'd taken at the Ritz. Before leaving that room he'd turned off every light and pulled the drapes all the way open. Now, those windows were like a black slash in the facade of the hotel, their darkness accentuated by the light coming from surrounding rooms and suites. A nervous ball started to form in the pit of his stomach as he stared at the darkened windows. His breathing quickened and his vision tunneled in on the room, every nerve buzzing, every muscle tensed as he waited for the traitor to reveal himself.

"Hand me the binoculars, please," he said, holding out his hand. He heard rustling behind him, and then the glasses were pressed into his palm. He peered through them.

He leaned forward when the light in his suite went on. He pressed closer to the window and watched as a man crossed the room to sit at the desk. The laptop flickered on. "Bingo."

"What's happening, Jack?" Laine asked.

He backed up a step, handed her the binoculars and waved her forward. She stood in front of him and peered through the narrow opening.

"What am I looking for?" she asked.

"See those windows, the ones with the curtains pulled back on the top floor?" When she nodded he continued. "That's my room." He heard her sharp intake of breath.

"Who is that?" she queried. She looked at him over her shoulder. "And why did you leave the computer?"

Jack looked over the top of her head into the room across the street. "I don't know who it is but I know who it's *not*, and the computer doesn't matter anymore. The files Ripley wants were sent to every aforementioned Federal agency before I copied them to a flash drive and wiped the memory. And, the camcorder is going to tell me who the traitor is."

She turned to face him, her eyes wide. "You think that person is the one who betrayed you?"

"Has to be," he replied. "Why else would he be in my room?" He met her gaze. "Ten to one he used his badge to get the suite number. The desk wouldn't give it out otherwise."

"How do you know it's not one of Ripley's men?"

He saw the lines of fear tight about her mouth. "I know Ripley's men. He's not one of them. Once Ripley realized we were heading to Denver, he would've called his mole and had him do reconnaissance. That's what I was counting on." He paused as the faintest scent of her shampoo drifted to him. "I'm sure Ripley has men in town by now, but it's easier to let the guy with the badge do your footwork rather than risk exposing yourself. After all, the lawman will get farther." Jack returned his gaze to the hotel across the street. "As soon as I booked that suite with my credit card I was pretty sure the rat would know about it. I figured he'd be the only one monitoring me, since nobody else at the Bureau has a reason to, or even knows I'm in trouble."

"And if there's more than one rat?" she asked in a whisper.

Jack pressed a hand to her cheek. "Don't worry, Doc. There is *one* guy I trust, and you're going to meet him tomorrow. Once *you're* safe, then I'll tackle the rest."

"By yourself?"

"No," he replied, "but I'll do it without you."

"Jack—"

He saw the anxiety so clearly reflected in her eyes and wished he could take the fear from her. "That's the way it's supposed to be, Doc." He ran his thumb over her lower lip, and found his eyes drawn there. The curves of her mouth fascinated him. "You don't belong here, Laine. I wish I could undo what's happened, change things back, but I can't."

"I don't wish that," she said in a hushed voice. "If I could go back, even knowing what I know now, I wouldn't change a thing. I would still have picked you up off the side of the road."

"Why?" he whispered.

His pulse skipped a beat when she turned her face and pressed her lips to the palm of his hand. Then she looked at him with those wide, hazel eyes, and he watched as they began to change from gold to green. She covered his fingers with hers and took a step back.

"Because that's who I am," she replied simply. "It took you coming into my life for me to remember that."

"And the woman in the photo?" he had to ask. "Have you remembered *her* yet?"

Laine backed away another step and let her hand fall. He wanted to grab that hand and pull her back, but he forced himself to remain motionless. She stared at him for a moment, a ghost of a smile playing about her mouth.

"You already met her," she said as she walked toward the bedroom. When she reached the entry, she paused and looked back at him. "She was the woman in the cab."

He felt as if the floor had dropped out from beneath him and all the oxygen had been sucked from the room. He stared at her. A small, sad smile curved her mouth, and she walked through the doors and out of his field of vision.

Jack fought to keep from following her. He fisted his hands at his sides and clenched his jaws until his teeth ached, and still his body wanted to go to her. He had pushed her away at the river because Agent Vaughn had asserted himself, and rightly so. He had spurned her in the cab because her nearness was clouding his thinking, and he had needed a clear head. Now he didn't have those excuses. For the next few hours at least they were relatively safe, and the thought of being in this room with her but not *being* with her tested the very limits of his endurance.

Tomorrow would be the end of their involvement. What had happened up to now was something he trained for. What came next ... he was *not* equipped to deal with. And worse, he wasn't sure Laine was equipped to deal with it either. He knew she thought that after the files were delivered, after they met with the only man he trusted that everything would be fine. He'd get the bad guy and she could just go back to Montana and her life as it had been pre-Jack. He knew better.

If they managed to reach safety at all, they would be separated, and then they'd be interviewed, which could take hours. After that she'd be placed in protective custody, and then Witness Protection at least through the trial, and possibly forever. She'd be given a new name, new identity, and relocated to a city only the WITSEC inspectors knew. Jack gulped. Once she was given over to the U.S. Marshals he would probably never see her again outside a court room, and that knowledge sent a shaft of pain through him. He'd waited all his adult life to meet a woman like Laine – strong, compassionate, and beautiful – and now that he had, fate seemed determined to keep him from her.

The sound of music reached him and Jack looked toward the bedroom. Laine must have turned on the stereo. During his time in Denver planning this undercover operation, he had heard a lot of country music, and he immediately recognized Keith Urban's voice. He also recognized the song, *Tonight I Wanna Cry*. Oddly enough, Jack wished he could do just that.

Keith sang about the way it could have been, and never being able to get over the woman who had walked away from him. Jack planted his hands on his hips. Keith then admitted to keeping his feelings hidden and believing that strength was never losing control. Obviously Mr. Urban had been reading his mail, and Jack's eyes stung. When Keith sang the line about damning his pride and giving in to his urge to cry, Jack could barely draw a breath. His lungs burned and his chest ached, and despair threatened to choke him.

He pressed his thumb and forefinger into his eyes and tried to rein in his emotions. The song didn't apply right now because Laine was still with him. But tomorrow it would. Once she'd been debriefed and handed off to the Marshals, the song would be his testament.

Jack faced the window and looked through the gap in the curtains, hoping to distract himself, but Keith kept on singing. He watched as the lights in the suite across the street went out, and it was like the light in his heart went out as well. He turned and glanced toward the open bedroom door, expecting Agent Vaughn to speak up and say something logical. He waited, but the familiar voice was strangely silent as Keith Urban sang the closing line.

Suddenly, the thought of fulfilling the song's prophecy was like a gunshot to the gut, raw and painful. He remembered her words. *I wouldn't change a thing . . . .* The ache in his soul grew and he wondered if she'd feel the same tomorrow when everything came to a head. He knew his feelings wouldn't change, but hers certainly could.

He straightened as another thought hit him, and he wanted to smack himself upside the head. He'd been so busy regretting her involvement that he hadn't paid attention to what she'd been telling him, both verbally and non-verbally.

Maybe he couldn't have forever with her, but they could share the next few hours . . . if she still wanted to. He knew this was an opportunity that would not present itself again, and he doubted he'd ever meet another woman like Laine. Jack held his breath and to his surprise, the consistent, analytical voice that had ordered him to keep his distance said three words he knew would change him forever.

"Go get her."

The binoculars fell to the floor as Jack strode across the thick carpet and walked into the bedroom. She wasn't there. He looked to the right and saw her standing next to the tub, staring out the huge window. He allowed himself a moment to admire her shapely silhouette; the sleek length of her legs, the high, rounded bottom, the narrow waist, the luxurious waves of hair that nearly reached her waist. His eyes widened when he realized he'd crossed the distance between them and now stood at her back, and he wasn't sure how he'd gotten there. He looked up and saw their reflection in the pristine glass.

"Laine . . . ."

The word was a softly spoken plea. She closed her eyes and he saw the tears fall, their tracks turned golden in the candlelight. When he touched her shoulder, she turned and wrapped her arms around his waist as she pressed her face into the crook of his neck. Jack held her tightly and closed his eyes. His gut clenched and he mentally kicked himself for hurting her. He tightened his hold and made a vow. Never again.

"I am sorry for pushing you away," he whispered, his cheek against her hair. "I've been hiding for so long I forgot how not to." He pressed his lips to her temple. "I want to be with you, but when this all plays out we may not be given that opportunity."

Her reply was hushed. "I know."

He pulled back and cupped her head in his hands. "It may be that all we have is the next few hours, Laine." He searched her eyes. "Tell me what you want."

"I want you," she said in a low voice. "What do *you* want?"

"You." Jack's gaze fastened on her mouth. "I've never wanted anyone more." He lowered his head and kissed her, expecting Agent Vaughn to interrupt, but he didn't.

Heat pulsed through him, and the urge to protect her nearly overwhelmed him. She melted against him when their tongues met and he took his time, tasting her, savoring her, exploring her mouth as she explored his, her fingers clutching his shirt. His senses went into immediate overdrive and he became hyper-aware of her; the shape of her mouth, the feel of her breasts against his chest as she moved closer, the taste of tears on her lips, the way she fit him. He realized with surprising clarity he'd never wanted a woman as much as he wanted her.

His lips moved over hers as he backed slowly out of the bathroom toward the bed. When he felt the edge of the mattress behind him he slowly turned until he and Laine had changed places. His mouth left hers and trailed with leisurely intent down her slender throat. She seemed unaware they had moved, her eyes closed and her teeth worrying her lower lip. As he nibbled her earlobe his fingers worked the button and zipper of her skirt open. When the garment puddled around her slender ankles, Laine pulled away from him, her eyes smoldering with desire. She stepped out of the tangle of material and gracefully ascended the steps to the bed. Jack watched her as she moved onto the edge of the mattress. Laine leaned forward, wound her arms around his neck, and pulled him closer. A sensual smile curved her lips as he stood between her thighs. When she lifted her face to his, he accepted the invitation and kissed her deeply. Fire raced through him when she moaned softly. He felt himself harden.

Laine made quick work of the buttons on his shirt. When her fingers contacted his skin, he drew back, startled by the heat her touch generated. She met his gaze as she slid her hands up and over his shoulders, then down his arms. Her movements were deliberate, careful, and all he felt as she undressed him was unadulterated lust. The shirt fluttered to the floor, the pain in his shoulder little more than a memory.

He remained motionless and she turned her attention to her own clothing. He gulped as the buttons of her blouse came undone and each new inch of skin was exposed. The silken material fell from her shoulders, her skin gleaming beneath the warm lights. That wasn't what caught and held his gaze, however. Her eyes were a swirl of gold and green, beckoning to him. Even when her bra joined the discarded blouse, he couldn't look away from her. Never had he seen anyone so beautiful. She was a siren, seducing him with a sensual smile, a shy but passionate glance, her skin flushed and glowing.

His abdominals clenched involuntarily when he felt her fingers at his waist. She unfastened his belt and pulled it from the loops. The tip of her tongue appeared at the corner of her mouth as she unbuttoned his pants and slid them past his hips. He continued to stare at her, his heart beating in staccato against his sternum, until he felt cool air on his bare buttocks. She gave him a sinful smile and looped his belt around his neck. With one hand clutching either end of the stitched leather, she pulled him toward her. He didn't fight.

He captured her mouth and heady desire flamed into unbridled passion. She lay back against the mattress and he followed, relishing the feel of her skin against his. He stretched out beside her, plundering her mouth with ruthless abandon. His left shoulder was injured, but that didn't mean his arm was completely useless. He cupped her breast in his left hand and smiled when she moaned softly. His thumb moved over the taut peak and she arched her back, pressing herself more firmly against his fingers.

Jack lifted his head and let his gaze wander over her face. Her cheeks were flushed, her lips swollen from his kisses, her lashes a dark, sweeping arc above her cheekbones. Her breath came in short, shallow gasps, and when he took one nipple into his mouth her body jerked in response.

"Oh, Jack . . . !"

Those were the most beautiful words he thought he'd ever heard. He swirled his tongue around the rosy nub as he let his fingers drift down over her belly. He curled his hand over the soft mound at the juncture of her thighs and let it rest there. She was trembling again, but when he slipped his fingers beneath the top of the lacy panties she froze, whether in anticipation or fear, Jack didn't know. He kissed the swell of her breast, then her jaw, then her cheek. Her eyelids fluttered open and she looked at him. He met that golden-green gaze and smiled.

"Trust me, Laine," he said in a hushed voice. He dipped his head and captured her lips in a long, slow kiss. When he pulled away, she whispered:

"I do, Jack. I do trust you."

He kissed her deeply and realized the song now coming through the speakers was another Keith Urban hit: *Raining on Sunday,* a song about a man spending a stormy Sunday in bed with his woman and putting everything else aside. Perfect. Keith really *was* reading his mail.

Jack explored her mouth as his fingers explored farther south. He moved slowly, carefully, gauging her reactions by the pace of her breathing and her soft moans. His thumb grazed her clitoris and her hips jerked. He smiled.

He began a slow, methodical stroking of that nub of flesh and was rewarded when her legs started to quiver. Jack kissed his way back to her breast and her hands stroked his head. He suckled her as he continued his tender assault. She moaned and her hips moved in rhythm with his fingers.

Jack slipped one finger inside her. He sucked in a breath as the ache in his groin sharpened. She was hot and tight and ready for him. He was swollen and heavy, he wanted with every fiber of his being to lose himself inside her. However, he knew the harder won victory always tasted sweeter. He wouldn't let himself have what he wanted until he'd shown her what she meant to him. Her pleasure was first and foremost on his mind, and the need to hear her moan his name as she climaxed solidified his resolve.

Jack trailed his lips down over her taut belly, pausing at her bellybutton for a moment as he moved to stand between her legs. Her abdomen contracted and her fingers fisted in the bedcover as he swirled his tongue around her navel. With another kiss to her belly, he hooked his fingers in the waistband of her panties and pulled them slowly down the length of her legs, his lips following closely behind. He glanced at her and smiled when she reached for him.

Ignoring her entreaty, Jack took one foot in his hand. Inch by inch, he trailed his tongue from her ankle to her knee. He continued until he was kneeling between her thighs, and her hushed gasps told him more than words could. Jack paused and looked at her, and a smile curved his mouth when she let out a moan. Her entire body was flushed and trembling, and when he nibbled the flesh of her inner thigh, she jumped. He made slow, lazy circles on her skin with his tongue, moving ever closer to his goal. Her leg muscles shook and her abdomen quivered. Her eyes were closed, her hands clenching and unclenching the bedcover, her breasts rising and falling with each rapid breath.

"Oh, Jack," she said in a hushed voice, "what are you doing to me?"

Instead of replying he covered her with his mouth. His tongue started a slow, deliberate massage of her most sensitive spot and she covered her mouth with her hands, as if she didn't want him to hear her. He teased her for several minutes, but when he increased the pressure, she squirmed and tried to scoot away from him. Jack planted his good hand on her belly to hold her still while he backed off just a little. She remained poised for flight, but he swirled his tongue lazily around that tender, fleshy button and she arched her back, her stomach muscles quivering. Her head thrashed back and forth on the bed, her hair like red ribbons on the white cover.

He sensed the tension in her, sensed her holding back, and kissed the inside of her thigh. "Don't fight it, Doc," he whispered. "You've taken care of me. Now it's my turn."

He covered her with his mouth again and sucked lightly on her clitoris. He kept the pressure constant and rhythmic, his tongue flicking back and forth. She moaned and a wave of exhilaration rose inside him. Her back arched, her legs tensed and she started to shake. Her cries increased in volume and pitch. Each gasp and whimper only fueled his need. His penis throbbed, but he was in no hurry. He closed his eyes and continued his intimate kiss. A few moments later her entire body coiled like a spring. She went completely still and silent, and then the dam burst.

His name was wrenched from her lips and that wave of exhilaration rose higher, pushing his desire for her, and his feelings, to heights he'd never before experienced. He imagined it was something akin to what fighter pilots feel when catapulting off an aircraft carrier: excitement, elation, and anticipation. He continued to make love to her with his mouth as she climaxed, her body shuddering, her fingers clutching his head. When the last spasm left her, she went limp and covered her face with her hands, her breath coming in short, ragged gasps. Jack sat back on his heels, watching her, and an intense satisfaction welled up in him as color flooded her cheeks.

He ignored her embarrassment and kissed his way back up her body. Her breasts were of particular interest to him and he focused on them, nibbling, licking, caressing.

Laine felt as if she'd just been turned inside out, ripples of pleasure pulsed through her. She hadn't been with a man since Nick, and this tender, deliberate attention was much more than she'd expected. Jack continued to torment her and, try as she might it was impossible to catch her breath. The climax he'd given her had been beyond intense, but despite her recent release her body still hummed with desire. His touch left a trail of fire wherever it went, and his mouth set her nerves tingling. Only moments had passed, but she wanted him again.

"Jack, stop," she gasped. "Please . . . stop."

Before the words finished leaving her mouth he kissed her. Laine's body betrayed her and she found herself kissing him back. He was like a narcotic, and her head spun as his tongue explored her mouth and his fingers her breasts. When he pulled away, she was breathless and dizzy.

"What did you say?" he asked in a teasing voice.

Laine met his silver gaze, and the tenderness she saw reflected in his eyes brought her up short. Mindful of his shoulder, she pushed him onto his back and came up onto all fours over him. They stared at each other for a moment, and then she lowered her head until her lips were no more than a hair's breadth from his.

"I said," she whispered, "stop it . . . some more."

He lifted his head and captured her mouth, his kiss stealing what little sense she had left. Her breasts brushed his chest and electricity shot through her. A pulsing ache settled between her thighs, and while he was very good with his mouth, she needed more. The thought of having him inside her made her ache. Unable to stop herself, she reached down and wrapped her fingers around him. She moaned softly as the heat and hardness of him sent desire shivering over her skin and sizzling along every nerve.

He went still as she straddled him, and when she rubbed herself against him he closed his eyes and growled deep in his throat. The animal sound only excited her more, and for the first time since meeting him she felt like she was the one in control. He gripped her waist with his good hand, and when she swiveled her hips and bore down on him he sucked in a breath. His gaze flew to her face. She gasped and paused, warm tingles fanning out from where their bodies joined to every part of her.

She started to move, slowly and rhythmically. The feel of him inside her sent her heart racing as he filled her completely, his hips moving in rhythm with hers. The tension between her legs intensified and roiled outward, expanding exponentially when he moaned her name. She closed her eyes and threw her head back. *This* was what she had needed.

"God, you feel good," he growled.

She looked at him, but his eyes were closed. His fingers flexed and relaxed at her waist. When she started to move faster, his grip on her tightened. He opened his eyes and met her gaze, and she gasped when he drove his hips upward. A shock of pleasure traveled all the way to her toes. She froze for a moment. When she moved again, he matched her pace. With each thrust of his body into hers, she felt her climax building.

She was lost in a haze of sensation so complete that when he put a hand behind her neck and pulled her to him she didn't realize she was moving. Then he kissed her and everything came back into razor sharp focus. She gasped as he devoured her, his tongue matching the thrusting of his body.

Jack was overwhelmed, and the sensation was what he imagined drowning would feel like. It was hard to breathe, he felt heavy with need, and helpless to stop it. Never in his life had he imagined the quiet, unassuming doctor would be such a firebrand. They moved together as if they were perfectly calibrated for each other, though there was nothing mechanical about their lovemaking. Wave after wave of pleasure rushed through him, and he fought to maintain control. She was hot and tight and felt so damn good it was hard not to just let go.

This was the woman from the photos, the woman he'd glimpsed in the cab. She was sensual, brazen, and unashamed. He felt her tremble as he buried himself inside her, and then pulled back. He moved fast and hard, and she buried her face in the crook of his neck.

"Oh, God . . . Jack . . . ."

Her muscles began to contract around him, but he couldn't stop, not now.

"Come with me, Doc," he whispered in her ear as his fingers wrapped around her hip. "Come with me."

When her orgasm hit he was unprepared for the shock of sensation that exploded inside him. As she cried out against his neck he gave one final thrust and closed his eyes as a pleasure that was nearly unbearable burst through him like lightning through storm clouds. He clenched his jaw and wrapped his arm around her, holding her as tightly as he could. His body shook with the intensity of his climax, and it was several minutes before the last tremor left him and he was able to draw a full breath. When it did, he lay limp and motionless. He clung to her, and she to him, both of them panting as if they'd just run a marathon.

Had Ripley himself walked into the room at that moment, Jack would have been unable to move and quite content to stay where he was. He could feel Laine's heart pounding in tandem with his, and at the moment nothing else mattered but her. He ran his hand up her back, amazed at the silken texture of her skin. He threaded his fingers into her hair and sifted through the riotous strands. Yep, the rest of her was just as soft as her neck.

Laine didn't move. She couldn't have if she'd wanted to, and she didn't want to. It felt so right, being with Jack. In fact, she hadn't felt this right since before Nick's death. The sensation of his fingers in her hair was pleasant and familiar, and she closed her eyes with a sigh.

"Does this feel as right to you as it does to me?" Jack asked in a low voice.

Laine's voice failed her and her heart flip-flopped. All she could do was nod. His fingers traced lazy circles on her shoulder, and she suddenly remembered he was injured. She sat up and looked at him in dismay.

"Did I hurt you?" she asked.

When she reached for the bandage he grabbed her hand. She bit her lip as he shook his head and kissed her palm. Heat flooded her cheeks, and other parts of her, as she realized he was still inside her.

"No, you didn't hurt me," he said in a low, husky voice. "But, you could still kiss me and make everything better, if you felt so inclined."

Laine didn't need a second invitation. She'd wanted to kiss him for so long it seemed, and now he wasn't pushing her away. When his tongue demanded entrance to her mouth, she gave it, and a soft moan escaped her as desire began to pulse through her yet again. Her eyes flew open and she looked at him in surprise as he hardened inside her.

"Well, lookee there," he said, with a wicked smile. "I'm better already."

Chapter Twelve

Laine closed her eyes and leaned back against Jack's chest, warm water swirling around them. He trailed a washcloth lazily over her breasts, and a sigh escaped her. When the tub was full, she used her toes to turn off the faucet, then flipped over and settled against him, her head on his chest. He chuckled and brushed a strand of wet hair from her cheek.

"Y'know," Jack said, "I've been dreaming of this ever since you bathed me back in Montana. Personally, I think bathing *you* is a lot more fun."

"Hmm," was all she said. Laine closed her eyes and allowed herself to believe, if only for a few moments, they could stay here just like this. For the time being, there was no man named Ripley, no team of mercenaries hunting them down, no tomorrow. There was nothing and no one else but this huge tub with her and Jack in it. She knew it was dangerous to even entertain the notion, but she couldn't help herself. She imagined, for the briefest moment, a life with Jack and couldn't stop the smile.

"Why are you smiling?" he asked, rubbing the washcloth over her back in wide, leisurely strokes.

"How do you know I'm smiling?" she asked in return.

"I can see your reflection in the window." He kissed the top of her head. "So, why are you smiling?"

Laine couldn't tell him the real reason. She turned to face him. "I don't know," she lied. "Maybe it's because I'm relaxed for the first time in nearly four days."

"Relaxed." He put the washcloth aside, put a finger under her chin and tipped her face up. "I hope I had something to do with that." His silver eyes searched hers for a moment before he lowered his head and kissed her.

If he'd had hair she would have wound her fingers through it, but as it was she contented herself with rubbing the velvety stubble on his head. The soft friction against her palms was strangely arousing, and when he pulled away, it took her a moment to catch her breath.

"You had everything to do with it," she whispered.

He smiled. "Good. Mission accomplished."

Jack kissed her again and his mouth moved over hers with painstaking deliberation, as if in slow motion. Unlike the furious passion which had claimed them both earlier, this was different. Instead of a wildfire, this was a slow burn, and Laine was helpless to fight it. Not that she wanted to. In a few hours they would go their separate ways, and she'd probably never see him again. Until then, she intended to enjoy every second.

The entrance of his tongue into her mouth was tentative, hesitant, and it reminded her vaguely of her very first kiss. She'd been a sophomore in high school, and neither she nor the boy kissing her had known what they were doing. That first kiss had been so awkward that a second kiss wasn't even attempted. In this situation, however, Jack knew exactly what he was doing, and as he deepened the kiss there was nothing awkward about it. This was intentional, as if he was memorizing her, and she was pretty sure much more than a second kiss would follow.

"God, I love your mouth," he whispered against her lips.

Laine couldn't find her voice. She felt him harden against her stomach and the ache between her thighs sharpened. Jack put a hand on her lower back, pressing her closer, but his kiss remained gentle, probing. The languor of his movements was in sharp contrast to the urgency she felt. She rubbed against him and he sucked in a breath, pulling back to look at her. His eyes darkened as she nibbled his lower lip and moved her hips again.

"Suddenly, I'm not so relaxed," he said.

Laine smiled. "I hope I had something to do with that." She straddled him, planting her knees on the bottom of the tub. He was hard beneath her, and she started a slow, methodical movement, back and forth. Her breath caught as delicious shivers shot through her. The muscles in his jaw clenched and unclenched as she pleasured herself, the friction of their bodies sending liquid heat along every fiber and nerve of her body.

"You had everything to do with that," he replied in a low, husky voice. "It's all your fault."

He cupped her breast and she gasped when he took the sensitive tip into his mouth. Pulsing waves traveled from her aureoles to her vulva and back. As he suckled her, his sex grew larger and harder, and Laine couldn't wait any longer.

She put her hands on his chest and moved her hips. "Then let me help you . . . ."

He came into her powerfully and she froze as her body adjusted to him. He sat straight in the tub, bringing them eye to eye, and she couldn't look away from that stormy gaze. Their bodies were wet and slick, which seemed to accentuate the friction as they began to move. Her breasts raked up and down his chest as he thrust into her, his pace deliberate and unhurried. Water splashed over the sides of the tub and onto the floor. Laine wrapped her arms around his neck as he kissed her throat, her body alive with sensation. His hands, his mouth, the feel of him inside her; it was all too much. When he slipped his hand between them and his fingers found her clitoris, she couldn't silence the moan. He seemed to know exactly where and how to touch her, and it wasn't long before she felt the familiar tension begin to build.

Laine needed to kiss him, and when he thrust his tongue into her mouth, a bolt of pure pleasure shot all the way to her toes. She cupped his head in her hands as his lips crushed hers.

Jack placed his feet on the wall of the tub and used the leverage to move deeper inside her. He savaged her mouth and groaned. There wasn't an inch of him that wasn't on fire. His fingers moved against her in time with his body and her soft mewls only fueled the blaze. His lips left hers to trail down her throat, and he pressed his face between her breasts as her arms encircled his head. He kept things slow and steady. The tightness in his groin continued to build and expand. He sensed the urgency in her, but she felt so good that he wanted to prolong their lovemaking, make this last as long as he could.

This was pleasure beyond what he'd expected, and he didn't want it to end. The pressure increased until it went beyond what he thought the human body could endure. When her muscles contracted around him, he couldn't hold back. Her muffled scream was music to his ears as she shuddered violently.

Jack gripped her hips and buried himself deep inside her, groaning as wave after wave of pleasure washed through him. His climax seemed to go on and on, but just when he thought he'd lose his mind, the sensations softened to pleasant ripples. Eventually those, too, waned, and he was left breathless and completely wrung out. Laine clung to him, trembling and gasping.

"You okay?" he asked softly, his brow resting on her breastbone.

Her chin rubbed against his head. "No," she replied in a whisper, "but I will be."

***

Laine pretended to be asleep as Jack slid beneath the covers and curled himself around her. That now familiar ache throbbed between her legs, but she couldn't let him know she wanted him again. He would be more than happy to oblige her, she knew, but the doctor in her was wary. She already felt guilty that he'd exerted himself as much as he had. He'd been injured less than forty-eight hours ago, and what he really needed was rest not sex. Nevertheless, she couldn't help but smile when he snuggled closer and nuzzled her ear.

"Aren't you tired?" she asked him. A glance at the clock told her it was nearly 3 a.m.

"Exhausted," he replied, his voice a husky whisper in her ear. "And hungry."

The throbbing between her thighs intensified. She turned over and looked at him. "You need to rest, Jack. You lost a lot of blood that your body hasn't had time to replace it yet. I'm surprised you can maintain . . . ." Her voice died off and heat suffused her cheeks. Laine turned her back to him and bit her lip.

"Maintain what, Doc?" he teased.

His arm snaked around her waist and pulled her tighter against him. Laine steeled herself against the heat springing to life in her, but it was a losing battle. She closed her eyes.

"It's three in the morning, Jack. What time are we supposed to meet your friend?"

He chuckled and relaxed his hold. "Boy, you really know how to dump cold water on a guy, don't you?"

"I learned from the best," she replied. As soon as the words were out of her mouth, she wanted to pull them back. Regret and shame sent heat into her cheeks, and she covered her face with her hands. She felt him stiffen and held her breath, but to her relief he didn't move away.

"Ouch."

"I'm sorry, Jack. I didn't mean that."

"Yes, you did," he said. "But it's okay. I deserved it."

Laine turned to him and was caught by that silver gaze that seemed to see her more clearly than she saw herself. Candlelight cast a golden glow on his skin and darkened his eyes to a steely grey. Her throat closed up as she thought of never seeing him again, and a band of pain tightened around her chest. "No, you didn't." She pressed a hand to his cheek and looked at the cleft in his chin. "I know there was a line you were trying not to cross . . . ." Her voice died and she closed her eyes. "I shouldn't have pushed it."

"Stop it." He nudged her chin up with his knuckles. "Look at me."

When she did, she was surprised by what she saw in his gaze. He was looking at her with unabashed, uninhibited emotion, as if she was the most beautiful and important woman in his world. Her heart flip-flopped and then expanded until she thought it would burst.

"If I could go back," he said, "even knowing what I know now, even knowing what's to come, I wouldn't change a thing." A smile curved his mouth. "Well, maybe one thing."

"What?" Laine asked, breathless.

His expression turned pensive. "I would've kissed you the first time the thought crossed my mind." He picked up a damp lock of her hair and rubbed it between his fingers.

"And when was that?"

"When you first scrubbed my back," he replied, "in Montana." He traced the line of her collarbone. "You were so close and so pretty, and the way you touched me . . . ."

Her pulse leapt and she dropped her chin. She didn't want to feel what she was feeling, and her guard immediately went up. "Yeah, well, I suppose if you went around kissing every pretty girl when the thought entered your head, you'd go through a lot of Chap Stick."

"No." He shook his head. "No. As far as I'm concerned, kissing is more intimate than sex, Doc." His eyes narrowed when she looked at him. "All animals mate, but humans are the only ones who kiss."

As if to show her, he leaned over and covered her mouth with his. She tried to fight the emotions roiling inside her, tried to keep herself from returning his kiss, but her body wasn't listening. His lips were at once hard and soft; the touch of his tongue, delicate and cautious. In her head she knew this tenuous thread between them would soon be severed, but her heart wasn't listening and didn't care. With a sigh of surrender she let herself fall, heedless of the inevitable end. She reveled in the feel of him, the hardness of his body next to hers, the tenderness of his kiss. When he finally pulled away, he rested his forehead against hers and looked into her eyes.

"That's how I kiss someone I care about," he whispered. "That's not something I do with just anybody." He rolled onto his back and gently pulled on her shoulder. "Now, get over here."

Laine was speechless. She tried to swallow the lump in her throat, but it was too large. Without a word she moved into his embrace and settled against him, her head on his shoulder. His fingers made lazy circles on her arm.

"Go to sleep, Doc," he said. "It'll be morning soon."

The band around her chest tightened a little more, and she silently cursed her mortal state. She didn't want to sleep next to him. She wanted to make love to him again, talk to him, get to know the man behind the muscles and the tattoos and the hawk-like gaze. That she would probably never get the chance made her want to weep. Pressing her face into his neck, she squeezed her eyes shut and fought the tears that wanted to come.

***

Laine felt warm and safe, and gradually came awake with the knowledge that Jack was spooned around her. She felt his breath on her neck, deep and even, his arm draped over her hip. She looked at the clock and her eyes widened. It was after nine a.m. and this would probably be their last day together. A pang of regret stabbed through her and her eyes stung. She wanted to imagine that somehow they could beat the odds, but she wouldn't allow herself to hope. Having that hope dashed would be too devastating.

Slowly, so as not to wake him, she slipped out of his embrace, though she would've been happy to stay there forever. A small smile tipped up the corners of her mouth as she sat on the edge of the bed and watched him. He looked much younger asleep, and much more relaxed. She reached out to touch his face, but pulled her fingers back just in time. A heaviness settled on her heart as she contemplated the coming hours, and forced herself to get up.

She had just slipped into one of the hotel's plush, complimentary robes when there was a soft knock on the door. Laine jumped, her eyes flying to Jack's sleeping form. Slowly, cautiously, she approached the door. The image of some unknown assailant shooting through that thin panel made her pulse leap, and she pressed herself against the nearest wall.

"Who is it?" she called out.

"Room service."

"What's going on?" Jack asked from behind her.

She glanced over her shoulder at him. He stood in the bedroom door, the sheet draped about his waist, and she remembered another time when she'd seen him so adorned. She shook herself and came back to the present.

"Room service," she whispered. She faced the door. "I'm sorry, I didn't order room service."

"I'm sorry, Ms. . . . Garrett," the person said. "Your employer, Mr. Forrester, called this morning and ordered for you. Said to have the works delivered to your suite. You can call the front desk to confirm if you like."

Laine looked at Jack and he shook his head. That was when she realized he was armed, the pistol barely hidden behind the edge of the sheet.

"Hold on a moment," she said. Laine crossed to the phone and dialed the front desk. After a brief, terse conversation, she looked at Jack and shrugged. "Mr. Curry, the front desk manager I met last night, says it's legit." She waved him back into the bedroom. "Go on."

He strode to her and slid the pistol, a Glock 9mm, into the pocket of her robe. "Be careful."

Laine nodded and waited until he was out of sight to open the door. As the young man wheeled the large cart into the room, she retrieved her wallet, keeping a close eye on him as she did so.

"That's fine there," she said before he'd taken more than half a dozen steps into the suite. She walked to him, a twenty in one hand, her other on the Glock. The young man smiled brightly at the size of his tip and left without incident. Laine watched through the peephole until he got into the elevator, and then she dead-bolted the door and put the gun on the kitchen counter. "It's okay, he's gone."

She started to pull domed lids off the large trays and her eyes widened as she revealed piles of fluffy scrambled eggs, pancakes, plump sausage and crisp bacon, home-fried potatoes, toast, and fresh fruit. There was a carafe of orange juice, one of grapefruit juice, and a large thermos of coffee. Next to those sat a thermos of hot water and a selection of tea bags with cream, sugar, and lemon on the side.

"Wow," Jack said from beside her, clothed in one of the hotel's robes. "Why do I get the feeling your brother-in-law thinks you're either *really* into breakfast, or you aren't alone in this fancy suite?"

Laine looked at the abundance of food and shook her head. "I don't know what he's thinking, but that's Brian. He's always over the top." She picked up a huge, ripe strawberry, bit into it and savored the tangy sweetness. "He doesn't send his wife a dozen roses on their anniversary, he sends *six* dozen, inside the stretch limousine he's hired to take her to the restaurant he's rented out for the entire evening so they can dine alone with their personal chef in attendance, and have the dance floor all to themselves."

Jack whistled softly. "*She* married well," he said. "Must be nice to be rich."

"Yeah," Laine agreed.

He bumped her shoulder and smiled. "Hey, for the moment we're rich. At least, we're pretending to be."

Laine pursed her lips. "We're two people on the run hiding in a very expensive suite in a very expensive hotel," she said flatly. "That hardly makes us rich."

"Can we make-believe?" he asked with a childlike exuberance. "Only until after breakfast, of course."

Laine chuckled and poured a cup of coffee. "Go sit down and I'll bring you a plate."

His expression sobered. "You don't have to wait on me, Laine."

She met his gaze. "It's what I do for people I care about," she said with a small smile. "It's not something I do for just anybody."

His expression didn't change, and that raptor's gaze seemed to look into her soul. After searching her eyes for a few moments, he leaned over and kissed her soundly. Then, he smiled and sat down at the head of the dining table.

Laine wheeled the cart into the dining room and prepared him a plate. He watched her, and the sensation gave her goose bumps. After she'd served him, she sat at his elbow with her own plate of food, and they started to eat. The silence was comfortable, broken only by the sound of silverware on china, or the pouring of coffee or juice. When she was full, she pushed her plate away and watched him over the rim of her glass of OJ.

"So, what's the plan?" she asked. "You said I get to meet the one guy you trust today. Who is that, exactly?"

"Special Agent Ted 'Bear' Bristol," Jack replied as he finished his eggs. "He and I got to be pretty close while we were planning this op.

I call him the brother I got to choose. You have to get to him, and get him to come here."

Laine frowned. "How do I do that? I don't know him, he certainly doesn't know me. How am I going to convince him to come to my hotel room?" He lifted one brow and gave her a lusty look and Laine scowled. "Honestly, Jack. Do you really think he'll be so interested in my feminine charms he'll just trot right over? He's a federal agent, for God's sake."

"*I* fell for you."

That brought her up short. She stared at him for a moment then turned her eyes to her plate. "Yeah, well," she stammered, "I . . . um . . . I didn't dig a bullet out of *his* shoulder."

He chuckled. "Bear wouldn't need that much motivation." He took a drink of coffee and watched her over the rim of his cup, a self-satisfied smile on his face.

"Okay," she began, flattening her hands on the table, "exactly how and where do I meet him?"

"Well, every Saturday and Sunday at noon he has lunch at a café about a mile from the Federal Building. He lives a couple of blocks from there in a converted loft." He leaned back in his chair. "You be there when he arrives and you should have no trouble meeting him. Just make eye contact and smile, and let Bear do the rest."

Laine was far from confident, but she realized Jack was counting on her to do this. She straightened her spine and stood, grabbed her dishes and put them on the tray, and then wheeled the cart closer to Jack. "Why don't you finish eating and I'll call one of the boutiques downstairs, have them send up a few outfits, something more appropriate." She held the neck of the robe together and dared a quick look at him. "All I have are sweats and blue jeans."

He grinned and took another sip of coffee. "Those would be fine. You were wearing jeans when I first met you."

Her heart fluttered. "I remember, but again, I didn't dig a bullet out of your friend's shoulder. *Him* I may have to impress." She felt the flush creep into her cheeks and again swore silently at her fair-skinned predecessors. "Since I have Brian's company card and a license to spend, I think the shops will be happy to accommodate a private fitting."

"Knock yourself out, Doc," he said, watching her over the rim of his cup, "but I'm telling you, you won't need fancy clothes to attract Bear. He likes them all shapes, sizes, colors and persuasions. All you have to be is female, and that you *definitely* are." His gaze swept over her appreciatively. "Take my word for it."

Heat flooded her face, but her voice had deserted her. She gulped, nodded, and spun on her heel. He laughed softly as she walked toward the bedroom.

***

Laine strode into Bridges' Café shortly before noon, relieved to see the place was only about half full. She wore a red linen skirt that fell about an inch above the knee, a white linen tank with a low, square neckline embroidered with delicate red flowers, and a pair of white strappy sandals. She pushed her sunglasses back on her head as she looked for a table. The butterflies in her stomach calmed somewhat when she saw several men look her way and give her an appreciative once-over. She exhaled slowly and nodded when the waitress behind the counter told her to sit anywhere.

It looked like Bridges' Café had time-warped back to the 1950s, right down to the 45s tacked to the walls and pictures of Elvis and Frankie Avalon. Laine was surprised the waitresses weren't wearing poodle skirts and saddleback shoes. It was a cozy place, with large, plate glass windows lining one wall and framing about ten booths. In the center of the room were roughly a dozen square tables of white Formica edged in chrome, and a long counter with low-backed stools stretched the length of the opposite wall.

She slid into a booth and absently perused a menu, her fingers nervously tapping the table. The waitress, dressed in short-shorts and a white blouse which read "Bridges' Café" over the right front pocket, hurried over.

"Can I get you something to drink?" the perky brunette asked.

Laine absently wondered if there was an attractiveness quotient required to work here, noting that all members of the wait staff were fit and attractive. No wonder Jack's friend ate here a lot.

"I'll have an iced tea with lots of lemon," Laine replied. "I should be ready to order by the time you get back."

The pretty twenty-something smiled and nodded as she walked away, and Laine went back to the menu. Her heart rate was slightly elevated, but when she saw the 6'8" man grab the door handle with hands the size of dinner plates, her pulse jumped and started to race. Jack had said he'd be the tallest guy in the room, blonde, blue-eyed, and muscular. The newcomer fit that description exactly and her heart leapt again. The moment of truth was at hand. She was about to find out if she was as good at this as Jack said she was.

Laine took several deep breaths. As he walked through the door, he almost had to turn sideways because he was so broad, but there wasn't an ounce of fat on him. If she hadn't known he was an FBI agent, she would've guessed Marine. His hair was cut in a high and tight, and he walked like someone with formidable military training. He had steely blue eyes, and his jaw was so square she had no doubt she could open a can with it. His features were sharp, but he didn't look hard or jaded. He wore a pair of jeans and a white Denver Broncos polo shirt which completely hid the evidence of the pistol Jack had told her he always wore. He paused near the cash register, smiled, and said hello to her waitress. The girl giggled and gave him an adoring look. When he turned to scan the rest of the establishment, Laine focused on her menu, leaned back in her seat and crossed her legs gracefully.

In her peripheral vision she saw him hesitate in his perusal, and his body turned toward her. Pretending to look for her waitress, Laine started at the far end of the counter and moved her gaze toward him. When their eyes met his stare was arresting, and Laine had no doubt many a suspect had been cowed into confessing by that laser-pointed look. She smiled, tipped her head slightly, and then went back to her menu as a blush rose in her cheeks.

She went to steal another look at him and jumped when she realized he was standing at the end of the table. She pressed a hand to her heart.

"Oh, goodness," she said in a low, breathy voice, "you startled me."

"I apologize, ma'am." He nodded curtly. "That was not my intention."

His smile transformed his appearance from forbidding to stunning. The change was dramatic, and Laine found herself momentarily distracted by his movie-star smile and bright blue eyes. When he extended his hand, it was a moment before she slipped her fingers into his, and the heat in her face intensified as he brushed a kiss across the back of her hand. He immediately released her, but his gaze continued to hold hers captive.

"A gentleman," she commented.

"Always, ma'am," he replied, "and I don't mean to intrude, but I don't believe I've ever seen you here before."

Laine leaned her elbows on the table, giving him a good view of her cleavage, but his eyes never left her face. "No, you haven't."

"And, until now," he said, "that has been my misfortune. I am extremely glad my luck has changed for the better."

Laine didn't think she'd ever met anyone so charming. There was nothing smarmy or sleazy about his manner. Every word that exited his nicely shaped mouth conveyed warmth and sincerity. This man would easily give Jack a run for his money when it came to like-ability and sex appeal.

She gave him a demure smile. "Are you staying for lunch, my good sir, or are you here for take-out?"

"May I ask if you are alone?" When she nodded, his smile widened. "I don't believe in take-out, ma'am."

While married to Nick, Laine had learned law enforcement officers, no matter who they worked for, never liked to sit in a public place with their back to the door. She rose in one fluid motion, and even in heels, the top of her head only came to his chin. Her heart leapt into her throat and it took superhuman effort to swallow it. She forced her eyes upward, smiled, and gracefully indicated the seat she'd just vacated.

"If you would join me," she began, "then I can say my luck, also, has changed for the better."

"You didn't have to give me your seat," he commented, his brows drawing together, "but thank you. I admit I do not like to sit in a public place with my back to the door." He took her seat and she slid in opposite him. The waitress showed up with her tea and a glass of water for Bear.

"Are you ready to order, miss?" the girl asked.

Laine met Agent Bristol's intense gaze. "There are so many choices. What would you recommend?"

"Do you have any dietary preferences?" he asked. "Are you vegetarian, vegan . . . ?"

"Carnivore," she replied. "I hope that's all right." His expression told her it was more than all right.

"Forgive me for asking," he said, "but you're not watching your figure, are you? If you are, I must say you have no need."

She silently applauded his tact and smiled. "No, I'm not."

He nodded and looked at the waitress. "Bridges' bacon cheeseburger for the lady, half fries, half rings, and I'll have the usual, Becky."

The girl almost sighed. "Ok, Bear. You got it."

After she hurried away, Laine gave him a knowing look. "I think

Becky likes you."

He smiled. "She'll outgrow that," he replied. "Besides, she's a tad young for an old man like me."

Laine laughed. "Old. We can't be more than a couple years apart."

His brows drew together. "I beg to differ. You can't be more than 30. Besides, women are like fine wine. They only get better with age."

One corner of her mouth rose. "I'm nearly forty, and you have more charm than any one person should be blessed with." She propped her chin in her hand. "And yet, you haven't told me your name, although I'm assuming it's Bear, unless that's just Becky's pet name for you."

He extended his hand again, and her fingers were engulfed. His grip was warm and firm. "Ted Bristol, but my friends call me Bear, for obvious reasons. That includes you now, at least it will if you would do me the honor."

"Laine Wheeler," she said. "Pleased to make your acquaintance, Bear. Jack told me I would like you."

"Jack? Jack who?"

They went silent as their food was delivered, and Becky gave Bear one last wistful look before walking away.

Laine lowered her voice. "Special Agent Jack Vaughn, ATF," she replied. To his credit, his expression never changed.

"I'm afraid I don't follow."

She smiled. "He said you were good, Special Agent Bristol, but I'm not here by accident. Jack's in trouble and he sent me here to get you."

His posture remained relaxed, but she saw his expression harden just slightly. As a doctor, she had learned to observe people carefully, and while no one else might have noticed the change, she certainly did.

"I don't know what kind of game you're playing—"

"I'm not playing a game," she interrupted. "His cover's been blown, he's been shot, and he's on the run." She paused and reached across the table to take his hand. He didn't pull away, nor did he acknowledge her. His gaze was sharp, but she forced herself to continue. "He needs your help, and so do I."

His eyes narrowed. "You?"

"Yes, Bear. Jack's not the only one in trouble."

Chapter Thirteen

"Why didn't Jack just call me?" Bear asked.

His tone was light, belying his pointed gaze. Laine felt impaled by those piercing blue eyes, but before she could reply her cell phone rang. His brows rose. Laine retrieved the phone from her purse and answered the call.

"Hello?" She listened for a moment and then handed the phone to Bear. "It's for you."

Bear looked at her, then took the phone and put it to his ear. His eyes never left hers and his expression never changed, until the end. Laine felt a spurt of hope as the man smiled, then said:

"Yeah, you sure know how to pick 'em. She doesn't have a sister, does she?"

Laine sighed and closed her eyes in relief. Bear said his goodbyes, then handed her the phone. Before she could say a word, Bear signaled the waitress, and Becky rushed over.

"Box this up, please, Becky," he said as he pulled out his wallet and handed her two twenty dollar bills. "Thanks, sweetheart, and keep the change."

Becky appeared thrilled, and rushed away with their untouched plates. Laine watched her go and turned back to Bear. He looked at her closely for a tense moment, stood, and extended his hand to her.

"C'mon, beautiful," he said. "Let's go take Jack some lunch. I'm driving."

They left the restaurant and Laine was surprised when he walked to a car parked across the street. It was a black Cadillac Escalade with tinted windows, and when he saw her expression, he smiled.

"I guess Jack told you I only live a few blocks from here," he said. When she nodded, he unlocked her door and opened it. "He's right. I just wasn't planning to go home after lunch. Wasn't planning *this* little detour, but I wasn't planning to go home."

Laine got in and took the bag of food from him. He closed the door, jogged around to his side and got in.

"Where were you planning to go?" she asked.

He gave her a sidelong glance. "When I saw you I thought perhaps dinner and a movie, but that's all shot to hell." He chuckled and started the engine. "Jack always has been—"

"One lucky SOB," Laine finished for him. "So he's told me."

"Yeah, well, it's only a football game I'll be missing," he said. "The Broncos will just have to survive without me."

"Who are they playing?"

"San Francisco," he replied with a grimace.

Laine smiled and bit her lip, and when he saw her expression, his brows drew together.

"Tell me you're not a fan," he said.

"Sorry," she said, raising her hands. "Spent three years at UC Davis. They kind of grew on me."

He stared at her for a moment before he started the engine. "Well, I suppose you're to be allowed a few flaws." He put the Escalade in drive. "After all, no one's perfect."

"Not even you?" she teased.

He flashed a grin that made him look more like a mischievous boy than an intimidating special agent with the FBI. "Nope, Laine, not even me." He wiggled his eyebrows at her. "I suppose that means we're still friends."

"Good," she said as he pulled into traffic, "because I wouldn't ever want to be your enemy." He gave her a once-over, but there was nothing overtly sexual or rude in the way he looked at her. Nevertheless, Laine felt stripped and shifted uncomfortably in her seat.

"Trust me," he said, turning his eyes back to the road, "that will never happen."

***

Jack sat on the couch as Laine finished redressing his shoulder. Bear sat in one of the wingback chairs, though he barely fit, watching with his usual unreadable expression. He hadn't asked any questions yet, deferring to Laine's wish to check Jack's shoulder before the debriefing began. After she finished dressing his wound, she helped him into his shirt and his sling. She gave him a solemn look, then rose and started to walk toward the bedroom. Jack grabbed her hand and smiled when she turned to him.

"Thanks, Doc," he said. She merely smiled and nodded, then walked into the bedroom and closed the door. Jack watched her go, and then he looked to his friend. Bear was scowling.

"Tell me you didn't fall for the doctor," Bear growled. When Jack said nothing, Bear ran a hand over his face and swore. "Dammit, Jack. What the hell are you doing?"

Jack wasn't intimidated in the least. "Maybe I should be asking you that."

"And what the hell does that mean?" Bear demanded.

"It means somebody in your office sold me out," Jack shot back. "Ripley nearly killed me out there, and if it wasn't for *her* I would not be here."

Bear looked furious. "How do you know it was one of my people?"

Jack stood. "The ATF assigned me to you to plan this operation, and the only people who knew with whom and where I was work in *your office!*"

Bear also rose. "And Ripley said it was someone here?"

"Not directly," Jack said, squaring his shoulders. "He rousted me and a bunch of the men out of bed one night, and gave us this grand speech about loyalty and shared ideals. He went on to say that those who didn't share our ideals would always sell their loyalty for a price, and that it was always a good idea to have that kind of person working in the offices of our enemy." Jack stood toe to toe with him. "After that he marched us all out into the woods. He walked us for more than a day before separating me from the rest of the men and telling them I was a federal agent. How else could he know that if not for one of your people?"

Bear put his hands on his hips and chewed his lip, his expression troubled. Finally, he met Jack's furious gaze. "Do you have any idea who it is?"

"Last night when we got into town, I rented a suite at the Ritz with my personal credit card." He saw the light of understanding dawn immediately.

"Did you get a bite?" Bear asked.

"Oh, yeah," Jack replied. "And I hid a camcorder in the room, so it will all be on video."

"Any chance the maids will find the camcorder?"

"Doubt it," Jack said with a shake of his head, "unless they clean inside the air conditioning vents."

Bear rubbed his chin and walked over to the windows. The curtains were open a couple of feet, but the sheer liners were closed. He scowled. "Which one?"

Jack went to his side. "Top floor, third set of windows from the right."

The curtains in his suite were almost completely closed. Jack thought it strange, but the maids could have done that.

"Question now is, how do we get the camcorder back?" Bear mused. The muscles in his jaw flexed. "You can't get it. I can't get it without alerting the rat we're onto him, and until I know who the traitor is, I can't call anyone else to come get it."

"A friend, someone you trust, could rent the room and retrieve the camera."

Bear's brows rose. "Put *another* civilian in danger? Really, Jack?"

Jack frowned. "Maybe a metro cop, local sheriff?"

Bear shook his head and stared at the windows across the street. "Not with stuff like this." He glanced at Jack. "This is national security we're talking about here. My superiors would skin me alive if I let sensitive material like this get into the hands of anyone outside of our respective agencies."

"Somebody at ATF here," Jack offered.

Bear lifted one blonde brow. "Ripley said 'offices,' meaning plural, correct?" He rubbed his eyes. "For all we know he could have moles at every agency in the Federal Building." He swore again and stalked to the desk. He planted his fists on the polished surface and hung his head. "Shit, Jack. This is one hell of a hornet's nest you've stirred up."

"Hey, don't shoot the messenger," Jack said. He eased down on the couch and looked at Bear's broad back. "We could call in someone from outside Denver."

"We don't have that kind of time."

Bear stalked back to the window, and Jack saw his posture change.

"Laine would do it," Jack said absently. "I swear, there were times I forgot she was a civilian, Bear."

"Apparently, so did she," Bear said, his gaze aimed downward toward the street.

Jack looked at him and a stone of dread settled in his stomach.

"What are you talking about?" He moved to Bear's side, and followed the direction of his gaze. Below, crossing the street as if she didn't have a care in the world was Laine. Her flaming hair was visible even from this height. Jack's heart twisted. "No." He ran to the bedroom, hoping he had been hallucinating, but the room was empty. He saw his pants hanging over the back of a chair and reached into the pockets.

"Shit." He walked back into the living area. "She took my room key."

Bear's posture had changed again, and so had his expression. His eyes were narrowed dangerously and focused like a hawk on something.

"We have bigger problems, Jack."

Jack practically flew to the window. "What?"

Bear pointed towards the windows of his suite. "The curtains in your room just moved."

Jack's head spun with the possibilities, and he suddenly felt lightheaded. "It's the maids," he whispered. "It has to be the maids."

He heard a rustling and looked toward the sound. Bear had the phone book out, and when he found what he was looking for, he pulled out a cell phone and dialed. He looked at Jack, and the seriousness of his expression was light years from the voice he affected.

"Yes, my name is Jack Graham," he said in a genteel, Southern drawl, "and I was wondering if I could reserve a special suite. It's my anniversary. What suite?" He looked at Jack.

"3687," Jack said softly.

"Room 3687," Bear said into the phone. "My wife and I spent our honeymoon there, and we'd like to celebrate our anniversary where we started our marriage." He paused. "Wonderful, but we're at the airport. Is the room available now, or will we have to wait to check-in?"

Jack closed his eyes when Bear shook his head and gave him a look that told him it wasn't maids in the suite. He got to his feet and retrieved a pistol from the suitcase he and Laine had packed. He stuffed it inside his sling.

"What do you think you're doing?" Bear asked from behind him.

"She saved my life, Bear," Jack said in a terse voice. "There's no way I'm not going to return that favor."

"Well, if you think you're going alone you're nuts." Bear gave him a grudging smile. "Hell, maybe once we save her she'll realize I'm the better man and decide to defect to the FBI."

Jack smiled, in spite of the circumstances. "Of all the people I know,

Bear, you're the one man I think would be capable of handling her." He checked his pistol to make sure it wasn't visible. "Let's just make sure we get her out alive so she can make a choice." He pulled the silenced .45 out of the suitcase and tossed it to his friend. "Here, you might need this."

Bear easily caught the gun and turned it over in his hand. "Nice. Always wanted one of these."

They rode the elevator down in silence and crossed to the Ritz Carlton. His nerves tighter than bow strings, Jack kept his head straight, but his eyes were always moving, looking for any sign of Ripley's men. He knew Bear was doing the same, looking for the traitor. They walked into the lobby, which was just as busy as it had been last night, and made their way toward the elevators. Just as Jack pushed the button, Bear grabbed his arm.

"They'll be watching the elevators," he said. He looked around then jerked his head to the left. "Come on. I have an idea." He walked toward a maid, pulled the woman aside and discreetly showed her his badge. "Where are your service elevators?"

"Down that hall to the right," the woman told him. "Should I call the police?"

Bear gave her one of his charming smiles. "I am the police, ma'am, which means they're already here." He looked at Jack and strode in the direction the woman had pointed them. When they were out of her range of hearing, Bear said, "She's going to call the cops."

Jack was on his heels. "Oh, yeah. Probably dialing as we speak."

They took the elevator up to the thirty-third floor, and Jack remembered how Laine's gaze had been so focused on the flashing numbers the night before. He closed his eyes briefly and tried to shake off the cloak of dread that threatened to overwhelm him. They exited the elevator and took the stairs from there, Jack's pulse ratcheting up with each step he took. As they neared their goal, he started sending fervent prayers heavenward.

Bear went first, moving slowly and silently, the pistol held close to his chest. When they got to the thirty-fifth floor, Bear paused, then looked at Jack and held up one hand. Apparently, there was someone on the next floor landing.

Jack held tight to the wall as Bear leaned slowly out over the railing, his eagle-eyed gaze focused above and to his right. He moved with the coiled efficiency of a python, smooth and seemingly effortless, but oh, so deadly. Jack watched as Bear moved his index finger from the barrel to the trigger, and whistled softly. Jack heard movement above them and Bear squeezed the trigger. There was the familiar "pfft", a startled exclamation, and then Bear squeezed off two more rounds. To Jack's surprise, two men, dressed like tourists, heavily armed tourists, fell down the stairs, and when they came to a stop at the landing, neither of them moved. He recognized them immediately as Ripley's men. Bear approached him.

"Stay here," Bear whispered. "I'm going to go down a level and check the stairwell on the opposite end of the hall. Wait five minutes, and then proceed."

The last thing Jack wanted to do was wait any longer, but he knew he needed to follow Bear's lead. Between the two of them, Bear's thinking was far less muddled. Jack nodded. "Got it."

They checked their watches. Bear gave him a nod and took the stairs down three at a time. Jack took the dead men's weapons, stuffed one pistol in the waistband of his pants and another behind the sling. He moved up to the 36th floor access door and waited. When five minutes had passed, he slowly opened the door and peered out.

The hallway appeared deserted, so he slipped out of the stairwell and closed the door silently. With slow, measured footsteps he walked toward his former suite. He was surprised to find the door to the room propped open with a book. He took a closer look and recognized the Gideon's Bible. He looked up and down the hallway, but Bear hadn't shown up yet. He took a deep breath, then opened the door with his foot and stepped into the room, making sure not to disturb the makeshift doorstop.

The first thing he saw was Laine, seated in a chair facing the door. She blinked when she recognized him, and he saw the fear in her eyes. Relief at seeing her alive flooded him, and then all of his insides cramped. Behind her stood Calember. He had one hand on her neck, and the other held a military-style hunting knife. At least she wasn't tied to the chair, which was a plus. She just sat there with Calember's considerable presence at her back.

It wasn't the knife at Laine's neck that really worried him; it was the fact Calember had a gun somewhere, of that much Jack was absolutely sure. More than likely, it was within easy reach. Calember was nothing if not careful.

"Nice of you to join us, Agent Vaughn," Calember said in a cordial voice.

His friendly tone belied the cold fury in his eyes, but Jack only looked at him for a moment. Laine was his primary focus.

"I'm sorry, Jack," she whispered.

"Don't worry, Laine," he replied. "Everything's going to be okay."

She nodded and moved her eyes to her right, in the direction of the bedroom, and blinked slowly, twice. Jack dropped his chin a bit, to let her know he understood. Then she looked left. There was a dining/meeting room behind that set of closed doors, and she blinked twice again. Jack pursed his lips and nodded once as he met Calember's eyes.

"So, what's it going to be, Calember?" he asked. "You've got me here. Why don't you let her go?"

"Who? The good doctor?" Calember laughed. "You must be joking, Jack. You, of all people, know how this works."

Jack tried not to scowl when Calember stroked her neck, but the man wasn't Ripley's second in command for nothing. He paused in his movements, one sandy brow shooting skyward. A sly smile curved his mouth and he leaned over to whisper in Laine's ear, keeping his eyes on his former colleague.

"I think Special Agent Vaughn has feelings for you, doctor," he said. "Did you see that spark of jealousy in his eyes when I touched you?"

Laine blinked and a tear slid down her cheek, but her expression was far from weepy. She gritted her teeth and turned toward Calember just slightly.

"Perhaps it's just his personal distaste for *you*." Her chin lifted a notch. "Believe me, I understand his intense dislike."

Calember chuckled, kissed her cheek, and straightened. "So, Jack, is this where you play the hero, sacrifice yourself for the lovely doctor?" He clucked his tongue. "Such a waste."

"The police are on their way, Mike," Jack said, using Calember's first name. "This is going to draw you and CAG a lot of unwanted attention. Are you sure that's what Ripley wants?"

Calember continued to stroke Laine's neck. "Maybe Ripley thinks it's time for our organization to go public."

"And he wants CAG's first foray into the public arena to be connected with the murder of an innocent woman and a federal agent?" Jack actually laughed. "I doubt that."

"He said to do what's necessary," Calember replied in a tight voice.

"I imagine his *exact* orders were to do whatever was necessary to neutralize the threat and retrieve the information I stole," Jack argued. "I *have* spent some time with the man."

"Well, I think this is what's necessary."

"Fine," Jack said with a shrug, "but it won't get you the information back."

Calember sneered. "We already have the laptop, Jack."

"Yeah, and even you should be able to figure out that what you want isn't there anymore." Jack looked around the room, but the laptop was gone. "Wherever it is, whoever has it, you may want to call them and have them double-check it."

Calember eyed him for a moment and released Laine's neck. That in itself was enough to make Jack want to sigh in relief. They weren't out of the woods yet, but hopefully there was a bear in the woods that would help get them out.

The man pulled a satellite phone out of his pocket and dialed.

"Yeah, check the laptop," he said.

Jack could hardly suppress a smile when Calember's face started to turn red.

"Check it *again*," he seethed. A few more moments passed before Calember snapped the phone shut and tossed it aside. "Where are the files, Jack?"

"There's at least one copy of them in my e-mail inbox," a familiar voice said. Bear had his weapon drawn as he stepped around Jack. "You might as well give it up, Calember. Your boss and your fledgling terrorist organization are done." He glanced at Jack. "Sorry it took so long. Had several unwanted visitors in the stairwells and next door I had to take care of." He looked at Laine. "Hello, Laine."

"There's two more in the bedroom," Jack said.

Calember yanked Laine's head back, and she stifled a cry of pain. He smiled and laid the knife against her neck.

"Drop your weapons or she dies."

"Don't do it," Laine said from between clenched teeth. "Kill him."

What happened next was chaos. The door to the bedroom seemed to explode from within, shards of wood whistling through the air. They moved lazily, as if they were passing through water and not air. Then two men burst through, their movements also oddly sluggish and exaggerated. Sounds were muffled, and Jack had the oddest feeling that he was underwater. Bear swung slowly around and got off three shots, taking out the first man and wounding the second. Unfortunately, the second gunman also fired and hit the rather large target that was firing at him. Bear jerked, spun, and seemed to hang in the air for a moment before he fell to the ground, the gun flying from his hand. Jack started to reach for his friend, until he realized that the second man was still shooting.

Jack somersaulted to a position behind the couch and ground his teeth together as agony shot through his shoulder. He took a knee, caught a breath, and a glimpse of something in his periphery. He leaned left, pulled the gun from his sling and shot the second man just as the crosshair found him. The gunman's arms were flung wide as the bullet impacted his chest, and he seemed to float to the ground. He bounced a couple of times then went still, his head lolling to the side.

The couch wasn't much good as cover, but it was all he had. Jack crouched behind the heavy piece of furniture and took a breath. He saw movement out of the corner of his eye and his head snapped around, the gun tracking with his gaze. It was Bear. The taller man pressed a hand to his neck, blood seeping from between his fingers, but he managed to give Jack a nod. Jack nodded back then turned to face Calember.

Ripley's second had Laine on her feet and pulled against his chest. He was using her as a human shield. Jack saw the fear in her face, but he also recognized the resolute determination and something inside him recoiled. He couldn't take a shot without risking her life, but that's exactly what her eyes were telling him to do.

"Let her go, Mike," Jack said in a low voice that was no longer distorted. "This is done."

With his left hand fisted in her hair, Calember moved his right hand across her throat to position the blade beneath Laine's left ear.

Jack stood and shouted, "Don't!"

"Why not, Jack? After all, it's like you said. This is done."

Jack lifted his gun, but his arm felt weighted down. He closed his eyes briefly and prayed Laine would forgive him for shooting her. He carefully aimed, focusing on the upper right side of her chest below the collarbone. At this distance the shot would probably go right through her and, if he placed the round correctly, hit Calember in the middle of his chest. It might not kill him, but it would most definitely incapacitate him.

Before Jack could fire, Laine dropped her chin and clamped her teeth onto Calember's forearm. The muscles in her jaw worked as she bit down, *hard*. Calember screamed and blood rushed down his arm, but with her teeth firmly dug into his wrist he couldn't draw the knife across her throat. All he could do was release her hair and jerk, the action sending her spinning from him. Jack didn't wait. He squeezed the trigger and kept firing until the gun was empty. Calember was launched backward by the force of the barrage and hit the window. Jack heard the cracking of glass, and it seemed minutes passed before the clear pane gave way and gravity began to take over. As Calember fell backwards over the sill, Jack saw the gun he pulled from his back. Calember focused on him and fired, then disappeared from sight.

Jack saw the flash and the bullet as it left the muzzle. It was the strangest thing. He could see the air move as the projectile penetrated it. It rippled, as if the air was water and the bullet a pebble. Jack tried to move out of its path, and while his brain was processing information at the normal pace, the hands of time refused to move any faster. It wasn't until the bullet was only several feet from him that time seemed to return to normal, and by then it was too late. He felt the impact in his chest, felt the immense pressure, a burst of pain, and dropped like a stone.

Laine saw Jack fall back and screamed his name. Heedless of everything else, she skittered across the floor to his side and immediately pressed her hands over the wound in the center of his chest. Blood squeezed from beneath her fingers, but she kept pressure on it. Jack's jaw worked soundlessly, as if he was trying to speak but was unable, his eyes searching the air above him for something she couldn't see.

"Jack," she said loudly. "Jack look at me."

She had reverted back to doctor mode, her voice clear and strong. That seemed to penetrate the fog he was in, and he finally focused on her.

"Laine," he whispered, "you're okay." He coughed and blood burst from his mouth, spattering his face.

Behind her it sounded like the Apocalypse had descended. The local police had arrived and were shouting, the myriad of voices like a shrieking, unintelligible chorus. She heard Bear shouting back, but she couldn't pay attention to that now. She felt fingers grasp her arm, as if to pull her away from Jack. She whirled, struck out blindly and was released. She immediately covered the bleeding wound in his chest again and shouted:

"I'm a doctor, dammit! Get an ambulance. *Now!*"

Her announcement seemed to deter whoever had grabbed her and no one else touched her. The riot continued in the background, but she had learned long ago how to tune that out.

"Jack," she said again, "Jack, you need to look at me. Focus on me, Jack. Focus on me."

He blinked and tried to swallow, which only resulted in more coughing and more blood from his mouth. She got up on her knees and put as much pressure on the wound as she dared, hoping to stem the bleeding, but it didn't seem to help. She was up to her wrists in the thick, coppery-smelling liquid.

"Somebody get me an ambulance!" she screamed. Her stomach twisted when she saw the growing blood stain on the shoulder of his shirt. Had he been shot more than once?

"What can I do, Laine?" Bear asked as he knelt across from her.

The front of Bear's shirt was soaked in blood, but the concern in his eyes was obvious, as was the steely determination. She grabbed onto his strength and calm and blinked as she realized the ungodly choir had faded to a dull roar. "Are you hurt?"

"Bullet grazed me," he replied. "I'll be fine. Now what do you need?"

"An ambulance."

"It's on the way. I think they're pulling up as we speak. What else?"

Laine nodded. "Do you have a knife?"

He grunted. "Do you know any self-respecting cop who doesn't carry one?"

"Get his shirt open so I can see his shoulder."

Bear did so with quick, sure movements. She sighed in relief when she saw the bleeding came from where he'd ripped his stitches and not because he'd been shot twice. Just as she started to relax a hair, Jack started coughing violently, and she felt his blood spatter her chest and neck. He took a great, gulping breath and closed his eyes.

"No, no, no, no," she said, fighting back a wave of panic. "Jack, look at me! Look at me, Jack! Dammit, Special Agent Vaughn, *look* at me!"

His eyelids snapped open and she leaned closer. He focused on her and tried to smile. His usually bright smile was red with blood, a gruesome sight. Laine smiled back and then remembered she had Calember's blood all over her face. She probably looked as macabre as he did.

"That's it," she said, "focus, Jack. Don't try to speak, just look at me, okay?" He nodded. "Good. Just listen to my voice, focus on my face. You're going to be all right, do you understand me? You're going to be fine."

A few moments later, more voices joined the cacophony and Bear backed away. A paramedic dropped a bag and knelt on the spot Bear had just vacated.

"What have we got?" the young man asked.

Laine took a breath. "White male, approximately 6'3", 240 pounds, single GSW to the chest."

"Ok, back off so I can get a look."

"No," Laine replied flatly. "If I release pressure, he'll bleed out before you can get him to the ambulance. I need a central line, two milligrams of epi . . . ." She continued giving orders just as she had in years past, without even thinking about it. It was an automatic thing, and the EMT moved as he listened.

"You a doctor?" he asked.

Bear actually slapped the man in the back of the head. "No, numb nuts, she watches a lot of ER reruns. Do what she says or *I'll* shoot you."

Five minutes later the EMTs were loading them onto the ambulance, Laine on the gurney straddling Jack's waist so she could keep pressure on his chest. He was in and out of consciousness, but she kept talking despite the lump in her throat. He seemed to respond to her voice. Laine was glad for that because it was the only thing keeping the tears at bay.

The ambulance screamed into the hospital, and medical personnel were waiting when the EMTs unloaded them. She stayed astride Jack, hands pressed tight to his chest, until they were inside the hospital.

"I hear you're a doctor," a man in green scrubs said as they were wheeled into a trauma room.

"Yes," Laine replied. "I'm Dr. Wheeler."

"Dr. Winslow," the man said. He started a cursory exam as the nurses rushed around preparing the room, hooking Jack up to monitors, and then he looked up at her. "We were told he had one GSW. I see two."

"The shoulder is four days old," Laine replied. "The one in his chest is the one you need to worry about."

"All right, what have we got?" Another man in scrubs said as he strode in. He took in the picture of her on top of Jack and his eyes widened just a bit. "Wow. I'm sure there's a great back-story here, but I'm not even going to ask." He approached Jack's side and met Laine's gaze. "Dr. Shepard. I'm the surgeon. Why don't you get down so we can take a look?"

Laine nodded, but she kept pressure on the wound until her feet were on the floor. Then she stepped back and moved out of the way. As they started working on him, flashbacks of another day assaulted her, and it was all she could do not to run from the room screaming. It seemed to take forever, and yet time flashed by with unnatural swiftness. She leaned against the wall until a nurse took her arm and gently ushered her from the room. Laine stood at the door and watched through the window. All too soon the doctor and the surgeon stepped back. Laine's heart hit the floor.

Chapter Fourteen

Laine stood at the doors which read *Authorized Personnel Only* in large red letters. She peered through the square, mesh reinforced window as they wheeled Jack into an operating room. When they disappeared from sight, she sighed and shuffled to a chair. People walking by her looked, and then did double-takes, but Laine paid them no heed. She knew she looked like a survivor from a horror movie, but she had more important things to worry about.

"Dr. Wheeler?" a vaguely familiar voice said from beside her.

She looked into the face of Dr. . . . Winslow, that was his name. "Yes?"

He sat in a chair beside her and handed her a pair of surgical scrubs, a towel, and a toiletry kit with shampoo, soap, lotion, a toothbrush and toothpaste. "Thought you could use these," he said in a low, kind voice. "Looks like you and your friends have been through thirteen levels of hell today."

"You could say that," she said, weary to the bone.

"I talked with the EMT who brought you in," Winslow went on. "He said you were the reason our patient was stable enough for transport."

"Just doing what had to be done."

"Well, he has a much better chance, thanks to you," Winslow said. "Shepard is one of the best surgeons in the country. Your friend is in good hands."

Laine closed her eyes. "Thank you."

"If you want, I'll show you where the women's locker room is," the doctor offered. "You can clean up there. Your friend will be in surgery for a while."

"Then tell *me* where it is, and she can find it when it suits her," Bear said from a few feet away. The doctor looked up, nodded, and walked over to Bear. Laine watched as they exchanged a few hushed words, and then Winslow disappeared down the hall.

Laine looked up and couldn't help but smile. Bear looked ridiculous. He had a large bandage on the right side of his neck and was wearing a hospital gown over his jeans. He sat down next to her.

"Didn't have scrubs big enough for me," he groused. "Guess I'll never wear *that* shirt to a game again."

She laughed. Bear looked askance at her, and when her laughs turned to tears, he put one tree-like arm around her shoulders and pulled her onto his considerable lap. It was like being hugged by a grizzly, a warm, strong, friendly, protective grizzly. He leaned back in his chair and just let her cry, as if this was the most natural thing in the world. He said nothing, did nothing, just held her. When she was cried out, he looked down at her.

"Feel better?" he asked softly.

"This is all my fault," she said with a sniff. "If it wasn't for me—"

"Jack would be dead on the side of the road in rural Montana," Bear interrupted, his voice low and even. "You didn't shoot Jack, you saved his life."

"If I hadn't gone over there—"

"Y'know, I really hate that word," Bear said. "*If.* If my aunt had balls she'd be my uncle. If I was two inches shorter I'd be flying military aircraft instead of carrying a gun and chasing scum. If you hadn't gone over there, we wouldn't have gone over there, and it could be you laying down in the morgue instead of . . . now let's see . . . two in each stairwell . . . two in the dining room and two more in the bedroom . . . Calember . . . wow. Between Jack and me, the coroner has nine bodies to look at. Hey, hey, not bad for a day's work."

He actually sounded pleased and Laine looked up at him. He smiled at her, and again she saw the handsome, mischievous youth.

"Almost ten terrorists down, and we'll find out how many more to go once we start digging into the information Jack sent us." His eyes narrowed on her face, and just like that, the FBI agent was back. "We'd never have gotten that information if it wasn't for you, so quit beating yourself up. Quit focusing on the bad things, trying to rationalize it with 'if's'. Concentrate on what's good and worth living for. You spend all your time saying 'if', and you'll get to the end of your life and realize all you ever did was talk, and none of it was particularly good conversation."

He chucked her under the chin. "You did great, Laine. Now why don't you let me show you the ladies locker room so you can get cleaned up? I have to admit, it bothers me to see a pretty girl covered in blood."

She was so shell-shocked all she could do was nod. Bear kept her close to his side as they walked slowly down the hall. He stopped in front of the women's locker room and sat down in a chair directly across from it. He gave her a nod and a small push.

"Go on, Laine. You're freaking people out."

Laine was numb as she entered the bathroom and stood in front of a mirror. Her reflection was truly ghoulish. She stared, not recognizing herself. Her lips were stained with blood, making her look like a vampire who had serious drinking issues. Calember's blood left a dark swath from the corners of her mouth over her chin, and down her neck. The white tank was now a bloody rag. The spatters and droplets scattered over her face, chest, and arms were from Jack, and her hands looked as if they'd been dipped up to the wrists. Her nails were caked with the stuff. Tears welled as she pictured Jack, bleeding and gasping for air. She went to the door and stuck her head out, and Bear was there in an instant.

"What is it, Laine?" he asked, concern etched on his granite features.

She couldn't take her eyes from her hands. "Um, could you ask a nurse for a nail brush? I don't think this is going to wash off." Without waiting for a reply, she stepped back into the locker room and plopped down on a bench.

What had happened finally started to register with her on an emotional level, and she felt herself spiraling downward. It was a terrifying, dizzying sensation that left her trembling and nauseous. Tears filled her eyes as she stared at her hands, and she choked back a sob as the picture of Jack bleeding out on the floor hung in her mind's eye. If he died . . . Laine moaned softly and tried to get a hold of herself. Breaking down now would do no one any good, especially Jack. She had to keep it together.

A few minutes later someone tapped on the door, but they didn't wait outside. Laine looked up as Bear walked right in, took her by the hand and led her to the sink. Without saying a word, he turned on the water, thrust her fingers beneath the faucet, and then soaped her hands between his much larger ones. In the middle of his efforts a woman walked in and froze in the doorway, a startled look on her face.

"Do you mind?" Bear asked, as if it was the men's locker room and not the women's. "I'm working here." The woman left as if Laine was chasing her, vampire fangs bared.

Bear sudsed her hands, took the nail brush and began scrubbing. For such a large man his touch was amazingly gentle. He worked the brush up and down each finger, bending and unbending them so he could get the nooks and crannies. He scrupulously cleaned each nail, taking as much care as any surgeon would have but with a much lighter touch. He worked the brush up and around, scrubbing in soft circles until not a trace of Jack's blood remained. After rinsing her hands, and then his, he grabbed some paper towels and held them out to her.

"There," he said, sounding quite pleased with himself. "All better. I'd offer to scrub the rest of you, but I think Jack would take offense."

Laine stared at her pristine hands, turning them over and back again. She nodded, met his gaze and gave him a tearful smile. "Thank you."

"Finish getting cleaned up, Laine," he said quietly. "You'll feel better when you do, and so will I." He stood behind her as she looked at her reflection again. "You're starting to freak *me* out." He wiggled his eyebrows at her and turned and left the room.

Laine took her time showering, hoping the hot water would wash away all that had happened. She scrubbed herself until she was squeaky clean and pink, and as she toweled her hair dry she still couldn't get Jack out of her mind. She hadn't seen Calember fire; she'd heard the shot and instinctively looked at Jack, praying she was wrong. When the blood stained the front of his shirt, she'd realized her prayers hadn't been answered. She didn't want to go through this again.

She dressed in the clean scrubs, but when she looked around for her clothing, it was gone. She searched the locker room, but it was all gone, her shirt, her bra, even her shoes. Then it hit her. Her clothing was evidence.

Laine stepped into the hallway and Bear stood up.

"So, did you take my clothes into evidence, or did you have someone else do it?" she asked.

"I did it," he said. He held up a large, printed plastic bag with a red strip across the top that read EVIDENCE. He whipped out a pen, signed something, and then signaled for a uniformed officer who was waiting down the hall. The officer walked over, took the bag and went back the way he came. "Sorry, Laine. Your clothing is part of a criminal investigation."

"I get it," she said with a sigh as they strolled back to the chairs outside the operating rooms. "I was married to a cop once."

"I know," he said, "and I'm sorry for what happened to him."

"Thank you." She paused and turned to him, startled. "Wait, what?"

"I had a colleague do some checking on you while I was downstairs getting stitched up," he admitted without being sheepish or apologetic. "Standard procedure. You're a witness in a federal investigation. The men at the top of the chain want to know what kind of witness you'll be." He sat and rested his elbows on his knees. "I told them what kind of witness you'd be, but they weren't in the mood to simply take my word for it." He shook his head and looked at her. "Imagine that."

"Go figure," Laine agreed, sitting next to him.

"Y'know, Laine," he began, "they've already called wanting your debrief."

"I'm not going anywhere until I know he's going to be okay."

He rested a hand on her shoulder. "I know. I told them not to get their panties in a bunch, and we'd be there when we got there." He smiled and gave her a wink. "Sound good to you?"

Her eyes stung and she smiled. "Sounds perfect."

"By the way, we got the guy from Jack's recording. Caught him at the airport trying to board a plane for Mexico City." He chuckled. "As soon as they got him into interrogation he folded like a house of cards. Ripley has more to worry about now than the dirt Jack had on him."

All Laine could do was nod.

Bear studied her face for a moment. "You look kind of tired, Laine. My shoulder makes a great pillow, if you've a mind to catch a few winks."

Laine looked at him, and realized with no small amount of surprise that she was about ready to drop. She'd pulled long hours during medical school and residency, and had gone through some hair-raising experiences, but nothing like what she'd experienced the past several days. With a tired sigh she put her head on his lap and pulled her feet up. Bear seemed startled for a moment, but he rested a hand on her arm and said, "That works, too. I'll wake you as soon as there's word."

Laine hadn't believed she'd be able to sleep, but Bear's lap was warm and his hand on her shoulder was a comfort. Within moments she drifted off and, thankfully, didn't dream.

***

She didn't know how long she'd been asleep, but she bolted upright when Bear gently shook her. Laine raked her fingers through her hair then looked at Bear.

"How long was I out?" she asked.

"Nearly two hours," he said with a smile. "Nurse just came by and said the surgeon's on his way out."

As if that had been his introduction, Dr. Shepard pushed through the swinging doors, pulled the surgical cap off his head, and held it in one hand as he approached her. Laine rose, Bear at her side, and listened as Shepard described the surgery. She didn't realize she'd been holding her breath until he said Jack had made it through. She exhaled forcefully and took a deep breath.

"Thank you, Dr. Shepard," she said, shaking his hand firmly. "Is he awake?" The surgeon's expression changed and Laine was instantly alert. "What? What are you not telling me?"

"The bullet grazed the pulmonary artery and nicked the esophagus before lodging in his right lung," Shepard told her. "He lost nearly two-thirds of his blood volume."

"Oh, God." She blinked. With that much blood loss, oxygen circulation was seriously compromised. "So there could be brain damage."

Shepard nodded. "We won't know until he wakes up, and he hasn't done that yet."

"Can I see him?"

"He's in recovery right now," the surgeon said. He put a comforting hand on her shoulder. "As soon as we get him in a room I'll have a nurse come get you."

"Doctor," Bear broke in, "I'm going to be posting a twenty-four-hour security detail on that room. Let your people know."

Shepard nodded. "Of course." He gave her a small smile, and turned and walked back the way he'd come.

"Jack's a fighter, Laine," Bear said in a voice filled with confidence. "He's going to be fine, so just hold onto that."

She looked at him, and he appeared every bit as confident as he had sounded. "How do you know?"

"Because no one puts themselves through what he did to make this investigation work without having brass balls the size of Rhode Island." He planted his hands on his hips and sharpened his gaze on her. "Jack is one of the most dedicated agents I've ever worked with, and there is no way he is checking out before he sees this through." A smile softened his features. "Besides, I know he'll want to see you again."

A short while later, a nurse approached them and escorted them to Jack's room. Once they entered, two uniformed agents took up posts on either side of the door. Laine looked at Jack's unconscious form and her breath hitched.

He was pale, his eyes like dark craters in his face. He was shirtless, a large bandage covering the center of his chest, and he had IV's running into his left arm. She listened to the soft 'beep beep' of the heart monitor and watched the dancing line.

"Well," Bear said, "he's still alive."

"Yeah," Laine agreed, "but is he still Jack?"

There was a knock on the door and Laine jumped. Bear turned and opened it, and two men in suits walked in. The first guy gave Bear a withering look, then fixed his eyes on her.

"Dr. Wheeler?" he asked. "Dr. Laine Wheeler?"

"Yes?"

"I'm Inspector Paul Gilman, and this is Inspector Ben Guarnere," the man said as he held up his credentials. "We're U.S. Marshals."

Laine examined each man's badge and ID, and then fixed Gilman with a pointed stare. "And?"

"We're here to escort you to the Federal Building, ma'am," Gilman replied. "There you'll be questioned, debriefed, and put into protective custody."

She looked from one Marshal to the other, and back. Anger flared in her chest as they watched her, and she realized that once she left with them, they would have virtual control over her life. Well, she was tired of doing as she was told. Frowning, she crossed her arms over her chest and said, "No." Laine turned away from the Marshals and sat in a chair at Jack's elbow.

"What?" Gilman seemed momentarily taken aback, and Bear's amused chuckle did nothing to ease his discomfiture. "That wasn't a request, Dr. Wheeler. I am under orders to escort you downtown."

She looked at him over her shoulder. "I'm not going anywhere until Agent Vaughn wakes up and I speak to him," Laine said flatly.

"This isn't a joke, Dr. Wheeler," Gilman argued. He took a step toward her, but Bear stepped neatly in front of him.

"Leave. The lady. *Alone*," he said in a tone that chilled her.

She glanced at him, but his back was to her.

"I have orders, Special Agent Bristol," Gilman insisted. He peered around Bear's girth and looked at her. "Don't force me to remove you physically, ma'am."

"I'm sorry," Bear said, "*what* did you just say?"

Gilman puffed up his chest and craned his neck to meet Bear's gaze. "If I have to, I'll put her in cuffs and carry her out of here."

"Like hell you will." Bear towered over the man, and even Laine felt intimidated.

"Oh, throwing your height and weight around, eh, Bristol?" Gilman sneered. "Big man thinks he's the cock of the walk."

Bear growled, grabbed the Marshal's arm, and steered him into the hall. Even through the door Laine could hear them.

"Keep it up and I'll be throwing *your* height and weight around, and you won't even *have* a cock when I'm done."

"Think you can take us both?" Gilman asked.

Laine glanced at Guarnere, who was still standing silently in the corner, and saw he didn't possess the brash bravado of his partner. He stood expressionless, but alert.

"Pack a lunch and bring a few more friends," Bear said, "and then we'll just about have an even fight."

"We need her statement."

"Why?"

"You were there and you're asking me why?"

"Yes, I am," Bear replied. "I know what went on at the Ritz. What I want to know is why you think her statement is so important you're willing to handcuff a *federal witness*, and force her to do something when it isn't immediately necessary!"

"And why don't *you* think it's necessary?"

"Because all the suspects in the aforementioned action are, how shall I put it? Oh, yeah. They're *dead*. Therefore, unless you really need her to swear out a statement against a bunch of corpses, whatever you think you need, can wait."

"Bristol!"

The cacophony was back, like after Jack had been shot, and it was suddenly too much. Laine grit her teeth and rose in one fluid motion. She felt Guarnere's eyes on her, but he never moved as she crossed the room, opened the door, and stepped into the hall. "Enough," she said, moving to Bear's side. She looked at Gilman. "I'm sorry to be such a pain in the ass, Marshal Gilman, but I am *not* leaving this hospital room until I see and hear for myself that Agent Vaughn is going to be all right." She shrugged. "You can either wait in the hall until then, or I'm sure Agent Bristol would be more than happy to escort me to your offices once Agent Vaughn wakes."

Bear nodded. "More than happy to."

"I could always arrest you for impeding an investigation," Gilman said.

"You could," Laine agreed, putting a hand on Bear's arm when he tensed and growled again. "However, you may want to tell your superiors that if you do that, you'll never get the encryption key for the files you are so anxious to dig into." She gestured at the door to Jack's room. "I don't see him talking, they're not even certain he'll wake up. The only other person who knows the encryption cipher is me. Therefore, you may want to take that to your bosses before you slap the cuffs on."

She stared hard at the frustrated Marshal, arms crossed over her chest, and finally he spun on his heel and walked down the hall several yards. He pulled out a cell phone and had a brief, hushed conversation, then walked back over to her. He looked at Bear and tried to appear official.

"As soon as Special Agent Vaughn is awake and coherent, we expect you to escort Dr. Wheeler to our offices for debriefing."

Bear cocked his head to the side. "What, no *please?*"

A sense of relief engulfed her and she smiled. "Bear."

"Done," Bear told Gilman. "Now leave." He stood with his hands on his hips as Gilman opened the door to Jack's room and gestured for Guarnere to follow him. When the two Marshals had disappeared down the hall, Laine and Bear returned to Jack's bedside. Then, Bear looked down at her. "Do you really have the encryption key?"

Laine merely looked at him, smiled, and returned to her chair.

"I'll be damned." He laughed. "Jack said he sometimes had trouble remembering you weren't an agent. I'm beginning to see why." He stood behind her and kneaded her shoulders. "I know he's going to pull through this, Laine. Do you want to know why?"

She laid her hands over his much larger ones and leaned her head back. "Why, Bear?"

He grinned. "Because Jack has always been one lucky son of a bitch."

***

Jack fought the brightening light behind his eyes, because he knew it meant the pain was coming. He wanted to stay in the peaceful blackness of sleep. Then he heard a familiar voice, a voice that made him want to come out of the darkness.

Gray swirled, turning brighter until his eyelids fluttered. He waited for the pain and it was right there, as he'd expected. His throat hurt, and he felt like he had been kicked in the chest by a horse. Then it all came back. He remembered the shattering of glass and the bullet racing toward him as Calember fell to his death, the taste of blood and the sound of Laine's voice as he struggled to breathe against the pressure in his chest, the golden-green of her eyes as she ordered him to focus on her. The rest was pretty much a blur. He knew there had been an ambulance in there somewhere, and unfamiliar voices as Laine's face faded into the background, and then, nothing.

He began testing various body parts, starting with his toes. Those seemed to work, so he moved up. Knees, legs, those were good, too, but he couldn't move one of his hands. That forced him to open his eyes. Even smiling hurt, but when he saw Laine's face, her cheek resting on top of his right hand, the dark fringe of lashes and the gentle flare of her nostrils as she breathed, he couldn't help himself. He didn't realize he'd said her name until her eyes fluttered open. That golden-green gaze pulled him in, and he was only too happy to go.

She lifted her head just a bit. "Jack?"

He dragged his knuckles over her cheek. "Hi, Doc."

A smile blossomed on her mouth as she grabbed his hand and held it under her chin, tears welling in her eyes. She bit her lip and a single tear slid down her cheek. The warm droplet plopped onto his wrist. "Hi." She paused and took a hitching breath. "How are you feeling?"

"Like hell," he replied, "but seeing you makes it almost bearable."

"At least they got you to do something I never could."

His brows drew together. "What?"

"Morphine."

She pointed to the machine to his left and Jack scowled. When she reached for the plunger that would administer a dose, he stayed her hand.

"Don't, please," he said. "I just woke up. I want to look at you a while longer."

Her chin trembled and she closed her eyes. "I'm so sorry, Jack. This never should've happened."

"It was bound to happen, Doc." He squeezed her fingers. "I'm just glad you were there to save me, again." He paused and sucked in a breath as a wave of pain rolled over him. "Are you ever going to let me return the favor?"

"But you did, Jack," she whispered. "Remember the woman in the photos? You brought her back from the dead."

"She wasn't dead, Laine. She was just . . . lost."

"Well, you found her, and she repaid you by getting you shot."

He gripped her hand tightly. "You didn't get me shot, Laine, I did. I walked into that room with the full knowledge I would probably be shot and killed, but I did it anyway. And I'd do it again, in a heartbeat."

"So you forgive me?"

"Forgive you?" he repeated, incredulous. He lifted his right arm. "Hey. Come here."

Laine looked at him uncertainly and bit her lip.

"Doc, come *here.*"

She watched him for another few seconds before she stood and carefully stretched out beside him. Her movements were cautious, tentative, and he knew it was because she was afraid to hurt him. Once she was pressed to his side, her face resting against his shoulder, he draped his arm around her and sighed softly.

"Ah, now this is more like it."

That was how Bear found them half an hour later. Jack was awake but Laine, on the other hand, was asleep. He looked up when Bear walked in with two large cups from Starbucks and smiled. Bear put the cups on the window ledge and moved to his side.

"She's been awake pretty much since you were moved in here," Bear said.

"How long has it been?" Jack asked.

"About 18 hours." He shook his head. "I tried to get her to rest, but, well, you know how she is."

"Yes, I do," Jack affirmed, closing his eyes and pressing a kiss to her brow. "And I'm the better man for it."

"You're setting yourself up for a major heartbreak, you know that, don't you, Jack?" Bear asked, his brow furrowed with concern.

A flutter of apprehension bounced around the pit of his stomach and he closed his eyes.

Bear sighed. "The Marshals have already been here. They want to debrief her and move her into protective custody, but she refused to go anywhere until she knew you were all right. Now that you're awake, I have to take her in."

Jack swallowed the lump in his throat and held her closer as he nodded slowly. "I know, Bear." He met his friend's solemn gaze. "Give me just a little while longer, please?"

"Of course," Bear said immediately. "Take your time, Jack. I'll wait outside with the security detail, and you haven't even woken up yet." He smiled and walked toward the door.

"Hey, Bear," Jack said.

Bear stopped with his hand on the door pull. "Yeah, Jack?"

"You know the saying, 'It's better to have loved and lost than never loved at all?'"

Bear nodded. "Yes, Jack. It's Tennyson."

Jack met Bear's gaze and gave him a pained smile. "I finally understand what that means."

Bear looked away, nodded, and then left the room without a word.

***

Laine stared out the frosted glass window as she gave her statement, again. A deputy U.S. Attorney named Joanna Slate listened and took notes. She was the fourth U.S. Attorney Laine had met with. Bear was sitting to her right, his chin propped in his hand. There were several other people in the room, but she had no idea who they were and she didn't care. She didn't want to be here; she wanted to be at the hospital.

She began with where she'd picked Jack up and continued from that point, leaving out no detail. She saw the startled looks the agents exchanged when she talked about killing Mr. Clean, and knew they had questions, but she didn't give them a chance to ask. She only wanted to repeat this story once more before she had to formally testify. It seemed she'd already told it a dozen times to a dozen different people.

"And is that everything you can recall?" asked Slate.

"Yes," Laine replied in a wooden voice. "Did you not read the other dozen statements I've given?"

The woman gave her a tight smile. "We just want to be sure the story doesn't change, Dr. Wheeler."

Laine lifted one brow. "Well, if you want to compare the statement I just gave you to the others, knock yourself out. The story won't change because truth doesn't change. I'm not in the habit of embellishing, exaggerating, or dramatizing the facts. I find it's a lot neater and more efficient to stick with the truth."

"Well, thank you for your candor," Slate said as she gathered her papers and tossed an annoyed glance at Bear. "The Marshals will escort you back to your hotel."

"I don't think so," Laine said, rising and placing her hands flat on the table. "I've given you what you wanted, and now I want to see Agent Vaughn."

Joanna Slate looked hard at her. "I'm afraid that's impossible."

"Why?"

"Special Agent Vaughn is still in the hospital, and his visitors have been restricted to family," Slate replied in a cool voice.

"I'm his doctor," Laine said. "I was the attending physician at the scene."

Slate opened her briefcase, started putting her papers away, and fixed Laine with a bored look. "You're not an MD anymore, *Dr.* Wheeler. You're a veterinarian now."

Bear ran a hand over his face. "Aw, hell."

"That's like saying you can't be a *judge* because you're a *lawyer*," Laine shot back, sounding just as bored. "I earned every credential I have. Just because I received a degree in veterinary medicine does not mean my credentials as an emergency physician are null and void."

"Lady has a point," Bear said with a yawn and a stretch.

Slate shot him a withering glare and turned her gaze back to Laine. "In the past five years you've done the bare minimum requirements to maintain your certification."

"Yes, but I *have* done them." Laine crossed her arms over her chest. "I did not spend nearly 15 years of my life in school so some low-level U.S. Attorney can tell me I'm not a doctor." When Slate didn't reply, Laine looked at Bear. "Agent Bristol, am I *required* to remain in protective custody? Can the government . . . *compel* me to do so?"

Bear steepled his fingers beneath his chin as a smile curved his mouth. "No, ma'am, they cannot."

Laine swiveled back around and stared at the U.S. Attorney. "Well, then, either I get to see Agent Vaughn, today, or I will respectfully decline your protection and see him whenever I wish."

Slate gaped at her. "Your life is still in danger, Dr. Wheeler."

Laine gaped at the woman, incredulous. "*You* are telling *me* that?" She glanced at Bear, who merely shrugged and remained silent. "You're kidding, right? You think I don't know that my life is in danger?"

"Obviously not if you're willing to risk your own safety, and that of Agent Vaughn," Slate replied. "We cannot completely secure the hospital, and his enemies know that."

"What place, aside from the Pentagon, the White House and Fort Knox *are* completely secure?" Laine frowned. "Even the hotel you have me in, comfortable as it is, is not completely secure."

"Special Agent Vaughn *has* been asking to see her, Ms. Slate," Bear interjected.

Joanna Slate looked between the two and threw her hands up. "Fine," she said.

She gathered her briefcase and walked over to Bear. He stood, and she poked a finger in his chest. "You, Special Agent Bristol, are responsible for her."

Bear pursed his lips. "Tell me something I don't know." He smiled as the attorney and her assistants huffed past him. "Been a pleasure, Ms. Slate. You have a nice day now, you hear?" When the woman was gone, he rolled his eyes and looked at Laine. "Come on, beautiful. Let's go take Jack some lunch."

Chapter Fifteen

Jack looked at Laine's profile, astounded that nearly two weeks had gone by since the incident at the Ritz. It was more than he could have hoped for. As they sat on the wooden bench with birds chirping, water gurgling, sun shining, and other patients strolling around, Jack watched her and wished yet again he'd met her in another place and time. He had expected to have just the one night with her, but for some reason God had seen fit to give him some extra time. He prayed the Creator continued to be so generous.

"I'm going to be getting out soon," Jack said. "The doc says I'm healing remarkably well. I've gotten nearly all the strength in my arm back, and he sees no reason to keep me here. In three days, barring any unforeseen complications or assassination attempts, I'll be a free man." He watched her face carefully, unsure what he was looking for.

Laine smiled and laid her head on his shoulder. "That's wonderful, Jack. I'm sure the nurses will be sad to see you go."

"Hey," he reproached her. "I'm not interested in any of the nurses."

"Maybe you should be," Laine said in a low voice.

Dread pooled in his stomach, and he pulled back so he could look her in the face. "Why would you say that?"

Laine took a deep breath and slipped out from under his arm. "I'll be leaving soon," she said, her voice barely above a whisper.

Jack looked across the small pond in the center of the hospital's tiny garden, the sunny day no longer as beautiful as it had been. He had known this day would come from the moment she'd picked him up on the highway. Whenever she had been with him, he had managed to put it out of his mind, concentrating on living in the moment with her. Now, it was over. He took a deep breath and asked, "When?"

"I'm not sure," she replied. "They won't tell me, for obvious reasons." She sighed and clasped her hands in her lap. "They did tell me today would be my last visit." She glanced at him. "I'm surprised they let me visit you as much as they have ."

He kept his face impassive, unwilling to show her how much it bothered him. The last thing she needed at this moment was for him to cave. Hopelessness loomed – dark, damp, and oppressive – but he pressed it back. He had no right to complain or bemoan his lot, especially given what she was facing. A new city, new name, new life. She had enough to deal with.

"Jack?"

"What?" He wanted her to look at him, but her gaze was fixed on the pond.

"I need you to do something for me."

"Anything."

"Don't say that until you know what it is," she said, dropping her chin until it almost touched her chest.

"I said anything, Laine."

She closed her eyes and took a deep breath. "I need you to go to Grant and tell him I'm okay." She glanced at him. "He knew something was wrong when I dropped Maverick off. I can't have him thinking I just . . . drove off and . . . never came back." She paused and looked into his eyes. "Tell him to live his life and forget about me."

His throat tightened. "No." He shook his head. "I'm sorry, but I can't do that."

She turned wide, stricken eyes to him. "Why not?"

Jack turned toward her on the bench and took her hands in his. His lungs refused to function, and it was several moments before he could speak. When he did, his voice was little more than a hushed whisper. "Because I know, from personal experience, he will never be able to forget you."

Tears welled. "Then tell him to be happy, and live his life without me."

The pain in her face imprinted itself on his heart like a brand. Jack clenched his jaw and looked away from her. "That I can do, Doc." He put a hand behind her neck and pulled her to him. "That I can do."

He felt her tears hot on his skin as she took a shuddering breath. She clung to him briefly before she pushed him away and jumped to her feet. With two long strides, she was at the edge of the pond, her hands thrust into the pockets of her jeans. He rose and stood at her back wanting to touch her, but not certain if he should. She stood still and straight-backed, and then her shoulders started to shake.

He put a hand on her shoulder, and she turned into his embrace, pressing her face against his neck. "Don't cry, please." She wept silently, and it felt like his heart was pushing through his sternum. She trembled and clung to him, and he tightened his embrace. After weeks of having only one good arm, he could finally hold her with both, and he used his arms to try and shield her from the pain he himself felt. It did little good. Loss pulled on him, cutting deeper than the sharpest knife, and there was nothing he could do to stop it. He blinked rapidly, his eyes stinging.

"Everyone I've ever loved has been taken from me," she said, her voice muffled and tear-filled. "I can't do this again, Jack. I just can't."

Anguish rolled through him like a wave of broken glass, ripping and shredding his insides, but what could he say? The last thing he wanted was to let her go, but her safety was more important than his own selfish desires. During the weeks since the shooting, law enforcement agencies had rounded up or killed most of Ripley's men, but the man himself had eluded capture. Until Ripley was dead or in prison, neither of them would be safe.

He pulled away and framed her face with his hands. "You have to do this, babe. You have to." Those golden-green eyes had darkened to a deep emerald and were swimming with tears. The tortured look she gave him nearly buckled his knees. His resolve started to disintegrate and he closed his eyes, fighting desperately to be strong.

"I don't want to leave you," she whispered.

"And I don't want you to," he said fiercely, clenching his jaw as his emotions threatened to overwhelm him. "But if anything happened to you, Laine, it would kill me." He looked deep into her eyes. "It would *kill* me, do you understand?"

"Jack . . . ."

His name from her lips was almost his undoing, and he realized he was losing this battle. Before she could say another word, he kissed her and poured every ounce of frustration, anger, and despair into it. He molded his fingers to her head as his lips moved over hers. Her lips tasted of tears. He explored her mouth, memorizing her, her scent, the way her body fit against his, the silky texture of her hair. He knew this would be the last kiss they shared. Anger burst to life in his chest, but it was quickly overwhelmed by sorrow. Every beat of his heart was a painful endeavor, every breath a laborious task. Against his better judgment he had allowed himself to fall in love with her, and now they were both paying the price. The worst part was he knew he'd do it again in a second if given the chance.

"Laine," Bear said from behind them.

Jack heard the sadness in his friend's voice, and it was as if Death himself had manifested. For a few moments his heart didn't beat. In a final show of rebellion, he took his time ending the kiss and then pressed his brow to hers, his eyes closed, his breathing ragged.

Bear sighed. "Jack."

It almost sounded like a plea. Jack opened his eyes and met Laine's grief-stricken gaze. He desperately wanted to see her smile again, and hoped the woman in the photographs wasn't truly gone this time.

"Live your life, Laine," he whispered. "Live it well, be happy, and know I will *always* love you."

***

Laine stared out the window of the hotel room, her heart like a million shards of glass, broken and scattered. Behind her she heard the rustle of plastic, as the two agents who'd been assigned to watch her unloaded dinner from the take out bags.

"Hey, Doc," Agent Patton called, "you hungry?"

Laine simply shook her head and continued to stare out the window.

The sun was setting. During the past few weeks she and Jack had fallen into the habit of watching the sun set from the garden. As the sky was cast in hues of pink, gold and crimson, she wondered if he was watching it too. He had told her sunset was his favorite time of day.

"Mine, too," she whispered. A tear slid down her face and she wiped it away. With one last, lingering look at the twilight sky, she turned and walked into the bedroom, closing the door softly behind her. With a dispirited sigh, she flung herself on the bed, rolled onto her side and pulled a pillow to her chest.

The feeling of loss was familiar. It pooled beneath her sternum, thick, dark, and viscous, and pressed heavily on her heart. The only thing keeping her breathing was the fact Jack was still alive. Unlike the utter devastation of Nick's death, the unchangeable permanence of his passing, she still felt a connection to Jack. A faint wisp of hope rose from the ashes only to be extinguished by cruel reality. Laine covered her mouth and sobbed.

About an hour later, there was a knock on the outer door. She heard

Agents Patton and Wyler scramble to their feet, and she imagined they were drawing their weapons. When no gunfire ensued, Laine guessed it was either their relief agents, or another inquisitor from the U.S. Attorney's office. At that moment, she didn't care which.

A few moments later, the edge of the bed dipped sharply beneath someone's considerable weight. She didn't have to look to know who it was.

Bear spooned himself around her. Laine sighed and wrapped her fingers over his forearm as he draped it across her chest. She settled her chin in the crook of his elbow and closed her eyes as his familiar warmth leached into her.

"I know this is hard for you, Laine," he said softly, "but your bodyguards tell me you're not eating."

She looked at him out of the corner of her eye. "Really. They told *you?*"

He smiled and the dark clouds receded just a bit. Bear was connected to Jack, and somehow that connected *her* to Jack. It made no sense logically, but his presence was soothing nonetheless.

"Actually," he said, "they told their boss and their boss called me." A low chuckle rumbled in his chest. "Personally, I think you're doing this just to make them grovel at my feet."

"You know it," she replied. "After the way Inspector Gilman talked to you, I couldn't let that go unpunished."

"You need to eat."

"I'm not hungry, Bear," she said. "But I could use some company."

"You got it." He settled himself more comfortably and pulled her closer. "Think I should open the door?"

"Nah," she answered. "Let them wonder."

***

Jack stood in the window, hands fisted on the sill, watching as the sun disappeared in the west and darkness laid claim to the outside world. His dinner sat untouched on the bedside table. He heard the door open, but he didn't bother to turn around.

"Agent Vaughn."

He recognized the voice of Amy, one of the night nurses.

"Agent Vaughn, you really need to eat."

He was numb. "I'm not hungry," he said. "I told them that before they brought it in here."

"If you want to go home, you have to keep your strength up."

Darkness loomed inside him, and this time he didn't bother to fight it. "I have nothing to go home to."

"Doc Shepard isn't going to like it if I tell him you're not eating." There was a brief pause followed by a heavy sigh. "Ok. But don't say I didn't warn you."

He heard a brief scrape of plastic against wood as the nurse picked up the tray.

"Last chance, Jack," Amy said.

When he didn't acknowledge her she left, the door whispering shut behind her.

The 18 months he'd spent in San Quentin to build his cover had been easy compared to this. The year it had taken him to be invited to "hang around" the Marauder's Motorcycle Club, and the three years he'd slaved to move up in rank high enough to be introduced to Calember seemed like a cakewalk now. Then there was Ripley. Jack had worked his way up in the organization, and it had taken him more than two years before he found himself in the position where he could gain access to the kind of information that would bring CAG down. All totaled, he'd given almost eight years of his life to this assignment, but it seemed so unimportant now. He'd give eight more if he could have her back.

Across the room, a radio was playing Laine's favorite Denver station. He heard the distinctive vocalization of Gary Levox, lead singer of the popular country band, *Rascal Flatts*. Laine had told him she loved this man's voice, so when he started to sing, Jack's ears perked up. His vision blurred as the words impaled him. The lyrics spoke of a love cut short, of feelings so intense and deep that time was immaterial. Pain seared through him as his lungs refused to draw air. The woman Levox sang of had left her mark on the man's soul, just like Laine had left her mark on Jack's. And no matter how brief their time together had been, he, too, would remember her forever.

Jack closed his eyes and let out a shaky breath as the tears ran down his face.

As Levox continued to sing each verse, the tide of volatile emotions rose and morphed into something more angry than sad. It sparked inside him and started to burn in earnest – white hot, roiling, and relentless – until he couldn't control the fire. He clenched his jaw, strode over to the radio, picked it up and threw it against the wall with as much force as he could muster. The cheap plastic exploded into a million pieces and peppered his face with shrapnel. He stared at the shattered remains, his chest heaving as claws of sorrow and rage shredded his insides. The gunshot had been nothing compared to this, and for a moment he wished Laine hadn't been so successful in helping to save him. If he'd died in the hotel, at least her face would have been the last thing he saw.

By the time the door to his room opened, he was back at the window. The door swung shut and one of the agents outside his room shouted, "Nurse!" Moments later the sound of hurried footsteps reached him and the door opened again. He heard a sharp intake of breath and ran a hand over his face. To his surprise, his cheeks were warm and sticky. He looked down and frowned when he saw blood on his fingers. He felt a presence at his elbow and turned, and Amy's eyes widened.

"What did you do?" she asked.

Jack planted his fists back on the sill and stared into the western sky. "Nothing," he said in a low voice. "Nothing worth a damn."

Amy rushed away, probably to summon a doctor. Once the door closed behind her, Jack reached into his pocket and pulled out the pictures he'd stolen from Nick's box. He ran a finger over her visage and tears gathered again.

***

"Laine," Bear whispered. "Laine, wake up."

Laine rolled over and curled up against his chest. "Why?"

He eased away from her and off the bed. When she looked at him, he held out a hand.

"Come on," he said quietly. "Let's take Jack a late night snack."

For a moment she thought he was joking, but when he smiled, joy bubbled up inside her. She grabbed his hand and sprang out of bed. She stayed behind him as he slowly opened the bedroom door and peeked out into the living room.

"Follow me, and keep quiet."

Laine held his hand and tiptoed behind him, barely able to contain her excitement. He closed the bedroom door and moved with unnatural stealth to the door of the hotel room. One of the agents dozed on the couch, his face turned blue by the light from the television. As they passed the bathroom, she heard water running, which told her where the other agent was. The knob disappeared inside Bear's huge hand as he turned it and eased the door open. He stepped into the hallway and she quickly followed. She stepped aside as he slowly closed the door and wiggled his eyebrows at her. Laine couldn't help but smile as a weight evaporated from her shoulders.

"Let's take the stairs in case they realize you're gone," he whispered. "The elevator and the lobby will be the first places they look."

"Why are you doing this, Bear?" Laine asked as they moved quickly toward the stairs. "I don't want to get you in trouble. You've already stuck your neck out for me more times than I can count."

"Well," he began as they descended, "the head Marshal asked me to come take care of you, so I'm just following orders." He glanced over his shoulder as they descended the stairs. "They can hardly bust me for doing that, can they?"

She smiled. "You really walk a fine line, don't you?"

"It's amazing, isn't it?" A chuckle escaped him. "You wouldn't think someone as big as me would be a tightrope walker. I'm surprised Barnum and Bailey aren't knocking down my door."

Laine giggled, and was surprised by the sound. She hadn't laughed in what seemed like ages, and it actually felt good.

They came out of the stairwell and went through the exit to the parking lot. When they reached his Escalade, Laine felt a tug of hesitation. He was putting his career on the line for her and overwhelming gratitude made her eyes tear. He stopped and looked at her, his brows drawing together. Before he could speak, she threw her arms around his neck and hugged him. He seemed startled for a moment and then embraced her and lifted her off the ground. Laine dangled there, tears trickling from beneath closed lids. After a few moments she pulled back and took his head in her hands. He continued to hold her aloft, as easily as if she weighed nothing.

She met those piercing blue eyes and sniffed. "Thank you, Bear." Her gaze wandered over his face for a moment. "It's the strangest thing. It took all this for me to find some of the best friends I've ever had."

Bear's gaze was hawk-like. "Yeah, well, if you ever get tired of Jack you know where to find me."

"Yeah, I do. And if I show up at Bridges' some Saturday afternoon, I'll let you take me to dinner and a movie. Or a football game. I'll even root for the Broncos."

He smiled as she hugged him again, and then he put her feet gently back on the ground.

They strode into Memorial Hospital at a quarter past two in the morning. It was well past visiting hours, the lights were dimmed and the halls quiet. Each time someone approached them, Bear simply flipped out his badge and kept walking without even stopping to acknowledge the person. When they reached Jack's room, Bear gave the guards a look, and they let her in without a word.

"I'll be right outside," he said in a low voice. "You won't be bothered." He gave her a wink and pulled the door shut.

The room was dark, illuminated only by the pale, orange glow from a streetlight coming in through the window. She walked to a chair by the bed and eased down. Jack appeared to be sleeping, and she didn't want to wake him.

"Hi," she whispered. "You can thank Bear for this. The Marshals didn't know what to do with me so they called him. I told him I didn't want him to get in trouble, but he just smiled and said he was only following orders. And so, here we are."

Jack didn't move or speak, his breathing deep and even. Laine watched the steady rise and fall of his chest, and thanked God he was still alive. She stood and moved the chair a bit closer to his bedside, careful to be quiet.

She looked at him for a while, his face cast in shadow, and it brought her joy just to be this close. Suddenly, she needed to touch him, so she carefully slipped her fingers through his.

"You asked me a question once." She paused and stared at his hand. "I hated you that night, you know, but now I think . . . I think I'm finally ready to answer you. Do you remember what you asked me?"

He didn't respond, not that she had expected him to. A lump formed in her throat, but she choked it down and took a breath.

"It had been a long night, a long, cold night. I was almost to the end of a 36 hour shift and I couldn't wait to get off." She smiled wistfully. "It was the first day Nick and I had had off together in almost three weeks. We'd made plans to get breakfast, and then spend the rest of the day in bed." A sad chuckle escaped her. "It's funny how life doesn't always go along with your plans, isn't it?"

She blinked back tears as the memories threatened to overrun her, and she squeezed his hand just a little, needing his strength. He squeezed back and her head snapped up. Her eyes had adjusted to the gloom and she looked at him, but he still appeared to be sleeping peacefully. She shook herself and then continued.

"Around 3 a.m. we got a call from dispatch that there had been a shoot-out with multiple casualties. Since we were the closest hospital, they were sending us the most critical patients." She sighed and shrugged. "That was nothing new. We simply got things ready and waited for the ambulances to show up. Boy, when they did . . . talk about a perfect storm."

"The first patient in was a kid I knew, a gang member, DeWayne Johnson. I'd treated him probably a dozen times over the past few years; broken bones, black eyes, concussions, stab wounds, you name it. This time he had a bullet hole in his chest. The chief resident recognized him and assigned him to me since I'd treated him before, and like a good little soldier I went right to work."

She paused and ground her teeth together. Fragmented images of that night flashed in her head. With the memories came pain, a pain she felt every bit as deeply now as she had then. Laine took a deep, shuddering breath and exhaled slowly as the tears started.

"I knew just by looking at the wound he was bleeding out, but apparently *he* didn't know that. The paramedics had put him in restraints, and he was fighting them, yelling, 'I got that pig! I got him good!' I didn't really listen to him at the time. When it's that chaotic you learn to tune out the noise and focus on the important stuff. I didn't really care what he was saying. I just knew I had to get him stable enough to be transferred to surgery, or he was going to die."

Laine stopped and leaned forward, laying her head on the mattress next to his hand. She had intended to tell him everything, but the weight of that night pressed down on her chest, constricting her airways. Repeating the story was something she had purposely avoided ever since Nick's death and it reminded her with agonizing clarity how much she had lost in a split second of time. However, she knew if she didn't get it out now she probably never would. She closed her eyes, pressed her cheek to the back of his hand, and finally managed to take a breath.

"I almost lost him, but with the help of my interns and the nurses we got DeWayne stable enough to be moved upstairs. I waited in the ER with him until one of the surgical team took him up, and I went into the next room to see if I could help in there. There were so many doctors and nurses around the gurney all I could see was the patient's feet." She paused and licked her lips. "The monitor was flat-lining, and

Dr. Grayson was performing CPR while the paddles charged. I remember the whine, the sound of the discharge, and the jerking of the person's feet. Nothing happened." She sniffed, tears dripping sideways down her face. "They shocked the patient three more times, until Dr. Fraser finally called . . . time of death. For a few seconds everything went really still, as if time had stopped for a moment. Then, one of the nurses turned, saw me, and dropped the tray of utensils she was holding."

Laine sat up and covered her mouth with her hands. The memory washed over her until she thought she would drown in it, her heart thundering like a runaway train. Panic roiled in the pit of her stomach. She grabbed Jack's hand and held his fingers to her chest, taking in great gulps of air until the sorrow receded enough to let her breathe. When she finally regained her voice, she didn't have the strength to muster more than a whisper.

"After the nurse dropped her tray, I suddenly noticed all the cops standing by the door, cops I hadn't even realized were there, cops I recognized. They were looking at me with the strangest expressions, and just like that I knew. I looked at the shoes again and realized they were . . . ." Her voice broke and she gasped as grief ripped through her, as fresh and violent as it had been that night. ". . . They were Nick's."

Laine squeezed her eyes shut tightly and pressed her lips together as she fought the sob that wanted to burst from her throat. She wept softly, her insides quivering.

"I don't remember the people leaving, but it seemed like one moment the room was overflowing and the next, it was just me and Nick. He'd been shot three times in the chest at point blank range. DeWayne Johnson's words came back to me and I understood exactly what he'd been yelling about."

Suddenly she couldn't breathe. An invisible hand punched through her sternum and raked around inside her chest cavity. Unseen talons slashed, clawed, and grabbed, as if looking for her heart. A tormented cry escaped her when she remembered Nick's blue eyes. The eyes that had once looked at her with love and desire and even annoyance had become flat and lifeless. Laine squeezed Jack's hand and pressed it to her cheek, guilt and self-recrimination crushing down on her from all sides.

Her shoulders shook as the words burst from her mouth. "God, I hope he forgives me for saving his killer while he lay dying in the next room."

"He never blamed you," Jack whispered. "He *loved* you."

She bolted upright and met his eyes, eyes that brimmed with unshed tears. His tears were her undoing. Her face crumbled, and when he pulled on her hand she threw herself against him. He grunted and she immediately pulled back, horrified at what she'd just done.

"Oh, Jack, I'm sorry! I'm so sorry! I didn't mean to hurt you!"

He gave her an annoyed look and pulled her back against him. "You just startled me." He scooted over in the bed and settled her against his side. "I don't think you're capable of hurting me, at least not *physically*."

"What about when I slapped you in the cab?" she asked.

"That *stung*," he said with a rueful chuckle. "What hurt was the way you looked at me."

"I'm sorry."

He put a hand to her cheek and turned her face to his. He scowled at her, his brows drawn together ominously. "*Stop* apologizing," he said in a fierce whisper. After a moment, his expression softened and he traced the outline of her lips. "You don't ever need to apologize to me."

It was then she noticed his face, and her eyes widened. "What happened to you?"

He grimaced. "Cut myself shaving."

"You shaved your forehead and eyelids?" she asked in disbelief. "You've got three stitches here, four here, three more here. What did you do?" She started to examine the wounds, and he took her hands in his.

"Stop. I just had a little disagreement with the radio." He kissed the backs of her fingers. "I didn't like the song it was playing." He chuckled. "You think I look bad, you should see the other guy. Now stop examining me and come here."

She snuggled against him and the anguish that had threatened to suffocate her receded. He pressed a kiss to her temple and rested his cheek on top of her head. They lay like this for several minutes then he said, "I'm sorry for what happened to Nick."

Laine gulped as the raw emotions washed over her again. "How much of it did you hear?"

"All of it," he replied. "I woke up the moment the door closed behind you."

"Why didn't you—"

"Hush." He pressed a finger to her lips. "I didn't say anything because I thought it would be easier for you to get it out if you didn't know I was listening. Now, shut up and let me kiss you. They're going to take you away from me soon enough, and I want to enjoy every moment we have left."

Hazy sunlight was invading the room when Laine was jerked from a sound sleep by raised voices. She shook her head, disoriented. Jack kissed her brow and held her tightly for a moment. When he released her, he whispered, "You'd better get up quietly and get dressed. I have a feeling your ride is here."

Outside the door the argument continued. "What the hell were you thinking, Agent Bristol?"

"It's *Special* Agent Bristol, *Inspector* Montoya, and I was doing what you asked me to do."

"What I asked you to do? This is *not* what I asked you to do!"

"Hey, you said you had a problem you wanted me to take care of. I took care of it."

"This is not what I meant!"

"Then perhaps you should've been more specific. You wanted me to fix things, I fixed things. Stop bitching."

"You took a federal witness from protective custody without telling anyone anything."

"Hey, I called Agent Patton to let him know."

"Yeah, *forty minutes ago.* You've had my witness in the wind for more than *four* hours! Anything could have happened in that period of time!"

"You're kidding, right? She's in a hospital, or didn't you notice all the medical personal when you walked in here? There are security personnel and cameras on every floor and you have three federal agents sitting outside the room. The only other way in or out, unless you're a snake and sneak in through the plumbing, is through a reinforced, sealed Plexiglas window. If that's *in the wind,* I'd hate to see your definition of *confined.*"

"You are out of line!"

"Does this mean I don't have to worry about you asking me to do you any more favors? Gee, darn."

"Agent Bristol . . . !"

"Enough. Your witness is inside, perfectly safe and healthy." There was a brief pause, and when Bear spoke again his voice was tightly controlled. "Don't you get it? The two people in that room love each other, and as soon as you take her away from here, they'll never see each other again. Are you really that much of a bastard you can't bend the rules a little?"

"The rules are there for a reason."

"Well, maybe they should be revised. Jack Vaughn has spent the last *eight years* working undercover, putting his life on the line every day so we could bring down CAG. Laine Wheeler has done everything you and your people have asked, and then some. She's giving up her life, her credentials and her career, which she spent close to fifteen years working for, and the man she loves all in one fell swoop. Even *you* had to have been in love at least once. Don't you remember what that was like?"

"Of course, but—"

"So, why don't you cut them some slack and do what you came here to do. Standing here shouting at each other isn't going to change anything."

"Fine."

"When you speak to her, you'd better be respectful or I *will* clean this floor with you."

There was a tense silence, followed by a soft knock on the door. Laine was dressed and sitting in the chair by Jack's bed when Marshal Montoya stuck his head into the room.

"You've got two minutes, Dr. Wheeler," he said. "We've got to get you to the airport. Your flight leaves in just over an hour."

Laine felt the floor drop from under her and for a moment she felt dizzy. She took a breath, held it, and then gave the Marshal a nod. He nodded in return and closed the door.

She stood, turned to Jack, and was immediately enfolded in his arms. They didn't speak, they just held each other. Nothing more needed to be said. After about a minute Jack pulled back.

"Marry me."

The room dropped several more feet and her knees went weak. Stunned, she stared at him. "What? That's not funny, Jack."

"Am I laughing?" He searched her eyes and framed her face with his hands. "Marry me."

She gaped at him for a moment. "What do you want me to say? We *can't* get married."

He ran a thumb over her cheekbone and a small, pained smile curved his mouth. "I know, but it would still be nice to hear you say yes."

The door came open. "Dr. Wheeler, we have to go."

Tears welled and she stared at him, disbelief and joy wrestling inside her rib cage. She gasped softly, shook her head, and turned to leave. Jack grabbed her arm and pulled her to his chest. He kissed her deeply, branding her as his. Then he pulled back and met her gaze.

"This isn't over, Laine," he whispered, his lips nearly touching hers. "I *will* find you."

"Dr. Wheeler."

Alarm raced through her as strong fingers closed about her arm and pulled her toward the door. She watched Jack over her shoulder and with every step her anxiety grew. When the door closed she nearly panicked. It was as if her lifeline had been severed once Jack was out of her sight. She reluctantly allowed the Marshal to lead her down the hall, but they hadn't gone more than a dozen paces when she jerked away from him. Suddenly, leaving without answering Jack's question was not an option. Part of her knew if she did, she would regret it forever. Laine ran past a grinning Bear and back into Jack's room. He stood at the window, his expression pensive.

"Jack."

He turned to her, eyes wide.

"Yes."

Chapter Sixteen

"Remember to study chapters 26 & 27," Laine said as her students scrambled to load their backpacks. "Study group meets tomorrow morning, and don't forget finals start Monday. Have a good weekend."

She sat on the front edge of her desk as the rambunctious teenagers made their escape. Out of the corner of her eye, she saw Greg Pearson, one of her best students, loitering at the back of the line. He was a handsome kid, typical Californian with blonde hair, blue eyes and a complexion tanned the color of mocha. He was putting his text and notebooks into his backpack, and he was moving much slower than he normally did. When the door closed, he looked up, his eyes wide with surprise. She silently applauded his acting. Laine lifted one brow and crossed her arms over her chest.

"What do you need, Mr. Pearson?" she asked. Beneath the tan she saw him blush and hid a smile.

He walked over to her and sat down on top of one of the vacant desks. "I . . . I wanted to thank you, Miss B," he said at last, his voice low. He focused on his Nikes.

"For what, Greg?"

"Well, thanks to you, I'm ready for my finals," he said with a quick glance at her. "I mean *really* ready." When he saw her smile, it seemed to give him courage. "Without all the time you spent tutoring me, I never would've been able to get through the sections on RNA and DNA . . . ." He paused and took a breath, his toe tapping the floor. ". . . and I wouldn't be applying to Stanford and my dad and mom would be really upset with me because they want me to go to a good school and I've always wanted to be a doctor and—"

Laine put a hand on his shoulder. "Greg, take a breath, kiddo. You don't have to thank me. You did the work."

"Yeah, but if you hadn't explained it to me the way you did, I never would've gotten it." He looked tongue-tied for a moment, then reached into his backpack and pulled out a sealed pink envelope. "I really, *really* appreciate everything you did to help me."

Something warm and soft expanded in her chest, and she took the envelope from his outstretched hand. "You're welcome, Greg, but you didn't have to do this."

"Yes, I did, Miss B," he said.

He looked at her, unsure for a moment, then ducked in quickly and lightly kissed her cheek. Before she could even react he was off like a shot. Surprise was the first emotion to register, then happiness and pride jumped in and the warmth inside her grew. She stared after him as he pushed through the door and took off down the hall, a blur of long arms and legs. Her eyes misted as she read the card, and a sense of wistful satisfaction made her smile. Greg Pearson would make a wonderful doctor someday. When she pulled out the gift certificate for a full day of spa treatments at a very exclusive, very expensive spa in La Jolla, a tear rolled down her cheek. She wiped it away and slipped the card and certificate into her purse.

"I think he likes you," a familiar voice said from the back of the room.

Her heart nearly stopped as she recognized Bear's voice.

"Then again," he said, "what's not to like? None of *my* teachers ever looked like you."

The emotions that flashed through her were varied and intense: hope, fear, joy, despair, all at once and unfiltered. She hadn't seen or spoken to him since before she'd been put in Witness Protection, and there were only two reasons she could think of to explain why Bear would be here. Either Ripley was gone, or Jack was. Contemplating one made joy burst inside her like a super nova, while thought of the other made her throat tighten in apprehension. It took her a moment to gather her courage. She took a deep breath and faced him.

"Bear."

He looked very professional in his suit, tie, and government-issue sunglasses, his hair cut in the familiar high and tight. How he had managed to slip in without her realizing she didn't know, but he always had moved with unnatural stealth for a man of his size.

"You look good, Laine," he said. He walked forward, unbuttoned his jacket and sat down on the desk Greg Pearson had vacated. "You always did." When she didn't reply, he pulled off the sunglasses and she saw the concern in his sapphire eyes. He studied her face before asking, "What's wrong?"

She stood less than two feet from a man she had the utmost regard for and loved deeply, yet she was scared witless. Dare she hope he was the bearer of good news, or should she brace herself for the worst? Her emotions see-sawed wildly between the two possibilities and she closed her eyes briefly. "I don't know whether to hug you or hide beneath my desk."

He smiled. "I'd prefer a hug, but that's just me."

She didn't need a second invitation. Leaning into him, she wrapped her arms around his neck. He held her tightly and she closed her eyes with a sigh. "Why are you here, Bear? You're not supposed to know where I am, much less *be* here." A lump formed in her throat and she fought to swallow it. "The fact it's you tells me this visit has something to do with Jack, and it's something I'm not going to like."

She pulled back to look at him, but he kept his arms looped around her waist.

"It's about more than Jack," he said. "It's about you as well."

"What about me?" she asked. "I've done everything I was instructed to, I've been very careful . . . ."

He chuckled. "You've done great, Laine. In fact, from everything I've read, you seem to have taken the lemons the government gave you and made some pretty tasty lemonade."

She blinked at him, thoroughly confused. "Then what is this, Bear?" she pleaded. "Please just tell me."

She studied his face, but there was no reading Bear if he didn't want to be read. His expression was neutral, his gaze warm and steady, his posture relaxed.

"It's over, Laine," he said at last.

For a moment she was sure she hadn't heard him correctly. She frowned and stared hard at him. "What do you mean 'it's over'?"

He tipped his head to the side and his gaze wandered over her features. "Ripley is dead. The members of his group who weren't caught in the initial raids have been either hunted down or killed. The money used to finance him was traced, the accounts frozen and seized by the U.S. Government." He rose from the desk. "CAG is gone, its backers scattered like roaches in daylight."

She stared at him for a few moments. "So . . . it's . . . *over*, over," she said at last. He nodded and Laine was unable to look away from him as she digested this bit of news. Hope started to bloom, but realization crushed it. She dropped her gaze. After a few moments, she lifted her chin and asked in a whisper, "Why are *you* here, instead of Jack?"

His expression darkened just a little. "We don't know where Jack is."

Her breath caught. "What do you mean you don't know where he is?"

Bear released her and ran a hand over his brow. "Well, after you left Denver, he made it his personal mission to hunt down Ripley because he knew you'd never be safe until the man was dead or in prison. It took him almost 11 months, but he finally tracked the bastard to Cyprus, holed up with one of his former financiers." He paused. "Jack was supposed to wait for backup from Interpol, but his last transmission said he thought Ripley was going to rabbit, which means—"

"I know what it means, Bear," she said with a wave of her hand. "I was married to a cop, remember?"

"Right." He smiled. "Anyway, he went in, alone. Backup arrived a few minutes later, but it was already over. There were six down, including Ripley, but Jack was gone. I saw pictures from the scene. There was one hell of a fight."

"Are you sure he was there?" she asked, her mind cycling desperately to come up with a plausible explanation. "Maybe something happened to him before the shoot-out."

Bear walked to the window that overlooked the football field. "We found his blood at the scene, Laine."

Her knees gave out and she sank down on the closest desk.

Bear looked over his shoulder at her. "He was *there*, just not when Interpol arrived." He spun around. "Don't worry. This is a good thing."

She gaped at him, her pulse thrumming violently against her windpipe. "A *good* thing?" she repeated, incredulous. "How can you say that?"

"Because we didn't find a *body*." He approached her slowly and put a hand on her shoulder. "Have you forgotten so quickly? Jack is the luckiest SOB I've ever met."

Tears welled and she squeezed her eyes shut as fear shot through her. "Oh, God, Bear. Are you sure?"

"As sure as I am that he loves you." He put a finger under her chin and tipped her face up. "Now, let's go somewhere we can talk. You have some decisions to make."

***

"This is a great place, Laine," Bear said, his gaze wandering over the beach front cottage. He glanced over his shoulder. "Right across the street from the sand," he looked back at the small house, "Craftsman architecture, porch and porch swing, palm trees and bougainvillea." He gave her a smile as they ascended the three steps to the porch. "I'm surprised WITSEC put you here."

"They didn't." Laine rummaged in her purse for the keys. "They had me in an apartment in Carlsbad. I found this place and bought it myself."

Bear looked around the property again. "Wow. How did you afford this place on a teacher's salary?"

She shrugged. "My salary didn't pay for any of this." She opened the front door and preceded him inside. "I've had the misfortune to be the beneficiary of two sizeable life insurance policies." She tossed her briefcase and purse on a large chair near the door and kicked off her shoes. "The first was from my dad when he was killed in action, the second from Nick. Even today buying any kind of insurance makes me sick to my stomach."

"That's understandable," Bear said. "I'm sorry."

The note of regret in his voice gave her pause, and she slowly turned to face him. When she saw his solemn expression, her stomach clenched and a wave of uneasiness swirled around her. "What are you sorry for?"

Bear met her gaze for a moment, and then sighed and looked at the floor. "Before Jack left for Cyprus, he changed his insurance policy."

Laine backed away from him, that clenching sensation expanding to the rest of her internal organs. "No."

He nodded. "He doubled the payout and made you the beneficiary." He must have recognized the anguish in her expression because his brows drew together and he cupped her chin in his hand. "Don't worry. You *won't* be collecting because he's *not* dead."

Her knees wobbled and nausea roiled. "Even if he were," she whispered, "I wouldn't want it, Bear."

Bear hooked an arm around her neck and pulled her against his chest. "I know, Laine. I told him as much, but he wouldn't be deterred. Said he owed you at least that much for all the destruction he'd brought to your life." He rested his chin on top of her head. "He once told me he hated to see you cry, and he felt bad because it seemed like all he ever did was hurt you."

"He's still doing it," she said against his shirt.

"Not intentionally," Bear said in a low voice, his hands rubbing in circles over her back. "He wanted to make sure everything you went through wasn't all for nothing."

Laine looked up at him. "If he's dead, then it *was* for nothing, and no amount of money will change that."

"You're right," he agreed. "If he's gone, money can't bring him back. He had hoped, if something happened to him, the money might make things easier for you." He searched her eyes. "Take it at face value, Laine. He wanted to make sure you were taken care of, and until Ripley was gone, this was all he could do. He was thinking about you."

A horrible thought crackled to life inside her head. She turned it around and mulled it over for a second or two, and a heavy knot of dread coiled in the pit of her stomach. If Jack had been focused on the job instead of her, none of this would be happening. She had made the choice to go into Witness Protection to protect herself, but also because she'd decided it was better to be apart from Jack and know he was alive than the alternative. The knot inside her doubled in size and she sank down onto the closest chair. The possibility that she was the reason he had chased Ripley halfway around the world was soul-crushing.

"Laine," Bear said, "whatever it is you're thinking you're wrong."

"Am I?" She looked up at him. "If it weren't for me . . . would he even have *gone* to Cyprus?"

He frowned. "Of course he would have, that was his *job*. He dedicated years of his life to this investigation. Do you think he would stop now, when he was so close to finishing it? If you think that, you don't know Jack at all."

"Once Ripley left the country he became *Interpol's* job," Laine shot back, jumping to her feet. "Jack doesn't have any jurisdiction in Cyprus."

Bear put his hands on his hips and fixed her with a pointed stare. "The government of Cyprus doesn't want terrorists on their soil any more than we do. It's called a *joint* operation for a reason." He pinched the bridge of his nose and sighed. "Jack was determined to bring Ripley to justice or kill him long before he met you. *You* just gave him a reason to keep fighting."

Tears trickled down her cheeks. "Please tell me . . . tell me this isn't my fault."

"God, Laine," he exclaimed, "how could you even *think* that?" His expression was incredulous. "I suppose in the context that he was alive to go to Cyprus because you saved his skin before, then yeah, in that sense it's your fault."

He grabbed her shoulders and shook her once, but that was enough to make her teeth rattle in her head. He looked angry, something she'd never seen in him. If she hadn't known him, his intensity would have frightened her.

"Jack went to Cyprus because he wanted to bring Ripley down." She was taken aback by the vehemence with which he spoke. "He also went to Cyprus because bringing Ripley down would mean the threat to your life was gone. Loving you made him *determined*, not *careless*." He fixed her with that piercing gaze. "This is *not* your fault." He stared hard at her, but then his expression softened and he dragged his knuckles over her tear-stained cheek. "There is no fault, because Jack Vaughn is alive."

"I'm sorry, Bear," Laine said in a hushed voice. "I don't know what's wrong with me."

"I do," he replied. "You're frightened and worried. Me, too. I wonder what he's going through, and I wish I could help him. Since I can't, I have to believe he's out there somewhere doing everything he can to get back." He took a deep breath, held it, and then let it out slowly. "Does he feel gone to you?"

Laine's head snapped up. She had detected a note of fear in Bear's voice, and it rifled through her at warp speed. Only moments ago, Bear had spoken with such surety about Jack being alive. Although his face was as blank as she'd ever seen it, that surety had evaporated. Nevertheless, she wouldn't allow herself to believe Jack was gone. She couldn't. Laine took a deep breath and closed her eyes. After a few moments, she looked at him.

"I still feel him," she said as she laid a hand over her heart, "in here."

Bear nodded. "Me, too. That's why I will continue to say he's alive. Until that feeling goes away or somebody shows me a body, not a word to the contrary will exit my mouth." He tucked a strand of hair behind her ear and his expression changed. "You're not a redhead anymore."

"You're just noticing?" she asked wryly. "That's some attention to detail, Special Agent Bristol." A voice from the past echoed in her head. *I love redheads.* She ran a hand over her hair. "Should I change it back?"

"Don't change a thing," he said. "I wouldn't want Jack to be confused when he returns."

Just like that, the atmosphere changed. The storm clouds lifted and life regained some of the color it had lost.

"Where are you staying?" she asked.

One blond brow rose. "Some place downtown," he replied. "Why?"

Laine pursed her lips and fingered the silky material of his tie. "If you stay here, I'll make you dinner. Afterwards we can take a walk on the beach and talk about all these other things you say we need to discuss." She gave him a hopeful look. "Please. The spare room is already made up."

"You drive a hard bargain, Laine. I'll get my bag."

***

Laine kicked her foot up on the railing and sipped her beer, the porch swing moving slowly back and forth. Bear sat next to her, his beer resting on his knee. The sun had just vanished below the horizon, the sky a vivid rainbow of scarlet, pink and gold. The moon rose behind them, the contrasting light casting the beach in alternating ripples of silver and amber.

"Jack told me this was his favorite time of day," Laine said softly.

"*Is*," Bear corrected her. "It *is* his favorite time of day."

She laid her head against his shoulder. "Right. Sorry."

They sat in comfortable silence, each lost in their own thoughts. Laine's head was spinning with everything Bear had told her over dinner, and she didn't think she'd ever felt so conflicted.

"So," he began, "do you have any idea what you want to do?"

She sighed. "You're kidding right? I'm still trying to process what you told me. Making a decision isn't even a blip on the radar right now." She looked up at him. "Is there a time limit?"

He smiled. "No, but it can't be that hard, can it?" He waved a hand at the idyllic scene before them. "You can either stay here in beautiful Oceanside, or return to Montana." He gave her a sideways glance. "Which do you prefer, Laine, sparkling beach and the vast Pacific, or pristine wilderness and abundant wildlife?"

"It's not that simple, Bear," she said.

"I know," he said with a rueful chuckle. "I'm just giving you a hard time."

"Well, don't," she said with a pout. She moved closer and he put his arm around her shoulders. "Regardless of what I choose . . . ." Her voice died and she looked at him.

"Don't worry," he said, giving her a squeeze, "I'll be there, right behind Jack, of course."

"You better." She gave him a light jab in the ribs. "I've grown rather attached to you, you know. Right now, you're the only one keeping me from losing it."

"You give me too much credit," he said. "You're one of the smartest, strongest, most level-headed people I've ever met."

She chuckled. "I like how you said *people* and not *women.*"

"My mama didn't raise no fool," he said flatly, a twinkle in his azure eyes. "Besides, you're stronger, smarter, and have more sense than a lot of people I work with." His expression sobered. "That's what Jack fell in love with." He turned his head and looked down at her. "It wasn't your pretty face or figure, it was who you were. He told me he'd never met anyone like you." A pensive smile curved his mouth. "I know how he feels."

She hugged him and his arm tightened around her. "Thank you," she said in a hushed voice. "I'm really glad you're here."

"Me too, Laine."

It was several minutes before she spoke again. "Can I ask you something?"

"Of course."

She pulled back. "You never call me Doc. How come?"

"That's what Jack calls you," he replied simply.

She studied him. "Why aren't you married?"

He leaned over until their noses touched. "Because you're going to marry Jack."

Laine's eyes widened and she pulled away. She searched his face, and when his mouth widened into a grin, she pursed her lips and gave him a withering glare.

"Very funny, Bear," she said with a roll of her eyes.

One brow went north. "Who said I was being funny?"

Laine crossed her arms over her chest and scooted away from him. "You're terrible."

He followed her on the swing until she had nowhere left to retreat. "I am, but you love me anyway." He put her in a head lock and playfully ruffled her hair. "Admit it."

Laine laughed and wriggled out of his grasp. "Fine," she said as she jumped to her feet. "I admit it. Just don't tell Jack."

"It'll be our little secret," he said with a conspiratorial wink, "one I shall take to my grave."

"Don't talk like that."

"I meant forever, Laine," he said with a shake of his head. He took her hand and laced his fingers through hers. "I don't plan to find a grave until I'm old, gray and toothless."

"Good, because if something happens to you, I'm going to bring you back so *I* can kill you."

"Are you threatening a federal agent, ma'am?" he asked with a smile and narrowed eyes.

"Yes, I am," she replied. "Now, come on. Let's take a walk."

***

A phone rang somewhere and tugged Laine from sleep. She rubbed her eyes, rolled over, and looked at the clock. It was after two in the morning. She yawned and sat up, and the sound of a hushed, one-sided conversation reached her. The words were unintelligible, but she recognized the deep, rough timbre of Bear's voice.

As she kicked back the covers and got out of bed, she heard a door open, then another door open and close. Laine walked out into the hall and glanced in the spare room. Bear wasn't there. She checked the bathroom and the kitchen first, and then made her way through the dark house toward the front door. The sound of his voice reached her, and so did a squeaking. He was sitting on the porch swing.

She thought about eavesdropping and quickly chided herself for considering such adolescent behavior. Bear obviously didn't want to disturb her, or he didn't want her to overhear the conversation. Given his line of work, there could be a hundred explanations for such a late phone call, and if he wanted to tell her about it he would. If not, she had no right to pry.

Laine turned to go back to bed, but she hadn't taken three steps before the front door opened. She paused and looked over her shoulder.

Bear was a magnificent sight, and she wondered how many women had been rendered speechless and spellbound by him. He filled the doorway, literally.

"Hey," he said as he flipped his cell phone shut. "Did I wake you?"

"The phone did," she admitted, facing him.

He had a strange look on his face. "Why are you smiling?"

She hadn't realized she was. "I'm smiling?

His eyes narrowed. "Yes."

Lying would be useless. He'd pick up on it immediately. She decided to go with it and hope she embarrassed him. "Sorry. I was just admiring your shorts."

"What's wrong with my shorts?"

Laine leaned against the door jamb. "Well, the 90s called and they want them back, even if you *do* have the physique to pull them off." She gave him a smile and a wave. "Night, Bear. I'm going back to bed."

"Don't you want to know who was calling me at this hour?"

She yawned. "Not really."

"Good," he said with a scowl. "Wasn't going to tell you anyway."

Laine laughed and closed the door behind her.

***

"So, you're sure about this?" Bear asked again.

Laine nodded. "Yes. I'll stay at the school until finals are done and report cards are finished, but after that . . . I want to go home."

He leaned back in his chair and took a drink of coffee. "What about this place?"

Laine looked around the quaint kitchen of her beach front cottage and shrugged. "I bought it fair and square, so the government can't make me give it up." She gazed out the window into the small but lush backyard. "Maybe this will be where I fly south for the winter. Montana can be awfully cold."

"Yeah," Bear agreed with a wry twist of his lips, "we get snow in Denver, too." He watched her over the rim of his cup. "This wouldn't have anything to do with being some place you know Jack can find you, would it?"

She met his gaze and lifted one brow. "No, Bear. Not at all."

A grin curved his mouth. "I didn't think so."

"Of course I want Jack to find me, but I also miss Grant, I miss trees, I miss my dog." She contemplated her unfinished pancakes and felt the familiar ache. "I miss Jack, Bear. I wish he'd come home."

Bear reached across the table and covered her hands with one of his. "He'll be back before you know it." He squeezed her fingers and gave her a jaunty smile. "Just remember, you know where to find me when you get tired of him. I'll be waiting."

He grinned at her, finished his coffee, and rose. She tipped her face up as he towered over her, and he leaned over to brush a kiss across her cheek.

"I've got to notify the Marshals," he said. "If they don't get started on your paperwork *now*, you'll be spending Christmas in Oceanside."

"How long will you be gone?" she asked. "It's Saturday after all. Will Montoya even be in?"

Bear wiggled his eyebrows. "No, but I thought I'd give the little man one more reason to hate me."

"He doesn't hate you," Laine reproached him.

He grabbed his suit jacket and slung it over his shoulder. "When I tell him you've decided to resurrect Dr. Laine Wheeler, he will." His grin widened. "God, I *love* my work."

Chapter Seventeen

"Hey, Dr. Wheeler," Ruth called. "I've got a package for you."

Laine was surprised, but she approached the reception desk. It had taken almost three months for the Marshals to restore her identity. It had been just over nine months since she'd returned to Evergreen Springs. Once she'd moved back and gotten unpacked, she'd started working at the hospital, and had fallen into the role of doctor without so much as a hiccup. She still managed to squeeze in some veterinary work on the side. Busy was an understatement, but she liked it that way. She smiled at Ruth and took the tall, rectangular box from the older woman's hand. She looked it over, looking for the return address, but there was none.

"Where did this come from?"

Ruth shrugged. "The UPS guy dropped it off about half an hour ago." She leaned forward in her chair, eyes alight with interest. "Are you going to open it?"

Laine pursed her lips, put the box on the counter and stared at it. What was in it? Should she open it?

After a few moments, she looked up and said, "Letter opener, please."

Ruth handed her the tool like it was a scalpel. Laine made quick work of the tape holding the container closed. She lifted the box flaps and peered inside. Her heart somersaulted. Something in her face must have changed because Ruth stood up.

"What's wrong, Dr. Wheeler?" she asked. "What is it?"

Laine pulled the bottle of Laphroaig from inside the box.

Ruth returned to her chair behind the counter. "What's that?"

Laine looked at the label and realized this was a bottle of Laphroaig's 30 year-old scotch whisky, the *good* stuff. It was the same year as the whisky she and Jack had enjoyed at the Hotel Montbleu in Denver. Goose bumps shivered over her skin. No one but Jack would know about that. Her heart leapt as she remembered what had followed that drink, and then sank as more memories sprang to life. She didn't know if she should be elated or apprehensive. Schooling her face into an expressionless façade, she stared at the bottle.

"Wow," Dr. St. Pierre said from beside her. "Is that what I think it is?"

Laine's gaze was glued to the label. "What do you think it is?"

"Well," he began, "it looks like a $700 bottle of scotch."

"Then it is what you think it is."

Dr. St. Pierre whistled. "That's some anniversary gift."

It was far more than a gift, it was a message. But why? Why send a bottle of whisky instead of calling? Laine shook herself and glanced at him. "What are you talking about? What anniversary?"

"The nine-month anniversary of you working here," he replied, as if she should already know. "You came to us November of last year and now it's July. If you'd been pregnant, you'd be due." He grinned and chuckled at his own humor.

Laine was not in the mood and focused again on the bottle, as if it would grow a mouth and reveal the sender. When it didn't, frustration and uneasiness worked their way up her esophagus. Was Jack trying to tell her he was okay and this was the only way he could do that? She took a deep breath. "Ruth, was it the regular UPS guy who dropped this off?"

"Yes, dear," Ruth replied. "Is something wrong?"

"Hey, is that a bottle of Laphroaig?" Dr. Singh asked. He stopped, put his chart on the counter and picked up the bottle. He looked at Laine. "Where'd you get this? Do you even drink scotch whisky?"

"It was a gift," Ruth volunteered. "I don't see what the fuss is all about. It's just a bottle of whisky."

Laine's mind was firing off questions faster than her synapses could process them, and her co-workers only added to the noise. Troubled and more than a little irritated, she put the bottle back in the box. "You're right, Ruth," Laine agreed. She put the box under her arm. "It's just a bottle of whisky."

"Hey," St. Pierre protested, "aren't you going to share?"

She ignored him and walked slowly toward the women's changing room, her mind going at warp speed. Bear. She needed to talk to Bear. In the year since she'd left Oceanside she and Bear had kept in close contact, but she had heard nothing from Jack. Bear told her he'd gotten one phone call, but it had cut off before he'd been able to get any pertinent information. He'd tried to run a trace, but the line hadn't been open long enough. His efforts since then had been fruitless. At least they knew

Jack was alive . . . somewhere. The Laphroaig was additional proof of that, but the thought of letting herself believe frightened her so much she was almost unwilling to hope.

Laine strode into the changing room, made sure it was empty, and locked the door behind her. She placed the bottle on the bench, which ran in front of the lockers, and straddled the seat facing the whisky. It wasn't going to talk to her, that much she knew, but she was transfixed by the dark, curved glass and the memories it triggered. She stared at it for a little longer before pulling out her cell phone.

"Bristol."

"Hey, Bear," she said. "It's me."

"Laine," he declared. "How are you, beautiful?"

"I'm good," she replied. "You?"

"Better now. How are things in Montana?"

"Good. I see the Broncos picked up that new quarterback. Think he'll be any good?"

There was a brief pause. "Yeah," he said, "I think he'll do well, but that's not why you called."

"It's not?"

"Laine, this is me you're talking to. Spit it out."

"Have you . . . ." Her voice died and she had to swallow several times before it returned. "Any news?"

"Nothing concrete." He sounded discouraged. "I got a call a couple of days ago from an old contact in Edinburgh who said he thought he'd seen Jack."

"Edinburgh, as in Scotland?"

"Yeah. Crazy, huh?"

Laine looked at the bottle. "Oh, I can think of crazier things."

There was some noise in the background, and he said, "Hey, Laine, I'm going to have to call you back. You be up later?"

"I'm pulling an 18 hour shift, big guy," she replied affectionately. "I won't be home until after midnight."

"Then I'll call you tomorrow," he said. "Around noon?"

"Okay. Love you."

"You too, sweetheart. Be good."

The line went dead and Laine held the phone to her chest for a moment. "Always."

She picked up the whisky, ran her hands over the glass, and then stuffed it in the back of her locker. Light glinted off the bottle as if it was winking at her. Laine squeezed her eyes shut and closed the locker door. Exhilaration, anxiety, hope, and terror swirled inside her, but she could do nothing about the strange emotions rioting through her. She spun the dial on the combination lock, took a deep breath and returned to her rounds.

***

Laine drove home via auto-pilot, thoughts of Jack haunting her. She'd driven this road so many times she could do it blindfolded, and the monotony allowed her to think. She wasn't sure if that was a good thing or not. Her brain cycled through various, disjointed images from the time she'd spent with him. Some of the memories made her eyes well with happy tears, others made her want to weep.

It was half past midnight, the sky awash in stars when she pulled into the driveway. She looked up at the stars for a few moments, smiled at Venus, unlocked the door and went inside. After tossing her bags on the couch, she took the bottle of whisky into the kitchen and put it on the counter. She absently wondered if this was the first of several messages, or if it was a solo effort. Maverick padded over to her and nuzzled her hand.

"Hey, boy," she said, crouching to scratch his ears, "how you doin'?" He licked her fingers and buffeted her chin with his head. Laine chuckled and rubbed his belly. "Oh, that feels good, doesn't it? Yeah, boy."

When she rose, Maverick walked over to the dog bed by the fireplace and plopped down, his chin on his paws. She turned and grabbed a scoop of dog food from the canister next to the refrigerator, but when she moved to pour it in his bowl, she saw the bowl was already full. Startled, Laine froze and her pulse jumped a notch. Maverick's head came up. She tossed the scoop back into the container and put her hands on her hips.

"You figure out how to get your own food without opposable thumbs?" she asked the dog. Maverick tipped his head to the side and looked at her.

"Did Grant come by and feed you, boy?" Laine stared at the full bowl of kibble for another moment, then sighed and ran a hand over her face. She snapped the lid back into place. "Hell, maybe *I* fed you and don't remember." She looked at the canine. "I'm losing it, Mav. And listen to me. I'm talking to a dog and expecting a reply. I need a shower . . . and a drink."

Maverick tipped his head to the other side and gave her a brief doggy smile. Laine chuckled and made her way to the bedroom.

After showering, she put her hair up into a loose braid. Then she pulled on a pair of sweat pants and a T-shirt and walked toward the kitchen.

When she reached the end of the hall, flickering orange light was visible through one of the windows near the back door. Laine stopped in her tracks. The propane-fueled fire pit in the backyard had been lit. Had Grant come by for a late-night chat? While it wasn't likely, it also wasn't completely out of the realm of possibility. She chose to err on the side of caution. A mixture of anxiety and curiosity swirled inside her as she moved slowly and silently to the sideboard.

Her gaze locked on the flames, she reached into a drawer and pulled out a Springfield XDS .40 caliber pistol. Next to that was a Lady Smith .38 caliber revolver. She slipped the smaller gun into the waistband of her sweats at her back and made sure her t-shirt covered it. Being armed settled her nerves somewhat, but not completely. She took a breath and walked toward the kitchen, the .40 in hand.

She briefly entertained the thought that Jack was messing with her, but discarded the idea as quickly as it had come. Jack wouldn't do this sort of thing. If anything, he would have joined her in the shower rather than engaging in some elaborate cat-and-mouse game. As she passed the kitchen counter, she realized the bottle of Laphroiag was gone. Her heart nearly stopped. Panic climbed into her throat. She stared at the empty spot for a moment, and the hairs on the back of her neck prickled. Part of her reasoned that Grant could have fed the dog, lit the fire pit, and taken the whisky, but the rest of her knew he would never do that to her, not like this. So, who?

Laine spun around. Her eyes darted back and forth, but there was no one else there. Turning her eyes to the window, Laine reached behind her and picked up the phone. It was dead. Now she knew neither Jack nor Grant was involved. A surge of adrenaline hit her bloodstream, and her heart jumped in response. Her palms went clammy and she put the handset back.

She watched the flickering orange light for a few moments. She took a step toward the back door, but stopped. Someone had been in her house, possibly more than one person. She wanted to run, but her father had taught her not only to face her fears, but also how to defend herself. Deciding it would be better to ensure the house was clear before heading outside, she backed up. Her gaze turned down the hall to her bedroom and the closed door to the exam room. Moving slowly and carefully, she approached the short corridor.

A glance in the bathroom revealed it was empty, so she faced the exam room door. Her breathing turned rapid and shallow as she grasped the knob and turned. When she felt the mechanism disengage, she opened the wooden panel a crack and pushed it back. The .40 came up and she stepped into the doorway. When she saw the room was vacant, her knees went weak. Laine leaned against the jamb and took several deep breaths and then she straightened. She glanced over her shoulder toward the window.

It suddenly dawned on her that Maverick was not on his cushion by the fire. Perhaps he'd gone outside to see to their unannounced visitor. Laine closed her eyes and listened, but the night was quiet and still. Maverick didn't usually take to strangers. If an intruder had ventured onto the property when she was home, Maverick's wolf DNA would have instantly asserted itself. She shot straight past worried to fearful and prayed the dog was okay.

Holding the gun down alongside her leg, Laine crossed the room to the door leading to the garage. She briefly thought of looking in there, but decided against it. Instead, she flipped the lock and the deadbolt. The mechanisms were sturdy, Grant had installed them, but she knew they wouldn't keep a determined intruder out. However, if her nefarious visitor was in the garage, or had a friend in the garage, the locks would give her time to take aim.

Now that the house was as secure as she could make it, the only place left to check was outside. Light from the fire pit turned the white painted window frames a pale orange color, and her heart rate started to pick up pace as she slowly approached the back door. She could feel it thrumming violently against her sternum. It was an odd sensation, and it made breathing more difficult than normal, as if her heart was fighting with her lungs for space in her chest. Laine stared at the door for a moment before she opened it and peered outside.

The fire pit was about 30 feet from the back door on a patch of closely cropped grass, encircled by half a dozen wooden Adirondack chaise longues. She glanced around for Maverick, but she didn't see the dog anywhere. Carefully, she stepped onto the patio and pulled the door shut behind her. Holding her breath, she walked slowly and silently toward the circle of light.

She'd gone about a half dozen paces when she realized someone was sitting in one of the chairs, his back to her. She could see the outline of a person's head, but from this distance all she could tell was it was a man. She didn't think it was Jack, and the person wasn't big enough to be Bear. At his elbow, on a small wooden table, was the bottle of whisky and two glasses. She blinked, focused on the tumblers, and then refocused on the back of the person's head. *Was* it Jack? The very possibility made anger blossom in her chest. If it was him, she was going to take the Laphroaig and break the bottle over his head.

Slowly and silently, she walked up to the back of the chair. Her pulse skyrocketed and odd tingles shivered over her skin. Unless he'd gone gray since she'd seen him last, the man with the silver at his temples who was sitting on the chaise was *not* Jack. Laine lifted the pistol.

"If you like your brains where they are," she said in a deadly whisper, "you'll show me your hands and get up . . . *slowly.*"

The person's hands came up immediately. She kept the gun aimed at his head as he rose with the grace of a jungle cat. When he was fully erect, she moved her finger to the trigger. Her heart was knocking against her breastbone in earnest now, and it was definitely winning the battle for space inside her ribcage. Her chest ached from the pounding.

"Well," the man said, "this is a warm welcome."

Laine didn't recognize the voice. "Turn around."

He did so, and she found herself looking into the coldest eyes she'd ever seen. They were dark and seemed to absorb the dim light rather than reflecting it. He was older, but exceptionally distinguished looking with sharp features and a fit physique, and he stood with a military bearing that was unmistakable. He looked down the barrel of her gun for a moment then met her gaze.

"You may want to put that down," he said.

"Who are you?"

His smile was cold, reptilian, and it made her shudder. Suddenly one of the crystal tumblers exploded and she jumped. Apparently, he wasn't alone. In the split second it took her to jump, he disarmed her and she found herself looking down the barrel of her own pistol. Her heart stopped pounding against her sternum. Coldness flooded her insides. It was as if her blood was frozen in her veins. He pointed the

.40 at her forehead for a moment before he slipped it into the waist of his pants at the small of his back. Staring at him, Laine exhaled sharply as her body realized he wasn't going to shoot her, at least not yet. She realized she still had the revolver. If worse came to worst, she might need *that* particular ace.

"That's better," he said. His tone was almost cordial. "Now, we can talk." He gestured to a chair.

Part of her wanted to run, but Laine stood her ground. There was still a sniper out there. No doubt he, or she, could pick her off if she chose to flee. She lifted her chin a notch. "Who are you?"

"My name is Ripley, Dr. Wheeler," he replied as he eased down onto one of the chaises. "Now, sit."

The coldness returned and nearly drowned her. She blinked. "You're supposed to be—"

"Dead?" he offered. "I am relieved to say reports of my death have been greatly exaggerated. I was laid up for a while, Jack always was an excellent shot, but I'm all better now." Again he gestured to a chair. "Sit, Dr. Wheeler. You and I have some things to discuss."

That, oddly enough, sparked her temper. This was the man who had nearly killed Jack, not once but twice. This was the man who had turned her life upside down. The very idea that he thought the two of them could just sit down and talk like rational adults infuriated her. Caution said to tread carefully, to hold back her anger. Instead she decided to fan the flames. The coldness started to recede and now it wasn't fear that increased her heart rate. If she was going to die tonight, and chances were good she would, she was going to do it on her feet. She glared at him.

"No," she said flatly, "we don't."

He leaned back and laced his fingers over his taut abdomen. "I see now why Jack took such a liking to you." He looked her up and down. "Attractive, intelligent, fiery. Heady combination."

Laine said nothing. Ripley stared at her, his gaze even more penetrating than Bear's. She clenched her jaw, imagined herself gently blowing on those angry embers, and forced herself to return his gaze.

"It's sad," he said, "because none of this is really your fault. I suppose I should've known Jack wasn't truly one of us from the start. You see, he didn't have the indiscriminate tendencies of his fellow CAG recruits. When they went into town to drink and carouse with loose women, he would stay behind, clean his weapons, and ask West to teach him more about the technical end of running an organization such as mine."

"A *terrorist* organization," Laine spat. "Terrorist. Organization. Sounds like an oxymoron to me. Terrorists aren't about organization, they're about chaos."

"*Controlled* chaos, Doctor," he corrected her. "We use chaos to return control of a government run amok to the people who should be running it."

A tiny flame burst from the coals. "Thank you for the civics lesson, *professor*," she sneered. "Now, why don't you tell me why you're really here?"

"I am here for retribution," he said. "You see, Doctor, life is all about balance." He rose, clasped his hands behind his back, and moved to stand toe-to-toe with her. "Jack took something from me. Now I'm going to take something from him."

"Jack isn't here."

His smile widened, and the firelight transformed that smile into something ghoulish. Internally she recoiled, but kept her expression cool.

"I know," he said, "but he will be."

Laine gazed into those cold eyes and took a deep, steadying breath.

Men like Ripley were predators, and the smell of fear was the scent they most enjoyed. She refused to look away, and returned his stare with one of contempt.

"What did you do to my dog?" she asked.

He actually looked amused. "Your dog is fine, Dr. Wheeler," he replied. He spun on his heel, walked to the opposite side of the fire pit and sat down in a chaise facing her. "I don't believe in punishing animals for their owners' bad choices, especially such a handsome canine as yours. In fact, I took the liberty of feeding him, in case you hadn't noticed. A few hours from now he'll wake up and be none the worse for wear." He lifted one brow and smiled. "I may even take him with me when I leave."

"You won't be leaving here," she said, "unless it's in a body bag."

He laughed. "Spoken with such confidence." He clapped several times. "Bravo, Doctor. Perhaps you should have gone into the theater instead of medicine."

"Then I wouldn't have been able to save Jack so he could kill you," she spat. "No. I think medicine was the correct choice. Call it . . . providence."

He crossed his legs at the ankles and smiled at her. "Providence.

Interesting choice of words."

"If Jack doesn't kill you, I'm going to."

"You?" He arched one brow. "You're a doctor. You wouldn't hurt anyone. It goes against everything you stand for."

The flame burned a little hotter. "I may be a doctor," she began, "but that does *not* mean I'm a pacifist. I've already killed one man. What's one more?"

"Exactly whom did you kill, Doctor Wheeler?" His expression said he clearly didn't believe her. "And losing a patient doesn't count."

"I believe he was a friend of yours." She smiled. "Tall, bald, liked to hurt women. Ring a bell?"

His expression told her this was indeed a surprise. He narrowed his eyes on her, and she saw something in his face she couldn't identify. Was it respect? Anger? She didn't know and she didn't care.

"Even a mouse will fight back when cornered," she said with a small smile.

"Indeed," he conceded. "Very neatly done, by the way. Two shots to the heart: quick, clean, effective. I'm impressed."

"I'm glad you're impressed," she said, her voice laden with sarcasm. "It makes me feel all warm and fuzzy inside."

He chuckled. "You are nothing if not entertaining, Doctor. Waiting for Jack won't be nearly as tedious as I imagined."

"Speaking of waiting for Jack," she said in a bored voice, "how long are we going to wait? A day, a week, a month?"

"I imagine he should be along any time now," Ripley said with a glance at his watch. "From what information I was able to gather Agent Vaughn is on his way here as we speak."

That hit her like a fist, and she knew the impact registered on her face when Ripley smiled. She whispered, "What are you talking about?"

He laced his fingers and laid them over his stomach again. "Well, since he thinks me dead and you've left Witness Protection, his next move will be to make contact with you."

"And why would you say that?"

"He is in love with you, is he not?" Ripley asked. "What else would spur him to pursue me so mercilessly?"

"Maybe it's because you're a crazed killer who needs to be put down like a rabid dog?"

This time she recognized the spark of anger in his eyes, and a split second later he leapt to his feet. He strode over to her, his face a thundercloud.

"Tread carefully, Doctor," he warned her. "I am a patient man, but that patience is not infinite. I would prefer to have Agent Vaughn watch as I kill you, but I imagine your death will hurt him just as deeply either way."

The realization Ripley was using her as bait so he could kill her and then Jack sent dread spinning her insides like a top. Laine took a breath and decided to eliminate the man's trump card. Taking a step toward him, she tipped her face up and gritted her teeth. "So do it."

His eyes narrowed then a smile spread over his face. "Very clever." He returned to his seat. "The more time I spend with you, the more I like you, Doctor Wheeler. It's too bad we're on opposite sides of the fence."

"As long as that fence is 20 feet high with concertina wire and armed guards, I think she'd prefer it that way. I know *I* would."

She snapped her head around to the right and toward the sound of Jack's voice, her heart nearly bursting with joy, fear, amazement and relief.

Her eyes searched the darkness where his voice had come from. He materialized out of the gloom dressed in black TAC gear and carrying an MP5. Her mouth dropped open and her eyelids fluttered as she stared at him, shockwaves reverberating through her.

"Hi, Doc," he said softly, a faint smile hovering on his lips.

Her eyes welled with tears. He looked bigger than she remembered and his hair was a tad longer, but that gaze captivated her just as completely as it always had. His jaw was shadowed with stubble and there were dark circles underneath his eyes. When he looked at her it was all she could do not to run into his arms. He walked to her side and positioned himself between her and Ripley.

"Well, here I am," Jack said, facing the man. "Show me what you've got, Ripley."

"He's got my .40 in the small of his back," she whispered.

"What are you waiting for, *Commander*?" Jack taunted. "Isn't this what you wanted?"

Ripley uncoiled himself from the chair like an anaconda. The smile he wore gave him a sinister look. There was a self-satisfied light in his eyes that chilled her.

"All I have to do is twitch my hand, and your lovely doctor will be dead before she hits the ground," Ripley said. He nodded at her. "My sniper has her targeted at this moment, see? He's simply waiting for my signal."

Her throat closed up when she looked down and saw the red dot on her chest. She lifted her gaze to Jack's. He gave her a wink.

"Actually, that's *my* sniper," Jack said, turning back to Ripley. "We took your guy out the second he fired at the whisky glass. And, if you notice, the laser sight is no longer on *her*, it's on *you*."

Laine's eyes widened in amazement as Ripley's chest lit up like a Christmas tree. There were at least six red dots dancing across his torso, and after a moment they all settled into an area about the size of a quarter.

"By the way," Jack added, "I brought more than one shooter, just in case. Sucks to be you."

"How did you . . . ?" Ripley's voice died off and he clenched his fists at his side. "This isn't over, Vaughn."

"But it is," Jack replied. "See, I'm *hoping* you'll try something, *anything*, so I have an excuse to put a bullet in the left frontal lobe of your brain. Barring that, making sure you spend the rest of your life in a super-max prison will have to do."

As if on cue, half a dozen men dressed in matching TAC gear appeared like they had materialized out of thin air. Laine realized with sudden clarity that none of this had been chance. It had been choreographed down to the last detail.

Ripley stood stiff and defiant as one of the men walked forward, handcuffs at the ready. Another approached from the opposite side, and the rest of the men, all but one, holstered their weapons.

"He's got one at his back," Jack called out.

The men nodded. The first agent reached for the gun, but Ripley moved in a blur of arms and legs, his elbow jerking back and impacting the agent's face with a sickening crunch before Ripley spun away. The agent went down hard, blood streaming from his nose. Ripley grabbed the second man and spun him around, his arm snaking about the agent's neck. He pulled the agent close and used him as a shield. It happened so quickly no one had had a chance to react.

Time slowed to a crawl as Laine saw the .40 caliber pistol Ripley had taken from her materialize in the man's hand. Slowly the muzzle came up and pointed straight at Jack. Laine sighted down the barrel of the .38, heard the shot, and felt the jolt in her arm. Odd. She didn't even recall drawing her weapon.

Multiple gun barrels turned on her, but her eyes were locked on Ripley. He looked at her in shock as his body jerked backwards. His mouth opened in a silent scream as blood trickled from the hole over his right eye. The gun fired, but the shot went into the ground a few feet away, sending a cloud of dirt and grass into the air. He stared at her and she stared back as the agent he'd grabbed escaped his hold and scrambled away. Ripley hung there, seemingly suspended in mid-air, not standing but not falling, as if there were invisible wires holding him aloft like some kind of disjointed marionette. When he finally fell to the ground, time resumed its normal pace.

In the background she heard Jack shouting for them to lower their weapons, but the sound was vague, as if it came from far away through a very bad phone line. She lowered her arm and dropped the .38 on the ground, her eyes still focused on Ripley. She saw one of Jack's men bend over him and check for a pulse, and then the man shook his head to indicate there wasn't one.

"I said, 'Lower your weapons!'"

Laine jumped and the fog cleared as Jack shielded her with his body, his back to her. The burst of noise was sudden and painful. Everyone seemed to be shouting at once, and she clapped her hands over her ears.

"Hey! Lower your weapons *now*!"

The voice was Bear's, and it cut through the cacophony like a hot knife through butter. The ensuing silence was almost eerie. She looked for him, the one person besides Grant who had been a constant in her life during the last year. When she saw his towering form appear on the far side of the fire pit, she flew at him. As she did she realized she should be running for Jack, not Bear, but she didn't stop. Right now she needed to grab hold of someone who was real, someone who could be an anchor in this hurricane. Even though she'd seen and spoken to Jack, part of her still couldn't believe he was real and that he was here. It was just too much to process.

Bear's expression was grim, his brow furrowed in a scowl, but it wasn't directed at her. She threw herself against him and closed her eyes as he held her with one arm, the other arm waving the officers away.

"Back off," Bear snapped. "Everything's good. Mitchell, get started on the scene."

"Yes, sir."

Bear pushed her back, one hand on each shoulder, and looked her up and down. "You okay?" When she nodded, he hugged her again. "Nice shot."

"Laine."

She turned at the sound of Jack's voice. Her eyes filled with tears.

When he pressed a hand to her cheek she walked into his embrace with a sigh. His arms closed around her and she clung to him.

"Thank God you're all right," he whispered. He held her tightly. "You saved me again, Doc. For the last time I promise."

Joy bubbled up inside her like a spring that flowed through her and filled the empty space that had haunted her since she'd last seen him. She was almost afraid to believe she was finally in his arms again. But as her mind replayed what had just happened, the flow waned and another strong emotion erupted in the pit of her stomach. If this had been choreographed, as it must have been, that meant Ripley wasn't the only one who had used her. The man she loved had used her, and so had one of her closest friends. Two of the people she trusted most in the world had betrayed her, and she felt that betrayal slice through her like a scalpel. The knowledge they'd been lying to her for only God knows how long registered like a fist to her middle. Her diaphragm spasmed in response and she exhaled sharply. All too quickly that emptiness inside her was filled again. Something black and angry crowded out the elation she'd felt. It bubbled and expanded, morphing into red, livid fury that seeped through her until she felt like it was being forced out of her pores.

She pulled away from Jack. She met his gaze and felt the drawing down of her brows and mouth. His expression changed when he saw her face.

"Laine, what—"

Her hand cracked sharply across his cheek, and the stinging in her fingers reminded her of another night she'd hit him. He looked at her in surprise as she backed up a step and turned to Bear, whom she punched in the gut. Air hissed out from between his teeth, but he managed to stay upright.

"What the . . . ?"

Her glare silenced them. She looked between the two, and didn't even make an attempt to hide what was brewing inside her. "Tell me," she began in a whisper, "that you two didn't just use me as bait."

She saw realization dawn in Jack's eyes, but Bear remained as unreadable as ever. It didn't matter. Jack's reaction was confirmation enough. She turned an accusing stare on Bear.

"So it was all a lie, *everything*." Their silence was her answer. She backed away from them, shaking her head. "How long have you . . . ?" Her voice died and her eyes widened. "The phone call . . . that night in Oceanside." She pointed at Jack. "It was *him* wasn't it? You knew *exactly* where he was, didn't you? He's been *here*, watching, waiting for Ripley to show up." Her chin trembled and she clenched her jaw to stop it. The months of uncertainty, sleepless nights, and fear that she would never see Jack again stormed over her. The world spun crazily, the ground dropping out from under her, and she squeezed her eyes shut as nausea roiled. She took several deep breaths and then looked at Bear. "It was never *over*, was it? You *used* me, both of you, to draw Ripley out."

Her gaze shifted to Jack, and he looked down at the ground. His expression snuffed out any hope she'd harbored that this was all some cosmic coincidence. The knife plunged deeper. She pressed a shaking hand to her mouth and tears streamed down her cheeks, but she didn't bother to wipe them away. She didn't have the energy.

"Wow. How gullible am I? I never suspected a thing." She took a deep, hitching breath. "Nice work, gentlemen. You two should be very proud."

She looked at them for another moment and then spun on her heel and walked away.

Chapter Eighteen

Jack watched her go. In a split second every negative emotion he'd experienced since meeting her manifested with Herculean strength – shame, regret, guilt, fear – and they showed him no mercy. Hard, powerful fists pummeled his internal organs, and they only seemed to increase in intensity and speed with each step she took away from him. For several moments he couldn't even breathe, his lungs burning and struggling to inflate against the enormous pressure in his chest. When he started to walk after her, Bear grabbed his arm.

"Don't," Bear said.

Anger flashed inside him, heating his blood, and Jack glared at his friend. With a growl he shook off Bear's hand and took another step. Bear stepped in front of him and Jack tensed, his hands fisted.

"Jack, *don't*," he said again, more firmly. "She's pissed off and she has every right to be. Going after her now will only make things worse. Give her a chance to cool off."

The tone of Bear's voice cut through the blazing heat in his chest, and he realized Bear was right. Jack stared after her. Everything inside him wanted to run after her, take her in his arms and tell her he loved her, but she was angrier with him than he was with himself. She needed time to process what had happened. Still he had to physically stop himself from pushing Bear aside and chasing her down. He'd been watching her for more than three weeks, but this was the first time in nearly two years he'd been close enough to touch her. The look she'd given him had laid his heart open and scored it like the sharpest blade. Despite that, he ached to hold her, bury his face in her hair, and run his fingers over her skin.

"We should've figured out another way, Bear," he said. "We should've done something else, anything but what we did."

"It's a little late for that, Jack," Bear replied. "It worked. The only one who got hurt was Ripley."

"No," Jack said with a shake of his head. He remembered the anguish in her eyes as he'd watched her try to come to terms with their betrayal. Regret and shame choked him, and he had to fight to speak. "He *wasn't* the only one who got hurt."

"Hey," Bear said, putting a hand on Jack's shoulder. "We tried to get him for more than a year, and he was always able to stay one step ahead of us. This plan wasn't perfect, but it was the only way to get in front of him. Now Laine is safe, you're safe, and *he's* dead."

Jack gripped his forehead with one hand and tried to concentrate on something other than the sick feeling in the pit of his stomach. "And who shot him, Bear?"

Bear planted his hands on his hips and stared into the fire. "Yeah. That wasn't our finest hour."

"We did what Ripley did," Jack said. "Overconfidence was always his biggest flaw, and it's what finally brought him down. We got overconfident, too, and she's paying for it." He ran a hand over his hair.

"No op is perfect," Bear replied, "and no operative is perfect. All things considered, the higher-ups will look at this as a great success."

Jack scowled. "Well, I don't."

The sound of sirens pierced the relative quiet as two patrol cars and an ambulance rounded the house and skidded to a stop outside the yellow tape Mitchell had set up. Jack watched as Grant Donovan launched himself from his sedan. The sheriff ran toward him.

"Where is she?" he demanded, his face tight with fear.

Jack nodded toward the house and Donovan spun on his heel. A lump formed in his throat as he remembered the day he'd delivered Laine's message. Donovan had taken the news with quiet stoicism.

"Give her some time, Jack," Bear said, following the direction of Jack's gaze. "Once you explain it, she'll understand."

He stared at the back of the quaint cabin. "I wouldn't blame her if she never wanted to set eyes on me again. After what I've done to her life . . . if I were her, I'd hate me."

"She's not capable," Bear stated. "She loves you."

"Does she love you, too?"

Bear lifted one brow. "I certainly hope so. I love her."

Jack looked at him out of the corner of his eye. "Is that why she ran past me into *your* arms . . . because you love each other?"

He stared at Jack for a minute. "She's like a sister to me, and even if you don't trust *me*, you should trust *her*. Jealousy doesn't become you, Jack."

Jack met his friend's disdainful gaze before looking away. "I'm sorry, Bear," he whispered. He ran a hand over his face. "I didn't mean that."

"I know. Now, come on. Let's get this shit wrapped up, so we can get on to more important things."

Jack nodded and looked toward the house. Grant Donovan appeared in the back door, his eyes scanning the yard. When they stopped on him, the man's face hardened. He marched toward him with long, purposeful strides.

He knew what the sheriff was going to do, and he knew he deserved it and then some. In fact, Jack found himself looking forward to a good, old-fashioned pounding. Maybe, if he was lucky, the physical pain would distract him from the ache in his soul.

Donovan didn't say a word. The sheriff stopped a couple of feet away, then hauled off and hit him with a right hook that sent Jack sprawling. Fireworks exploded inside his head. He felt the air whoosh by as he flew backwards. The bone-jarring impact when he landed on the hard ground knocked the wind out of him. He lay there for a moment, dazed and struggling to catch his breath. When his vision cleared, he saw Bear holding the brawny sheriff back.

"Grant, no!" Laine called out.

"You son of a bitch!" Donovan seethed. "You used her as *bait*? She could've been killed!"

Jack tested his jaw and blinked, flashes of light still dancing behind his eyes. He eased up onto his elbows and pain radiated through the lower half of his face. Sadly, the physical discomfort he felt did nothing to lessen his emotional turmoil. For a moment he thought about taunting Donovan, goading the man to hit him again, but then Laine appeared.

"Grant, stop!" She stood in front of the sheriff, her hands on his chest as Bear continued to restrain him from behind. She put a hand on his face. "Grant, look at me." After a few moments, the sheriff turned his eyes to her. "Stop it. It's done and I'm fine. We're all on the same side here."

"Listen to the lady, Sheriff," Bear advised him in a low, calm voice. "I know you're angry, and that's understandable, but it's over."

Grant looked at Laine, his eyes searching her face. After a few moments he relaxed and said, "I'm okay," and Bear released him. Grant put a hand behind Laine's neck and pulled her into his arms.

Guilt rose like bile as Jack watched the two embrace. Bear extended his hand and helped Jack to his feet. Clapping him on the shoulder, Bear turned and walked away. Jack looked at Laine for a few more seconds, fighting against the utter despondence that threatened to pull him under. Finally, he turned and followed Bear.

"Hey," Donovan called out.

Jack paused and looked back over his shoulder. Donovan met his gaze over Laine's head, his eyes blazing.

"You ever hurt her again, I'll kill you," Grant said.

Jack nodded once. "If I ever hurt her again, I'll let you."

***

"Really, Grant, I'm fine," she said. "You don't have to stay with me."

"Are you sure?" he asked, his eyes dark with concern.

She smiled and patted his arm. "Your girlfriend expects you home, and I don't imagine she'd be pleased if she found out you spent the night here. She wasn't very happy I returned to town at all, remember?" She looked at the nearly half dozen black SUV's parked around her backyard, agents coming and going as they processed the scene. "Besides, the FBI and ATF are still here. I think I'll be all right."

"They're the ones who got you into this mess," Grant pointed out.

Laine eased down onto the top step of the porch. "Please, Grant, it's after three in the morning. I'm exhausted and you have to get back to work." She leaned against his muscular leg. "Finish your shift and go home to Sherri. *That's* where you belong."

"You call me if you need *anything.*" He squeezed her shoulder. "Understood?"

She smiled up at him. "Understood. Now get out of here."

He leaned over and brushed a kiss over her brow, then walked toward his police cruiser. She watched him until his patrol car disappeared from view.

"Laine."

It was Bear's voice. She looked up at him, and he returned her gaze with one of cool composure. Angry embers flared until she reminded herself that was just Bear. Right now, it was all about business. When business was finished he would return to his normal self, but *only* when business was finished. That was how he worked, and she'd expected nothing else.

"Yes, Bear?"

He clasped his hands in front of him. "I need to get your statement, and then we'll be able to get out of your hair."

While Laine didn't see the point, they'd obviously been witness to everything that had happened, she didn't argue. Procedures were procedures. Before she could move to get up, Bear extended a hand to her, as if he'd read her mind. She looked at his fingers for a moment. The hurt was still palpable, but she sensed he was offering her more than just help up. She placed her hand in his, and he tugged her to her feet.

"Why don't we go inside?" she suggested. "I'll make some coffee."

"That would be great," he replied.

Laine glanced around the scene with a dispassionate eye, until she saw Jack watching her. The expression on his face tore at her heart. When she realized he was standing over Ripley's body, her breath caught. A rush of jumbled emotions blended inside her, moving so quickly and fluidly there was no way she could individually define them. Part of her wanted to run to him and throw herself against his chest, the other wanted to grab the Laphroaig and bash his skull in with it. She faltered and Bear's head turned. It took her a moment to regain her composure. Bear waited silently. When she was finally able to make her feet move, he followed her into the house.

Bear made small talk as she made coffee, and the mundane task helped her focus on something other than her see-sawing emotions. As she poured the dark brew and retrieved the cream from the refrigerator, she felt a flicker of relief as the numbness finally started to set in. Her mind drifted back to her meeting with Joanna Slate, U.S. Attorney. The only difference between this scene and that one was the fact Bear was asking the questions. She took a deep breath and shook off the sensation of déjà vu. The interview progressed and Laine suddenly realized she felt nothing, not the chair beneath her, not the counter her elbows rested on, not the warm mug in her hands. She sent a silent prayer of thanks heavenward and focused on the deep timbre of Bear's voice.

It took an hour and two cups of coffee for Bear to get her statement. As Laine moved to pour him a third cup, he waved a hand at her.

"Thanks, but I'm good," he said. He slid his pen into the notepad and put it on the counter. "How are you?"

Gone was the stalwart professional. His azure eyes were filled with concern and regret, and he made no attempt to hide his feelings. That brought her up short. Laine took a deep breath and put the coffee pot back.

The conflict between her love for Jack, her friendship with Bear, and the anger she felt toward both of them warred in her chest. "I don't . . . I don't know," she replied. She walked around the island and slid onto a barstool next to him. "I understand what you did, at least . . . intellectually." She stared at the wall without seeing it. "It's just . . . all these months . . . not knowing if he was dead or alive . . . thinking Ripley was dead and I was safe . . . and suddenly realizing it was all a lie." She rubbed her temples. "It's a lot to process, Bear."

"We didn't enjoy deceiving you," he said in a low voice. "Jack least of all. This whole thing has been hell for him." He dropped his chin. "In my defense, that call in Oceanside was the first time I'd heard from him since he disappeared, so it wasn't *all* a lie. He asked me not to tell you because he didn't want to get your hopes up if something else happened."

Laine didn't know what to say. Bear glanced at her and sighed.

"This whole thing was my idea, Laine, so if you want to hate someone, hate me. Jack didn't like it, but he wasn't given much of a choice."

"I don't hate you," she whispered. She blinked back tears. "I could never hate either of you." She ran a hand over her eyes. "I love you both." Laine looked at him, but Bear was looking out the window into the backyard. "Y'know, you could've just asked for my help. I'd have been more than happy to be your bait."

"We couldn't take that chance."

It wasn't Bear who had spoken. Laine turned and met Jack's hawk-like gaze. He stood in the doorway, nearly filling the frame, his grey eyes on her. She hated the leap in her pulse but was helpless to control it. He still affected her just as he always had.

Jack glanced at Bear and Bear nodded and rose.

As soon as the door closed behind Bear, Jack approached her. "I *wanted* to tell you," he said softly, "but it would've been too dangerous."

Laine felt tightness in her throat that expanded through her chest and she gaped at him, "How much more dangerous could it have gotten?"

"Ripley was an exceptionally intelligent man, and a brilliant tactician. More than anything else, he was a cold-blooded predator who would slaughter his own men for the smallest of mistakes." He stopped a few paces away. "Your reactions had to be completely natural, because if he had, for one *millisecond*, thought you were part of a trap he would've simply killed you and run." His brows drew together and he shook his head. "I couldn't let that happen."

A strange tingling started at the base of her skull and wound tightly around her neck. For a moment she couldn't breathe. "You led him to me," she accused.

"No," he said from between clenched teeth. "You've been under surveillance from the *moment* Ripley set foot on U.S. soil. For more than three weeks my men and I have been shadowing you around the clock, at the hospital, the clinic, here. We were prepped and ready for Ripley to make his move." The look he gave her begged her to understand. "I would never have let him hurt you. Never."

"He was in my house!"

A small smile curved his mouth. "So was I." His smile widened just a bit. "And then you locked me in the garage."

Her stomach dropped. She blinked at him, her vocal chords frozen, and then her brain grabbed hold of something he'd just said. "Wait. You've been watching me for *how* long?"

He walked over to the couch and sat down, his elbows on his knees. "Longest three weeks of my life. I can't tell you how many times I dialed your number and hung up." He lifted his gaze to her, and the pain she saw there made her heart twist.

"I wanted . . . *so* much . . . to hear your voice," he said in a whisper, "to let you know I was okay, to tell you . . . tell you how much I . . . I *love* you." Her chin trembled and she pressed shaking fingers to her mouth. His declaration pierced the ball of anger pulsing inside her ribcage and the rage began to drain. Jack pressed his fingers into his eyes. "It had to be this way, Doc. I'd rather have you alive and hating me than have you dead."

He looked up and when she saw the sheen of tears, the roiling ball diminished, and she had the oddest sensation of open space inside her chest. Her heart and lungs ached, but at least they could function normally now.

Jack took a shaky breath and dropped his chin, looking at the floor. "Ripley is gone. You're free, and I hope you can forgive me someday." He swiped at his eyes. "Please . . . please forgive me."

His request was barely audible, but it crumbled the last of her defenses. She stared at his bowed head for a moment and the desire to touch him, comfort him, overwhelmed her. Laine slid off the stool. She stood in front of him, but he wouldn't look at her. Her eyes swam with tears and she put a hand on his head.

"Oh, Jack . . . ."

His arms snuck around her and he pressed his cheek against her stomach. She ran her fingers over his hair. It felt like velvet against her palm and she closed her eyes.

"God, I've missed you," he whispered. "And I am *so* sorry."

The simple apology sealed the deal for her. She blinked and tears dripped slowly down her cheeks, plopping down onto the top of his head. "I know," she replied, "and you're forgiven." She framed his face with her hands and forced him to look up at her. "I've missed you, too."

He searched her eyes. "Tell me I haven't lost you."

Laine ran a thumb over his brow, then lowered her head and kissed him. He kissed her back, but he was tentative, hesitant, as if he was afraid she'd bolt. He was leaving it up to her to set the boundaries.

She was unprepared for the firestorm that ensued. Like tossing gasoline on banked coals, heat flared up inside her and roiled from her core to every part of her body. Even her fingers and toes were warm and tingling. His hands splayed over her back, pressing her closer as her lips moved over his. She had dreamt of this moment for so long, imagined what it would be like, and it was beyond what she had expected. He took her breath away, his touch as gentle as the caress of the sun's rays at twilight.

"Special Agent Vaughn, we have to . . . oops. Sorry."

"Hey! Get out of there! Didn't I tell you not to bother them?"

Laine didn't recognize the first voice, but she did recognize Bear's voice. She smiled and pulled away. Jack stood, pulled her back as if he hadn't heard a thing, and recaptured her mouth.

It was almost too much; the feel of him, the taste of him, the strength of his embrace. Desire swirled in her belly and she wanted nothing more than to be naked in his arms, skin against skin. The night they'd spent in Denver flashed in her mind and her limbs went rubbery. She had resigned herself to living without him, and part of her worried this was all a dream, that she would wake up and be back in Oceanside living a life created for her by the government. It hadn't been a bad life. She had enjoyed teaching and had really liked her students, but Jack Vaughn couldn't be part of that life. He *could* be part of this one. She ended the kiss slowly, her eyes closed, her forehead against his.

"You haven't lost me," she whispered.

She wrapped her arms around his neck and pressed her cheek to his. Jack let out a shaky breath.

They stood like this for several minutes, until there was a light rap on the door. Laine turned her head toward the sound and smiled when Bear stuck his head inside, one hand over his eyes.

"Is everyone decent?" he asked.

Laine rolled her eyes. "Bear."

He peeked through his fingers, dropped his hand and gave Jack a disappointed look. "Dude. I figured you'd have her in bed by now. You're slipping, buddy."

"Bear!" Laine said in a gasp.

He grinned, stepped through the doorway, and walked up to them. "At least you're smiling, which is a good sign." He looked from one to the other. "Are we okay? Everything better?"

Since he had admitted to being the primary conspirator, she didn't want to let him off the hook just yet, but she couldn't conjure her earlier anger. She rolled her eyes and chuckled. "As long as you both swear to never do anything like that again," Laine said, "we'll be fine. You guys do your jobs, and just leave me out of it, okay? These undercover operations are *not* for me."

Bear put his hands on his hips and stared at Jack. "You . . . didn't . . . tell her?"

That churning ball was back, and it had grown. "Oh, for goodness sake, what now?" she asked, looking from one to the other in disbelief.

"I didn't get a chance," Jack said, as if she hadn't spoken. "She was too busy kissing me."

Laine crossed her arms over her chest. "Fat chance of *that* ever happening again."

Bear choked back a laugh and Jack glared at him. Ignoring his friend's humor, Jack took her hands and looked into her eyes.

"What Bear was referring to is the fact I am giving up field work. No more undercover ops for me." He looked at the floor and then back up at her. "Once this case is officially closed, I'll be pushing a desk for a while, a *long* while. Shortly before my cover was blown, I put in for an inter-agency transfer and it was approved. I'll probably be assigned to the L.A. office, but once I've done six months there I can transfer some place closer."

Laine's eyes widened and she glanced at Bear, who nodded, his expression solemn. She looked at Jack, but he appeared to be studying the floor.

"Is that what you want?" she asked.

He met her gaze. "I'm looking at what I want."

She stared at him and when her lungs started to burn, she realized she was holding her breath. "Jack, you can't give up something you love because of me." She squeezed her eyes shut and fought the anxiety winding tightly around her chest. "You'd only end up resenting me."

"I'm not giving it up because of you," he stated, "and it's not the job I love. I'm giving it up because I'm done. I've spent nearly half my career, almost ten years, working for this day." He traced the line of her collarbone. "Besides, even if I wanted to return to field work, the department requires a certain amount of downtime between assignments." He chuckled. "You wouldn't believe how many vacation days I've accrued while on this particular job, and I intend to put every one of them to *very* good use."

He looked at her and the implication was clear. Laine's face went hot, and then that heat coiled low in her belly. Her breasts tingled. If Bear hadn't been standing there, she probably would've ripped Jack's clothes off and had her way with him on the couch. However, Bear *was* standing there. She pursed her lips and looked at him out of the corner of her eye.

"Don't give me that look, Laine," Bear warned her with a smile. "I know you've been waiting for this day for a while, but Jack and I still have some loose ends to tie up." He looked at Jack. "Hate to break you two lovebirds up, but we need to get to Missoula so we can catch our flight back to Denver. The sooner we leave, the sooner we can officially close the book on this one, and the sooner you can be back here."

She stared at Bear and blinked, her mind refusing to process what she'd just heard. Her synapses fired again. Her brain did an instant replay of Bear's words and her mouth dropped open as realization hit her like a fist in the gut. "You're . . . you're *leaving*?"

Jack sighed and rubbed his forehead. "Give me a minute, Bear."

"Ok," Bear agreed, "but first I have to do this."

Bear wrapped his arms around her and lifted her off the floor, hugging her tightly. A startled cry escaped her, and then she relaxed against him. "It's over, Laine. It's finally over, and you can take that to the bank this time." He held her close for nearly a minute before he put her feet carefully back on the ground. His gaze wandered over her face for a few seconds before he cupped her chin with one hand and pressed his lips to her brow.

"I apologize for the circumstances of our meeting here tonight," he said. "Forgive me?"

"Of course," she whispered her eyes stinging. "I love you."

Bear grinned. "Love you, too, sweetheart." He released her and lifted his eyes to Jack. "Say goodbye, partner, and say it well. Leave her wanting more. I'll be in the car."

When the door closed behind him, she turned to Jack, her insides heaving and quivering. She understood the concept of making personal sacrifices for one's work, but this was almost too much. For a moment she was back in the garden saying goodbye. The scab on that wound was ripped off, sending ripples of sorrow radiating outward from her heart. Not wanting him to see how distressed she was, she kept her chin down and focused on one of the plastic clips on his TAC gear. "I can't believe you're leaving already."

"We have to meet with the Director of Homeland Security in the morning, or I wouldn't be." He nudged her chin up with his knuckles. "I will be back as soon as I can, and then we'll have plenty of time together, I promise."

"I'll miss you," she whispered.

"Not half as much as I'll miss you," he said in a voice that set goose bumps plumping on her skin. He covered her mouth with his and Laine clutched the front of his vest as her pulse quickened and her knees threatened to give way. His arms wound around her waist, his lips playing over hers with exquisite delicacy. Their tongues met with a gossamer touch and a small sigh escaped her. Jack took full advantage of the opening. Her breasts tightened as he explored her mouth with languid intent, and when he pulled away, she whimpered in protest. Jack chuckled.

"Oh, what I'm going to do to you when I return," he said softly. He framed her face and feathered kisses over her brow, her cheekbones, her nose. "I love you, Laine Wheeler."

"And I love you," she replied, breathless. "Hurry back."

"You can count on it."

Chapter Nineteen

"Go home, Jack," Bear announced in a voice that said he wouldn't take no for an answer. He tossed down the handful of case files he'd been holding and took a seat opposite Jack's desk. "Leave."

Jack bit back a scathing retort, ignored his friend, and continued scribbling. It was becoming a daily affair; Bear telling him to go home and him not obeying for at least an hour. If they weren't such close friends Jack would have strangled him by now; at least he would have tried.

Because his home during his pursuit of Ripley had been various hotel rooms around the world, and prior to that a CAG camp in the woods, Jack was staying with Bear temporarily. Although they got along better than most people, being in Bear's loft only drove home the fact that he wasn't with Laine. It had been nearly a week since he'd watched her shoot Ripley on her back lawn. Even though they spoke on the phone or via webcam every night, it wasn't enough for him. He wanted to be with her. Just when he thought he was finished with the paperwork, Homeland Security or the Attorney General's office would request more information on the case. And they couldn't just pick up a phone. The requests were all done in writing and required written responses in return. Since Ripley was dead and the organization mostly dismantled, Jack didn't see the point. Nevertheless, the higher-ups demanded it and it was the way the Federal government worked, so he did it.

He frowned and battled visually with Bear for a few moments. It was useless; the set of Bear's jaw told him that. The rest of the paperwork would have to wait until tomorrow . . . again. Hopefully, that would be the last of it. Laine was all he could think about, and concentrating on work was the only way he got any peace.

"I have to get these reports and briefs finished, Bear," he growled. "It's been almost a week since... I want to get this case wrapped up and put away for good. The sooner I'm done, the sooner—"

"You can get back to Laine," Bear finished for him. "I know, but it's late, and you're exhausted, *again*." Bear reached over and plucked the pen from Jack's hand. "If you wear yourself out, you won't be any good to anyone, including Laine." He returned Jack's frown with a scowl. "I'm your boss, and I said go home, now. As of this moment, you are officially on vacation. Enjoy it."

Bear stood and turned to walk away, but Jack grabbed his arm. "Wait . . . vacation? What are you talking about?"

"Well," Bear said, stuffing his hands in his pockets, "as your superior I have the power to compel you to take vacation, especially if you haven't taken one in . . . oh, I don't know . . . almost a *decade*." He shrugged. "This case is mostly wrapped up, minus some unimportant paperwork that I or Mitchell or anyone else who was at the scene can do. It doesn't have to be you, so I've decided it's not going to be you. If you won't take vacation, I'll put you on administrative leave pending the psychiatric evaluations and get rid of you that way."

A spurt of anger burned in his chest and Jack rose. "You can't just remove me from the case like this, not *now*."

"Hey," Bear interrupted, putting a hand on Jack's shoulder, "the case is over, so there is nothing to remove you from."

"But . . . ."

"Jack." Bear's brows drew together and he frowned. "Get out of here, or I'll call Dr. Calvert myself and tell him you are anxious to begin the post-op psych evals. I'm getting tired of doing this with you every night. You're burning the candle at both ends, and everyone knows *you* need the downtime."

Jack stared at his friend in disbelief. "Bear—"

"Enough," Bear said, pinching the bridge of his nose. "You're officially off the clock. Why don't you head back to the loft, have a beer, and relax for the first time in years. I'll see you later tonight, and then we can work on getting you back to your girl."

"So, you get to stay and I have to leave?" Jack asked. "What kind of shit is that?"

Bear started to walk away and tossed him a jaunty grin over his shoulder. "It's one of the perks of being the boss, my friend. Trust me, there aren't many, so I take full advantage of the ones I have. Now get out of here, before I pick you up and toss you out." He chuckled and shook his head.

Jack clenched his jaw and squared his shoulders. "I'm not going on *vacation* until this is *done*." Bear stopped, turned, and Jack saw the determination in his friend's eyes, and the spark of annoyance.

"Don't push me, Jack," Bear warned. "We both know I can throw you out of here if I really want to. Remember who trained you in advanced hand-to-hand and mixed martial arts before you joined CAG. You may have beefed up during your hunt for Ripley, but I still have five inches and at *least* 50 pounds on you. And if I don't feel like breaking a sweat, I'll just tase your ass first to make it easier."

Jack knew Bear was serious, and correct, but that did little to lessen his frustration. When he finally went back to Laine, he didn't want *any* interruptions. If there were foul-ups his superiors would recall him in a heartbeat.

"Fine," Jack said at last. He pointed a finger at Bear and grabbed his jacket. "But I will be back tomorrow to finish the rest of this crap, no matter if it takes all day and all night. *Then* I'll go on vacation." He shrugged into his coat. "I plan to be in Evergreen Springs before Sunday, even if it means I have to quit my job." He paused, looked at his desk, then looked at Bear and sighed. "If you need anything . . . ."

"It's all good, bud," Bear assured him. "And, if we do need you for something, I know where to find you. We are roommates after all."

Jack tossed him a disgruntled look and walked through the nearly empty office to the elevator bay. As he stood there waiting for a car, Bear stuck his head through the archway.

"Hey, Jack," he said as the elevator doors slid open.

Jack stepped inside and tossed him a petulant glare. "What?"

Bear grinned, a wide, ear-to-ear grin so unlike him that Jack was taken aback for a moment. "You're welcome," Bear said just as the doors slid shut.

***

Jack walked up the final set of stairs to Bear's third floor loft and pulled the keys out of his pocket. When he slipped the key into the lock, the door whispered open and his senses immediately went on high alert.

There was a special trick to shutting the door to the loft that Bear had taught him, and if it wasn't closed just right the bolt mechanism wouldn't fully engage. A brief examination told him the door hadn't been forced, but the locks could have been picked by someone who knew what they were doing. Jack put his keys away, unholstered his weapon, and slowly opened the door with his foot. Once inside, he shut the door, dead-bolted it, and engaged the chain. It wouldn't stop an intruder from getting out, if the person somehow managed to get around him, but it might slow them down long enough for him to catch up.

Bear's loft was basically one open space, so a single scan of the dimly lit room told him there was no one there. That left the two bedrooms, the bathroom, and the upstairs loft overlooking the living area that served as Bear's office. The door to Bear's bedroom was open so he approached it first, moving over the wooden floor on silent feet. After checking behind the door, he glanced in the closet, and then walked back out to the living room.

The bathroom was between the two bedrooms, and as he approached it he saw the knob start to turn. Jack took a few steps backward through the door into Bear's room, clicked the safety off the .40, and waited. The person in the bathroom walked into the main living space and paused. Jack silently counted to five and then walked through the door, weapon raised and pointed at the intruder's back.

"Don't move," he said in a deadly calm voice.

The person froze, and even in the dim light he could tell it was a woman. She'd obviously just gotten out of the shower. She wore a red satin robe that fell to just above her knees. Her hair was wet and hung down her back, her feet were bare. As his gaze roved over her, his eyes narrowed. There was something familiar about her, but he kept his gun on target.

"Turn around," he said.

The woman raised her hands and slowly turned to face him. His heart started to thump when he met those familiar golden-green eyes, eyes that were wide with fear as she looked first at the pistol, and then at him. He blinked, certain he was hallucinating, but she was still there. He saw the anxiety in her expression, the rapid rise and fall of her chest as she stared at him, and finally his brain caught up.

"Oh, my God." He gaped at her and shook his head. "Laine."

Jack holstered the gun and crossed the distance between them in two long strides. Without a word he thrust his fingers into her damp hair and covered her mouth with his. He molded his hands to her head, and his heart jumped as her arms sneaked around his waist. It had been so long since he'd held her; the brief moments in Evergreen hadn't even qualified as an embrace. He wanted to taste, touch, and feel all of her. Jack released her long enough to scoop her into his arms, walk to his bedroom door and kick it open. Once in the bedroom he tossed her onto the bed.

Laine was dazed as he stood over her, her lips still tingling from the ferocity of his kiss. That raptor's gaze locked with hers as he slowly removed his jacket and flung it over a nearby chair. His eyes wandered over her face, his expression unsettling in its intensity. She watched him and licked her lips. Heat surged through her when he undid the buttons of his shirt, took it off, and tossed it next to the jacket.

He was beautiful. She remembered thinking he'd seemed bigger last week when he'd shown up at the cabin, and now she knew why. It was obvious he had not been idle during his time under the radar. Laine reached out and touched the ridged abdomen, tracing each sharply defined muscle. If he were five inches taller, he'd look like a slightly less muscular version of Bear. When he smiled and unfastened his belt, her breath caught. When he removed his pants, she closed her eyes, her senses in overdrive. Fear, longing, desire, a love so intense it was painful all roiled within her. Her heart thrummed against her breastbone, and she wondered if he could hear it.

A small gasp escaped her when the bed dipped and he knelt over her on all fours, his muscular thighs warm against hers. Laine took several slow, deep breaths and tried to slow her pulse. Summoning all of her courage, she looked at him and was immediately captivated by that silver gaze.

"I'm sorry for holding you at gunpoint. I didn't realize ..." His voice trailed off as he traced her cheekbones and the line of her jaw, apparently distracted from what he had been about to say. "God, you're beautiful." He outlined her mouth with the tip of his finger. "What are you doing here, Doc?"

Laine's brows drew together. "Bear didn't tell you?"

Jack shook his head. "The only thing Bear told me was to go home. He said nothing about you being here."

Uncertainty churned and she stared at him. He seemed happy to see her, but she wondered why Bear hadn't said anything. Heat surged into her cheeks and she dropped her gaze. "Maybe . . . maybe I should have called first."

"No," he whispered. "No." He nudged her chin up with his knuckles and forced her to look at him. "No. This is the best surprise since . . . well, since *ever*."

When he kissed her this time, it was a sweet kiss, soft, slow, and gentle, totally unlike his previous assault. Laine couldn't decide which she liked more. She sighed softly as he stretched out beside her, his mouth never leaving hers. Her breasts tightened and an ache settled between her thighs, an ache she knew only he could cure.

His mouth left hers and trailed down her neck. "Even though I can see you," he said, his voice low and husky, "even though I can touch you," he nibbled her ear, "I still can't believe you're here, and you're *real*." He paused and looked up at her. "Tell me this isn't a dream, Doc."

Laine could think of nothing but getting his hands on her skin. She untied the sash of her robe and slowly pulled it open, and his eyes darkened. She gave him a sensual smile as she took his hand, placed it on her bare breast, and then leaned up to kiss him deeply. He growled, the sound rumbling low in his chest.

His animal reaction only turned up the flame in her. Her breasts tingled, her nipples hardened, and her vulva throbbed. "Does that feel like a dream?" she asked in a throaty whisper, her lips still touching his.

His eyes were smoky with desire. "No."

He ducked his head and took one sensitive nipple in his mouth, and pleasure spiraled through her. His tongue swirled around the rosy nub for a moment, leaving her trembling, goose bumps shivering over her skin. Heat and cold bathed her body in alternating waves, tingling pulses coiling low in her belly. Laine moaned softly and he lifted his head to look at her.

"It doesn't feel like a dream, it feels like paradise." A wicked smile twitched about his mouth. "When Bear told me I was officially on vacation, I had *no* idea this is what he meant." His smile widened and he feathered kisses over her face. "Thank you, Bear. I will never again argue with you when you tell me to leave the office."

Laine chuckled and ran her fingers over his short hair. "Bear said if I didn't come down here, *he* was going to strangle you. I hear they've started calling you Little Bear, and *not* because you're a smaller version of him."

His expression sobered and he framed her face with his hands. "I just wanted to get everything done so I could get back to you. Every time I think I can finally put this to bed, the powers that be come up with some other form or report or brief they want finished ASAP ..." His voice died and he searched her eyes. "I feel like I'm going crazy here,

Doc. I've been away from you too long."

"Well, you don't have to worry about that anymore," she said. She blinked rapidly as her eyes stung, but she refused to cry. "You're not getting rid of me again, not ever."

"I requested a transfer to Missoula," he blurted out. "I'll have no trouble getting the spot and it's only a few hours from Evergreen—"

A thrill of anticipation went through her and Laine put a finger to his lips. "I know. I asked Bear to pull it."

His eyes went wide. "What? Why?"

"Because once your transfer to the FBI was approved you were assigned to the Denver office instead of Los Angeles," she replied. "A couple of days ago I called to talk to you, but you were in a meeting and Bear told me.

"But . . . ." His voice died and he stared at her in disbelief. "I want to be with you, Doc. I can't do that from Denver." His expression shifted and he moved away from her. "Unless . . . unless you don't want me that close."

Laine scowled. Placing a hand on his chest, she pushed him onto his back, and straddling him, she slowly slid the robe off her shoulders. Once she was completely nude she leaned over, her breasts brushing his chest, and started planting small kisses on his face, his brow, his jaw. He was hard beneath her and she rubbed herself against him, that familiar tension building between her legs. She saw the conflict in his silver eyes, uncertainty and desire. Part of her wanted to put his mind at ease, but for the first time since meeting him she was completely in control. She gave him a sinful smile and kissed him.

"You're right," she whispered against his mouth, "I don't want you in Missoula."

Jack put his hands on her upper arms and pushed her back. His expression was incredulous, and hurt. "Why not?"

Laine decided to have pity on him and gently pried his fingers loose. She kissed each palm, then slid his hands around her waist and held them there.

"Well, since *I'm* moving to Denver, *you* moving to Missoula would be sort of . . . self-defeating, don't you think?" The look on his face clearly said he didn't understand, so before he could say anything, she continued. "Last week, after you left, I started making some phone calls." She let go of his hands and was relieved when his fingers splayed over the small of her back. She leaned closer. "One month from today, I take over the E.R. at Memorial Hospital. Apparently, my helping to save your life in such a dramatic fashion left quite an impression."

He blinked at her, and then a hint of a smile appeared. "I'll bet." Jack tucked her hair behind her ear. "You left quite an impression on me, even before the drama at the hotel."

Laine ran her fingers over his brow. "You sure hid it well."

"A mistake I do not ever plan to repeat." His expression sobered. "I'll spend the rest of my life making up for it, and for everything else, if you'll let me."

Laine bit her lip and traced the line of his jaw. "So . . . you're okay with me moving to Denver?"

For an answer Jack put a hand behind her neck and pulled her head down. When his lips captured hers, there was no sweetness, no hesitance. His kiss was ruthless, demanding, and it made her dizzy. His tongue melded with hers. He grew even harder and her nipples throbbed. The ache between her thighs sharpened intensely, and she moaned in protest when he pulled back.

"Are you kidding?" he asked in a harsh whisper. "I love you, Laine Wheeler, and I don't care where we are as long as we're together."

"Then make love to me, Jack," she said softly. "We have a lot to talk about, but right now I don't want to talk. Right now, you have some physical therapy to do, doctor's orders."

Laine cried out in surprise and giggled when he flipped them over and settled between her thighs. She could feel him, hot and throbbing against her flesh, and she wrapped her legs around his waist, trying to draw him closer. Jack held his ground.

"I don't usually follow doctor's orders, as you well know," he said with a shameless grin. "But this time . . ." he paused and kissed her, ". . . this time I think I'll make an exception."

"Really?" she asked, breathless. "You'd do that . . . for me?"

He slowly entered her body and began to move his hips in a languid, sensual rhythm. Laine closed her eyes and clung to him.

"Anything for you, Doc," he said, kissing her again. "Anything for you."

THE END

About the author

Leslie McKelvey has been writing since she learned to write, and her mother still stores boxes of handwritten stories in the attic. Her debut novel, Accidental Affair, was published in 2012.

Leslie is a veteran of the Gulf War who served with the U.S. Navy, and she was among the first groups of women to work the flight deck of an aircraft carrier.

Leslie lives in California with her husband and has three sons.

Also by Leslie McKelvey

Right Place, Right Time

While shooting pictures of a mama bear and her cubs in Rocky Mountain National Park, wildlife photographer Beth Drummond witnesses a murderous shootout and the violent deaths of four men. When those responsible realize they've not only been seen but also photographed they give chase, determined to tie up loose ends. Praying she can outdistance her pursuers Beth dashes headlong through the woods, intent on nothing but reaching safety.

When Special Agent Bear Bristol, on leave from the FBI, hears gunshots and sees the woman running for her life, he knows he must intervene. He recognizes those who are chasing her and realizes that things are much worse than they seem. A vicious cartel with a mole at the FBI has put a target on Beth's back, and there is no one they can trust. Unable to call for backup, Bear must keep Beth safe until they can figure out who the inside man is.

As they struggle to stay one step ahead of both corrupt law enforcement and the killers they learn to trust one another, and realize there is more between them than just friendship born of necessity. Can they overcome the obstacles they face, or will they win the fight to live only to lose the battle to love?

Coming soon from Leslie McKelvey

Her Sister's Keeper

Latest titles from Black Velvet Seductions

Playing for Keeps by Glenda Horsfall
Playing by His Rules by Glenda Horsfall
The Love She Wants by Mila Winters
Holly's Big Bad Santa by Starla Kaye
Punished! by Richard Savage, Nadia Nautalia & Starla Kaye

See more of our titles at
www.blackvelvetseductions.com

Our titles are available from:
Amazon
Smashwords
LuLu
Nook
Blushing Books
All Romance eBooks
Bookstrand
and other retailers